Beyond the Stars

A Planet Too Far

Edited by Ellen Campbell (http://ellencampbell.thirdscribe.com)

Cover art by Julie Dillon (http://www.juliedillonart.com)

Cover designed by Kendall Roderick (www.RMind-Design.com)

Formatted by Therin Knite (http://www.knitedaydesign.com)

The stories herein...

Venatoris (*G. S. Jennsen*)

Humanity may have colonized much of the galaxy, but space remains as dangerous as ever, and so do the people inhabiting it. When Alexis Solovy—space explorer, freelance scout, recalcitrant wanderer—lands the contract of a lifetime, the race is on to claim the prize. Now she must not only outrun but outsmart her rivals to uncover the secrets of an ancient, mysterious pulsar. For deep in the void, far beyond the reach of civilization, wealth and renown matter little absent the ultimate reward: survival.

Hope 91 (*Nick Webb*)

A child escapes Earth aboard a NASA spaceship, one of the few chosen to settle a new world thousands of lightyears away. With only a few robots as companions and decades of space travel ahead of him, the boy soon learns there is another space traveler nearby in another ship, and will do whatever it takes to talk to her. To see her. To console her. To laugh with her.

And hopefully, against all odds, to love her.

Symbiosis (*Rory Hume*)

Mariana Soto arrived in orbit around Verdu with one job: to observe the elevator taking cargo down to the planet. When the job ended up being more than Mari expected, and she was in the middle of an interplanetary war she knew nothing about, the only way out might be her coworker… a symbiote without a name.

War Stories (*Samuel Peralta*)

You don't really want to hear about war. You want to hear about courage and honor. You want the medals, the bugles, the drums. You want to hear about starships on fire off Orion's shoulder, plasma beams glittering as they slice through inertial drives. I'm sorry. This isn't that story.

The Mergans (*Ann Christy*)

They are almost legend, but not quite. In a galaxy as vast as ours, it's easy to miss one planet laid to waste. And if a few centuries pass and history remarks on the changes on that planet somewhere, who is to say what—or who—caused it? Are they pirates or rescuers? Fanatics or bringers of justice? The answer depends on who is asked.

To those who see the dark, round shapes in their sky, they are not legend. They are harbingers of the end.

The Immortals: Anchorage (*David Adams*)

Recruited into the mysterious Synapse Foundation, Nicholas Caddy—still bearing the scars of an interstellar war—is dispatched on his first mission with the Immortals. A passenger liner, the *Anchorage*, has gone silent. Their task is simple: find the ship, salvage what they can, report what happened. Simple.

Simple.

This is Part two of *The Immortals* series set in the Universe of War, thirteen years before the events of *Symphony of War: The Polema Campaign.*

Pele's Bee-keeper (*Annie Bellet*)

A pilot crash lands on a faraway moon and discovers a solitary woman living there, trying single-handedly to terraform this barren world. Somehow the woman, layered in veils and mystery, is more than she seems. Somehow she knows that there was an explosion… a loss… a death.

There are sides to every fight, and secrets in every war. And sometimes it's impossible to know if someone is an enemy or a friend.

Services Rendered (*Theresa Kay*)

Li'hanna, a member of the prized and elusive Kotkaa race, is prepared to do anything to keep the secrets of her clan out of the hands of the evil imperial fleet.

Captured by one of the imperial hybrids and his human associate, she's smuggled aboard a transport ship that belongs to the vengeful Jeren Skalos. When she manages to break free, she finds herself assisting the human crew to outwit the enemy—instead of running for her life.

What starts as a desperate escape attempt engenders something else—a partnership that could be the beginning of a rebellion against the empire.

Spike in a Rail (*Logan Thomas Snyder*)

Trouble is brewing aboard Over/Under Station. Returning to the station after an extended absence, the huntrex Xenecia of Shih'ra is summoned by an elderly mystic known only as "the Grom." The Grom has had a vision, she explains, one that speaks to the station's imminent destruction… and only Xenecia can prevent it. How this catastrophe will come to be, however, the vision did not reveal. Is the station doomed, or can Xenecia discover the truth behind the Grom's vision in time—even when all is not as it seems?

The First to Fall (*Sabrina Locke*)

When Fallan Jin-Dahl was six years old, her father gave her a child's toy she named Paladin. Ten years later when Paladin goes missing, Fallan discovers there might be a whole lot more to the object than she believed. She might not be the person she's always thought herself to be. The hunt for Paladin brings two mysterious guys onto her ship—Alden and Finn Hendrix—but are they her protectors or her jailers?

Fallan's journey to find a lost toy leads her into adventure and tragedy. She will have to choose whether to cling to her family and her past or leave her old life behind in order to find out who she is—and more importantly—who she can become.

The Ivory Tower (*Elle Casey*)

In a world where the human race is at risk of extinction, the future is in the hands of the last four girls in existence. Each is kept in isolation, her every hour scripted and controlled by a team of men who call themselves fathers. Zelle has accepted her fate until one day someone offers her a choice: remain in her ivory tower to become a mother to future generations, or escape and perhaps live another life where free will is no longer just a dream.

CONTENTS

Foreword

by Patrice Fitzgerald

SO WHAT EXACTLY *is* space opera?

The term was coined in 1941 by a writer named Wilson Tucker... and he didn't mean it as a compliment. His idea of a space opera was a "hacky, grinding, stinking, outworn, spaceship yarn."

A more flattering description comes from science fiction anthologists and authors David G. Hartwell and Kathryn Cramer, in their 2007 collection *The Space Opera Renaissance*, who defined the genre as "colorful, dramatic, large-scale science fiction adventure, competently and sometimes beautifully written, usually focused on a sympathetic, heroic central character and plot action, and usually set in the relatively distant future, and in space or on other worlds, characteristically optimistic in tone. It often deals with war, piracy, military virtues, and very large-scale action, large stakes."

To me, that describes space opera pretty well… and the collection of short stories in *Beyond the Stars: A Planet Too Far* surely fits the bill. Here you'll find drama, larger-than-life heroes and heroines, and everything from classic "pew-pew" military battles to gargantuan starships traveling across the galaxies to make peace and settle planetary squabbles.

What should also be mentioned is that these stories are *fun*. Space opera gives a writer the biggest canvas possible… the entire universe! Whatever bizarre alien creature anyone could imagine can come to life in one of these stories. Conflicts and relationships of every conceivable type can be played out against a background of invented worlds and weird civilizations. There are no limits. The only boundaries are the walls of our brains.

The authors in this anthology managed to fit all these qualities into the short story format. Concise but powerful tales, each like a precious gem mined fresh from the writer's imagination, are lined up here before you, one after another, in a string of mesmerizing stories.

Now it's time to take the pilot's seat and strap in for the ride. The g-forces are about to hit you. We're powering up and heading… beyond the stars.

Patrice Fitzgerald
April 1, 2016

About Patrice Fitzgerald

Intellectual property attorney, part-time opera diva (meaning real opera… she's a mezzo-soprano), and CEO of a boutique publishing company, Patrice Fitzgerald has been happily self-published since Independence Day, 2011. Her books include *Karma of the Silo*, based in Hugh Howey's world of *WOOL*; *Running*, a standalone political thriller about the U.S. Presidential race; and numerous short stories that have been anthologized in The Future Chronicles as well as in other collections. She's currently writing a space opera trilogy, *Star Crimes*, featuring aliens, spaceship battles, and an investigator with an unnerving ability to penetrate minds and read memories.

Patrice publishes other authors who write in the cozy mystery, romance, and fantasy genres, and is the founder and series editor for *Beyond the Stars*. She also writes some very different kinds of books under two pen names.

Patrice is the one asking the questions in the Q&A segment after each story. The curious will have no trouble finding her on Facebook (far too often). She lives in New England with her husband and tries to keep up with the adventures of her four children, two of whom came to her by birth and two by marriage.

Venatoris
by G. S. Jennsen

"The fast lane I am flying down is one
with no end in sight
filled with reckless adventure and
paved with dangerous delights."
— Ashley Young

YUZHOU LI ORBITAL STATION
Shi Shen Stellar System
1,080 Parsecs from Earth
March 2317

"DOUBLE BOURBON, STRAIGHT up. Double everything. Except the ice. Don't double the ice."

Alexis Solovy glanced down the bar in idle curiosity at the source of the dramatic pronouncement. A woman with frizzy black hair and pale, bleached skin sagged off a stool and onto the bar, arms splayed out in defeat. She looked familiar, but damned if Alex could pull a name out of anywhere. "Bad day?"

The woman didn't lift her head from where it lay propped sideways on her elbow. "My ship is trashed. A mangled heap. Bloody asteroid spun out when I tried to grapple it. I limped back here like a crippled monkey, jack shit to show for my trouble."

Alex raised her glass in contrived sympathy and turned away. If the woman didn't have any useful leads, it wasn't worth the pain of engaging in conversation, polite or otherwise.

Intel was the only reason to come to this godforsaken place, the sleaziest bar on the sleaziest space station for two kiloparsecs. Tidbits. Information. Leads. On a good night, contracts.

Her eyes roved over the room in search of better prospects. The bar was nearly two-thirds full—loud and busy, but not so full as to preclude card and target games and the occasional display of bravado. Bad synth blaring out of the speakers made it feel rowdier than the reality.

Alex knew half the people on sight. Some she was on a last name basis with; others, an epithet basis. Many were interstellar scouts, freelance—same as her, while a few were traders, smugglers, or both. But she didn't see any corp reps or brokers. Was no one in this cursed place doing business?

"Alex, doll, you need something stronger than… what *are* you drinking?"

She leveled an unimpressed scowl in Bob Patera's direction as he leaned on the bar beside her. "A Carina Nova.

They make it in civilized places like Earth. Luckily, the bartender's visited civilized places."

He nodded with as much vigor as his inebriated state allowed. "Still need to get you something stronger."

"Can't. I'm working."

He stared at her skeptically but couldn't seem to think of a suitable response. Finally he took a long, fulsome sip of his drink, a dark and frothy concoction. "Go on a date with me."

It had to be at least the seventy-fourth time he'd asked in the two and a half years since she'd met him. "No."

"Why not?"

"Because you think you're a space pirate, Bob."

"But I am a space pirate."

She laughed in spite of herself. "My point exactly."

"You dated that Ethan Tollis guy, and he thinks he's a synth star."

"He *is* a synth star." And the dating happened years ago, before Ethan found well-deserved fame, but she wasn't inclined to correct him.

He looked genuinely offended. "I am a space pirate."

Patera was a good guy; a functioning drunk and a righteous lech, but a good guy nonetheless. He took the odd scouting job mostly to entertain himself and to have tales to brag about at any of a staggering variety of bars, of which this was only one.

"Oh, clearly. But—"

She recognized the man the instant he stepped in the bar and made sure she was the first person he made eye contact with. "Sorry, Bob, got to go. Working."

The man sat down at a table in the corner near the door. She stood up and headed for it with an air of deliberate casualness. It wouldn't do for anyone else to notice him and beat her there, but she also didn't want anyone else to notice her running for him.

She made it to the table scot-free and slid in opposite him. "You have a job?" Perhaps not the smoothest greeting, but she rarely had the patience for pleasantries.

He didn't appear to mind. As a respected and experienced broker for numerous Alliance corps, he presumably knew interstellar scouts weren't always the most socially well-adjusted people.

"Astral Materials is getting ready to post an open contract for rare, high value elements at a newly discovered pulsar in Messier 71."

Messier 71 lay a considerable distance from Shi Shen, out in the void beyond settled space. She was okay with that.

"What's special about it?"

"It's a millisecond pulsar with three suspected planets identified. The scientific data is so promising they already gave it a name: Shanshuo. It's the Chinese word for—"

"Scintillation. I know. And it's an open contract?"

"Should hit the boards in the next hour or so. You did a great job on the contract for Palaimo last month, so I thought you'd be interested in a little forewarning."

Pulsar planets were rare, and rare was interesting. Better yet, millisecond pulsars were very, very old, which meant lots of opportunities for elements to bake, mature and transform. The odds leaned toward something lucrative waiting at Shanshuo.

She harbored no doubts she would find that something

if it was there to find, but she also had to find it *first*. "What's the payout?"

"Depends on what you find."

Her gaze bore into him until he made a prevaricating motion. "200K to 1.2 million."

She managed to stand up without sending the chair skittering across the floor. "Appreciate the tip."

Then she slinked out the door, hoping no one noticed her exit, and hurried down the curving walkway of the station's outer torus as she messaged Kennedy.

Ken, where are you? It's time to quit partying and start working.

The response took several seconds to come in.

Are you sure? I literally just met a delicious merchant from Arcadia. He sells custom wide-band decrypters fabbed onsite.

And he needs you to come to his hotel room so he can show them to you?

Actually I suggested the hotel room.

Alex reached the transfer lift and hopped aboard as it departed.

Hey, it's your vacation, but you said you wanted to come on a job with me so you could, and I quote, 'See what I did with all my free time.' Here's your chance. You can stay and bed Don Juan if you want, but I'm clamps off in twenty.

Oh, fine. I'll meet you at the ship. I've got to disentangle myself here.

Twenty, Ken.

* * *

The hangar deck did not look to be in compliance with any

safety regs from this century, and certainly not Earth Alliance regs, which Shi Shen claimed to be subject to. Maybe the jurisdiction got fuzzy once one breached space? Alex knew better, though. Her mother—Queen Admiral of the Universe, Earth Alliance Strategic Command Division—would have an apoplectic fit if she saw the wreck this place was. But her mother did not deign to frequent places such as this.

A third of the bays were filled with half-broken ships while their owners, bots and assorted mechanics tried to put them back together. Two men were busy installing a new impulse engine in the ship next to hers, right there on the deck. She shook her head and strode past them.

The *Siyane* sat at the end of the left row. Sleek, aerodynamic lines gleamed panther black, giving it a predatory appearance. It wasn't the largest ship in the bay, but by God it was the most beautiful. As well it should be, since she'd designed it herself. Built to spec by the company Kennedy worked for, it represented nothing short of perfection.

…Except for all the upgrades and customizations she desperately wanted to make but could not yet afford. *Step by step, day by day.*

Kennedy came rushing up behind her, a mess of golden curls bouncing around a flushed face as she repositioned the straps of her jade slip dress on her shoulders. She skidded to a stop in a huff. "You're not on board yet? I could've gotten—"

"You can tell me on the way, Ken. Come on."

"Where are we going?"

"On an adventure. Trust me, it'll be fun."

* * *

SIYANE
Messier 71
PSR J1952+1846
4,220 Parsecs from Earth

Many people believed humanity's mere presence in the stars beyond its home planet had rendered space civilized.

Superluminal travel allowed them to hopscotch over the void on their way from one colony to the next. Half the time they didn't even bother to glance out a ship's viewport and note it was the *stars* they journeyed through.

But out here, twelve hundred parsecs from the nearest settled world—which happened to be the most uncivilized world of them all, run by gangsters, murderers and thieves— space revealed its true nature. Vast. Untamed. Dangerous.

In other words, her playground.

Alex noted all this with a brief smile of anticipation as she increased the thrust of the impulse engine and accelerated into the stellar system hiding in a far corner of Messier 71. Not the venue for idle musing.

The race was already on. Word of the contract had spread across the width and breadth of the freelance scout network by now, and she'd be deluding herself if she thought she'd be able to close this deal without competition.

The rules for claiming 'property' in unexplored, unowned space were straightforward: plant a beacon at the location detailing the extent of the claim and the name of the claimant. Once the broadcast reached the relevant authorities—a matter of seconds—the claim was certified. Period, full stop. It was the only practical way to handle development of the forty billion star systems still unexplored in their little corner of the galaxy.

The various governments generated much to-do about their new discoveries. Corporations, however, simply took what they wanted.

Well, it would be more accurate to say corporations paid people to find and claim what they wanted for them. People like her….

"Oh, *chyertu*." Alex groaned as the long-range scanner picked up the telltale signs of another vessel in the system. A database check identified the owner of the ship bearing that particular emission signature.

"Problem?" Kennedy muttered as she ascended the spiral staircase from the personal quarters below wearing far more appropriate sweats and a tee.

"Joaquin Kyril's here."

Her friend leaned against the cockpit half-wall and crossed her arms over her chest. "Who?"

"Asshole extraordinaire. Not a scintilla of hunter skills to his name. He wouldn't recognize a neutron star glitch if it sauntered up and slapped him across his peevish face."

Kennedy's eyes narrowed in contemplation. "Wait, is he that guy we bumped into on Demeter last year? He was cute."

"Really, Ken? I offer a string of insults by way of introduction, and you go straight to 'cute'?"

"I didn't say he was nice or upstanding. Just said he was cute. I can't believe you haven't put a second chair in the cockpit yet. Where am I supposed to sit?"

Alex shrugged. "The floor? The couch back in the main cabin? You're the only person who ever comes out with me."

"What about Malcolm?"

She snorted. "We're nowhere near the stage where he goes with me… anywhere that isn't on Earth. Seriously, he hasn't even seen my bedroom."

"Here on the ship or at your apartment in San Francisco?"

"Either." She'd been on two dates with Lt. Col. Malcolm Jenner in the past month; the third might have happened this week, were she not out here in the void. Perhaps it would happen next week, if she didn't die out here in the void.

He wasn't her type. For one, he was military—a Marine of all things—which she'd been swearing off since… since a long time. He was upstanding and proper and gentlemanly to a cringe-inducing fault.

But he was also smart, considerate and funny in a self-effacing way. And handsome, even if he did have to keep his hair shorn in an annoying military close-crop. For reasons she hadn't yet found the words to articulate, she liked him. Maybe. She'd worry about it later. Right now she had to work.

Kyril wandered around five AU out from the pulsar… searching for the outermost planetary body? If so, he was searching in the wrong place.

Shanshuo hadn't been receiving scientific attention long enough for the eccentricity to be accurately measured, but the orbit appeared wildly erratic. Kyril was guessing.

Alex studied what data existed on the sequential orbits of the third body.

ORBIT 1: *Inclination: 12.3°; Ω: 147°; Period: 3.8 years*
ORBIT 2: *Inclination: 17.6°; Ω: 132°; Period: 4.1 years*

ORBIT 3: *Inclination: 9.5°; Ω: 153°; Period: Incomplete (859 days as of yesterday)*

She ran through some calculations then killed all the screens to stand and stare out the viewport.

They weren't able to *see* the pulsar, of course, as it emitted primarily X-rays. A spectrum filter engaged over the viewport to rectify the deficiency in their eyesight.

"Ooh, that's pretty."

"In a manner of speaking." Like a lighthouse on an *ampaKhat* high, the X-ray beam spun madly, strobing across the viewport faster than she could blink. It was hypnotizing, and she let it cast its spell. She watched without seeing as her vision blurred under the mesmerizing rhythm.

There.

She dropped back into the cockpit chair, strapped in and set a course for *there.*

* * *

Cold gas giant, 0.8 the size of Jupiter, sporting a standard hydrogen and helium composition. Likely a captured planet, although with an orbit this close it must have been falling into Shanshuo for billions of years. Still, gas giants, whether cold, room temperature or hot, ranked among the most common non-stellar bodies in the galaxy.

"Ugh. Boring."

Kennedy now sat on the floor, propped up against the wall eating roasted almonds. "Are you kidding? Look at those colors, at the way the clouds swirl together. This planet is spiffing art."

She didn't disagree, but.... "I know, but we're not here

for art. We're here to find elements worth money to Astral Materials, and as lovely as this planet may be, it's not lucrative. One day I'll have earned sufficient credits to be able to spend days gaping in wonder at such sights, but that day isn't today."

"I'm sorry, I didn't mean...."

She spared Kennedy a quick, closed-mouth smile. "And I didn't either." Kennedy, or more specifically her family, was wealthy beyond the numbers to count it, but it hadn't mattered since seven minutes after they'd met as freshmen at university.

With a sigh she started to pull away and shift her focus to the inner bodies when the scanner beeped to inform her of another vessel in proximity.

She glared at the screen incredulously. Kyril was *ghosting* her?

Shit. His ship was faster than hers, one reason she desperately needed the proceeds from this contract. If he could track her, he'd be able to leapfrog her the instant she struck figurative—or possibly literal—gold and sling a beacon. He could steal the discovery out from under her while she watched in impotent fury. And he would do precisely that without a moment's hesitation.

"Dammit, I should have spent last month's money on a real dampener field instead of a new ionized gas analyzer." The dampener field was on the list, but the list was a busy place. And now she floated out here with no way to mask her engine's emission signature and no way to shake Kyril's tail.

"You know, IS Design recently introduced a new prototype dampener field which is nineteen percent more effective at eighty-one percent the power requirements of the previous gen model."

"Did you design it?"

"I helped. A lot, in truth, but I'm still too low on the corporate ladder to get the credit for it." In response to Alex's questioning gaze, Kennedy grinned smugly. "Soon."

"I've no doubt."

Alex pretended to be scanning the planet below, like there might legitimately be something worthy of finding, while she racked her brain for a solution to the problem that was Joaquin Kyril.

It seemed she was not going to be allowed to explore the system, investigating every object for possible valuable elements. She'd only have one real shot at finding and claiming the mother lode.

So where could the mother lode be hiding?

She leaned down and grabbed a handful of Kennedy's almonds. The second suspected planet had, by the timing measurements, a notably strange orbit. She considered it a minute… and palmed her forehead with her free hand.

"I'm an idiot."

"Not usually."

"The second object the researchers detected isn't orbiting Shanshuo. It's orbiting this planet. It probably got brought along for the ride when the gas giant was captured."

"So?"

"So regardless of whether it's a moon, planetoid or true planet, it'll be small and rocky. Small and rocky is—"

"Boring?"

Alex chuckled. "Well, yes. Okay, this leaves the innermost body. It's zipping around at an orbital period of 3.2

hours, which means it's close to the pulsar. Damn close." Dangerously close, at least for a puny little personal scout ship.

She imagined the *Siyane* protesting the insult with an aura of miffed indignation, and apologized silently. It certainly was not puny to her; it was, in point of fact, everything she had ever wanted.

"The type of relationship exhibited here—a tight, rapid orbit in the shadow of the pulsar—pegs it as a companion star rather than a planet. A white dwarf having its matter leeched away by the primary star?"

"Were you directing the question at me? 'Cause I'm an engineer, not a space junkie."

Alex mumbled a distracted reply. White dwarfs were a dime a dozen and as boring as the gas giant. But if it was a true white dwarf, the researchers should've been able to identify it as such relatively easily.

She swung toward Shanshuo in feigned casualness so as not to pique Kyril's interest, tuning out the *voom-voom-voom* strobe of the pulsar in favor of trying to catch sight of the orbiting companion.

She blinked.

There.

Blinked again. Gone.

But it *had* been there, a tiny dot of absence racing across the X-ray light. She readied the spectrum analyzer to take a broad spectrum reading. She'd filter out the pulsar's spectrum signature afterward to reveal the companion's data.

The scanner panned until she relocated it. Fantastic. Effective surface temperature estimated at….

She frowned. "That can't be correct." Either the white

dwarf was older than the universe—a dubious supposition—or the pulsar had siphoned off the outer layers completely, evaporating the star and leaving behind naught but its core.

Possibly its exotic carbon diamond-like core? What were the odds?

Vanishingly low, but higher than they had been a few minutes ago and doubtless higher than the first option.

Kennedy stood and peered out the viewport. "What've you got?"

"Maybe, just maybe, something wonderful."

She didn't elaborate for now; she'd been dallying for too long, and Kyril would be getting suspicious. And now she *really* needed a plan.

The small, rocky planet orbiting the gas giant had a thin atmosphere and varied terrain. Terrain she'd be able to lose Kyril in for several seconds at a minimum. Since her in-atmo pulse detonation engine didn't emit an identifiable signature, it might be enough.

"I need help. I need someone else. Who else is here?"

"I'm here."

Alex laughed. "I mean another ship."

Kennedy shrugged and returned to the floor. "Ah. Can't help you then."

The potential payout marked this as an enticing contract, if a marginally risky one. Pulsars didn't qualify as friendly environs for humans. The ionizing radiation alone, not to mention the powerhouse X-ray beacon, meant an early death for anyone not in a strongly shielded vessel.

Luckily for her, she did have those shields. The best radiation shielding last year's money could buy.

She tuned the emission sensor to its farthest range and filtered out the quite noisy pulsar radiation. Kyril's ship showed up immediately, right up her ass, leading her to growl a particularly colorful Russian curse under her breath.

"Your dad teach you that word?"

"Not intentionally."

After another pass two additional dots materialized, which earned another, nearly as colorful exclamation.

Once the targets were pegged, she refined the scanner's parameters until she had definable signatures then fed them into the ship database. The first one didn't match any entries, but the second....

Alex sent a secure comm hail. "Hey, Bob. What brings you to the void today?"

"Solovy? Dammit. Whatever brought me here, I'm not going to get it now, so I might as well turn around, head home and go get plastered."

He wasn't wrong. Bob Patera may be a better scout than Kyril, but that wasn't saying much. "Glad to see you accept the inevitability of my triumph, but don't rush off yet. I've got a proposition for you."

"Be still my heart."

She rolled her eyes. "Simmer down. It's not that kind of proposition. Joaquin Kyril is glued to my ass and I need to ditch him. Help me do that long enough for me to find elements which will satisfy the Astral contract, and you'll get ten percent of the proceeds."

"Fifteen percent."

"Twelve percent."

"Twelve percent and you have a drink with me next week."

She drummed her fingers on the dash. "All right. But a drink means a drink, nothing else."

"Oh, come on. We should at least have sex, if only to get all this sexual tension out of our systems."

Kennedy arched an eyebrow in interest, but Alex shook her head in a vehement *no*. "There is no sexual tension between us, Bob."

"Sure there is."

"Those are your dreams. This is reality. So are you in?"

"Point the way."

She exhaled in relief. "Terrific. You've got a Genyx VII impulse drive, right?"

"I won't ask how you knew that. Yes, the C2 model."

Alex toggled the comm and waved Kennedy up off the floor. "Can you figure out what he needs to do to his engine to make it approximate my emission signature?"

Kennedy nodded and jogged to the data center in the main cabin.

Her outward demeanor made it easy to forget—especially when the woman was in full-on vacation mode—but Ken was smart. Exceptionally smart. And she knew more about all the major components of starships than anyone Alex had met. Odds were she had the specs on the Genyx VII drive memorized, along with the specs for all the other commercial engine models.

Alex switched the comm channel back on. "In a minute I'll send you some adjustments you need to make to the power flow to your engine and a tiny tweak to its negative mass regulator."

"You want me to mutilate my engine?"

"Improve it, actually. You're going to pretend to be me.

Once you've made the adjustments, move to the far side of the middle body and wait there until I tell you to come in-at-mo. When you get close, I'll go dark. You'll take my place, then bail and get back to the gas giant."

"This body is… where? In case you hadn't realized it, I legitimately meant 'point the way.'"

It wasn't his fault he was a bad scout. Not even a bad scout, really—merely an ordinary one. "It's orbiting the gas giant, inclination 27.6° off the pulsar's reference plane at 1,722 megameters, give or take."

"I can work with that. What are you planning to do once I lead Kyril astray?"

She hesitated. She liked Bob as far as it went, but it didn't mean she trusted him. Not when hundreds of thousands if not millions of credits were at stake. "I'm going to go earn our riches."

Kennedy returned to the cockpit and, at Alex's gesture of approval, input the calculations and sent them to Bob.

"Fine, don't tell me. I'll just fly around jerking off until you decide I can stop."

"What you do on your ship is your own business."

"It most definitely is. Got your instructions. Give me five minutes."

Alex veered around a bit to make it look as if she were chasing down a potential find, shaking her head when Kyril followed like a proselyte. Still, he *had* to be getting suspicious by now. But what was he apt to do? Find anything of value himself?

Abruptly she stood and paced through the main cabin to burn off a fraction of her mounting nerves. She needed razor-sharp reflexes for what came next, not the jitters.

"So, where *are* we running off to once you lose this Kyril guy?"

Alex pointed out the viewport in the direction of the pulsar.

Kennedy canted her head to the side. "Sure. Why not?"

It took six and a half minutes, but Bob reported in. *"I'm on my way to you."*

She returned to the chair in a flash. "I see you. Come in under the planet's profile so he won't pick you up."

"Yep. You truly hate this guy, don't you?"

"Don't you?"

"He's a gilded-spoon prick, no doubt."

"He's a thief. He lets others do the work then finds underhanded ways to steal what he can from them. And he is brutal and unrepentant about it."

"Fair assessment. I guess I don't take it as personally as you do."

One of a thousand reasons why she was better at this than him, and would soon be the best.

Alex accelerated away from the gas giant and toward its satellite, and this time she smirked when Kyril followed behind at some distance. Did he honestly think she didn't know he lurked out there?

The atmosphere turned out to be even thinner than she'd expected. She glanced at Kennedy. "Will the pulse detonation engine operate in this weak of an atmosphere? I mean it should, right?"

Kennedy scrutinized the HUD screen displaying the gas percentages and cringed. "Uh... probably?"

"Good enough." She pointed the nose of the ship down and dove. When the atmosphere began to fight her she reached over and activated the transition from impulse power to the pulse detonation engine. They held their breath.

The ship jerked as the engine struggled for a minute… then began humming quietly.

The meager cloud cover dissipated to reveal a mountainous terrain. Perfect.

She leveled off a kilometer above the surface. "You'll want to strap in to the jump seat."

Kennedy's eyes widened. "Should I get a drink, too?"

"After."

Her face contorted into a grimace as she retreated to the main cabin.

Alex guided the *Siyane* toward the mountains, seeking out a path through the crests and valleys.

Kyril's ship was faster than hers in space; she had to assume it was faster in-atmo as well. But she could fly circles around him in her sleep using nothing but her left pinky. It wasn't arrogance; it was fact.

Perhaps a smidge of arrogance.

She cracked her neck and dipped until she cruised thirty meters from the sloping incline and tilted the belly of the ship toward it. No trees softened the scenery, and boulders rushed past in a blur.

Ahead, a ridge split into a deep fissure, more gorge than valley. She plunged into it, staying close to the ground.

Kyril emerged from the bluffs behind her. He'd drawn far closer, which represented a problem. He must think she was zeroing in on a find.

This gorge was doing nothing for her. She spotted a narrow cleft to the right. Too narrow? *Nah.*

She increased her speed, flipped the ship sideways and slipped into the gap.

"Alex, the hell!"

She gritted her teeth and tried to concentrate on flying. The gap hadn't widened yet. "I did tell you to strap in."

Reluctantly she spared a brief motion to activate the comm channel. "Bob, get down here and head to... 33.2° N, 114.1° W." The coordinates lay a hundred kilometers northwest of her current location. It should work.

"I'm not finished yet."

"Bob."

"Right. Heading there now."

Finally the terrain opened up, though the mountains grew far steeper. Jagged spikes jutting up from a dead landscape.

She swerved to the left to dart between two peaks then dropped down as low as she dared.

Kyril's blip followed. Motherfucker.

But it stayed more distant now. He was flying safely. "Coward."

Emboldened, she sped onward, dipping and weaving through the range. When another fissure came into view, she pivoted hard and raced through it, a mite too snugly for comfort. She was glad Kennedy wasn't up here to see how near to the cliff walls they flew.

On the scanner, Kyril slowed almost to a stop, handing her the break she needed. She found a basin on the topography map six kilometers to the northeast.

"Bob, shift to 33.8° N, 113.9° W and get ready."

"Yes, ma'am."

One last corkscrew turn... and....

She decelerated hard and plummeted toward the ground; when ten meters remained she killed the engine. "Now, Bob—17.8° N heading, then get back to space ASAP."

The ship shuddered roughly as it slammed to the ground. A couple of yellow warnings flashed across the HUD, but nothing critical.

"You are one crazy woman, Solovy."

"Thank you. I'm flattered."

Kennedy's voice sounded shaky behind her. "Um, did we crash?"

"Not technically. It's not crashing if it's on purpose."

Kyril had begun moving again and closed in on her location. Alex peered up as he passed overhead, but the paltry light didn't allow her to make out his ship. *Keep going. Keep going.*

He kept going, following Bob's blip into the darkness.

Bob did a surprisingly decent job of picking up where she left off. She was moderately impressed, not as if she'd tell him so.

But if she reengaged the engine too soon, Kyril's scanner might pick up the energy flare.

She breathed in. Out. Waited.

Slowly, cautiously, she lifted off the surface, spun and climbed through the atmosphere in the opposite direction from where Bob had flown.

They exited on the opposite side of the satellite from the gas giant, at which point she had no choice but to run the impulse engine for a minute or so.

"You can unstrap now."

Kennedy stumbled into the cockpit. "Okay, that sucked. What's next?"

Alex didn't answer. Better for her friend not to know until it was already done.

No time to reconsider. She activated the sLume drive and executed a pinpoint superluminal traversal to barely outside the not-a-white-dwarf-not-a-planet's orbit.

The warp bubble had hardly formed around the *Siyane* when it evaporated. Only then did the surge of adrenaline hit her.

A 2.7 AU superluminal trip was not a maneuver one did every day, mostly due to the fact it was dangerous as all hell. If she'd delayed another second—three-quarters of a second—before disengaging the sLume drive, they would've found themselves inside the pulsar. And dead.

"Did you… oh my God, you did. I think I'm… yeah, I'm going to go back to the couch and faint."

Alex grinned a bit wildly. "What? It worked, didn't it?"

"And if it hadn't?"

"We'd never be the wiser."

"Because we'd be vaporized."

"Yes. Now I don't have a lot of time, so hush."

Kennedy nodded weakly and wandered off. "Couch. Fainting. This is the worst vacation ever."

Alex blinked and worked to focus the adrenaline rush on productive endeavors such as catching up to the object, whatever it was, and matching its orbit. Something else guaranteed to be fun, since it was moving *fast*.

At such close proximity the pulsar taxed the radiation shield, but it would hold. She hoped. If this panned out, Astral-owned industrial vessels equipped with far stronger shielding would be able to hang out here for weeks at a stretch, but she couldn't risk staying more than… she checked the diagnostics… twenty-four minutes.

She had a solid bead on the orbital path of the object now, and she accelerated into a parallel trajectory. It gained on her from behind; she continued increasing her speed until she'd matched its velocity and it whisked along a sliver under four megameters off her port.

Trajectory stabilized, she blocked the massive X-ray radiation of the pulsar from the viewport and looked over.

She'd seen many interesting things in her three years of freelance scouting. Beautiful things, terrifying things. She needed a little sleep and a lot of drinks to process what she saw now, but she suspected this topped them all.

"Ken, get up here."

"But I'm still fainting."

"Whatever. Get your ass up here."

The planet-sized body—a quick measurement suggested a 40-50K kilometer diameter—appeared to be composed of a crystalline mineral so clear it was nearly transparent. The sole reason she was unable to see all the way through to the other side was that eventually, thousands of meters below the surface, the inner core darkened into an extremely dense form of carbon. Beyond the brilliance of the outer material, the body retained no more than a trace of natural luminosity. Plainly no longer a white dwarf; not for millennia.

The result of it being stripped of its outer layers then its stellar nature was a surface and outer core which looked a great deal like diamond but was likely something far more precious.

"What… ohhhh." Kennedy brought a hand to her mouth. "This is the most exquisite thing I've ever seen."

"Pretty much."

"You upgraded your radiation shield, right? Because I can get you a next-gen kit for cost."

"Let's do that. Soon as we get back."

Many white dwarfs had carbon-oxygen cores, but humanity thus far lacked the technology to harvest stars. Cold planetoids, on the other hand?

A dozen so-called carbon planets had been stripped bare to minimal riches for companies long forgotten, but only one other true 'diamond planet' had ever been discovered, orbiting the Fyren pulsar. A hundred twenty years ago the Magellan Aeronautics founder had made a fortune and funded an entire generation of interstellar private spacecraft by being the first to reach it and mine it.

Alex jerked out of the reverie. "Crap, the beacon!"

She'd been mooning over the splendor of the singular object speeding alongside them to the point of forgetting her mission. She hurriedly programmed in the details she hadn't known until now and launched it directly at the body.

The beacon plummeted to six kilometers above the ground, then decelerated and adopted a low-altitude orbit and began transmitting to everyone in the galaxy who mattered. Alex sank in her chair with an exuberant cackle.

"Bob, you and I are going to be rich—well, I'm going to be rich. You're going to be slightly more affluent."

Kennedy's face lit up in excitement. "If you're truly earning that much money from this find, I have got so many ideas—"

"Assuming you survive the next few minutes. Kyril just

turned tail and made a beeline for the pulsar. Or for you. I'm guessing for you."

Couldn't she spend five seconds enjoying her success in peace? Apparently not.

She straightened up in the chair and began to retreat from the planet. Her shield only had eight minutes worth of full functionality remaining before it started failing. She needed to move to a safe distance, and soon.

"Solovy, you bitch! You think you can get away with such a bullshit scam right in front of me?"

"Nice to talk to you, too, Kyril. Oh, wait. No, it's not. So sorry your plan to ghost then leapfrog me didn't pan out. Better luck next time. Or preferably, worse luck."

"Is that a bloody diamond planet? No. No way are you stealing millions from me. Not this time."

"He wouldn't dare try to shoot you down, would he?"

"Strap back in." She killed the heat and lights in the cabin and diverted the extra power to the defensive shield and increased the distance between her and the pulsar. Another couple of megameters and she'd be distant enough to engage the sLume drive and disappear—

—the *Siyane* shuddered as the laser hit it full-on broadside.

Kennedy's shocked gasp echoed behind her. "That bastard shot at you!"

"Not so cute now, is he?"

The shield held, but it had depleted to thirty-eight percent from the single hit. Kyril had top of the line everything it seemed, including weaponry.

Alex hit the comm. "Goddammit, Kyril, if you shoot at me again you will regret it."

"It would be such a shame if you accidentally got too close to the pulsar and met an unfortunate demise. Astral Materials will mourn your death while they pay me for the contract."

Fuck, no. Not going to happen.

She frantically pulled power from everywhere she could find it to recharge the defensive shield faster, located Kyril on the scanner and locked on.

She returned fire. The laser skimmed off his hull.

Nose down. Fired.

Hard port. Fired again.

She arced above him in a high-g maneuver, firing the whole way.

His shield had to be getting low. Hers had climbed to seventy percent, which was a good thing as he finally managed to track her and return fire. In a flash she was down to nine percent shields....

"Hit him again. I got your back."

Bob arrived out of nowhere above Kyril's ship, bless his drunken soul. She fired once more.

So did Bob.

Hers hit first, but it was Bob's shot that broke through the shield and caught the port rear of the ship. Hard.

The force of the strike sent Kyril's ship hurtling toward Shanshuo in an uncontrolled spin.

No blip on the scanner appeared to indicate the launch of an escape pod or chute as the ship was swallowed up by the pulsar.

Alex threw her arms on the dash and dropped her head onto them.

"Okay, Bob, twenty percent... and two drinks. You earned it."

"I didn't actually mean to kill him."

He sounded almost remorseful; she got that. "He intended to kill *us*. If you try to show mercy to someone like him, they will twist it back on you and use it to destroy you."

"When you put it that way... frankly, in your sultry voice it's kind of hot. Drinks—when and where?"

She sighed in weary amusement. "I'll be in touch. Promise."

When she lifted her head from the dash, Kennedy was standing beside her staring out the viewport. Her hands trembled at her sides. "Is it always like this?"

"Scouting? Nah. Sometimes it's dangerous."

Q&A with G. S. Jennsen

I loved the atmosphere you created in Venatoris. *We got the "feel" of it right away... the frontier vibe and the scent of unbridled competition. How do you go about envisioning an unknown world in an imaginary galaxy?*

All my writing is grounded in the core concept that no matter how much our technology advances, so long as keep these bodies of ours (however heavily augmented) we'll remain fundamentally *human*. This means whatever we find out there in the stars, we'll see it and experience it through the same human perspective we have now. This allows me to present what are often mind-blowing, nearly incomprehensible sights and experiences in a familiar, relatable way. The reader can put themselves in the world and imagine being there, because their perspective isn't so different from that of the character.

As for coming up with those sights and experiences, I've loved astronomy and space my entire life. I'm always researching, looking for wilder, more amazing creations I can bring to life, then throw characters into the middle of them.

What authors, past or present, got you jazzed about writing SF?

Goodness, I've been reading science fiction since I was a kid. In the old days, Isaac Asimov for the sweeping space exploration and fantastical future, Frank Herbert for the deep world- and culture-building. Later, Catherine Asaro for daring to mix serious, hard science fiction with romance and Lois McMaster Bujold for daring to have fun with science fiction. William Gibson for painting masterful imagery with mere words and Peter F. Hamilton for telling vast, grand stories.

Any Works in Progress?

Absolutely. *Dissonance: Aurora Renegades Book Two (Aurora Rhapsody #5)*, will be released April 2, 2016—so pretty much now. By the time it comes out, I'll already be working on the next book in the series, *Abysm*. If anyone wants to know more about *Aurora Rhapsody*, they can visit gsjennsen. com, or go directly to gsjennsen.com/aurora-rhapsody.

How can fans find you or follow you?

I love hearing from my readers. Seriously. They can email me at gs@gsjennsen.com; I'm active on Twitter, Facebook and Instagram, but I'm also on all the other social media networks (I'm easy to find—just try "GS Jennsen"). If someone wants to guarantee they'll find out about new releases, though, the best way is to subscribe to my mailing list (http://smarturl.it/gsjennsen-subscribe).

Hope 91

by Nick Webb

Day 715

MY NAME IS Alex White. I am nine years old, and I live on a spaceship called *Hope 91*.

Gertie told me I have to start keeping a journal, so here goes, I guess. She's mostly ok, but sometimes annoying. I told her she can't tell me what to do because she's a droid. But she tuts and laughs and makes me do the chores anyway. I hate it. But she's all right.

Let's see. I have to fill three whole pages, so I guess I should start typing. I've been on *Hope 91* for almost two whole years now. But I just woke up a month ago. It's very small. There's just room enough for me, Gertie, Max, Philae, and the other droids but they don't count because the rest of them only have one job, like the autopilot. I didn't name him, because he doesn't even talk. And Sally the chef. All she does is cook. But she doesn't even have a head. Just a bunch of robot arms in the galley.

Gertie's the nicest. Max is the funnest. And Philae is the weirdest. That's good because otherwise I'd be REALLY bored.

You see, I used to live in Baltimore, but, well, mom died. I still miss her a lot, but Gertie's been so nice to me. For a robot. Anyway, it's good that I'm up here. They say that I'll be one of the first people to live on Sephardia.

Who are *they*, you ask? They are everyone back on Earth. They are the ones who don't get to live on Sephardia. And the funniest thing of all is, they are all DEAD. Ha ha, I know, that's not funny. It's not like they all died in a big volcano or something. They all died two hundred years ago. There's new people living there now. People I'll never know.

They explained it to me once. You see, I was asleep for two years. And while I was asleep they fired the engines so the ship could speed up REALLY fast. I had to be asleep or else it would hurt me, or something. And now I'm going so fast that I'm TIME TRAVELING!!!! THAT IS SO COOL!

Anyway, I should get to Sephardia in about sixteen more years. But I'll have to sleep for two more whole years while we slow down. Eighteen years on a tiny spaceship. Yay. I can't wait. Gertie also says that I'm too sarcastic.

Anyway, Gertie's saying it's time for cleanup, then dinner, then more lessons with Philae, then a game with Max, then bed. I guess brave space explorers still have to do their chores.

Until next time!

Day 730

Gertie kept telling me to write in this thing, but I kept putting it off. Now I don't even know what to write about. I guess I'll describe the ship. It's called *Hope 91*. It's not big. I remember living in Baltimore. We had this house that was so big, I had my own bathroom, and the kitchen was big enough for mom and me to both sit down in, and there was a living room, and room to walk around. And a yard I could play in.

Hope 91 is mostly a lot of ladders. It's speeding up enough that I weigh half what I used to, but Gertie says that to grow right, I have to exercise a lot. I guess that's why they put all the ladders in. It makes me climb all the time, and makes me really tired.

The bottom floor is the engine room. I'm not allowed to go in there. The second floor is storage. It's where we keep all the food that I'll eat for the next thirteen years. Well, it's not *food* food. It's more like "add water" food. It tastes ok, I guess. Sally the chef does a good job. Better than mom ever cooked. She was always working and never had time for me anyway. She was always working so hard on something, which she never even told me anything about. Maybe it's best that she died and I left.

Now I feel horrible for typing that.

The third floor is where lots of machines are kept. Like the water recycler. And the air purifier. And all sorts of other stuff that Philae promised me he'd explain to me someday. He said that in a few years I'll get to choose my profession. He says I need to become good at all the spaceship's machines eventually, but that it would be best if I focused on one. I hope he doesn't make me learn to be a toilet expert. That would suck. Literally. The toilet here is not like the one in our house. It really sucks the poo out of you. I don't know why they just couldn't give me a real toilet.

The fourth floor is the kitchen. Sally the Chef's arms hang down from the ceiling and prepare all the food. But she doesn't clean. Really, people? You can design a robot that cooks me dinner, but that can't clean up after itself? I keep asking Gertie if she'll clean for me, but she just laughs and says I need to learn to clean up after myself. She says I have to be prepared for marriage. That's when I know she's just making fun of me. There's no one but me on this ship. And I won't get to Sephardia until I'm twenty-five. That's way too old to get married. Even if there are any girls there.

The fifth floor is my bedroom, and next to it is the game room where Max hangs out. He's the fun robot. Always inventing games for me to play with him. Sometimes he makes me invent games too, which is really fun.

The sixth floor is the school room. It's where Gertie and Philae both teach me my lessons. That is the most boring room ever. Every day. Four hours of Gertie. Four hours of Philae. Sometimes I wish the builders had packed me a gun.

The seventh floor is my favorite. It's the observatory. It has the most windows on the whole ship. The roof has windows too, and there's this loft I can climb up onto and lay on my back while I look up at the stars. It reminds me of laying in the back yard with mom in the summer, watching meteor showers. She always liked space stuff and astronomy, and we'd lay out there for hours. Sometimes she liked it so much that she'd even cry. I don't know why.

You can't see anything through the window but stars.

There are no planets or nebula or anything more interesting. Just stars and more stars.

So that's it, seven floors, three robots, an autopilot, Sally the Chef, and me. Alex White.

Wow, that was a lot. Goodbye!

Day 739

Gertie thinks she's my mom. Or at least that's probably how they programmed her. Sometimes she tries to hug me, but it's a little creepy. I let her anyway, because I don't have the words to tell her why it makes me uncomfortable, so I just let her do it. And she mentioned me getting married again today, which creeped me out. I asked her not to say that again, but all she did was smile and said something about Willow getting to meet me someday. Then she changed the subject really fast. I asked her who Willow was, and she said I must have heard her say something else, and then she made me go up to bed, an hour early! Ugh, I'm getting so sick of Gertie. Luckily, Max played a new game with me at bedtime. I think he sensed I was annoyed at Gertie. But now he's gone and I still had ten minutes before the lights turned out, so here I am.

Day 741

Today I tried to trick Gertie into telling me who Willow was. I lied and told her that Max and I talked about her last night before bed, and that he told me all about her. I thought she was going to cave and finally tell me, but instead she climbed up into the game room and punched Max in the back of the head. I think it was all worth it just to watch the two of them go at it. I think Gertie damaged one of Max's servomotors because his left eye has trouble blinking now.

Anyway, Gertie's not talking. She just makes me do my chores and does my morning lessons like normal. Every time I asked about Willow she just ignored the question and kept right on teaching. Today was all on commas and periods and punctuation. Seriously. Am I really going to need punctuation as one of the first settlers on a new world? So unfair.

Day 1010

Wow, so it's been awhile since I wrote. Like almost a year. I'm ten now, and the day after my birthday, all of the sudden Gertie starts blabbing about Willow! Like it was just part of her programming or something that she wasn't supposed to talk about until after I'd turned ten or something. She's a girl (duh!) who's in another spaceship called *Hope 92*. Gertie said I could talk to her sometime this year, but that first I'd need to prepare. I asked her what I needed to prepare, and she kept on saying stupid things like, *Oh, you need to be ready for her,* or, *all in good time, my sweet.*

I begged her to let me talk to her, but nothing worked. All Gertie did was continue with the morning lessons. Today it was ... I can't even remember. All I could think about was Willow. I think Gertie does the morning lessons because that's when I'm most awake and least likely to fall asleep. Philae's lessons are in the afternoon. That's when I'm already tired. But his are so interesting that I can't fall asleep. For robots, they're pretty smart.

Philae seemed pretty weird at first. He's still a little weird. He gets so excited about whatever our lesson is for the day. Like today, he taught me about seeds and germination and planting strategies and stuff, and I got to put on the VR headset and he showed me how to do it. He doesn't have to wear the headset since he's a robot, but we were both there, digging in the dirt and watering the seeds. He fast forwarded the time, and I got to watch our crops grow up in less than a minute. Then I learned how to run a harvester and chop and process all the wheat and corn. The whole time he was bouncing up and down in the tractor's seat next to me, telling me how combustion engines work, and just acting like Philae.

Then I asked him about Willow, and he said he wouldn't talk about her yet. Then he started talking about how learning how to grow all this food would help me feed my kids. That was weird.

I asked Max if I could move my bed from my bedroom to the top of the loft in the observatory. I want to fall asleep watching the stars. Even though they just look like points of light and nothing else, well, it reminds me of mom. I miss her.

He said no. Stupid robot.

Day 1121

It's been almost four months since Gertie first told me about Willow, and still, FOUR MONTHS LATER, she hasn't let me talk to her. Why are they making me wait so long? I've been sitting on this spaceship for over three years, and it seems like all I do is wait. That's the purpose of my life: wait. I'm waiting eighteen years just to get to my new home. And every day, all I can do is wait for the interesting lessons with Philae. Or wait for Sally the Chef to finish making dinner. Or wait through all my lessons to be able to play games with Max. And now, I have to wait months and months to finally talk to the only human I'll have gotten to talk to in years. I hate my life sometimes.

I finally convinced Max and Philae that I should get to spend two nights a week sleeping up in the loft in the observatory. Since there's three of us, we out-vote Gertie, who said that I couldn't sleep outside my bedroom. She thinks I might roll around in my sleep and fall off the loft. But I won't. I'm good with heights. I climb at least five hundred meters every day, since I go up and down those ladders over and over and over again.

Max calls the two nights I spend up there in the loft my slumber party. I asked him what that was, and he was surprised I'd never had a slumber party before when I was little. At least, I can't remember if I did. Mom moved us around a lot after dad left when I was really young. I remember living in three separate houses before she finally died. She never even told me why dad left. She said he was in the military, but never said anything else. She seemed really sad about it.

Anyway, I finally told Philae that I'd decided on a calling. I guess I should explain that. I'm supposed to choose a profession and a calling. The profession is some special skill that I'll learn and be an expert at that will be super useful to the colony when I get there. Farming. Building and programming computers. Being a doctor. That kind of stuff. But my calling is what calls to me. It's what I'm interested in doing and learning about that doesn't exactly help the colony, but is something that I want to learn about and be good at. For fun.

I chose astronomy. Well, actually I chose telescope building, but that's so I can look through the windows in the observatory and actually see stuff instead of just stars.

I get to start building my first telescope tomorrow. I'm so excited. I have a secret about the real reason I'm building the telescope, but I won't say it here because you-know-who is probably reading this.

Day 1128

I finished my first telescope. I spent a few days reading on the computer to learn how. There are lots of different kinds. I didn't know that before I started, so I chose the simplest one. Something called a refractor. It's just two lenses at different ends of a tube. After reading about what size lenses I needed and how far apart they need to be, I went to the printer and gave it the designs. A few minutes later I had the lenses and the tube, but then I realized I had no way to connect the lenses to the tube. So Philae gave me some hull sealant. That's the stuff they'll use if there's ever a hole in the wall of the spaceship from a micro-meteor. That's the biggest fear the robots have, is us hitting a tiny tiny piece of dust. Since we're moving at close to the speed of light, it'll hurt us bad. But there's no way to see one coming. Luckily, the robots say that deep interstellar space is super empty, and that we shouldn't have to really worry until we get close to the star system we're heading for. And right before landing on Sephardia will be most dangerous part of all.

Anyway, I used the hull sealant and glued the lenses in the tube. I took it up to the observatory, rested it on the loft pointing out the side window, then laid down to look through it.

AND IT WAS FUZZY! I was so mad. All that time I spent studying and printing and glueing, and it was fuzzy. I think I glued the lenses in at the wrong spot, or maybe I made the tube too short or too long.

But I think I figured out a way around that. Tomorrow I'll make a tube with two parts that slide against each other, so I can extend the tube or make it shorter. That way I won't have to glue the lenses exactly in the right spot.

Gertie has me doing stuff she calls "etiquette lessons." Basically, how to talk to girls. She's so weird. Aren't girls people? I used to talk to people all the time. Why can't I just talk to Willow?

Day 1129

I built the new tube. It works perfectly. Well, almost perfectly. I can slide the two parts of the tube in and out, and put them in just the right spot so the image is not too fuzzy. The thing is, it's still a little fuzzy, but I think it's from another problem. I read more about lenses, and I think it's something called astigmatism. That's when the lenses are crooked.

Man, this astronomy business is hard. Maybe I'll choose something else for my calling.

Hmm…. But if I change, I won't be able to do my thing I have planned. Gertie—stop reading my journal!

Day 1209

Over two months ago, I built that first telescope. It sucked. Now I've got a pretty decent one. It's still a refractor, but the lenses are a little bigger. The tube is not adjustable. That's because I figured out how to print out some lens holders that will clamp onto the tube. And I even printed out a tripod, and a clamp to hold the telescope on and move it around.

The bad news is, my plan didn't work. I tried to use it to find *Hope 92*. But I couldn't find it. I spent every night for a whole month looking for it, out every window of the observatory. Looks like I'll never get to talk to Willow, or see her or her spaceship. It's so unfair. Just like when dad left. Just like mom dying. Just like being sent out in this stupid spaceship. I should have never said yes. Why did I say yes? I was only seven. They can't just send seven-year-olds out into space, can they? Can they?

But now everyone back on Earth that sent me is dead, because for them, I left almost three hundred years ago. Life is so unfair.

I just want to talk to somebody. Gertie is annoying. Max is getting boring. Philae is the only interesting one, but I only get to talk to him for a few hours in the afternoon before he goes down to the engine room to take care of the ship. But he's not human, he's a droid. I mean, he has a human face, and he *looks* human. But it's just not the same. Not the same, and not fair.

I just want to talk to somebody.

Day 1210

I woke up today, and Gertie surprised me at breakfast.

She said tomorrow I get to talk to Willow.

I'm in bed now, but I can't sleep, so I'm writing in my journal. And I can't even concentrate to do that, so I'm going to read about telescopes. Goodnight.

Day 1211

I talked to her! Willow is a real person. She is ten years old. Like me. It is day 1213 for her, so she's been in space for two days longer than me.

I think that explains it. Since she launched two days before me, maybe it took us this long to catch up! That's why Gertie didn't let me talk to her, because we couldn't. And that's why I couldn't see her spaceship in the telescope, because it was in front of us.

Anyway, I got to talk to her for twenty whole minutes. It was the most amazing thing. We talked about everything. We compared our ships. We compared our robots. She has a mom robot, a fun robot, and a teacher robot, just like me. Her kitchen robot is like mine, except Willow calls him Jeeves. That made me laugh.

We even had a few minutes where we didn't say anything at all. But that was ok. It was just so nice to have someone real to talk to. So nice, that even that awkward silence was amazing. It was like I could hear her smile in the silence. I hope she could hear me smile.

I think I could get used to this.

I'm in bed already. I didn't even have time to do telescope work today! How can I have time for telescopes when there's a real person out here to talk to!

Day 1225

I've been talking to Willow for two weeks now. It's like I've known her forever. We're best friends, and we talk about everything. And I mean *everything*. We talk about our robots. We talk about what professions we think we'll have. It's still a few years before we need to decide, and I still have no idea what I want to do. Neither does she.

But she has chosen her calling. Willow is an artist. She says her mediums are colored pencil, watercolor, and electroglass. I thought it was funny she said mediums instead of saying, I like colored pencils. I laughed at her. But then she laughed at me for wanting to build a Cassegrain, so we're even.

A Cassegrain is a type of telescope. It's where light goes in one side, but instead of going through a lens, it hits a curved mirror at the other end. Then it bounces back and hits another smaller mirror at the first end. Then the light goes back to the second end and goes through a really small hole in the first mirror, where it comes out the tube and into a small lens in an eyepiece. I explained it all to Willow, and she's really excited for me. It makes me happy to know she's excited. It makes me want to see her art.

Day 1250

Gertie keeps on getting after me for talking to Willow so

much, but I can't help it. She and Philae tried to limit me to one hour per day, but me and Max outvoted them. Well, it's a tie, but we made a new rule on the spaceship that ties go in favor of the way something is already done, and since I already talk to her about two hours a day, that's how long I get to keep talking to her for. I love democracy. That's what Philae has been teaching me about. Democracy, monarchies, oligarchies, republics, theocracies, autocracies, military juntas, banana republics, it seems like it's one of Philae's favorite subjects. Except that every subject seems like Philae's favorite subject. Good old Philae. He asked me what system I thought we lived in on the ship, and I said Alexocracy, since I'm the only human onboard, I'm in charge. He did that snorting thing where his chest bounces while he laughs.

I asked Willow about her parents, about why they sent her up here to settle Sephardia without them. It was weird, Willow got all quiet and changed the subject. She's never done that before. We talk about everything. We don't keep secrets from each other. I'm worried I upset her, and then I realized what a stupid question it was, that maybe if I was sent up here because my mom was dead and my dad gone, maybe hers were dead too and I reminded her. Damn, I can be so stupid sometimes.

I just wrote damn. I think I can swear here. Who's going to stop me?

Gertie, if you're reading this, I swear I'll figure out a way to deactivate you.

Day 1252

I did it. I'm not sure why I did it, but I did. I asked Willow if her parents were dead. She said of course they were, because they died three hundred years ago. I guess she has a point. Even if mom hadn't have died before I left, she would have been dead anyway before I woke up from my two year nap. I asked her if they died before she left, and she told me to ask her again sometime, but not now. Ok, I guess. Whatever it is, seems like it's too hard for her to talk about.

We had a pretty big scare today. Philae thinks we passed through a molecular cloud. Now, when I hear the word cloud, I think of big white clouds back on Earth. But he said this was different than that. He says that there's hydrogen everywhere in the galaxy, like one atom per centimeter. And going so fast, we pass through a lot of it, but we have special equipment on the front of the ship that pushes it out of the way before we run into it. But this cloud was like a thousand times normal, so like a thousand atoms every centimeter.

Anyway, because we rammed through so much hydrogen, the outside walls started to heat up a lot, and the alarms went off. Gertie was scared that I got hit with too much radiation, but Philae thinks I'm fine. They're going to test me tomorrow to make sure. But it was just a nice reminder that we're in space, and space is dangerous. I sure hope we don't hit anything bigger than an atom, because that was scary hearing the alarms like that.

Day 1500

I thought I'd finally write again since it's a special day. Day 1500. I don't know why that's special, but round numbers seem special, so there. Willow thinks I'm a goon for saying stuff like that. If it were up to her, we'd celebrate day 1581, and when I ask why, she'd say, because One Five ate One! She's funny like that, always playing with words. She talks about her art every day. I wish I could see it.

We're both eleven now. I had my birthday a few weeks ago, and hers was a month before that. For her present I made her really simple plans for a telescope that will be really easy for her to put together. But she hasn't even touched the plans yet. For my birthday, she said she painted me a picture. But since I can't see it, she has to describe it to me. She explains pictures and things a lot better than me, I don't think I could describe the picture like she could. When she describes it, it's like I see it in my mind. She said it was a valley, with sunlight streaming through clouds. The light shines on a little house, and I'm in the front yard of a house digging in the dirt. I think she had me doing that because I chose my profession a few months ago. I decided I'm going to be a farmer. I used to love playing in the rocks and dirt in our backyard, and in all our VR simulations with Philae, I love the ones where we learn stuff about planting and harvesting and fertilizing and all that.

Day 1504

Willow woke me up today early. She was crying. She kept on saying she wished she had someone to just hold her, because she was really sad. Sadder than usual. Then she told me it was because today was her dad's birthday. She said that when her parents dropped her off at the launch, they made her promise to remember them on their birthdays, and they'd remember her on her birthday. And then Willow said something weird about them only getting a few birthdays after that. When I kept asking why, all she did was cry, so I tried to say funny things to calm her down.

I felt so bad I couldn't hug her and hold her and help her feel better. All I wanted was to make her not be sad anymore.

This is so unfair. Why did we get sent out here? Is starting a new colony halfway across the galaxy really so important that they need to make me waste my childhood locked on a spaceship? It seems so cruel.

Day 1505

Max had amazing news for me today. He likes to be the one to give me good news, and I even overhear the three droids fight over who gets to give me the news, whatever it is.

Instead of telling me, he took me up to the observatory, and pointed. I looked out the window, and didn't see what he was pointing at. Just stars. Look closer, he said. So I followed his arm and finger, and saw that it was pointed at a spot really close to the shield at the front of the ship. I still didn't see anything. Look closer, he said.

Then I understood what he was telling me to do. I grabbed my telescope and pointed it at the spot he was pointing to.

And there she was. *Hope 92*. Willow's spaceship. We finally caught up with it.

You know, for a year now I've kinda worried that Willow wasn't real. That it was too good to be true that there was actually someone else out here with me. I expected to wake up any morning and hear Philae tell me it was all a test to see if I would respond to a real human like I do to droids, or that Gertie would say that the whole thing was a dream.

But she's real. I can see into her windows. I can see pictures hanging up on her walls. Every wall that I can see is covered with pictures that she's drawn or painted. I even saw her. Not very well, because she never held still long enough for me to really see her. She never just stopped and stared out the window for me to get a good look.

But she's beautiful.

I didn't tell her what happened. I didn't tell her that I could see her. Instead, I'm going to surprise her. Today when we talked, I begged her to finish the telescope. The plans I sent her are so easy. She should be able to build it. I finally got her to promise me she'd finish it. Even though she's still really sad after her dad's birthday yesterday.

Then I'll have her point it at a certain spot in her window. And when she does, she'll see what I taped to my window.

I drew a picture last night of me and her. I'm holding her. Giving her a hug. Maybe seeing that will help her feel better.

Day 1506

She still didn't build it. Instead, she cried more. She must be really sad. I hope she gets over it, whatever it is.

Day 1507

Still no telescope. I made her triple promise me today that she'd do it.

Day 1508

Still no telescope. But she sounds better now. She didn't cry once when we talked today, but she still didn't sound happy.

I was thinking this morning. Why did her parents send her off in the spaceship without going with her? I mean, in my case, mom was dead, and I hadn't seen dad for a few years. I didn't have anybody there anyway, so it made sense to send me. Why her?

Day 1509

She built it! When she told me, I shouted over the radio, and whooped and hollered. I told her where to point it, and she did, and when she finally figured out how to focus and saw me through the window, she started yelling too. She sounded so happy. Then she saw the picture I drew, the one I taped to the window. And she got very quiet. I asked her if she was ok, and she said yes. She said she felt better than she'd felt since she left Earth. She said she felt loved.

That made me happy.

Day 2200

Happy birthday to me! I'm thirteen!

And, as a reward, Gertie started her lessons this morning talking about stuff a girl droid should never ever be telling a human boy like me. She called her lesson the birds and the bees.

Gertie, no. No, Gertie. Just … no.

I asked her if Philae could take over the lesson, and she

said he was programmed to teach me the hard sciences and history and practical things like farming. It was her job to teach me about penises and vaginas and why I keep waking up with wet sheets. No, Gertie. Just stop.

Anyway, I've been practicing my drawing, so I can impress Willow. I've been practicing on her. I'll stay up late drawing her face and her body. It's not very good, but it's a start.

I've started a big new telescope project. It's called a Newtonian Reflector, and it's going to be HUGE. All this time using the Cassegrain has been nice, but I can't really see very much detail when I look at Willow's ship. I can recognize her face, but it's still really small. I can see her drawings, but I can't really catch the finer details because the telescope is just too small. The Newtonian will have a seventy centimeter mirror. It'll be so big around that I won't even be able to wrap my arms around it. When it's done, it'll be like Willow is in the same room with me. It'll be so awesome.

Day 2234

Willow said something strange today. It's her dad's birthday again, and she was sad just like last year and the year before.

But she said she wished her parents had died before she left Earth, just like my mom. She said she was a little jealous of me, because she had to live with the knowledge that her parents lived for a few years without her, while my mom was already dead.

I asked her what she was talking about. Why would her parents live for only a few years? She said it was a secret, that she wasn't supposed to tell me. I asked her who was around to even tell her what to do anymore. I told her she didn't have to do what the droids said. It seemed like I was close to convincing her, but then she closed up and stopped talking. It's making me really mad that she feels like she can't tell me some things. Not mad at her, really, but mad at the droids. How dare they keep important information from me? It sounds like something was going on on Earth before I got sent away. Something about the clues Willow keeps dropping. It's like she's convinced there's not even anyone back on Earth anymore, that they're all dead. I mean, of course everyone we ever knew was dead, but those people had kids, and those kids grew up and had kids, right?

I'm about to finish the Newtonian Reflector. It's been harder than I thought. The printer can't print a mirror that large, so I have to print it in sections, and then I have to join them perfectly, and it's just a lot harder than I thought. But I'll get there.

Day 2235

I beat up Max today. I felt awful about it. But I did it, and I'm glad I did. When all the droids were together this morning, I asked them about what Willow's been talking about. Why her parents were alive while my mom was dead. Why we were launched into space. Why Willow keeps on talking like no one is left back on Earth.

They wouldn't tell me. They all clammed up. It made me so mad. So I started yelling really loud and throwing things around. Philae tried to make some big intelligent-sounding speech about some things being better not knowing about them and Gertie tried to hug me and calm me down, but I cracked. I exploded. I decided I was going to force the truth out of them.

So I tackled Max and started pounding on his head with one of my telescope tools. Not hard enough to really hurt him, but I yelled at them that I'd start hitting hard enough to really do some damage. And that when I'd broken Max, I'd come after the rest of them. I don't know what got into me. It just made me so mad thinking about my mom dead, but Willow's mom and dad alive.

So they finally told me.

I … I can't talk about it right now. Maybe tomorrow.

Day 2242

A week ago, they finally told me everything. Well not everything everything—they gave me access to a section of files in the computer that I didn't have access to before. The ones that told about The Disruption. That's what they called it. They even capitalized it, just like I did.

The Disruption.

A few years before I was born, astronomers discovered something called a brown dwarf. A really really small one. It's basically a star that failed to ignite, so you can't really see it from far away. But it's way bigger than Jupiter. And they discovered it was flying really fast from above the plane of the solar system, and was supposed to come really close to Earth. It wouldn't hit the Earth, but it would come about as close as the moon.

And because it was that big, and was going to come so close to Earth, they figured out that Earth was going to be ejected from the solar system. And within a few years the atmosphere would freeze. Most people would die when the brown dwarf flew by because of huge tides and shifting continental plates making volcanoes erupt and triggering earthquakes, and those that survived would eventually either freeze or suffocate or starve.

I felt like I was going to throw up.

I told Willow about it, and she said she knew the whole time, but her droids told her she was forbidden to tell me. That's just crazy. Why keep that from me? Philae told me that *they* (meaning the people on Earth that sent me up here) thought that it would just distract me, that it would be better if I didn't know so I could focus on my new life. But that's just stupid.

So that's why Willow's been so sad every time it's her mom or dad's birthday. They didn't live for very long after she launched.

And now I'm starting to wonder when my mom died. And why my dad left. I was only four, but I never remember them fighting. Not once.

This is so unfair.

Day 2250

The Newtonian is done. Of course, I've been telling Willow about it this whole time, telling her what it meant, that I could see every detail of her face, and I could really see and appreciate her drawings. She was excited too. I pointed it at *Hope 92*, and looked for her. She wasn't there. But I saw her painting, the one with me in the valley and the sun streaming down through the clouds, lighting up the green and yellow grass and the blue hills behind, and me in the dirt, digging.

And next to the painting, on just a plain piece of paper she'd taped to the window, was a message. One that I'd never have been able to read before the Newtonian. It said, *look closer*, and there was an arrow pointed at the old painting.

I looked closer. On the hill behind the house, really small, was a person. With a bunch of sheep or something. It was Willow. At the bottom of the painting, just above her name, she'd written, *I love you*.

I saw something else. On the wall, behind the pictures she'd taped to the window, was another painting. It was the exact same drawing I'd made of us a few years ago, the one where I was giving her a hug to help her feel better, only it was much, much better.

Then she

Day 2252

Sorry. I didn't mean to cut off like that. But something happened. Something horrible.

Horrible.

I don't know what I'm going to do.

The day we've been dreading came. I mean, it wasn't as bad as the droids feared. The piece of dust didn't directly strike the spaceship.

But it hit the antenna. A one-in-a-million shot. I mean, just hitting the spaceship would have been a one-in-a-million shot. This was one in a billion.

I can't talk to Willow. I can't talk to my best friend. My only friend.

I can't talk to Willow.

We looked at each other through our telescopes. I waved

at her. She waved at me. I pointed to my eye, then my heart, then at her. I saw her laugh. Then she did the same thing. All we can do is look at each other. She wrote me a little message that she taped to the window. It said, *We'll figure this out, don't worry.*

I hope she's right.

Day 2601

I'm fourteen.

Mom didn't die before I left. She lied to me. I guess she wanted me to feel like there was nothing left for me back there. I guess she wanted to make it easier on me. I mean, she was going to die anyway. She didn't want to have to face me on that launchpad like Willow's parents had to do. To say goodbye. Instead, she faked a disease and left.

I've thought about this for months. Can I forgive her? I don't know if I can. She's been dead for hundreds of years, just like everyone else back there. But for me, it was only seven years ago. I mean, that's half my life. I just don't know what to think about it, so I try not to think about it.

Dad didn't leave. Well, I mean, he did leave. But they didn't split up. And he might have even died before I left— the records are spotty. He worked for the defense department. In the decade before I left, Nasa and the defense department and every other government on Earth got together and tried to figure out how to stop The Disruption. Dad was in the marines, and he was also a tech guy. So he volunteered to go up in a big fleet of spaceships and try to land on the brown dwarf, and do something to push it far enough out of the path of Earth that maybe Earth would be spared.

It didn't work, of course. I read a few of the news reports after they tried. You can't land on a brown dwarf. It would be like trying to land on Jupiter. But they had to try anyway. And they failed.

Dad didn't leave me. He didn't abandon me. Not like mom.

Day 2602

Willow and I have worked out a pretty good system for talking. I can't hear her, of course. But we made up a sign language. I look into the telescope while she signs to me, then we switch and I sign to her. Our vocabulary isn't huge, but we learn two words a day. It's mainly a language she makes up, because since I have the bigger telescope I can see stuff she writes down on paper and tapes to the window. She can't see what I write. So she makes up a few signs, and writes the words next to the drawing of the signs, and tapes it up, then we practice it.

Her paintings have gotten really good. And she chose her profession. She's going to be a doctor. She says she likes the idea of helping people feel better.

Day 2603

In two years, we'll do the Big Turn. Philae is a little worried about it, and keeps checking and rechecking the original calculations *they* did seven years ago. The Big Turn is where we'll shut the engines off for a few hours, turn the ship around, carefully point it in just the right direction—straight towards Earth, then turn the engines back on.

That way we can start slowing down so that by the time we get to Sephardia, we'll be slow enough to enter orbit and land.

And this way I'll still have gravity.

But Gertie worries and worries, and pesters Philae to recheck again to make sure everything goes just right. She's been a nervous wreck ever since I beat the crap out of Max. I mean, Max is fine. He's as happy as ever. We still play games every night before bed. I switched my bedroom up to the observatory—I sleep there every night now, just staring at the stars, watching *Hope 92* through the Newtonian. I always go to bed later than Willow, so I just stare at her paintings.

Day 3302

Tomorrow is the Big Turn. Philae is confident we'll do it perfectly. Most of the systems are automated, of course, but he's agreed to let me help perform the actual maneuvers. We've been practicing in the VR, running through the steps over and over again.

Of course, if I do anything wrong, the autopilot will take over. But it'll be fun to actually get to fly the ship, even if for only a few minutes.

Willow's ship is doing the Big Turn at exactly the same time. She's not flying her ship, just watching. She's gotten really good with her art the past year. Like, she's taken it to a whole new level. I look at pictures from artists back on Earth, and I can't see that they're any better.

She's also a kick-ass … medical … person, ha ha. Not a doctor yet, of course, and she hates the word nurse. She fell off a ladder the other day and landed on one of her easels, and cut her arm open pretty bad. And she sewed it up herself, without help from her droids. Let me repeat myself. SHE SEWED HERSELF UP. That girl is bad-ass. And I love her.

Day 3303

The Big Turn happened today. I messed up. I can't talk about it yet. I can't believe what I did. It's all over. It's all over.

Fuck me, it's all over.

Day 3310

I don't leave the observatory. I can't. All I can do is search the stars behind us for *Hope 92*. It's back there, somewhere. During the Big Turn, I did something stupid. I accidentally pushed too hard on the accelerator, which means that for about an hour, without me knowing it, we decelerated much faster than *Hope 92*. By the time we figured it out, it was too late. For some reason we don't understand, the autopilot didn't kick in for me. I fear I accidentally shut it off.

Our nose is pointed towards Earth, our rear towards Sephardia, and somewhere back there is Willow, in the shadow of our own hull.

I've lost her.

I've directed the autopilot to decrease our deceleration so that we eventually catch up with her, but Philae says it could be a year before I see her again.

Day 3425

Still no sign of *Hope 92* and Willow.

I've started studying physics with Philae in the mornings instead of time with Gertie. Things are a lot different here than they were a few years ago. After my episode with Max, I think the droids all decided it was time to let me have more autonomy. Since then, it's basically been an Alexocracy. My word goes. So, last month, I decided Gertie's lessons were out, and Philae's physics lessons were in.

I just want to understand what my dad was up against as he tried to move that brown dwarf out of the way and stop The Disruption. I want to understand what my mom was trying to figure out—I learned she was a scientist too. She worked for Nasa in the decade before The Disruption, but I don't know what she was working on.

And I just want to understand what went wrong with my part in the Big Turn, and maybe figure out how to reach out to Willow again. I don't know how, or if it's even possible. But I've got to try.

Day 3499

Why didn't anyone ever tell me physics is hard? Seriously. This stuff is crazy. I've learned all about Newton, gravity, inverse square laws, Poynting vectors, flux and Green's theorem, and the Schrodinger equation, and wave-particle duality, and all kinds of stuff that I had no idea ever existed.

Still nothing on the Willow front. I look every day down there towards Sephardia, but no ship, no *Hope 92*.

I've kept up my drawings. I'm trying to get her face just right. I don't want to forget her.

Day 3700

I think I'm starting to forget her face. Some days I don't think it's possible, but others I have to go look at the pictures I've drawn to remind myself what she looks like. My secret fear is that I'll lose her, just like I lost mom, just like I lost Earth.

It's been over a year since the Big Turn, and still no sign of *Hope 92*. And now I'm seventeen. Seven years to go.

Physics is going great. I'm moving on to relativity soon. Just special relativity—Philae says that general relativity will be beyond my reach for a few years yet, so we'll stick to the basics. I already got the gist of it—I mean, I *am* aboard a spaceship flying at relativistic speeds compared to Earth, you'd think I'd have picked a few things up.

Day 3755

Everything is a lie. Mom lied to me. The people on Earth lied to me. Dammit, even the droids have been lying to me. I can't even trust Philae anymore.

I haven't been seeing real stars. I don't even know if I've been seeing Willow. Turns out, physics has consequences. I've been studying relativity with Philae, and combining it with my earlier studies of electromagnetism I figured out something pretty troubling.

We're traveling at a pretty large fraction of the speed of light. Something like 99.999%. There's this pesky little thing called redshift. If you're traveling away from something, its light gets redder. Traveling towards something, the light gets bluer. But we're moving so fast that the stars in the direction of Earth should be shifted far into at least microwaves, and the stars in front of us should be shifted well into the x-rays. All of them invisible. Instead, all I *should* see is a huge globe of light in front of us, the color depending on our exact speed. That globe would be the blue-shifted light from the microwave background of the universe. I should only be able to see the light from the universe's birth. That's all I should see. Nothing else.

These windows aren't windows. They're holographic projectors.

I've been looking through my telescope at a lie.

Please. Please let Willow not be a lie, too.

Day 3802

I finally confronted Philae about the holographic projectors. He said he was wondering when I'd figure it out. He said the people who designed the ship thought it would feel a lot better for me to be able to see stars. To see the outside of the ship. Otherwise, living for eighteen years closed up inside a box with no walls might make me go crazy.

Crazy or not, it was all a lie.

Philae swears Willow wasn't a lie. But how do I trust a droid that's already proven he has no problem lying whenever it suits him? Gertie tells me to trust them. Even Max got serious for the past few days and tried to convince me they were only doing what they're doing to help me.

I don't believe them.

Mom lied. Dad lied. The droids lied. Let me guess, is the Earth still there? Did they just send me away because they were tired of me? Or am I a guinea pig? To test out one of these spaceships, to make sure they work?

Day 3855

Philae convinced me to look through the telescope again. I don't know why I agreed to, but I did. There it was, *Hope 92*, finally caught up with us. Or us caught up with her. All I can see is the top of their shield. No windows yet.

I just don't know if I can believe them.

I mean, I see why they did it now. If all I had were actual windows, the x-rays would have fried me within a few days of leaving Earth. Behind the holographic projectors is a meter of lead and water shielding, with the water serving double duty as heat suppression. I'm literally in a lead box.

I think I liked my life better during the blissful lie. It was more beautiful, even if it wasn't real.

Day 3856

I've forgiven Philae. The more I look at the holographic set-up, the more I realize how necessary it was. It protected me from radiation. It saved my life, most likely. And really, the projector shows me what's out there—it just takes the light that it sees, and converts it to a wavelength that my eyes can actually detect. Those stars are real. *Hope 92* was real.

In a sense, it's like the truth was too horrible, too painful to accept, so the holographic projectors had to lie to protect me. They needed to give my eyes a version of the truth that wouldn't kill me.

It was all real.

It better have been real.

Willow better be real.

I hope she is. Hope is all I have at this point.

Day 3931

Yesterday was my birthday, and for my eighteenth birthday Gertie gave me The Letter. From mom. I'm still too numb to even talk about it.

And *Hope 92*'s windows are finally visible. But no sign of Willow. I can see her picture of the sunlit valley which is still taped up to the window, but she never appears next to it. There's another piece of paper taped up, but the ship is still at too steep of an angle for me to be able to read it.

I'll talk about The Letter tomorrow.

Day 3932

The Letter. I've read it about a billion times, just to be sure. Just to wrap my head around it. She goes into a lot of detail—lots of things I'd already figured out for myself. She talks about the brown dwarf, and how all of humanity mobilized against it, sending out mission after failed mission. She talks about preparations for The Disruption, and something she calls The Long Night. I guess, in addition to sending out a few thousand ships to Sephardia, each with a single person and a few droid companions, humanity also started up something called The Ground Initiative. The details were fuzzy, but they tried to dig a huge underground living space underneath North America, and another under France, and set up to keep the human civilization alive indefinitely underground. At least until technology would develop to get everyone off the planet, or steer the Earth back into orbit.

It failed.

But that wasn't the important part of The Letter. The real reason for The Letter was to admit to me that she lied. She said she just couldn't bear the thought of seeing me one last time on the launch pad, that she couldn't bear the thought of sending me off into space with me knowing that she sent me away. She thought it would be easier for me if there was a clean break. If she was already dead.

And she apologized for it. She realized she was wrong, after seeing me blast off and accelerate away.

She sent The Letter just before The Disruption. It was received by our computer after I woke up from my hibernation, when I was ten. Knowing that she realized she made a mistake, and wanted to go back and change things, well, I'm not sure if that makes me feel better or worse.

Anyway, I can't think about it anymore. All I can think about is Willow. I still can't read what she wrote. Maybe in a few weeks it'll come into view.

Day 3946

The note says: *Very sick. Have space sickness. In hibernation. I love you.*

I'm not sure what to think. Is she real? I want to think yes. I desperately want to think yes. But other times I think this is another lie that Philae has contrived, or a game that Max has invented, or some scheme by Gertie to keep me focused on something other than myself. If they can lie about everything else, why not invent a fake girlfriend for me? One I'll never meet, one I'll never touch. One I'll never get to have sex with. One I'll never really get to share my life with. Just a story to believe in. Something to get me to wake up in the morning and forge onward, thinking I'm not alone.

I have to believe I'm not alone. She really was there. We shared something. We shared our lives together. We grew up together.

I gave up on the idea of my mom a long time ago. And, years later, learning that she'd lied to me, I gave her up again.

But I can't give up on Willow. Even if she is a lie.

Day 5000

I'm almost 21. I've built telescopes. I've piloted a spaceship faster than any human in history. I've lived my entire life as a single, solitary pioneer. I'm a physicist. I've learned it all, from general relativity, to quantum mechanics, and even finally figured out how our engines work, how they scoop up energy from the virtual particle background. I've even learned how to draw properly, though I'm still but a shadow of an artist compared to Willow.

I've come so far. And now I'm sick. Came down with the same space sickness that Willow did. I'm no doctor, I don't really understand medicine and how the body works—that was my one area of academic deficiency. But something about the constant radiation combined with the lower gravity and the food I'm eating every day. I'm weak, shaky, have bad diarrhea every day, I'm lightheaded, I pass out a lot. The only solution is to go into hibernation early.

I'm still two years out from when I was supposed to enter hibernation for the Big Stop. That period of extreme deceleration is supposed to last two years. But I can't live like this. Philae says that going into hibernation will cure me.

Before I go, I'm drawing one last piece. I know I'll never, ever be even a thousandth as good as Willow, but I tried to get it right. I painted a picture of her, and me, holding each other. Just like that one stupid little stick figure drawing I drew all those years ago. But this time it's a masterpiece. At least, for my skills it is. I'm taping it to the window. If she's real, if she's still alive, and if she ever wakes up, and if she survives the Big Stop, then maybe, just maybe, she'll see it.

And remember me.

Day 6421

I'm awake.

More on this later. Damn, my head hurts.

Day 6422

Yesterday was awful. Today's still bad—I have to dictate this instead of type. Gertie finally got me the right combo of pills, and now I can actually think. I can move without screaming. Still so tired. I kept asking Philae how much time passed. If we made it. If Willow made it. He wouldn't say. He said it's best to discover these things by ourselves. He said something strange—he said the most devastating lies are the ones we tell ourselves, but the most liberating truths are the ones we discover on our own.

Sleep now. Hopefully tomorrow I can get out of bed.

Day 6425

I spent three more days in bed, down with a high fever. Something about the space sickness lingered, and triggered an immune response. But I'm better now. Much better. I'm out of bed, but there's no way I can climb that ladder. And no windows down here in the equipment room where they kept me near the hibernation chamber, so I hope I have strength to climb tomorrow.

Last Day.
6426

I climbed up the ladder. All the way to the seventh floor, to my observatory. When I looked out the window, I noticed something strange. The stars were there, just as it appeared they always were, but these looked different, somehow. And the observatory was lit with a strange glow. When I looked out the window, I saw the source of the light. It was so bright that it hurt my eyes—I saw a terrible black circle, an afterimage, for ten minutes afterward.

That meant one thing, and only one thing.

The holographic projectors were off. I noticed the edges of the window—the lead shielding had been folded away. I was really looking out the window. At real stars. At a real sun. When I pointed my Newtonian at a particularly bright star, it wasn't a star.

It was a planet. Finally, after all those years of studying astronomy, building telescopes, trying to find things to point my refractor at, and then my Cassegrain, and then my Newtonian, finally I found something different.

But I'd always had something worth looking at.

I turned my scope down, to where *she* was. To *Hope 92*. And there it was—it was so close, closer than it ever had been before, so close that I almost didn't need my Newtonian to look at it.

But I looked anyway. There was the picture of the valley glowing in the late afternoon sun. Behind it, taped to the wall, was the old stick figure picture I'd drawn. The one that made Willow feel loved. And near that was her refractor, assembled from the plans I'd made her.

She wasn't there.

But taped next to the valley painting, written in beautiful script, was a note.

Alex. I've been waiting for you for so long.

I'm real, I'm alive. And I love you.

You'll be a farmer. I'll be a doctor.

You'll be an astronomer. I'll be a painter.

You'll be glad to see me again. And I've waited so long to see you.

Welcome home.

Q&A with Nick Webb

Every once in a while an author comes across as story and says, "Darn it... why didn't I think of that?" Hope 91 is one of those stories for me. I'm thrilled to be able to include it in this anthology. Was there a specific incident or person that suggested the set-up to you?

I'm so relieved someone liked it! Honestly, it was a bit of a "left field" story for me. My standard fare, for novels at least, is shoot-em-up pew-pew military space romps. It's nice to take a break from that and do something completely different.

Several movies, books, and stories got me in the mood for *Hope 91*. I love the story devices of time dilation and cryo-sleep that are used to great emotional effect in both the movie Interstellar, and *The Dark Age*, one of my favorite short stories by Jason Gurley. The idea of separation from your loved ones in not only space, but time, for me evokes one of those gut-punch feelings—imagining missing not only the physical presence of a parent or a child, but missing out on large chunks of their lives because of a universal speed limit and the nature of space-time itself is something both terrible and poignant to think about, since it makes me appreciate and take more care for the time together we do enjoy. Another recent influence is Neal Stephenson's *Seveneves*, where the Earth is soon to be rendered uninhabitable by an exploding moon, and humanity's only hope is to send as many people as possible to live in orbit. I took that one step further and focused not on the apocalyptic event itself, but on the perspective of the lone, solitary journey of a kid who grows up in space, longing at first for his now-long-dead parents but eventually just hoping for human contact of any kind, and once finding it, then losing it, telling the story of what he will do to get it back.

What is your background, and does it inform your writing?

I am a scientist by training and a writer by hobby, but that has recently flipped. I'm now a full-time professional writer, and dream of doing science on the side. I have a Ph.D. in experimental physics and have done work for Los Alamos National Lab and a handful of other government agencies. Does it inform my writing? Yes and no. I mean, it's great to have a solid grasp of science and physical laws and it certainly makes "hand-waving" a bit easier since I'm fluent in the language of science. But on the other hand, this is fiction, and for me the characters and the story are far more important than writing a book with 100% accurate science.

What are you working on now?

I just finished up my Legacy Fleet trilogy, which was one of the bestselling SciFi series on Amazon last year, for which I'm both flabbergasted and grateful. Next up will be something similar: another space opera trilogy set in the same universe as the Legacy Fleet trilogy. After that I'm going to shift my focus to something more present day. For years I've developed the wonderfully addicting habit of Wikipedia surfing—I'll start on a benign page like "Solid Rocket Motors," and eventually, twenty pages later, will be reading up on the origins of Rosicrucian secret societies in late medieval Europe. For over a year I've planned to write my "Wikipedia surfing" technothriller—something where I can dump everything I've learned falling down the Wikipedia rabbit holes and cram them all into one novel, a hodgepodge of conspiracy theories, reimaginings of historical events, and in general explodey, shootey goodness against the backdrop of a present day societal-techno crisis.

So how can readers find you?

Come friend me on Facebook (https://www.facebook.com/authornickwebb), and/or sign up on my website at www.nickwebbwrites.com to receive all my short stories for free!

Symbiosis

by Rory Hume

MARI HAD SEEN the space elevator go down to the surface of Verdu too many times to count. From a holodisplay.

It was one thing watching the elevator take cargo to a planet from a flickering light on your desk. It was something else to be in the damn elevator.

It didn't help that Mari wasn't secured in one of the biped seats when she'd forced the elevator to drop. She'd had one strap on her shoulder and had been fumbling to put the other strap on when the pounding on the door started. Rationally, she knew that she had at least enough time to get the harness closed, and it would have taken more than five seconds to breach the door. But the box under her arm sloshed, Mari felt a flash of panic, and she hit the red emergency release button.

The elevator plummeted, and Mari slid off the seat.

She yelled, a deep-throated cry that echoed off the metallic walls. It sounded simultaneously raw and unreal. It didn't seem right that her yell was the loudest sound in the room, not with poorly-secured cargo rattling and a metal box plummeting to Verdu on a cable. It seemed even weirder that she cared how loud she was. After all, she was hanging out of a harness and clinging to a metal box so hard that she could feel the corners bruising her skin through her shirt.

I'm going to die, Mari thought. *I am absolutely going to die.*

The box slid out of her arms; when it hit the floor of the elevator, the glass shattered, and the forked-head symbiote inside slid out, a trail of water in its wake.

Mari might die, but it looked she wasn't going to be the only one.

Earlier

The space station was a lot like the other ones Mariana Soto had served on. There wasn't much need for variation when they were boxes with just enough space for a couple people to live in.

Of course, Mari had never served in a station meant for only one bipedal resident before.

"The glowing red line takes you to your cabin." The voice from her wristwatch wasn't joined by a hologram. Mari wouldn't get to see what the station's off-site manager looked like this time. "The glowing blue line will lead you back to the common area. You may have seen the kitchen and office on your way in."

Mari nodded before realizing there was no way for the manager to know she was acknowledging. "I did see," she said.

"Take a closer look." Was that a humming Mari heard under the speech? She'd heard Jovians often took these managerial roles because they couldn't live off world. They lived on gas giants, and their speech was more music than words. "Follow the blue line."

Mari did. It wasn't easy; the line was on the ceiling, and she was hunched over pretty severely. Most human stations had been built for early explorers, and they'd had a height restriction of 5'7" back then.

The blue line split into green, orange, and yellow. Yellow went to the lavatory, which was appropriate if gross. The two orange forks went to what Mari assumed was the office door—it had a "staff only" sign glowing on it—and a kitchen space with no door. Green went toward the airlocks.

"Your coworker is in the office," the manager said. "Would you like to meet them?"

Coworker? There was only space for one biped on the station. Would she have to share a bed with some stranger?

"Soto?" the manager asked.

What else would Mari say? "Yes, of course."

"Press your thumb on the scanner. Your skin print will be recorded."

Mari did as asked, and after some buzzing sounds, the door slid open.

The office was small and mostly empty. There were two desk spaces and a narrow gap between them. Mari would have to leave the office door open and keep her feet out to fit. The perils of being 6'3".

"Symbiote 22302, this is your new operator, Mariana Soto." Mari heard crackling from a speaker just above the rightmost desk, but no actual reply. "She begins her shift in four planetary standard hours."

Symbiote? Didn't those usually have bipedal hosts?

"Hello," a tinny voice called out. It was high-pitched, much higher-pitched than Mari when she spoke. "Hope you like small spaces."

Mari blinked. She couldn't see the symbiote anywhere. "Hi."

"Please step outside," the manager said. "The last part of the tour involves the elevator."

Mari shuffled out of the way as best she could. The door slid shut before she could turn away. She could feel the breeze of it on the tip of her nose.

The elevator door was in the room with the airlocks, down a level from the rest of the station. Mari had been told, when taking the job, that visitors hauling cargo would use the kitchen, but they'd keep to themselves otherwise. She should only engage in a professional capacity or if they spoke first.

"Open the elevator door," the manager said.

Mari pushed the button, and the door opened, revealing the inside of the elevator. It looked like a smaller version of cargo freighters she'd seen. There were four seats with harnesses for bipeds, with possibly more folded into the walls, and the rest was empty space for cargo. The walls were dreary metal, and the lights were painfully blue, which was even less pleasant than the metal walls and golden lights of the station.

She took a step forward. Or she tried. She hit something she couldn't see pretty fast, but red lights spread from her body quickly. A clear gate was blocking entrance.

"Humans are barred from entry on their own," the manager said. "In emergencies, Symbiote 22302 will assist you."

"How?" Mari asked.

The manager either didn't hear, or didn't care. "Close the elevator door."

Mari sighed heavily, stepped back, and hit the button again.

"You are not permitted to help with loading or unloading the elevator," the manager said. "Monitor the elevator's status and monitor the computer sending messages to HQ to ensure repair crews can be brought in if necessary. You may do maintenance on the interior computers from time to time."

It was a babysitting job. Mari had done some technical work in the past, and she had her spacewalk qualifications; part of the reason she'd gotten this job was because she could fix exterior parts of the elevator if it was broken. Or so she'd thought.

Computers on these kinds of stations never broke. She'd stare at the computer and do nothing for a living.

"Do you understand?" the manager asked.

"I understand," Mari said, even though she didn't. Why hire a human, drag them halfway across the galaxy, and pay them more than industry standard...to do nothing?

* * *

Mari didn't fit in her cabin. It wasn't a surprise. Mari hadn't fit into any of the cabins she'd been in since she'd been fourteen.

Back then, it had been that she'd been too wide to fit in the narrower doors, but she'd hit her last major growth spurt at fifteen and leaned out just enough that she could get through them. Many of her family members weren't so lucky.

"First station standard," Mama had said when Mari had been seven and seen Mama struggle with the height of the door. "They'd wanted shorter colonists so they could fit more of them in."

So Mari had to bend over if she was on her feet in her cabin, and she contorted to fit between her chair and desk, but it was actually the best room she'd had as an adult. Most spacious, for sure.

She squeezed into her chair and brought up her mother, who flickered in full color. That was another thing. Color diversity. Most of the holodisplays she'd worked with before had been black and white for contrast.

"Mari!" Mama said, beaming. She looked tired and pale, but generally okay. "You made it!"

"Did you think I wouldn't?"

"Of course I did." Mama was lying. She and Papa had worked in space all of Mari's life, and at many jobs on the level of Mari's. That Papa was dead and Mama was on a planet as part of a work accident settlement was proof that she knew the risks. "Settling in?"

Mari nodded. There wasn't much settling in to do. "Have you done elevator work before, Mama?"

"A very long time ago, mija. I didn't work with lower-gravity planets much, and they're more common on those."

"Verdu has Earth-standard gravity." Not that that meant much to Mari. She'd never been to Earth or on any planet surface. Mama had only been on one planet, and it was the one she was calling Mari from. She'd moved there three years ago. "Do you miss being in space?"

Mama laughed. "Absolutely not."

* * *

Everything on the station was automated. The ships that came in at the beginning of the shift docked without any input from Mari, and she watched from a holodisplay as their crews unloaded their cargo and traveled down the elevator, which descended on their go-ahead.

A small red light flashed, issuing a warning about the elevator. Mari frowned and brought up the computer's readout on the display.

"Gear replacement needed," she whispered. She always spoke to herself quietly while working alone. It filled the space.

"It's been needed for years."

Mari jerked, and her hip connected with the desk. She hissed. That was probably going to bruise.

"You okay?" the voice said. "What happened?"

"Nothing." Mari rubbed at her hip. "What did you say? Before?"

"Don't worry about the gear replacement." It was a tinny

voice...the tinny voice from the tour. The symbiote. "The station reports it every day, and HQ ignores it every day. Do you go by Mariana?"

"Um. Mari, usually. Sorry, what was your name again?"

"Symbiotes don't get names. My designation's 22302."

Mari didn't know what to say about that. The tinny voice sounded wry, and she didn't want to push.

"You're very quiet," the symbiote said.

"I am?"

"Most of the humans who've worked here call someone and talk the entire shift. I've learned a lot of different languages that way."

"You don't use a translator?"

"I have a converter. Translates electric impulses into speech, and those don't function well with translators." The symbiote laughed. "I'm glad you speak English. I know that one."

Mari made a wordless noise that could mean a lot of things. She was good at those.

"You can speak English with me. If you want." When Mari didn't say anything, the symbiote added, "To stay fresh?"

"Shouldn't I...work?"

"Oh yes. So much work for both of us to do."

Mari hadn't known a symbiote using a converter could sound sarcastic. "What's your job?"

"Emergency assistance." There was an oddly human snort. "It means, if someone's dying in the elevator, you can pick up my box and get inside."

"That's it?"

"What else can a symbiote do?" The symbiote sounded

bland and innocent. Almost like they were quoting something.

Mari flinched. "That's terrible."

"That's Space Station Management Corporation for you. Well, that's SSMC when there's no one to see them."

What a cheering thought. "Wait," Mari said as the conversation caught up with her. "Your box?"

"You didn't see? Look under the desks."

That was easier said than done. Mari had to stand up, push the chair out into the hall, and carefully ease down so she didn't brain herself on the tables. But sure enough, in the corner under the right-most desk, she saw a box with glass walls and a metal top and bottom. It was mostly opaque, but Mari could see a shadow and hear water sloshing.

"Hi," she whispered, grazing her fingers along the box's edge.

"Hello," the symbiote said back.

"Are you stuck in there? Even when I'm not working?"

"Oh yeah. System's solar power feeds me and runs the pump that filters my water. There isn't anywhere else for an unattached symbiote to go."

Mari got back to her feet and went to fetch her chair. Her throat felt a little thick. At least Mari could go back to her room when her shift was over. To give herself a moment, she watched the elevator signaling its return from Verdu's equatorial ocean.

"How often does the elevator go most days?" she asked.

"Solid dozen, at least," the symbiote said. A pause, and then, "They're putting in a lot of work to change the planet down there. You'll see if you're around long enough."

Mari suspected she didn't want to.

* * *

A ship docked as Mari was getting her breakfast. She was close enough to the docking ring that she could feel the rumbling under her feet. Ship rumblings were soothing, and the kitchen was the biggest one she'd had to herself. There were worse days to have.

"Biped."

The voice was stern and loud in the cramped space. Mari whirled around and nearly dropped her tea.

A person in a gray worksuit was standing behind Mari, hands on her hips. Probably a cargo hauler. The stranger was short enough that she stood comfortably in the space station, and her skin had a subtle green tinge to it. Her forehead had ridges that weren't human-like at all.

"Do you have anything to say for yourself?" the stranger asked.

"Uh," Mari said. "Hello. Can I help you with something?"

The stranger rolled her eyes. "The back of your *neck*, biped. Show me immediately."

Mari had no idea if the stranger had any authority. She didn't think twice about it; getting fired on her second day wasn't an option. She got on her knees since that was the only way to show her neck easily, and she lifted her black braid aside.

"Human," the stranger hissed, and Mari flinched.

Mari stayed in that position for a few moments, and when she looked up, the stranger was gone. She hadn't heard her step away.

* * *

"Treaty shit," was the symbiote's response.

Mari hadn't set out to tell the symbiote what had happened, but Mari hadn't been in a particularly talkative mood after the encounter in the kitchen, and the symbiote had asked why Mari had been silent. It would have been rude not to answer.

"Treaty...stuff?" Mari asked.

"Oh, should I not have said 'shit'? I'm still figuring out professional language."

"No, your language is fine. What treaty?"

"Humans are applying for symbiote candidacy. There's a lot of Ectos and not many hosts on their home planet, and apparently the human tests look good for both symbiotes and Ectos." The symbiote made a derisive noise. "Plus, the Ectos are offering financial incentive."

"What does that have to do with the station?" Mari was staring at the elevator's descent again. Hopefully, the woman she'd spoken to earlier was long gone.

"It's one of the steps to Ectosymbiote acceptance. Humans supply bodies for jobs, and maybe they can supply bodies for Ectos. But they don't like humans without hosts, from what I can tell."

Mari shuddered and stroked a hand on the back of her neck. "They won't make me be a host, will they?"

"Nah. Major interplantary violation to have non-consensual bondings."

Mari couldn't help her relief at that. She shifted in her chair as much as she could. "Is that why you're here? Lack of bodies?"

A pause. A laugh.

* * *

Mari was eating lunch in the office when the alarm sirens went off. She dropped everything and ran for the airlocks as red flashed throughout the station.

The elevator door was open when she arrived. There were a half-dozen cargo haulers grouped in front of the door, but Mari's attention was grabbed by two things: a three-eyed biped gasping and convulsing in the elevator, and an unattached Ecto on the floor just outside, flopping like the biped.

A cargo hauler scooped the Ecto and placed them in a bucket of water. Mari went for the elevator and slammed into the clear gate. It flashed red at her touch. She couldn't get inside without a symbiote.

One of the cargo haulers yanked her back, even as the biped inside reached for Mari desperately.

"Get away!" the cargo hauler said. Mari was close enough to her eyes to see the irises turn red. "Do you want to bring the planet's atmosphere in here? We'll all die!"

"We have to vent the elevator," another hauler said grimly. "Only way to clean out an atmosphere trap."

"Go! Report this to your superiors!" the first cargo hauler told Mari.

Mari wanted to ask what "venting the elevator" meant, but she wasn't used to speaking at work. Before she could summon up the courage to ask, the red-eyed cargo hauler was pressing buttons on the display generated by her watch, and the elevator doors slid shut.

The hiss that followed after told Mari everything she needed to know anyway.

They'd opened the elevator to push out the toxic air, and the biped inside had gone with it.

* * *

The symbiote didn't say a word to Mari when she went into the office to file the report. The symbiote didn't say anything when Mari dropped her head in her arms and tried to remember how to breathe.

It was probably for the best.

* * *

When Mari woke up a couple days later, there was a light flashing in her face. It was actually a word on her holodisplay, and not one she'd seen much.

"VIOLATION", it said. There wasn't a standard alert for "you fucked up at work" between companies, but it never took much work to figure out a new one.

Rubbing at her eyes, she pulled up the full message on the display. Apparently, she'd been reported by a cargo hauler for "inappropriate conduct". It didn't say when, but Mari figured it was from the elevator incident. She'd heard before that warnings were meant to be menacing and not actually helpful. Considering this one told her nothing about what she'd done, she was inclined to believe it.

Mari pinched the bridge of her nose. Two more weeks, and she would have enough money to get to her mother's planet. Three more weeks, and she could leave. Her contract would be over.

Just three more weeks.

* * *

"You haven't asked me about my reproductive cycle yet."

Mari hadn't spoken at all on the shift after her warning. She'd closed the door to the office at the beginning of the day so her legs weren't sticking out, and she'd stared at the holodisplay so intently her eyes were dry and painful. The most noise she'd made was a quiet grunt when the symbiote had greeted her that day.

But, to the symbiote's statement, Mari couldn't help saying, "What?"

"Ha, knew I could get you talking again." The symbiote sounded smug. "I bet it's just because you're quiet, but humans seem overly fascinated with reproduction and an individual's role in it. One person—I'm sorry, one *man*—who worked here was offended I didn't use 'he' to refer to him."

Mari sighed. "Nothing about your reproductive cycle is my business."

"You're the only one I've met who's said that. Even people who didn't ask about it seemed nervous with a lack of pronoun."

"There are reasons to care in a lot of human societies."

"Well, it's not important in my society." The symbiote sighed wistfully, but it didn't seem to be over lack of pronouns.

Mari bit her lip for a moment. She shouldn't be making

conversation. She should be making sure she didn't lose her job.

But she said, "I think more about your lack of name. I've been calling you 'the symbiote' in my head. I'd probably call you your species name if humans could say it out loud."

"I kind of like that. I'm *the* symbiote." Mari pictured a person with their chest puffed out. How would a proud symbiote look?

"There isn't something else you'd like to be called?"

"I don't get a name." A pause, and then, "We have different means of identification in my society. When we got to place where a name would have been helpful...the designation number works, I guess."

Something simmered in Mari. She wasn't sure what it was. It felt...big.

"You get a name if you want a name," she said, the edge of what she was feeling giving weight to her voice. "You can choose your name, and I'll use it."

For the first time since Mari had met the symbiote, the voice in the speaker was hesitant. "If it gets out..."

The "VIOLATION" light flashed through Mari's mind. It was in her contract that she would get taken to a transport hub and given her last paycheck if she was fired. What happened to a symbiote that was kept in a tiny box and not given a name?

Her first instinct was to apologize and drop the whole thing. Her mouth formed the beginning of the word "sorry", even. But there was something else there. Something that knew the symbiote deserved a damn name.

"Just us," Mari said. "I won't use it outside this room, if you want."

Silence. Mari held her breath and curled in as much as she could. If she'd had a little more room, she would have pulled her legs in front of her on her chair and hugged them. She liked hugging herself. It felt safe.

"Sym," the symbiote said, finally. "Short for 'the symbiote', but that's like a human name, isn't it?"

Mari couldn't quite manage a smile, considering everything. It didn't matter. Sym could probably hear the pleasure in Mari's voice.

"There's lots of ways for humans to have a name," Mari said. "But 'Sym' sounds like one I might hear."

* * *

The only alert that woke Mari up the next day was her standard alarm.

Usually, Mari started her day by getting breakfast, showering, and catching up on intersystem news in her room. She never fully woke up until she was at work. That was why, when the door didn't open from her cabin to the hallway, she spent several long seconds frowning at the door instead of doing something about it.

When she finally woke up a little, she tried again. The door was stuck.

She tried a third time, pushing the button with one hand and scrabbling with her fingers to find a gap in the door with her other hand. Nothing.

It was second nature for Mari to take the button's plate off the wall and play with the wires. She'd worked at enough stations where it had been necessary to open any door that way; doors tended to be low priority. She pushed the emergency release, leaving the button's plate hanging from the wall.

The door slid open like nothing was wrong. Mari froze at what she saw.

"GO HOME HUMAN" painted in ugly block letters on the ground in red.

She covered her mouth to suppress the yell that wanted to come out.

* * *

According to the station info, she was the only biped currently onboard. One of the cargo ships had to have waited until after Mari had left work to leave—it happened all the time—and someone onboard had taken the time to leave her a message. That would have been enough to give her a bad day.

But when she tried to check travel information on her cabin's holodisplay, she got an error message.

She went to the office a full hour before her shift started, ignoring breakfast and a shower to get to the holodisplay there. The lights weren't on in the room and probably wouldn't be until her shift, so she didn't say anything in case Sym was asleep. Or in a rest cycle? Mari didn't know much about Sym's biology.

As she turned on the display, she realized she hadn't learned about symbiotes' rest cycle. All she'd learned was the difference between symbiotes and Ectos in school. Ectos rested on the back of the neck, but symbiotes...her teacher had kept it clinical. The other kids chiming in on their displays had giggled about how gross "swallowing the slug" would be.

Mari had turned off her display after the lesson, went into the bathroom she and Mama shared with three other crew members at the time, and puked.

It had nothing to do with symbiotes and Ectos, but Mama had been turning off her display a lot during her talks with Mari lately. Sometimes, Mama managed to apologize before cutting the transmission short. One time, she hadn't managed before she'd started vomiting.

The glowing display brought Mari out of her head. She looked up passenger transports.

Transports didn't make it to that particular solar system more than once a week or so; Verdu, the only habitable planet, was still being settled, and the system was just a stop for most. Mari would have to summon a ship deliberately or book passage on one of the cargo ships that came to the station. That last one would be best for speed, but considering the paint outside Mari's cabin, it wasn't her favorite option.

She sat back in her chair as far as it would go, tapping her fingers on the edge of the desk. It was a terrible idea, but…

Pulling up information on Verdu confirmed what the elevator incident had suggested: no humans could go down and survive without gear. Mari hadn't been told about survival gear on the tour—or any evacuation procedures at all—which told her everything she'd needed to know about the possibility of bailing out in an emergency.

The interesting part was that only bipeds with Ectos or symbiotes were granted access by treaty. That seemed an odd distinction to make when buildings adaptable to different kinds of life were so common. Mama had told Mari about all the places on her planet with different levels of gravity and different median temperatures and different levels of humidity. There were undergrounds and bridges for the more common life populations that didn't fit surface standard. Her planet wasn't friendly to humans but was primarily settled by them, so the biggest tunnels were Earth standard.

"Took you long enough."

Mari squeaked before she could cover her mouth. She put a hand to her chest until her breathing settled. "Sym, you scared me."

"And you didn't scare me? I didn't expect you in here so early."

"Then why did you say 'took you long enough'?"

For the first time, Mari heard water sloshing. When all the computers were on, it was too loud to hear Sym inside their box.

"Because," Sym said, "you humans are always so curious about Verdu. Why is that?"

"They've probably never been on a planet before."

Sym didn't answer right away. Mari didn't realize how long it took Sym to reply at first because she was busy scrolling back through the travel feeds in case a ship's manifest had changed on the hour. That happened sometimes.

"Never been on a planet," Sym said slowly.

"Yeah."

"Ever?"

"There are a lot of humans, and only a few planets with places where humans can live."

"But there are so many planets. And there're ways to adapt buildings."

Sym was echoing Mari's earlier thought. For some reason, it made Mari clench her jaw. "People like me don't deserve to live on those planets." She made herself relax her mouth. Sym probably didn't know. "Why do you think I work a job like this? For fun? My mom worked for forty-two years before she made it to a planet surface, and it's because she's...she's not well."

"What about your home planet?"

"Earth?" Mari shook her head even though Sym couldn't see it. "My dad passed by it on a freighter once."

"So you've never been."

"My family hasn't set foot on Earth in...five generations? Six?" Mari had known the answer once. She rubbed her hands over her face. "Planets don't matter as much as the people on them, anyway."

"You said it." There was a pause. "Have you eaten yet?"

"What does it matter?"

"Maybe you should eat and call your mom."

"How do you..." Mari frowned. "Do you listen in on my calls?"

"I can't in your cabin. You should go there."

Something wasn't right. Mari felt weird about listening to Sym without asking what was going on, but she had her own problems. And maybe Mama *would* have some ideas.

"Okay," Mari said reluctantly. "I'll be back for my shift."

"I'm not going anywhere."

* * *

"Did I wake you?"

Mama looked like she was struggling to keep her eyes open. She was definitely lying down. "No, mija. I'm glad you called. What's wrong?"

"Wrong?" Did Mari look like she was upset?

"You never call me around this time."

"Oh. It's right before work, and I..."

Mari squinted at the display. Had Mama lost weight since Mari had last called? It was hard to tell on a holodisplay, but her face looked thinner. Mari had just called her three days ago.

"I missed you," Mari said. "How are you feeling?"

Mama sighed. "I need to talk to you about something. Can you—"

There was a thump. Mari didn't think it was particularly loud, but Mama stopped talking, and her eyes grew sharper.

"What was that?" Mama asked.

Another thump, and the room shook. Mari grabbed her desk to keep from tipping over.

"I don't know," Mari said, just as the alarms started going off overhead. She started to stand. "I need to find out, but..."

"Go. I love you."

Mari's hand hovered on the off button. Her mom had said it with an intensity that she couldn't ignore.

"I love you, too," Mari said. "More than anything."

She turned off the display.

* * *

The alarms silenced before Mari made it to the office, but Sym was already talking when Mari came in.

"It's fine," Sym said quickly. "It's okay."

"What's okay? The whole damn station shook!"

"We were hit by debris. The elevator was doing its daily test run, and the gear that was broken came off and broke a couple things. Whole elevator's down for the moment, but the station's integrity is good."

Mari sat in her chair as hard as the lack of space would allow. The feeling that something wasn't right still hung in the air. "I didn't know you could access the computer from in there."

"I can't. Your display announces emergency updates, and I can hear them."

Speaking of Mari's display, it lit up with an update that directed to her watch. Probably the station manager. She turned her watch on.

"A repair crew is en route," the manager's voice said. "Repairs are estimated to take two days. Cargo distribution has been suspended until repairs are complete."

"Wait," Mari said. "If a gear needs replacing, I'm qualified—"

"No. A repair crew is en route. Stay out of their way."

The transmission cut off. Mari kicked the office door, and thanks to her work boots, it thudded in a satisfying way.

"Feel better?" Sym asked.

Mari looked in Sym's direction. "The gear just broke off by itself. Magically."

"How else would it break? If HQ had listened to the warning—"

"Who got onto the station last night?"

Sym fell silent. Mari hated that she couldn't read the symbiote.

"What do you mean?" Sym said, finally.

"I got a reprimand, someone painted outside my damn cabin last night, and the gear that's been broken but doesn't mean anything shut the whole station down. What do you know?"

"I..." There were some sounds that weren't human speech of any kind, much less English. "The gear wasn't directed at you. I didn't know anyone was on the station last night, and not only would I not report you to HQ—"

"You have high turnaround, don't you? Where does that come from?"

"This is a shit job! I have nothing to do with it. HQ would never listen to a symbiote, anyway. They *don't want me here*."

Mari's shoulders dropped. She hadn't realized how mad and scared she'd felt until she'd heard it echoed in Sym's digital voice. Mari put a hand to her forehead.

"I'm thinking they don't want me here, either," she said.

Sym laughed. They didn't sound particularly amused. "Yeah. I'm beginning to get that."

* * *

It turned out doing a shift without an elevator to watch was even more boring than a usual shift.

Or it could have been. Mari, knowing that she and Sym were trapped together, asked Sym questions.

The first was answered simply.

"How many people have you worked with? Humans?"

"Month-long contracts are standard, so it's around twelve people a year," Sym said. "It's rarely fewer, and it's often more. I've been here three Earth-standard years, so you do the math."

The second answer was a bit more complicated.

"What's swimming like?" Mari asked. She had figured out that lying diagonally on her desks gave her more room in the office than sitting at the chair, so she was on her back, staring at the ceiling and listening to the occasional thump of the repair crew.

"You've never been swimming?"

"Water on ships and stations is for drinking," Mari said dutifully, in the same voice her mother had used when Mari was a child. "That's a nice way of saying 'rich people learn how to swim, and you'll drown and get me fired if you sneak in their pools'."

"How much water have you ever been in?"

Mari shook her head. "Shower's worth, I guess."

"I don't..." Sym made a frustrated noise. "What is it like to walk around in the air all the time without being inside another being?"

"Uh." It was what Mari had always done. She didn't know any different. "I get your point. What if I asked how swimming made you feel?"

"Depends."

"On what?"

"The size of the water."

Mari rolled onto her side so she could see under the desk. Sym's box was barely visible, and it looked small from her corner.

"Yeah," Mari said. "I can see that."

* * *

The monitors powering down for the day roused Mari from

a nap. She still wasn't sure what Sym's rest cycle was, so she slid off the desk as best she could and opened the door.

"There's a red button on the front of my box. Push it for three seconds, and my box will slide out. You can take it wherever."

Mari, halfway out the door, jumped. "Sorry?"

"The size of the pool, Mari."

"I don't understand."

"I haven't been on my planet for three years." Sym sounded matter-of-fact. "I lived in the oceans. Ectos came in and forced us out three years ago. They needed another planet to mine for resources, and when our planet denied their petition for immigration, they forced their way in and killed millions of us. Hosts, symbiotes."

Mari put a hand over her mouth.

"I was one of the lucky ones." A moment of silence, and then, "Do you remember what I said? If you need to get my box out..."

It took Mari a few moments before the words came out. "Red button," she finally managed. "Push and hold for three seconds, and slide."

"Sleep well, Mari."

Mari turned, wanting to say...something. What could she say?

"Good night, Sym," she finally managed, wiping a tear away.

She left the office, and the door closed behind her.

Once Mari blinked the tears out of her eyes, she could see that the repair crews were gone. Probably back on their ship for the night. Their tools were still scattered around, and that included a laser cutter in the middle of the damn floor.

It was turned off, but if she needed a reminder that safety didn't matter at all on the station, there it was.

She picked the cutter up, intending to put it in the toolbox, but she hovered before she put it down. A laser cutter could be helpful if she was trapped in her room again.

Mari shook her head at herself, but she took the laser cutter with her to her cabin anyway.

* * *

When Mama had told Mari that she was dying, she'd said, "I'll send you a vid of my own when I pass. None of those official ones. You'll hear it from me." Mari had replied that she would do her best to be there to say goodbye face-to-face, and Mama had said, "I know how hard it is."

Mari wasn't surprised to be awakened two hours after she'd gone to bed with Mama's message.

It was short. "Mija, if you're getting this, I've died. I'm so proud of you. Remember how worthy you are of everything you have and everything you don't. I love you."

Mari downloaded it to her watch and sent Sym a message on the station display saying that she wouldn't be going to work that shift. She didn't bother informing the station manager.

She stared out her small window at the green-red planet below until she was ready to sleep again.

* * *

"Mari. Mari. Do you hear me?"

"Mama?" Mari asked, rubbing at her face. She didn't

open her eyes. Mama would shake her awake if it was really important.

"Mariana, wake up."

She groaned, but Mari opened her eyes, and...

No, this wasn't one of the old cabins she'd shared with her mom. It was the one on the space station, and her mother's face wasn't on the display. Unless Mari played Mama's goodbye message, her mother's face wouldn't be on a display again.

"Mari."

She finally recognized the voice. "Sym?"

"You need to get to the office. There isn't much time."

Mari's mouth went dry, but her head was still thick with sleep. "Time? For what?"

"You have ten minutes. Maybe. Grab your things and come get me."

The transmission cut off, and Mari's heart started pounding.

* * *

Mari traveled light. An old superstition. When she was a child, she was convinced that, if she didn't have much and kept her things in her bag except for when she needed them, she'd get planetside one day. She'd be worthy of it. Mama had figured it was better to make the best of what you had and brought crates with her everywhere so she could decorate the cabins she and Mari shared. Mari had loved it, but she hadn't taken anything of her mom's when she'd started working on her own.

It meant that, after Sym's wake-up call, Mari was out

of her cabin and on the way to the office in less than three minutes.

All the overhead lights in the station were off. The only light was coming from Verdu outside the station. There weren't many portholes, but there were enough that Mari made her way to the office in the greenish-red light.

She paused at the office door. There was a pounding noise coming from the direction of the airlocks.

"Sym," Mari said, cramming herself inside the office so the door would close. "What the hell is going on?"

"Planetary coup." Sym sounded cheerful. "I need your help."

The words "planetary coup" rang in Mari's ears. "Help?"

"Yeah. Can't get to the elevator by myself."

"Wait, you're leaving?"

Sym spoke like she was reading off a recipe. "The Ectos will kill me if I stay. You might have a chance if you lock yourself in here and call one of your ambassadors. Oh, and if you grab some food from the kitchen. This door's reinforced, I think, but that won't do much good if you starve."

"Who is 'they'?" Mari's head spun. "Won't 'they' kill me for helping you?"

"'They' are Ectos." There was a *this is so obvious* tone to Sym's voice. "And yes, if they get their hands on you. A lot of Ectos would love to have a rebellious human to wave around, but they'll probably kill us both if you don't help me."

Put it that way. "So you want me to take you to the elevator? And then I come back?"

"Well, unless..." Sym fell silent for a moment. "Do you want to come?"

"To your planet?" The dying biped came to mind, choking on the trapped atmosphere in the elevator. "Won't the air kill me?"

"There's a group waiting for me at the bottom. Some of them have bipedal hosts, and their hosts have breathing gear in case they dislodge their symbiotes. You won't die."

Probable death on the station versus less likely death on the surface. That much looked straightforward. There was more Mari knew she should ask: would she be able to get off the planet later? Would the Ectos come after them on the planet? Would *humans* come after them, since they had the treaty with the Ectos?

What she did ask was, "Was the broken gear fixed?"

"What?"

"Will the elevator even work?" Mari hadn't been at work yesterday, so she didn't know if the crews finished.

Judging by the inhuman, wordless noise Sym made as the holodisplay turned on and showed the elevator, they didn't know either. "The gear's in place, but the controls weren't all turned back on. I think we can get it going from inside the elevator, but..."

"You don't know."

"No."

So probable death in the elevator versus probable death on the station. Neither sounded pleasant. There had to be a way to settle it.

"Do..." Mari pulled at her ponytail. There hadn't been time to braid her hair. "Do you *want* me to come?"

"I wouldn't ask you to come if I didn't."

That decided her. She had no family left who would care if she was seen as a traitor and went to an alien planet. She had to take a minute to let her throat tighten and her chin wobble. Her mom was dead. She didn't get to say a real goodbye.

But Mari had a friend, and she didn't want Sym to die.

"Okay," she said, pushing the chair out of the office and crouching. "Okay, I'll go with you."

"Fuck yes." Sym sounded relieved. "You won't regret this. I'll make sure of that."

Mari didn't entirely believe Sym, but she admired Sym's confidence. She paused with her finger over the button to Sym's box. "You won't be able to talk to me after this, will you?"

"Not until we make it to the planet."

Mari laughed. It was a slightly terrified sound. "Any last words?"

"Just push the fucking button."

"Good luck to you, too." Mari pushed the button and held it.

* * *

Mari's run to the elevator wasn't the most elegant set of movements she'd ever done. With her things on her back and Sym sloshing in the box under her arm, she was off-balance and hitting the sides of all the doors. Her eyes watered from the jolts of pain as she stumbled down to the airlocks.

Unauthorized station entries weren't common, so Mari hadn't seen what reinforced airlocks looked like before. Metallic doors had sealed the openings, and they looked thick and heavy. Someone was cutting into one. It was molten and melting.

"Elevator," Mari muttered. "Go inside."

She pressed the button to open the elevator door, and the blue lights inside flickered to life. Empty, of course. The shift that would have opened access to the elevator was still hours away.

"It won't kill me," she said to herself. "It won't kill me, it won't kill me…"

Holding Sym's box just in front of her, Mari stepped up to the clear gate. It glowed blue and let them enter.

She didn't have time to be relieved. A loud clattering sounded behind her, and Mari hit the button to close the elevator so fast she nearly fell over.

If she had been thinking rationally, she might have figured out that it would be better to secure Sym's box—and herself, for that matter—before anything else. She did put her bag down and sit in one of the biped seats, but the tapping she'd heard in the airlocks started on the elevator door, and…well, the only thoughts she had after that were "we'll get vented into space" and "I'm going to die", so she hit the red button for emergency descent before any securing was done.

The damn elevator had looked so sedate on the holodisplay. Speedy, but there was no reason to think it would be rocky. The display had read normal, minus the controls.

Which meant the speed it dropped, and the amount Mari felt it, had to be normal.

Whether it was or not, Mari was only partially in her harness. The elevator was built to maintain consistent gravity to protect the cargo, but the rocking of the elevator combined with Mari's precarious spot meant she slid…and Sym's box slid out from under Mari's arm, too.

The moment before it broke lasted for what felt like years.

Mari's fingertips grazed the edge, and she had just enough time to remember the Ecto being dropped in a bucket of water before the box shattered and a two-headed symbiote went sliding across the floor, a trail of water left in their wake.

It was the first time Mari had seen Sym. Sym looked so small.

The decision to get Sym was instantaneous. It was the easiest part. Look at the box? Check. Was it intact enough to hold Sym for the descent? Maybe. Did it have any water left? No, that had all tipped on the floor.

The elevator took ten minutes to get to the surface. Symbiotes died of exposure in four.

Mari could hardly breathe between the fear squeezing her chest and the artificial gravity, but moving her entire body was harder than breathing. A crawl was too ambitious. She tried anyway because she wasn't going to leave Sym to die. She pulled herself along by her fingertips and reached... reached...

Her height worked in her favor for once. She grabbed hold of Sym, and Sym flailed around in Mari's grasp. There was no way for a symbiote to sense anything in air as dry as the elevator's, and Sym was probably thinking "I'm going to die" as much as Mari. Did symbiotes panic the same way humans did? Mari had no idea.

"It's...okay," she said to Sym, even though Sym couldn't hear her, and she put Sym in her mouth.

* * *

The next few moments could be best described as "choking to death".

Mari had known before that Ectos took hosts by making connections through a biped's skin. She also had known that symbiotes made connections by going inside the body. "Swallowing the slug" was what she'd heard most often outside of the classroom. What she hadn't known was that symbiotes sat in a human's throat, making connections to a human's major systems through there and filtering air once they were settled.

Before then, the symbiote blocked all air to a human's lungs.

Sym settling in probably took only seconds. It felt like an eternity to Mari, one where she grabbed at her throat and choked and heaved.

Mari passed out before it was all done. The last thing she remembered before everything went dark was the shaking of the elevator and how lightheaded she felt from lack of air.

* * *

Water.

Mari was floating in... in some place where her skin felt kind of heavy and wet, but it wasn't until an echoing thought told her *water* that she understood what the sensations meant. She was submerged, a human floating, even though a flurry around her suggested the water was mostly filled with symbiotes.

The water wasn't anything like she'd ever seen before. It was green, for one thing. And there was so *much*.

She tried moving her hands. She flailed at first, but after a few twirls in the water, she managed to travel a bit. The awkward gliding was still freer than anything Mari had ever done in gravity. Water had a bit more resistance than zero gravity, and that was comforting. A nice balance.

Mari blinked.

The water was gone.

Grass.

Mari had seen grass on ships before. The grass she was sitting on was nothing like the green grass that she'd known; it was redder and somehow softer to the touch. There were symbiotes in the grass as well, sliding through wet pockets on their way to other things. The air felt barely less heavy than the water had, and there were water droplets on Mari's brown skin. She looked down on them in wonder, and—

"Are you finished?"

Mari looked around. She couldn't see any bipeds. "Who said that?"

"We did." It was in Mari's own voice. It took her a minute to understand.

"Sym?" she gasped.

"There you go." Sym laughed using Mari's voice. "Interesting mind you have. But it's time to wake up."

Mari opened her eyes.

The elevator door was open, and the green sky beyond was like the green sky she'd seen in her dream. Or memory?

"Memory," her brain agreed. It was louder and more defined than Mari usually thought. "Of course it's loud. You're not thinking this. It's Sym talking to you."

"Oh," Mari said aloud. Her throat was hoarse, and she gagged a little. Sym wasn't as thick in her throat as they'd been before, but Mari could still feel Sym there.

"Yeah, that'll take some getting used to. Whatever. I need to get to work. Do you mind?"

Mari's hand lifted slowly. Mari wasn't the one lifting it. Sym was asking for permission to do more.

"Oh," Mari said. "Sure."

Sym moving Mari's body was kind of funny. Mari was lurching, stumbling for her bag like she was drunk. But Mari could feel Sym's intense focus, and it only took a few moments of fumbling before Mari's hand held the laser cutter again.

"I can do that, you know," Mari said aloud.

"You can think at me," Sym thought. "No talking required."

"Fine," Mari thought. "Let me use the cutter?"

"Go ahead."

Mari moved out of the elevator. There were other bipedal hosts on the platform, their skin tinged with red. The water around was green, and Mari spotted movement that suggested other symbiotes in the ocean.

A host spoke in a high-pitched language Mari hadn't heard before. Sym used Mari's mouth to reply. It was odd, but exhilarating.

The other hosts helped Mari climb on top of the elevator. Mari turned on the laser cutter. It would take a while to cut the cable that connected the elevator to the space station, probably hours, but she was willing to take the time to do it.

Judging by the fierce determination that flooded through Mari, it seemed Sym felt the same way.

* * *

The hosts moved the platform through the ocean after the cable was cut. Mari still didn't understand their language, but Sym translated roughly. They were moving the platform to a place far away from any of the underwater settlements, and they would swim to find where they were going again. Sym added that, thanks to the symbiote in Mari's throat, Mari wouldn't need to surface for air.

Mari tried to care, but she couldn't bring herself to. She was sad, still, so sad that it weighed her down, and the movement of the platform on the water was also vaguely terrifying. It felt so *unstable*.

"How permanent is this host thing?" she asked Sym aloud.

"As permanent as you want it to be," Sym thought back. "But it's better than breathing gear down here, and..."

Sym didn't need to finish the next thought. The symbiotes had probably just declared war on the Ectos and humanity and a bunch of other aliens beside. Apparently, the symbiotes had allies as well, but Mari would likely be considered a traitor by Earth, if Sym's thoughts were any way to tell.

"So I can stay with you?" Mari thought at Sym.

Mari felt Sym's happiness that she would ask. "I'd like it if you did."

An image of an amphibious biped appeared in Mari's mind. She had learned about them in school when she'd learned about the symbiotes; her classmates had called them the "frog people". Their skin was red, their cheeks expanded, and their hands were webbed for swimming purposes, but they also had faces like humans. This particular face was an attractive one. Friendly, Mari might have said.

Grief flooded Mari, and it took her a minute to realize it wasn't hers.

"I'm sorry," Mari thought.

"And I'm sorry about your mom."

Mari looked down at the water. Sym was all she had. Sym, and a planet. After everything, Mari had made it to a planet.

The other hosts were jumping, barely splashing as they hit the surface. It was getting dark, so Mari couldn't see them well at first, but they turned on lights as soon as they made it underwater, and every host had a green halo around them. Mari looked up at the sky and saw the beginnings of stars. She'd never been able to see stars from space.

"Ready?" Sym thought.

"Yeah," Mari whispered aloud.

She jumped into the water.

Q&A with Rory Hume

This is a very powerful world you've created, full of conflict and danger. The way you've positioned humans is fascinating—and scary. How did you come up with the concepts?

Normally, when I write, I get a couple images in my head and make the story a bridge to connect them. For "Symbiosis", I didn't wait for the images to come to me; I wrote a list of things I like to either read or write in stories, and I played "what if?" until the main characters sprung into my head. Mariana Soto and her physicality in particular was the one who shaped the universe. I knew she was too big and too small for her place, and it didn't take me long to figure out humanity mirrored and influenced Mari. That's one of my favorite things about sci-fi: small stories in as big a space as we know.

What is your background, and have you been writing long?

I've been writing nearly as long as I could string words to-gether! A lot of that time was spent honing craft, especially in the recent past, but I was also having fun and figuring out self-expression in quieter corners. I'm happy to keep some stories in my metaphoric desk drawers—my actual desk doesn't have drawers—but I thought the SFF community looked pretty exciting right now, and I'm hoping to connect with it more in the future.

Do you have other stories in the works?

Nothing specific is in progress currently, but it never takes me long to get new ideas.

If readers want to find you, is there a place we can send them?

@roryhumewriting on Twitter!

War Stories

by Samuel Peralta

Dulce et decorum est pro patria mori:
mors et fugacem persequitur virum
nec parcit inbellis iuventae
poplitibus timidove tergo.
- Horace, *Odes*

SOME SAY YOU can't go forward into the future without letting go of the past. Sometimes, it's the past that won't let go of you.

Gravity will do that to you, too. You ride up to the starships in shuttles that burn against the g-forces, but gravity—it doesn't let you go. Not easily. One gravity, two gravities, three gravities press you back into your inertial restraints, the memory of the last tour made tangible, pulling you back.

You get past Saturn, past Jupiter, past Mars—you think you're finally headed home. And suddenly all the weight you carry is there, a system-sized gravity well of life and death, of comrades lost or left behind, of half-truths and lies, of choices made; all these fill your bones, marrow-cold and heavy, weighing on you like a war story.

But you don't really want to hear about war. You don't want to know about how the machine gun fire from Warthog armor drowns out the screaming as you mow down the enemy, or how loud your heartbeat sounds when a hunter-killer drone shines a ranging laser on your position. You don't want to know about the taste of ash and soot, the smell of blood, the scorching heat burning the small hairs on your body as a flash grenade detonates in the trenches.

You want to hear about courage and honor. You want the medals, the bugles, the drums. You want to hear about starships on fire off Orion's shoulder, plasma beams glittering as they slice through inertial drives.

I'm sorry.

* * *

We're waiting at the pickup point, about fifty clicks from where the drop-ship let us off, eight months ago. It's me and about half the crew I came to Titan with. That's pretty par for the course. Sometimes, in the mess tents, we forget and set up plates for those who aren't there anymore. We don't forget again.

We're mingling with other squads, here from different missions, our only commonality that we fight on the same side of this war.

Two hours to departure. From here a shuttle will take us up to the starship *Miyazaki*, where we'll go into hyper-sleep for the longest leg of the journey. For some of us, it's to Europa, for others, to Deimos. Already, other ships are on their way here from those settlements, bringing our replacements.

It's my third tour. I'm one of the lucky ones.

I scan the faces of the soldiers around me, but I don't see Sharkey around.

Sharkey and I aren't from the same mission team. We'd met on the *Aldrin* station on Deimos. All the cubs were at the terminals, reading anything that was sent to them, sending out their messages home. I was passing by, finishing a *Molson Canadian* lager when a private got up without warning from their seat and ran into me, upsetting what was left of my drink.

She was more distraught than I was over it, but I'd let her buy me a replacement. Hey, however you can get it. On her station uniform, the stencilled patch spelled out A. CHERENKOV. Her name was Anya, but her crew called her Sharkey, so I did.

We made a pact to see each other again, if we made it.

I decide to circle around, see if I could find her, if *she* did.

As I trudge through the encampment, I'm surrounded by snatches of stories from groups of soldiers, familiar and unfamiliar voices mingling like a congregation prayer.

* * *

A group is in a circle, cleaning their plasma rifles as I pass by.

One of them is talking: "So we're on Arwen Colles, by what looks like the dried up remains of a river. It's quiet and there's time, I duck into the trees for a piss. I'm done with my business and headed back through the brush and all of a sudden there's the barrel of a plasma rifle poking right in my ribs. It's this zook, except he's as shocked as I am. He's charging up his piece, but it malfuncks on him, and I zap him five—*boom boom boom boom boom*—before he can get the lead out. Alt history."

That gets a laugh from the company.

* * *

Sharkey and I had gotten to talking at the bar, and by the second lager she'd told me about how the last mail on her message list—and the reason for my spilled drink—had been from her Mars-based ex, suing for full custody of their daughter, who for the duration of the tour was with her parents.

"He might as well shoot me," she said.

She bit her lip. I offered her a cig-cap, and she pinched it under her nose, inhaling in the vapors. I didn't know really what to say, but I knew this was probably a good time to change the subject. What she'd said reminded me about Luther Myers, a guy I knew from my second tour, so I said, I'd been shot once, and memorably.

"Yeah?" she asked.

"See, there was this guy in my squad, Luther. First tour, didn't know any better, not listening to anything you said. He was just a kid, right? We were on a march into the Ettenmoors, about a day's travel across the plains from the drop point. Sarge called a break right at the edge of Eryn Vorn, heavy jungle with no sunlight, snakes, vines, quicksand, you name it. It would be slower going from here, you see, night vision, the works. While we were checking gear, Luther went off and started playing with an Aetna flaregun."

She cocked her head. "Aetna?"

"They're the ones that shoot re-usable flares. After you launched your flares, you track them to where they fell, pick them up when they'd cooled enough, and use them again. So Luther was standing maybe twenty feet away from me, holding an Aetna and zapping imaginary zooks in the jungle. And I told him, knock it off. He loaded, and fired the flare straight at me."

"Holy mack."

"Hit me square in the body armor. The goddamn heat through the chest plate insulation was just bearable, and I was cursing and tearing off my armor, and Luther stood there laughing as the flare sputtered and died."

"What did you do about it?"

"Cursed him out and said he'd better not sleep that night, or I'd shoot an Aetna up his ass."

It worked; she laughed. "For real?"

I took a swig. "No, not really. There were zooks in that jungle, and Luther took a sniper hit to the temple."

She thought about that for a moment, then took a swig of her own.

"War is hell," she said.

When hyper-sleep time came, Sharkey and I had chosen parallel sleep pods. After we woke, she told me that she wouldn't mind hooking up again, after both our tours were over.

* * *

Another group I pass is cleaning out the last of their rations.

"So Rizzo was driving us back to the base, we're the lead in a convoy. I'm the guy behind the driver, right? What happened next is a blur. The guy riding shotgun, Johnson, yells 'Truck right!' and Rizzo swerves right, but there's two bombs on the road, not just one, and we hit the second with a *BOOM*! The truck cartwheels and slams into the ground. Rizzo is dead, Johnson is dead, and I'm there with my goddamn arm blown off. Just because I'm the guy behind the driver."

* * *

When I find Sharkey, she's with a group sitting by the temporary comm station. She was talking, so I hang back, listening in.

"It was about halfway through my tour," she was saying, "We were out on a rescue mission in Chusuk Planitia for an advance patrol that hadn't reported in. We were headed east on our first pass when out of nowhere we were hit by gunfire. We lost control of the spinner, hit the surface at speed. It was twisted metal everywhere, the smell of burning. I was shouting 'Get out, get out!' but my leg couldn't move, and I had to drag myself out when suddenly I was hauled up. I looked up, and I was in between two zooks, and there were more of them, all around, kicking at my crew.

"Well they tried to stand me up but I couldn't, my left leg was bad off, and when I fell back down again they started shouting at me, and one of them jammed their handgun to the back of my head and I thought, here it is, I'm going to die. He pulled my helmet off and that's when they realized I was a woman.

"They tore off my weapons belt, examined my medical vest, and then they started shouting. Not at me, but at each other. It kept going for a little while, but then the guy with the handgun put it away. I think they realized this had been a medical mission, and that pretty much saved my life, I guess. They tied up my leg, threw me on a truck, and three of them took me to a hospital in the nearest zook town."

She took a whiff off of a cig-cap.

"Anyway, on the truck on the way to the hospital, that was when it happened. I was in the back, on the floor because I couldn't sit right. And there's the guy with the handgun on the side bench, guarding me, and he's looking at me like he still can't believe I'm a woman. I wasn't really thinking about anything in particular. I was thinking, I'm alive, and were my crew still alive, was anyone else still alive. And then this zook lowers himself from the bench to the ground, and he starts to kiss me."

Someone says, "Damn."

"I know," says Sharkey. "I mean, there I am, cut up and bloody, with my leg in a tourniquet and sitting in a pool of blood and dirt, and this is all he can think about? And before I know it, he's tearing at my uniform and starting to paw me. At that time I'm not doing anything, I'm thinking if I do something, am I going to die? And here he is groping me, pushing me to the ground, pulling the zip down to my pants."

"So what did you do?"

She inhaled another vape.

"I grabbed his hand, put it on my crotch, then snapped it back and broke his wrist."

"He screamed, of course. The truck stopped. I zipped up my suit, the others came running and when they saw him, cursed and switched him to the front of the truck, and we continued on. But no one ever touched me again."

* * *

That's when she sees me. She gets up, crosses the group, and hugs, saying nothing.

"Sharkey," I say, hugging her back. "Sharkey. I missed you."

She nods, and although she wasn't before, she is suddenly crying.

What we both know, in that moment that we are holding each other, that we didn't know a moment before, was that we are, the two of us, *alive*. It's a gift.

Someone else in her group starts telling a story—but just then the shuttle breaks through the clouds above us, looming like the hand of God.

Through the roar of the retro-rockets I shout to her that I have to get back to my squad, that we'd meet up again on the *Miyazaki*.

She nods, but it's a long time before she lets go.

"Thank God," she says.

* * *

Funny thing, that.

On our final mission before tour end, our squad receives orders to move in on a specific set of coordinates on Titan. We mobilize and head out, all we know is that the enemy had taken the target, and that we had to take it back.

It turns out to be this church in Echoriath Montes. There's even a goddamn cross on the top of the tower, and a bell in that tower. The guys hesitate for a second, and I know what they are thinking, we're going to hell for this.

Still, we've got orders.

We surround the place, cover all the exits. We train our howitzers on the windows, and then we hit them with everything we've got, plasma charges spitting out smoke like there's no tomorrow. We're raining fire on that church like God's own wrath.

When the zooks pour out we let go with the Weyman J77 machine rifles, yelling obscenities, shells spraying all over the place like they're fireworks, firing until there's nothing moving.

Sarge waves us forward, and we close in.

As we cross the threshold I remember, and here's the kicker, I remember that this is a place of worship, and for some reason I remember my Nana, who used to take me to church; I make the sign of the cross.

* * *

Thank God.

But does God have anything to do with it?

The odds were always against me surviving for a fourth tour. War is like Russian roulette; you pull the trigger, and if that chamber is a blank, it only means that the next time you pull the trigger, the odds have shifted considerably against you.

On my first tour, I was brought to the trauma centre at Faramir Colles, which was nothing more than three trailers at the base of a hill.

An hour earlier I'd been sitting down to Thanksgiving dinner with my regiment, when suddenly a spinner crashed through the perimeter. The sentries opened fire as everyone dived for cover, but it was too late. It turned out the spinner was loaded with explosives, primed to go within a minute after it had crossed the gates. Jack Eastbrook stood his ground, coolly firing at its tires. He hit one, the spinner veered away, but not enough—then it went off.

There was blood everywhere, Eastbrook had all his limbs blown off. But he was still alive when the med vehicle got there.

I had shrapnel in the legs, and they took out every excruciating piece in one of those trauma centre trailers. I screamed throughout. But they stopped me from bleeding to death, augmented me with cybernetic implants so I could walk again, fight again, kill again. As long as they could keep me alive they could keep on replacing my limbs, almost until I became indistinguishable from the zooks we were fighting.

I'll take trailer number two for five hundred, Jack.

In trailer number three, quietly, Eastbrook died.

* * *

I watched an old vid-reel once, about day-to-day life in a field military surgical hospital. In one episode there's this doctor talking to a chaplain.

He says, "Father, William Sherman was wrong." Sherman was a general in the Union Army in the first American Civil War.

The doctor is saying, "War isn't Hell. War is worse than Hell."

And the priest says, "How so?"

The doctor says, "Only sinners go to Hell."

And the priest goes, "And war?"

"War is full of the innocent," says the doctor. "Civilians, children, old people. Doctors and nurses. Factory workers. Soldiers. Almost everyone—except maybe for the weapons-makers and some generals—almost everyone in war is an innocent."

* * *

In the hyper-sleep hall on the *Miyazaki*, I fold my uniform neatly and put it in the drawer underneath. Now fully clad in a sleep-suit, I haul myself into the pod and wait for the fluid that would come in and cover us before we went into hyper-sleep.

"Sam."

It's Sharkey, on my right.

"I've been meaning to tell you. It didn't happen that way."

I nod.

"I mean, not all of it."

"I know."

She's lying down in her pod, looking up at the ceiling. All around us the soldiers are talking to each other, bantering with jokes, other stories. But on her right, the pod is empty, as on my left. She must have noticed that, one of those little things that push you to go further with your secrets than you intend to.

"After that zook touched me, I didn't break his wrist. I froze. I didn't do anything. I didn't want to make the situation any worse than it was. I didn't want to die."

I say nothing. Her eyes are still on the ceiling, as if that metal stretched far away into infinity. Her hands are clasped, as if she's praying, or in a confessional.

"He ripped my suit open and when he pushed my legs apart I screamed. And the truck stopped, and the others came. They were shouting, and at first I thought they were going to stop him. Then they started watching."

She is silent for a moment, maybe waiting for a sign from me that I'm listening, maybe for me to say something about forgiveness, or about penance. I don't know what to say, so I nod again, and maybe the movement is enough.

"They all did it. Raped me."

I watch her for a moment, but she's closed her eyes now, and presses the button on the inside of her pod. The lid slips down on her. For a while you can see her breath fogging up the glass porthole, then disappear as the hyper-fluid fills the tank.

* * *

Dulce et decorum est.

Sweet and glorious it is...

We've repeated that lie to each other for thousands of years. You'd think we would have learned better by now.

Yet here we are—on this godforsaken ship, circling the

moon of a godforsaken world, seven hundred and some odd million miles from home, three years' of travel in hyper-sleep to where our families and children weep for us, and everything we cling to—everything we tell ourselves is real, every story we tell each other—is either half of a truth, or a lie.

* * *

When Sharkey's pod is filled, I settle back in my own. The memory material form-fits to me, cushioning my human arms and half-human legs in a familiar embrace. I press my own button, and the casket lid closes on me with a hum.

Anya, I whisper to myself, and I repeat her name, because she's who I want to think about, she's who I want to see in my three-year-long dreams. But sometimes, the past won't let go of you. When I close my eyes, it isn't Sharkey that I see.

It's *her*.

I can still see her very clearly, the zook hiding in the confessional in that church in Echoriath. I'm pretty sure it was a confessional. I remember my grandmother taking me when I was eleven, because unlike my mother she hadn't stopped believing in a God.

At the rear of *La Iglesia de San Juan Bautista*, where Nana went on Sundays, there was a small, enclosed booth with a central chamber, where—in place of God—the priest sat, with two smaller booths on either side. You sat kneeling in the dark, until the priest opened up a small, latticed window to your small booth, which was a sign to start fumbling through your sins.

At the rear of the church in Echoriath there was also a confessional booth. I was the first one there, and I kicked open the middle door. Empty, as was the small booth on the right. I kicked open the one on the left, and there she was, hands clasped and kneeling, whispering through the lattice window to no one.

"You!" I said, and I motioned her outside with the rifle, but she ignored me, still whispering to no one. "You!" I said again, and she looked at me, and crossed herself.

She came out, arms and legs bruised and in a rag that must have once been a dress. She was the smallest thing. Her lips were ashen, her eyes were teary, and her face was smeared with soot. Her auburn hair was askew, strewn with caked mud. The smallest thing. So frail, almost inconsequential.

She raised her hands. There, on the palm of the little girl's left hand was branded a single letter: '*R*'.

I stood there, about as close to her as Sharkey was from me, three feet away from the face I see so clearly now, imploring, understanding but not understanding why.

Then Sarge's voice: "What the frag are you waiting for?"

I looked back, and there was Sarge and half my patrol on the altar platform, weapons ready, watching me. I raised my plasma rifle, touched it to her heart, and I fired.

* * *

The *Miyazaki* is turning.

You can feel the slow rotation of the ship as it turns, and the thrum of the ion thrusters readying their push against Titan's gravity.

But the secrets we keep, the lies of war honorable and glorious, they hew a gravity well deeper than for the planet and all of Saturn's sixty-two moons, an abyss from which there is no escape.

I close my eyes, and prepare for dreaming.

Q&A with Samuel Peralta

What does the Latin poem at the start of the story mean?

The verse from Horace translates as: "How sweet and honorable it is to die for one's country: / Death pursues the man who flees, / spares not the hamstrings or cowardly backs / Of battle-shy youths." Centuries later, the phrase *"Dulce et decorum est / Pro patria mori"* was used in a well-known poem by Wilfred Owen, what he called 'the old Lie'. That humankind still haven't learned this, now or in the time frame of my story, is part of the theme of "War Stories".

One of the many things I love about your writing is the way you tackle universal themes. This story is no exception. It's set in some mythical future and yet it could have taken place during the Roman Empire or today in Iraq. How do you manage to write stories that seem timeless?

I very often consciously choose those themes that are vital and important today - and those are themes that turn out to be universal - such as the inequality of different races or genders in today's society. Speculative fiction then enables me to use its particular vocabulary to say things about those themes and issues - using the inequality of robots and humans, for example, as a metaphor for today's inequalities - in ways that can turn out to be very powerful.

You have an interesting resume. Can you tell us a bit about what you do along with writing SF?

I'm still not a full-time writer. My day job is with a specialized engineering company that, among other things, provides complex high-tech tools for the nuclear industry, such as robots to do things in places where humans cannot go. I've been active in start-ups, in areas including software for handheld devices, advanced III-V opto-electronic semiconductors, and most recently in a gesture and image sensing. I've also helped produce and support over 100 short films, one of which recently received a Golden Globe nomination for Best Foreign Film.

Are you working on any new tales? And how can readers best find you online?

I have several stories coming up in many anthologies, a collection of my own stories later, and hopefully a novella. I'm continuing to produce my own anthology series, The Future Chronicles, which is up to fourteen volumes now. I'm most often on Facebook if you want to chat, but you'll get to know me best by my stories, and those you can find via www.smarturl.it/samuelperalta ... There's always some of me in my characters.

The Mergans
by Ann Christy

One

THE HAND WASHED the Voice's legs, smoothing away the dust from her knees and the bottoms of her feet. The Voice watched her work, trying to remain detached, as if it were not her body being tended with such care. Done with her legs, the Hand looked up, ready to wash the rest of the Voice's body in preparation for her first robing.

The Hand paused when she saw the Voice's face and the tears that marked her cheeks. Her alarm was real and immediate. Tears were for infants, unacceptable from anyone else. Dropping the wet cloth to the floor, she wiped away the tears with work-roughened fingertips, making sure to get every spot of lingering moisture.

When more filled the Voice's eyes, she gripped the

Voice's head and shook her a little. It wasn't rough or angry, only fearful and concerned, but it worked to make the Voice look at her. The Hand pulled away and signed the words, *Be brave.*

These two signs didn't help the Voice at all. How could this Hand know what she was about to go through? How could she understand?

Something of her thoughts must have been written on her face, because the Hand sunk back into her kneeling position in front of the bench and put a hand to the Voice's knee in comfort. When she leaned back her head, as if searching the ceiling far above for some answer, the Voice saw the tiny, pale line across this Hand's throat. She'd seen it many times, but tonight the old scar had greater significance than ever before.

The Voice leaned over as much as she could without unbalancing herself and whispered into the Hand's ear, "I'm afraid I'll do poorly. I cannot be a Hand if I fail. A Voice does not need hands and a Hand has no need of a voice."

The Hand's body stiffened when she spoke, and the Voice saw her eyes dart about as if looking for anyone who might have heard her speak. This was not allowed. Her voice belonged to her master and was for his use alone. Just as the hands of all Hands belonged to their master, all words from a Voice did too. The Voice relayed his words to others, but had none of her own.

At least, the Voices weren't supposed to have any words of their own.

The Hand pulled away and put a wrinkled hand to the Voice's mouth to stop her words. After another quick look around, she signed, *Your songs are beautiful. Your face is beautiful. They will accept you and you'll keep your voice. You will sing and read them stories from the Sky-God's books forever.*

The Voice straightened back up on the bench, a more difficult task than it should be. The Hand picked up the fallen cloth and resumed her washing of the Voice's body, pausing only when she reached the stumps where her arms once were. Her face hardened as she washed those, her eyes losing some focus as if she didn't want to fully see the damage that had been done to this Voice after her songs won her a place as such. The Voice didn't mind that so much. She couldn't even remember what having arms had been like since they'd been taken when she was three years old.

The Hand brushed the Voice's cheek and she smiled at her. The smile the Voice returned was weak, but it was there and would have to suffice. Her sadness would color her songs. It might make them beautiful or it might make them rough. It was best not to risk it this night.

Yet the Hand also knew the young Voice was right. A Voice did not need hands and a Hand did not need a voice. The deed had been done to the Voice already and if she did not debut her songs well tonight, she would be on the burning pyre tomorrow. Before sunset, she would be spread amongst the fields to help the crops grow.

All women had uses, even dead ones.

The Hand brought the robes and the Voice stood while she was draped with the exacting precision demanded by the evening. This was her first night wearing the robes of the Claimed. Her first week in the bleeding rooms was over and she was now a woman. She could be displayed as such and her songs heard by more than just her master.

As the crimson silk fell over her, the Voice watched the Hand and waited for her moment. When the Hand leaned close to tie the many elaborate closures on the robe, she put her lips to the Hand's ear and whispered the forbidden words, "I will be brave for you, Grandmother."

Two

Tango listened to the briefing, then nudged Delta in the next seat. "Let's just call it Douchebag Planet Number 40 or something."

Delta stifled a laugh and grinned widely. The grin didn't look good. It stretched the wide, white scar across a pair of lips already marred by a myriad of other such scars, making it shine under the briefing room lights. Lips and chins were often the victims inside the battle suits when a battle was in full swing. It was the only part of them that had significant freedom of movement inside their shells.

"Douchebag Planet, aye!" came her hissed response. Neither of them actually understood the origins of the reference, but it was a popular one and the word considered the ultimate insult.

A sharp glance from the Division command section up front hushed them and brought both soldiers' attention where it should be. There was nothing new here, nothing to be worried about. This would be just another planet that didn't pass muster. It didn't matter what name they chose for themselves or which Seed ship brought them to the planet. It didn't matter what they envisioned themselves to be, what they had deluded themselves into thinking was the right way to live. Their so-called faith and beliefs were of no importance.

What mattered is that they were douchebags and for that, they had to die. Or, as the Peace Force liked to call it, *reorganized*.

The Division Commander—called DC rather than any standard designator—eyed the crowded room, which held the leading elements of each Brigade, Battalion, and Company in their Division. Tango was the current Second in Third Company, while Delta was currently running in third for the Fourth Company of their Battalion. Not too high up in the command structure so that life was entirely without fun, but not so low that they didn't have opportunities to make their own fun. It was a nice balance and they were both very happy with their spots in the hierarchy.

The DC's next words put a hush on the room. "This will be a no-two-stones operation."

Tango and Delta looked at each other in surprise. There'd been no such operation since before either of them had come out of the crèche. It wasn't unprecedented, but it was rare. This planet must have gone very far off the beaten track to deserve a complete obliteration of their entire infrastructure, customs, and culture.

No-two-stones simply meant that no two stones in a building would be left together, an ancient reference that hardly worked when most planets were covered by buildings made of metal and glass. Still, the sentiment held. No-two-stones was bad news for the planet's current ruling parties.

"And the inhabitants?" asked the First for the battalion Tango and Delta both belonged to.

"That's where this operation gets a little sticky, so thank you for asking, Battalion Commander Xray-Mike-Four. We've got another year of ship time until we reach the system, which means you'll all be going back to sleep. That will give us about twenty-five additional years of planet time to evaluate them and figure out the details. Our current operational plan is being loaded into the learning modules. You've all seen the rather unique planetary conditions we'll be working under during your pre-planning sleep sessions. Extensive deserts and wind make this one an interesting environmental outlier. But there's also the social structure to consider, which is nothing like we've seen before. Our social engineers are still working on that part of it."

More than a few surreptitious looks were passed between particular friends or leaders. If it required even more study after the decision to intervene was made, then it had to be a seriously messed up system. But would it be messed up in the *oh, that's interesting* sort of way or the *I've really got to kill everyone I see* kind of way?

The battalion commander wasn't yet done it seemed, and asked, "And there are still no reports of significant military presence on the surface?"

The DC coughed a little at that question, which meant the answer wasn't truly known or wasn't going to be to the liking of the soldiers. Tango listened more carefully and tried not to be distracted by the close proximity of Delta.

"That's a difficult question. There are plenty of standard old-Earth style anti-air platforms, but they don't appear manned. Also, there are some indicators of underground activity, though we can't see through the bedrock to figure out exactly what that activity might be. It's possible that there won't be much fight here—"

The DC paused as low groans broke out from the assembled crowd. No one wanted to go to battle only to find no one to fight. "But—and I repeat, *but*—we should be ready for pop-up activity. It's entirely possible that they relocated all military structures underground to protect assets from the periodic activity in their asteroid belt. The planet is bombarded on a fairly regular basis, which would make underground assets a logical choice."

The groans faded at those words, but no one was very excited after that. Pop-up activity was nothing if not intense, but underground facilities would be boring. Orbital bombardment would get to have all the fun if that were the case.

As the briefing ended, Tango grabbed Delta by the arm and tugged, swerving them out of the flow of traffic toward a ladder access. Tango shouted a little to be heard over the noise a hundred pairs of boots created while clomping across metal. "Come. I've got a surprise!"

Delta's eyebrows rose at that. She liked surprises and especially liked Tango's surprises. Usually, it was something fun like a new combat move or an early look at some new weaponry.

They banged up the stairs for four levels, alone in the stairwell because no one used them. Most of the sailors and soldiers on this ship had probably never used stairs in their lives. Why would they? The chutes were faster and the ship was big. More than sixty thousand people lived and worked on this ship and it didn't seem crowded except when waiting for a chute. Tango had discovered the joy of the ladder-well echoes and never gotten over it. They were also a nice way to avoid waiting for the crowd after a battle briefing or during shift changes.

They left the stairwell at the level primarily reserved for suits and suit creation. Delta grinned again, thinking this might be a peek at some new weaponry for their suits. That would be good. Each planet they visited offered new opportunities to adjust their current weaponry to a new environment, a new defensive system, a new set of challenges. There was always something new being added.

Tango's face wore a mischievous look when they stopped in front of one of the Build Bay doors. It slid open and Delta followed along, passing racks of suits being refurbished or built. It was a constant process. A soldier was their suit. It was weapon, medical unit, habitation, transportation. It was all things to the person inside, and the soldier's suit must be up to date and in perfect working order at all times.

As the two soldiers passed the open stalls hung with suits, technicians called out or waved greetings. As they approached one such stall—an elaborately decorated suit in the final stages of battle preparation gleaming within—the technician popped out and smiled up at the two soldiers, leaning back so that there wasn't quite so much neck-craning required to see their faces.

Tango leaned over a little and said, "How's it hanging, Tech? This is Delta-Four-Bravo. Delta, this is Technician 440 assigned to the First Division."

The technician's small hand was lost in Delta's paw when they shook, but the shake was enthusiastic even so. Delta smiled at the short person, no taller than the bottom of her rib cage. The techs were small, but very nimble, very quick. And very smart. They were to be respected, but Delta always felt big and clumsy around them.

Before Delta was forced to figure out what to say, the tech clapped her hands and giggled, "She's going to love it. Go show her! Go show her!"

Tango boomed a laugh and grabbed Delta's hand to drag her down the row, the technician's high and delighted laugh following them. A few more technicians popped out of their stalls and clapped or shouted greetings as they walked. Delta marveled once again at how many people simply liked Tango. Was it the smile, the easy manner, the battle prowess that never returned to the ship as attitude after a battle was over? Delta could only shake her head at it and watch Tango return each wave and greeting.

Halting suddenly, Tango motioned into a stall and said, "Here it is. For you!"

Inside the stall was a suit, and it wasn't Delta's usual suit either. The last battle had seen her dented and damaged— so much so that her suit wouldn't even join the transport back up to the ship properly, requiring she be lifted with the wounded. Delta had expected a refit, but not a new suit.

She stood in front of the suit and took it in. Instead of gleaming metal or bright decorations like those on Tango's suit, it was all in shades of tan and brown, swirled about so that it blended beautifully. It wasn't a common color choice, but it was lovely even so. The exoskeleton that would encase her and join with her looked about the same in terms of general form, but it was smoother somehow. Elegant was the word that came to her mind. The weapons that covered every available surface almost seemed to flow like water from the metal body.

"It's beautiful!" she gasped.

Tango apparently couldn't hold back anymore or wait for Delta to explore the suit herself. Punching the button to rotate the suit, Tango opened the back and waved in invitation. "Get in!"

Delta slid into the suit and immediately felt the difference. This suit hugged her, pressing in where it should and giving her room where she most wanted it. It was fitted as only a long-time lover would understand she needed it to, as someone who knew her body as well as she did would create it to fit.

"Turn it on," Tango said from behind her.

Delta chinned the activation bar and the suit closed in around her, haptic feedback telling her exactly where the suit was touching the rack in exactly the right way. Even the chin-bar was padded on this new suit, an added touch that spoke of love and made Delta smile.

"Weapons," Delta said and the displays that came up in front of her eyes made them widen. She had everything. No, she had at least two of everything.

When at last she climbed out of her suit, Delta was overwhelmed and didn't want to sleep another ship-year away before she might use it. Tugging the sleeves of her bodysuit down, she asked, "How did you do this?"

Tango looked almost embarrassed, waving away the singular nature of the accomplishment. "I woke up a few months early, but the techs here did the hard stuff. Really."

Delta looked over at Tech 440, who was standing outside

the stall of the suit she was working on and shaking her head. She pointed to Tango as if to counter that claim.

"Well, I thank you. And the colors, how did you think of that?"

Tango shrugged and said, "During the learning about this next planet while I was sleeping, I saw all the deserts, the sand. I'm not sure why, but it stuck with me for some reason. I like it though. Do you?"

Delta nodded, suddenly shy again with all the techs sneaking glances at them from the stalls. This was unprecedented. Techs made suits, designed suits, maintained suits. Soldiers didn't do that. Tango was different and always had been, but this was almost too different.

"Why did you do this? The techs would have refitted my old one or made one," she asked, looking up at Tango, her eyes soft with emotion.

Tango shrugged and touched the pattern on the chest plate of the suit. "I don't know, really. I just wanted it to be right for you. Perfect. It seemed like something I could do for you that was special. I want you to be as safe as I can make you."

Delta shook her head, but she smiled even so. "I'm a soldier. So are you. Safety is for the ship, not the ground." She pushed the button that sent the suit back into the stall to wait for the next battle, eyeing it like the prize it was. Then she rose onto her tiptoes and kissed Tango's equally scarred lips and whispered, "But it's the best gift I've ever received and I love you for it."

"Well, anyway," Tango said, stepping back and eyeing all the grinning techs watching them, "we should get to sleep.

Lots to learn. Lots of battles to plan. It's going to take a long time for the ship to slow, so we might as well not get old while it's happening."

Later, as Delta felt the rush of cool gas filling her pod and the sleepiness washing over her, she thought about her suit and murmured, "Bang. Bang. Zap." Then she dreamed of battle.

Three

The Voice nearly tripped as she shuffled with unusual haste toward the women's quarters. The Hand assigned to her that day caught her before she landed on her face, a look of barely concealed panic marring her features. If the Voice were damaged, then it would be the Hand that paid the price.

"Thank you," the Voice said and the Hand cringed at the words.

This Hand was young, just out of the bleeding rooms and newly allowed into the halls of the palace. She was still fresh and fearful, which is why she'd been assigned. The Voice had grown old and weary, not so steady on her feet anymore. She needed a young, strong Hand to help her. But even with her advancing age, her voice was still pure and the notes she could carry higher than any other Voice in the land.

This ability had kept her alive for longer years than most, but she had one more advantage. She had also borne two Masters, an unprecedented accomplishment. That had made her master tender toward her, even lenient. He always ensured she had a Hand nearby to tend her. Even when she had been caught reading a Sky-God book for her own pleasure, he had only taken one eye instead of having her burned to feed the crops.

Though she had only borne five times, just one male had been culled during the Three Year selections. The other two had been sent to the Master's School, and when openings in the Great 5000 had opened, both her males had been chosen from their like number to fill the gap. The others were culled, but those she had borne had been made masters.

Of her two female bearings, she had no idea, for it was not considered important to the master, but she watched each new selection when it would have been their times, hoping to see some girl-child chosen to be a Voice that carried hints of her features.

Selections were always hard to watch, but those years had been particularly difficult. It would be the final time a child was whole. Each tap on a shoulder meant either the girl-child would have her voice or her arms removed. It was hard to decide which was the better outcome to hope for. Either choice was better than that which awaited all those not tapped on the shoulder. They filed out the other side of the choosing arena and their smoke darkened the skies within hours.

Even so, she'd looked for some hint of herself in those small voices and faces. She'd seen none, but that didn't mean they were both culled. It was possible that they lived.

Only now that meant nothing. Nothing in all the land meant anything now. The end was here. There were dark shadows in the heavens and the Masters were in a frenzy of fright.

Her master shifted between abject fear that it was the burning stars returning to blight the land again and ecstatic joy that the shapes might signal the return of the Sky-God. Eventually, he had settled on abject fear and that was that.

Grunting to avoid frightening her young Hand any further, the Voice nodded toward the door that led to the women's quarters at the end of the dim hallway. The Hand ducked her head and made the sign of obedience before hurrying ahead to open the door for her.

Two Enforcers bracketed the door and their eyes flicked toward her for only a moment. Like the Hands, they had no voices, but unlike every other person who was not a Master, they were male. Or rather, they had started as males.

Pausing at the threshold, the Voice looked down at the floor and said, "The Master calls for you. All Enforcers are to report to the sheltering place." They did not acknowledge her, but they knew of the dark shapes and hurried off, leaving the door unguarded for the first time in memory.

Like the women, some Enforcers were Hands and a few were Voices. These were Hands, and even though they were Enforcers, they listened to all Voices. Voices relayed the words of the Master and no others. They were trusted.

The hallways inside the women's quarters were stark. Bare of the decorations and frescoes that lined the halls on the master's side of palace, they were instead clean and bare, painted in shades of brown and tan to match the bareness of their lives.

The Voice hurried down the passageways, past the cells where pallets for women not on duty held sleeping forms, past the kitchens where they ate in silence. The bleeding rooms were up ahead and this was the only place a male would never venture to go, so it was where women went as often as they could. It was their only place of peace.

The Hand opened the door for her and she rushed in, her robes endeavoring to trip her feet with their many layers. It frustrated the Voice that she was unable to brush them aside or pick them up to make the going easier. Again, her Hand steadied her and as the door to the bleeding rooms shut behind them, she said, "Gather them all. Gather them here. There is no time. There is fire in the sky."

Four

Two divisions would be conducting the assault, which was a slender number when the number available was considered. Then again, this was a rather unique situation, the population skewed and the defenses oddly absent. Like all colonized planets, the Seed ship for this one sent out updates along the quantum buoys for millennia until finally launching itself into the system's sun to disappear forever.

And like all ships, this Seed ship did not concern itself with social development, only with ensuring that technological development remained within or below the allowed levels. It was a flaw in the original design, one that the Peace Force had been tasked with correcting long ago. It was the final task given to them before the Earth joined all the other planets whose times had come and gone.

Tango had learned the details of the planet while they all slept, troubled dreams and nightmares interrupting the long learning sessions. The Seed ship had not spared details or flavored the reports with opinion, but that only made the learning worse. Why this colony had become what they were was a mystery, but the asteroid impact that soured so much of their land had probably played a role. It didn't matter why, though. It only mattered that they had chosen this unacceptable path.

Like everyone else, Tango awoke disturbed. Angry. Ready.

As the suit tightened around Tango's body, the gel filled every crevice. The gel would sustain all bodily functions and protect its inhabitant from the vagaries of space and the planet's surface. The moment of breathing it in was hard—as always—but the moment passed. Now Tango was as mute as the majority of the planet's population, an irony.

Tango's throat made the motions of speech, and the suit created the sounds and transmitted them. An acknowledgement from the Company Communicator came rapidly, and soon all the members of the team were ready to form up. Testing weapons came last, each soldier passing through a testing chamber on the way to formation. The sizzling pops and hums were felt more than heard inside the suit, each one like a caress to a heart formed for battle.

Each company filed into the formation bay and the crowd grew, a thousand suited bodies standing on their markers and ready by the time their leadership filed in to take their places. More than twenty bays would be used for this launch, but that only accounted for the use of two ships and a mere twenty thousand troops. That was nothing in comparison with most. It was very few when considering the target was an entire planet.

As Tango crossed the bay, a final look brought Delta into view. She was far back in the formation, her tan and brown standing out in the forest of bright colors and patterns. Raising the suit's arm in a final wave, Tango's boots found their assigned spot and locked into place.

Two more ships stood at the ready in case of need, the bombardment cannons ready to destroy all of the surface that needed destroying, but this plan called for a more delicate operation. It was decided that though this would remain a no-two-stones operation, the vast majority of the population had been classified as victims in need of rescue. This was also an unusual wrinkle in the history of such planetary cleansings. Not entirely, because there had been others, but not at all common.

In practical terms, it meant that Tango and every other soldier deployed could not simply eliminate anyone they encountered within a set battle zone. Instead, each human would have to be cleared or targeted as individuals, a process that increased risk and delayed completion.

It was also a challenge. Tango liked challenges almost as much as battle itself.

The suit feedback probes attached to the bones behind each suited ear vibrated as the channel opened. "Brigade, prepare for deployment!"

The red lights of the opening bay door raised the pulse rates of all the soldiers. The anticipation of insertion and the battle that would follow heightened their bio-readings enough that the support techs in another part of the ship were highlighted in the red glow of their screens. Smiles and butt-fidgets inside their thousands of support pods followed the glow. For them this was battle too. Each soldier had a support tech, and each support tech lived the battle through their soldier.

As the bay floor lowered into open space, the planet loomed bright and wide around the edges of the platform. Too much brown, too much red, not enough green. Soured land. It would recover, but such things take time. The wide green strip to either side of the equator was jagged and broken by the seas, but already Tango could see tendrils of green stretching up along rivers and spreading abundance. Yes, the planet would recover in time.

But not with these people. Not with this society.

"Deploy!"

Like one thousand others, Tango's boots detached from the bay floor and the propulsion systems kicked on, pushing the suit over the edge and into space. With only the briefest pause, the matrix began to form, each suit connecting in its assigned spot, the ball growing around those suits in the center. Within moments, the Battle Ball was formed and propelling itself toward the atmosphere and planet below—one thousand suits meant to bring destruction and death. Other balls deployed, each one headed toward a known population center that the inhabitants called Palaces.

Once the spin began and the ball approached atmosphere, there was nothing to see as the face plates went opaque. Now, all they could do was enjoy the ride.

Five

The Voice crouched outside on the large platform roof above the women's quarters. Through the window, a crowd of women waited for her words, each ear ready and each body pressed forward. Her Hand steadied her as she gazed upward, though the girl would not look up at all. Perhaps she was even more fearful than the masters of the sky-fire, but she could be forgiven fear when her youth was considered.

"They are balls of fire," the Voice said. The awe she felt at the sight filled her voice and made the women nearby sigh. One of the many reasons she had lasted so long while other Voices fertilized the fields was her ability to tell a story with such feeling that the masters would cry at the telling. And that had been acting on her part. This was real.

"I see one coming this way. They are round, I'm sure of it. I do not know what they'll do, but if they bring that fire, we will be burned. That is nothing to us, is it?" She expected no answer, but she felt the trembling of her Hand through the arm around her waist.

One of the older Hands stuck her head out of the window and looked from side to side. The yard below was strangely empty. No Enforcers watched the un-bled Hands as they tended chickens and no Hands crossed the yard with food or water. Seeing her way clear, the Hand stepped out of the window for the first time in her life.

Even without a voice for speaking, the gasps of the other Hands drew the attention of the Voice. She smiled, creating a web of wrinkles around her eyes that spoke to her venerable years. At forty, she was long past the time for burning and she feared these balls of fire far less than the fire that would certainly take her soon in a much more personal way.

"Come. Come out. All of you. There is no one to see!" For the first time in her life, she gave an order that did not first come from a master's throat. It felt odd, strange… good. It was her duty to gather the Hands, to keep them together until the masters returned, but the Voice was quite sure that duty did not include standing outside against all the rules.

And her words were true. For the first time, there was no one to see, to judge, to send them for burning. The Voice knew where the masters had gone, at least the hundreds that lived in this palace complex. Her own master had grabbed a bag of gold, shocking the Voice into silence as she relayed his commands. No master touched an object in labor. No cup was lifted to their lips by their own fingers, no shoe shoved onto their own foot. And yet her Master had done so, nearly tripping at the unfamiliar action and putting the shoes on the wrong feet.

Her expression must have given her shock away, because he'd slapped her face and said, "Do not look upon me like that or I'll take your other eye."

She'd bowed her head and waited, no longer sure what she should do. The Sheltering Place was for the masters should another of the sky-rocks fall and scorch the land.

It happened every few years, but they were small, quick tails of flame that made no noticeable impact. Every few life-times the larger sky-rocks came, but even then the land was spared from any blighting like that which occurred long ago. That had been the time of darkening and nothing like it had happened since.

And these balls of fire did not look like any sky-rocks the Voice had ever seen. These giant balls of flame looked alive and filled with purpose.

Rock or no, the sheltering places were deep underground, each one far beneath the Palace it served. Her master had gone there with his enforcers and the breeders who had achieved Select classification through virtue of their many healthy births. All the masters would go. Deep underground, they would be safe.

The Voice could have also been taken, but she had hoped she would not and tried to be invisible as her master frantically gathered his favorite things. As the master had rushed through the passage away from her, the Voice held her breath, hoping that he would not turn back and tell her to come. When he did not, she'd smiled and run the other way.

Now, on this flat roof, she smiled again and said, "I tell you they are gone. Come out!"

The Hands came, at first hesitantly, but then like a flood. These were palace Hands, not allowed beyond the walls or outside like the Hands that tended the yards, gardens, farms, or animals. Most had never seen the sun save through the open sky-pit in the kitchens where smoke from the cooking fires escaped, or if they were fortunate enough to tend the master's palace, then through the windows there. But to feel the sun on their faces? No, none would have felt that before.

They crouched under the sun and sky, eyes squinting at the bright light after a lifetime of dim rooms and smoky fires. The balls were growing brighter in the sky, the flames surrounding them like coronas. They looked like the fires of a thousand children sent to the burning fields at once after a culling.

And the flames were growing closer. Quickly. Women did not fear fire. It was the end that all of them saw eventually, save for a few who died in other ways.

Let the Masters feel the flames now, the Voice thought and watched the fire.

Six

Right on time, the spin decreased and the heat dissipated.

Propulsion kicked on and the Battle Ball changed trajectory for the landing zone. The display on Tango's faceplate cleared, then overlaid the landing zone and deployment plans. It was going to be a tight one.

The palaces were nothing of the sort, but rather small and compact cities linked by endless walkways and roofed sidewalks. The buildings inside clustered in strange configurations that were going to complicate their plans for battle in significant ways.

A cluster of lights—huddled close the way animals and people often cluster—blossomed over a section of open space on the other side of the city. The Support Techs and the computer evaluated each bio-sign and the lights changed from the white of the unknown to the green of humans who were not legitimate targets and the blue of animals. Intel reported that all children were clustered in very specific locations, and now each of those locations glowed green, making all of those buildings off-limits for battle.

The land below approached quickly. When Tango first graduated the crèche into the life of a soldier, it brought a combined thrill of fear and excitement to see the planet rise in greeting like this. That thrill was still there, though tempered now by many battles in the years since.

The Battle Ball slowed and then hovered, the lowest suits no more than one hundred feet off the ground. As always, the outer suits rotated during that final descent and now weapons were brought to bear on any opposition. Yet there was none, or none worth the title. Old and almost useless anti-air guns belched smoke and clumsy projectiles in their direction, but those were almost too easy.

Tango frowned, unhappy at so little fight. Were these

people also stupid? Were they so arrogant they did not understand that even if they had control over every living thing on a planet, harm can come from elsewhere?

Each suit broke away, the landing pattern already established. Smoke and the bright lights of targeting lasers against the guns cleared under the wind's dusty power. Even before Tango's squad made it beyond the landing zone, the sound of weapons diminished, leaving only a few distant sizzling pops as old, combustion type ammunition burned off around the disabled guns.

The lack of fight made Tango's neck hair rise. It wasn't normal or natural. Who would create a culture so messed up that it begged for intervention, but do nothing to defend it? Waving the team forward, Tango's weaponry rose almost of its own accord, making the already-wide suit shoulders even more so. Laser weapons best used against small or moving targets flared from the forearms as if in sympathy with the disturbed feelings brought on by so little fight.

"Where is everyone?" Tango asked. It didn't matter if it was command or a support tech that answered, so long as an answer came.

A stone carved by the wind into a shape vaguely like that of a ground conveyance drew Tango's ire and the surge of energy from one of the suit mounted cannons sent a cloud of dust into the air. The rock was gone. Was this the extent of their battle? Rocks?

"All hold!" The command came from central, which meant the division leadership. It also didn't bode well. Never had an 'all hold' command been given once the battle was enjoined. It just didn't happen. It was one of those theoretical commands everyone knew, but never expected.

The ground trembled under the combined impatient steps of all the suits, the clomp-clomp of Tango's boots joining the beat while they all waited, sensors picking up and displaying everything. And nothing. The only bio-signs remaining were quickly coded into blue or green. Non-targets.

"Tango-Foxtrot-Nine, you have a command communications channel now open," said Tango's support tech.

The support tech seemed as disappointed with the battle as everyone else. While still professional, there was a glum tone that Tango could pick up. After a dozen battles paired with this tech, they knew each other's moods well.

"Roger, this is Tango-Foxtrot-Nine."

The channel burst with noise. The suits were big and unwieldy, but were like second skins to those that wore them. That didn't mean it wasn't a lot of work to carry them, however. Heavier breathing was the norm once planetary landing had been accomplished. The quick roll call as the channel was joined by others was another surprise. Instead of all command, the channel was being populated by a seemingly random assortment of soldiers from squad leaders like Tango to a fire team on the other side of the planet.

"Okay everyone, listen up. We've got a problem. Intel correlated over twelve-K signatures as confirmed hostile during pre-attack. Another eighty-K plus as potential hostiles. Not one of them is now locatable. They're all gone."

"What the sheeping hell?" Tango muttered, that prickly neck feeling rising again. Hostiles disappearing? Where did they go? "Off planet?" Tango asked, trying to think logically and not be spooked by this unusual foe behavior.

"Negative. These people have no ships," answered the division command communicator.

Division command took back up the reins and said, "We're going to have to think outside the battle box here. All of you on the channel are in close proximity to two specific indicators. First, you're closest to the last places the hostiles were located. Second, you're close to large masses of Greens that were in close contact with the hostiles before they disappeared."

Tango turned around and looked at the squad. Each had cleared their faceplates so that their expressions were visible, and each wore that same disappointed and slightly confused look that matched what Tango felt. Signing for them to wait and watch, Tango gave them the signal for intelligence passing and that seemed to settle them a little.

"We're sending survey and report instructions to most of the squads on the ground and assigning backup positions to others, but you will be receiving contact commands."

Tango took a step back at that, swiveling the suit to look at the cluster of ramshackle buildings behind the wall nearby. Made of stone and what looked like mud-brick, they were hardly imposing, but their sheer size and hodge-podge construction made them perfect for setting traps. Not to mention that contact commands using soldiers like Tango was also unusual. That sort of thing was limited to after the battle as a rule, and then usually assigned to the Administrators with their ability to communicate smoothly.

The unusual silence on the line was telling. Every person on this channel aside from command was a soldier like Tango. No one wanted a contact command.

"I know this isn't any specialty of ours, but we at command can't be sure that this isn't some sort of trap. We can't send Administrators down here with one hundred percent of the hostiles unaccounted for. So, you're to lead your squads to the Greens as directed by your support techs. Make contact. Find out what's going on. Then let's get it done and get the hell off this creepy planet."

Like everyone else on the line Tango *hoo-yahed* that final statement with whole-hearted agreement. This place was a shit-hole of brown dust, wind, and messed up behavior. They didn't even do battle properly. Who could respect that?

Once the line was clear, the support techs opened their squad lines and Tango briefed the team. There were a lot of raised eyebrows, but a command was a command. That was always good enough.

Leading the squad of five suits toward the wall, Tango said, "At least we can blow up this piece of crap wall. Who wants it? Give me any number between one and twenty. Closest pick gets to fire."

Seven

The Voice watched as the strange monsters walked about. The old icons of the metal-god were all gone. They were holy spots and not to be touched, yet these metal-men had simply erased them in great explosions of fire.

One of the Hands tugged at her skirts to get her attention, then signed, *The Sky-Gods have returned! They will bring more masters.*

The Voice shook her head, then returned her gaze to the metal-men—if that's what they were. Some were metal and she could hear the clang and bang of metal against stone even from where she stood, but most were colorful in ways not even the freshest of frescoes were. They were covered in chaotic patterns she could not discern from where she stood.

They were also huge. Far, far bigger than any male the Voice had ever seen. It was possible that these *were* the Sky-Gods. It was possible the Hand was correct and there would be more masters. It was equally likely that the Sky-Gods had returned because they were angry. After all, they were destroying all the holy relics they had given to the masters. Perhaps the masters would be punished.

That would be fine with the Voice.

The young Hand at her side nearly unbalanced the Voice when she jerked and then hid behind her wide crimson robes. The older Hand steadied her almost absently, then signed, *They come.*

The Voice looked where the Hand pointed and saw that she was right. A group of five metal-men were headed directly for the place where they stood. Their steps were long and loud, the ground banging with each heavy footfall. A glinting reflection off the head of one metal-man pierced her eyes. It was like brightly polished silver—no, brighter than that. Strange.

Fear made her belly flutter. There was too much unknown. Sky-Gods or perhaps something entirely new, like sky-devils or something. There was no way to know. The Voice had read every book in existence to the masters many times—all one hundred of the Sky-God books—and nothing like this was described in any of them. Yet, they were coming. Better to be ready should they be gods.

The Voice turned to face the huddled mass of women and said, "Listen to me. If these are the Sky-Gods, then we must be seen as obedient. If they are not Sky-Gods, then there is nothing we could do to stop them. We must know what they are, what they want. And even better, we should try to live to see the other side of it. The masters have made me their Voice, so I must do as they would command me."

A Hand near the front signed, *What should we do?*

"Follow me. Let's go into the courtyard where the masters who visit this palace come. Let us greet these metal-men as if they are Sky-Gods and see what happens."

Eight

"Tango, you've got movement ahead. Changing your view," the support tech said, voice tight and ready to provide.

"Go," Tango replied and blinked when the display changed. A mass of green lights seemed to be flowing like water from an upper area in the huge building ahead of them. The wall was still between them and the building, but just beyond it, the cluster of green moved closer.

"What are they?" Tango asked, letting those eager fore-arm guns rise a little more.

"Slave women. Oppressed class. Non-targets," said the tech.

"We'll see about that," Tango grunted.

Gender roles were often muddled on the planets colonized by the Seed ships. The humans first grown from the Seed had no history, no cultural context—things that the Peace Force worked hard to maintain in the thousands of years since they were put into action. The seed colonies developed strange ideas, but there was one thing all planets had in common—no one was exactly like anyone else and no one should be discounted. A non-target could be just as violent and dangerous as a confirmed hostile.

"Tango, it looks like they're forming up. Looks like a parade square. Nothing tactical."

"Roger," Tango replied, then said to the winner of the wall destruction draw, "Go ahead and blow it."

The section of wall disappeared in an explosion of mud-brick returning to dust. The thick brown cloud hindered their vision, but their visors shifted spectrums without a hitch.

"Go around the building in front of you to the right and the formation is in an open area just beyond and to the left. They barely moved when you blew the wall. A few fell down, but that's it," the support tech said.

"Roger," Tango replied.

Shifting the spectrum again, the forest of green dots turned into a forest of green silhouettes, each one a person easily sensed through the building in front of the squad. As support reported, they were simply standing there. Even as Tango tried to sort them, one of the silhouettes shifted, then another made many complicated hand gestures, then they shifted again. It was clear they were all facing the opening to the area, exactly where Tango and the squad would approach from.

The rest of the squad got the same visuals. Tango waved them onward and said, "Target detection is priority. Motion detection second. I want a full 360 in case this is a trap. Do it by the numbers."

Each squad member acknowledged. This was as standard tactic, with each of the four other members and their individual support techs responsible for a ninety degree arc around the formation. Tango would be focused on the action, which in this case was this strange group.

Tango opened an enhanced ambient audio channel and said, "Support, scan and parse."

"Roger."

Breathing. Lots of breathing came back from the audio. Quick, nervous breaths from the crowd of women.

Tango led the squad around the building, but they might as well have been on the mess decks inside the ship. There were no weapons, no troops, no defenses. The idea of non-hostile contact was nerve-wracking, such having happened in any context only twice in all the battles or cultural adjustments Tango had participated in.

Both times it was contact after the event and both contacts had been brief. Once, when their squad was assigned to dig out a non-hostile family from a basement under a building, a rescued man had hugged Tango's chest plate in gratitude. The other was when a non-hostile offered sex on a planet in which sex was rare and highly regulated before being liberated by the Peace Force.

Tango hadn't accepted the offer.

"Here we go. Keep your weapons up, but don't engage or direct weapons toward the non-hostiles unless I order it. I want a targeting offset of no less than fifteen degrees."

Tango turned the corner with the squad. In front of them was a garden, the color a shock after so much brown. Clipped green grass, flower borders tamed into regimented shapes, a fountain tinkling out a thin stream of water into a brightly tiled pool.

And women. Four hundred-seventeen of them according to the display. At Tango's appearance, the woman in front was lowered to her knees with the aid of a young girl at her side. As if the kneeling was a cue, all the rest did the same, each one bending entirely so that their hands were outstretched on the ground in front of them, their heads tucked down with their faces between their elbows.

It was an appalling sight to see.

"Give me a channel, support. Translate," Tango ordered, voice a bit gruff at seeing such undeserved obeisance.

"You're a go," came the near immediate reply.

Swallowing, Tango considered what to say. It would be easier to simply say *Show me the location of your hostiles so I can blow them up,* but that would also probably not be very effective. The words that protocol suggested flashed up on Tango's faceplate. Yes, this support tech knew exactly how to support.

"We are not here to harm you. Will you speak with me?" As the suit translated and transmitted the words, Tango made a face at how weak the words were.

The ambient noise filter picked up and translated the words, "Help me up." It seemed to come from the woman in front, the one wearing something that looked like a red tent. The young girl put her arms around the woman and helped to lift her. Something about the narrowness of her shoulders disturbed Tango and sent a chill rippling along the suit liquid.

Once she was standing, the woman looked up at Tango, her single eye flitting around as she took in the suits. Then her eye widened and she lowered her head again. Quietly, she said, "I don't understand. Will the Master tell this Voice why the Mergans are attacking the palace of the Euripeas?"

Tango didn't think that had translated properly. It made

absolutely no sense. "Support, what the heck is she saying? I don't get it. Is the translation messed up?"

The pause was noticeable this time. At last, support replied, "Translation confirmed. You're the first to make contact so I don't have anything from any of the other teams. Just ask what she means? Maybe it's code or something. Wait, Intel reports that Mergans is the name of one of the cities and... hold one... okay, that Yoorrippie-ass is the name of another."

Great, Tango thought.

Nine

The Voice waited while the strange metal-men stood entirely still and didn't answer. They were so large that they could not be human, yet they had to be Mergans, for the one in front—who must be their leader—wore the symbol of the Mergans upon the breast of his metal body. It was not done entirely correctly, but it was clearly meant to be that symbol. The entire metal body was covered in bright shapes and patterns, but that one stood out.

The red and white stripes, the field of stars upon the left side, the golden fringe like the sun. It was surely some artistic rendition of the symbol for the Mergans' Palace no more than two hundred miles away.

The Voice knew that symbol as well as every other palace symbol. The Mergans possessed the land bracketing a mighty river and had more than four hundred masters in their palace. They were feted when they came to the Euripeas Palace, treated as all masters were treated.

Why would they attack? And how did they create metal-men to do so? What Hand could perform such work? Confusion was replacing her fear. She would be burned for speaking to a Master unbidden, but this one had bidden her to.

No, this one had *asked* it of her. No Master that the Voice knew of had ever asked for anything. Commanded, yes. Asked, no.

At last, the strange booming voice from the metal-man answered her. "Protocol says I should ask for clarification of what you just said, but I'm going to be honest with you. I have no clue what you just said. I don't know what a Mergans or a Yoorippee-ass is other than the name of a city. We're not from this planet. We're the Peace Force and we're here to help… *uh*… liberate you."

The Voice understood the words, but the context was entirely wrong. Who are they liberating? The books the masters received from the Sky-God when they were made said that they were liberated from an eternal sleep. Is that what this metal-man meant?

"Are you the Sky-God?" the Voice asked. It was best to just get it over with. If she was to die, then let it happen and be done. If there were more masters to be woken by the Sky-God, then she'd rather not be here to live through it. New masters were terrible and cruel. Many new masters at once would be even worse.

"Sky-God? You mean the Seed ship? No, I'm not from there. I'm from the Peace Force. I need to ask you some questions," the metal-man boomed.

The Voice caught movement from the corner of her eye and saw that some of the Hands near the front had pulled back their hands to cover their ears. The metal-man's followers noted the movement too, because strange protuberances on their metal bodies rotated and followed some of the movements.

The words of the metal-man were confusing. Seed ship. Seed was the name given by the Sky-God to the magic by which masters were formed. The divine seed that had traveled the stars to create perfection in the form of the masters. Yet this metal-man had said the words as if speaking of nothing more important than a litter used to carry a master in the palace. Dismissive.

"This Voice will answer. If these Masters seek the Mergans as your symbol shows, then these Masters have come to the wrong Palace. This Voice will provide these Masters with a map to the Mergans if these Masters so desire it."

The metal-man boomed a laugh and said, "You've gotta quit talking like that. It's freaking my girls out here. Can everyone just stand up? It's weird. As for this symbol, it's just an old symbol from Earth that I liked. A country called America. It's one of the places where we originated, but it's long gone now. So is Earth, for that matter. You know it?"

The Voice nodded and said, "It is from the Sky-God, one of the many symbols for the Masters and their Palaces. The Mergans. You are not from the Mergans Palace? You are not Sky-Gods seeking the Mergans?"

"Mergans," the metal-man said. "It's wrong, but I get it. And no, we're not Mergans. Or Sky-Gods."

She had never heard any Master speak so. Ever. These could not be masters and if they were Sky-Gods, then they were strange ones. And girls? Girls are unclaimed Hands and Voices, never just girls. Peering around, the Voice looked for any sign of girls with the metal-men. She saw nothing of the kind.

A movement caught her eye and she saw one of the kneeling Hands—an old one known for her good counsel to young Hands—making signs. She read them, then turned to the crowd of Hands and said, "Everyone stand. Just stand and be still."

She was breaking all the rules today. A Voice had just relayed an order from a Hand! Yes, she would be burned if she survived this strange day.

The jostling around to get behind all the other Hands immediately commenced. No one wanted to be in front. The Voice shook her head and said to her young and trembling Hand. "I will go forward."

She took a few steps forward to show that there was nothing to fear, but the metal-men's strange objects all swiveled toward her. Though there were no spear points or arrows like the Enforcers used, the Voice was sure these were weapons.

She halted and asked, "How does this Master wish this Voice to speak?"

Ten

"Tango, you're not going to get anywhere like this. They don't understand. Intel reports are clear. They are an oppressed class, but it's more than that. They have no individual identity. She can't just talk normally to you. She doesn't know how," the support tech said, a hint of exasperation in her voice.

"Why does she keep calling me master?" Tango asked.

"She thinks you're a man. Men on that planet are masters, as you know. Well, some of them are. There are other slaves called Enforcers that are men, but they're still labeled as potential hostiles and potential non-hostiles."

"Gross. She thinks I'm a man? That's fucking insulting!"

"Yeah, yeah. Just tell her already. She can't see through your suit. I'm relaying your info to Division. Some of the other contact squads are having issues. Everyone just keeps running and hiding. It's freaking ridiculous."

Tango considered the woman in front of her. When those narrow shoulders kept bugging her, Tango had switched to infrared and seen the terrible truth. The woman had no arms and probably hadn't for a very long time. The narrow chest and shoulders were a clear sign that she'd never built up any muscle from using arms.

"Is this what they were talking about when they said the women here were mutilated? She can talk, but I don't think the others can at all. They keep signing to each other."

"It is."

"God, I hate this planet! No frigging fighting and this kind of messed-up crap."

The woman in red was looking more and more nervous, her feet shifting under that giant tent of cloth. Suddenly, an idea popped into Tango's head and she chinned the exterior channel, "Hold on a second. I'm going to come out."

Support broke in immediately with, "Go out? Are you de-suiting? No! That is not protocol. You may not de-suit on a planetary surface prior to the official end of hostilities."

Tango reached for the emergency de-suit button. It required that she maneuver her hand out of the glove, which was hard enough, but also use two fingers. It was meant to be difficult. While she wiggled her hand free, she said, "Support, this is not a normal situation. The hostiles are gone. The women are here. Just let me be. I'll keep my corona, so I'll still be in control of the suit." To the rest of the squad, she added, "Watch my back. Uni, you're in change if things go sideways."

When the release finally engaged, an immediate sensation of free space surrounded Tango. It usually signaled the end of a battle, not the beginning of one, but this time, it seemed like the way to get things moving in the right direction. These women probably had information, but the way they spoke made it clear they weren't in the habit of offering it. They probably didn't even understand that they could.

And if they thought the Peace Force suits were Sky-Gods, then Tango really needed to set the record straight. The last time a planet was rehabilitated—not a major battle, just a realignment of priorities—where they thought the Peace Force were gods, things did not go well. They started sacrificing each other all over the place to appease them. It was a nightmare.

As the suit fluid flowed out the back of her suit, Tango immediately began to cough. The probe unseated and her lungs fought for air. It probably wouldn't make the best first impression, but what can you do?

Eleven

The metal-man ejected a stream of bluish water from his back, making it look as if it had a sudden need to evacuate. If it weren't so frightening, it might even be funny, though the Voice would never dare to laugh at anything a master did.

Then the metal-man gave birth and the Voice stumbled backwards into the arms of her Hand. The other Hands also backed up, the gasps and shuffling feet loud. A giant blue infant landed on the ground behind the metal-man.

The Voice tried to look away, but could not. The infant coughed a terrible cough, blue fluid shooting from its mouth as it heaved on the ground. It was huge, taller than the tallest man the Voice had ever seen. Was this infant inside the metal-man? Was it an infant at all?

The infant ceased its heaving and breathed in deep breaths, making sounds like words as it did. The metal-man boomed out words shortly after the infant spoke and said, "Don't be afraid. I'm just coming out of the suit."

Suit? Like a master's suit, the one worn during congregations of the masters when a new master was selected? If so, then this was a very different sort of suit. No silk here. So, this giant infant was inside the metal-man the whole time. The infant stood, the legs as big around as the pillars that held up the ceiling in the great hall of the palace.

The infant wiped a hand down its face, flinging blue fluid from its hands onto the ground. Then it pulled away the blue covering from its head, exposing a shock of red hair the fell to its shoulders and framed the face. And finally, the infant stood and it was an infant no longer.

It was a woman. A very big, very beautiful, and smiling woman.

"You're a woman!" the Voice cried out, quite unnecessarily. Every Hand had frozen in place, all eyes wide upon the figure in front of them.

The woman spoke, but her words were gibberish. The metal-man—no, the metal suit—behind her spoke her words after a short delay. "Yes, I'm a woman. I'm not here to hurt you. I'm here to find the ones who have hurt you. We think they're the ones you call the masters. This world has failed to develop in accordance with Earth/Seed Peace Accords and must be re-organized or re-colonized. The culture present has been deemed toxic to human life, freedom, and the pursuit of happiness to all individuals outside the ruling minority. Complete re-organization has been determined to be the only proper solution."

The Voice shook her head, because most of those words were also gibberish.

The woman spoke again, this time only a few words. The suit said, "We're here to kill the men and help you rebuild a new culture that isn't complete shit like this one. Will you please tell us where the men are?"

The Voice stood stock still, everything else forgotten and the words she'd just heard spinning in her head. It couldn't be right. She must be ill? Perhaps even dead and dreaming. The giant woman had just said the masters' rule was feces.

"What?" she asked at last.

The giant woman flung more of the blue fluid from her body, exposing even more of the tight suit beneath. She rippled with muscle, more than any enforcer could ever hope to have and they were the strongest of all the Hands. She spoke again, and again the metal suit broadcast her words.

"Listen, don't take it personally or anything. We did this on another planet where women only kept three percent of the men alive for breeding. That was a shit planet too. Hardly any of them survived, but you women are totally safe with us. I promise. Will you tell me now?"

The Voice wished she had arms more than any other time in her life. She wanted to fling them wide and shout to the heavens. There were no Sky-Gods or if there were, they were not like the masters said.

That same old Hand, the one who helped many young Hands survive their first years of service, shoved her way forward in the group, tapping the Voice's shoulder with urgent pokes. The Voice turned and nodded for her to go on, trying to watch the giant woman at the same time. She was huge, like nothing the Voice had ever seen before. Even the largest enforcers would be small in comparison.

The old Hand signed for a long time, turning so that all the Hands would read her words. As she did, a smile lit her face that showed the gaps where her teeth had been lost. The light in her eyes was as bright as a woman's pyre at sunset.

When she was done signing, the Voice asked the crowd of Hands, "Do you all agree? Is this the bargain you wish me to strike?"

They slapped their hands against their thighs, the sign of agreement in the Hand quarters.

The Voice turned to the giant and said, "I know where the masters of this palace are. They are three hundred and fifty in number. With them are the Enforcers, whose number I do not know. Also with them are the Select Breeders, who are blameless. These Hands present here are but a small number of those Hands within the palace who are also blameless. I will show you where the masters are, if you agree not to kill them."

The giant woman looked confused for a moment, then

touched the wide golden band around her head as if listening to it. Then she shook her head and spoke for a long time, but the metal suit did not convey her words.

Finally, she turned back and spoke to the crowd of women, her eyes not without pity, and the metal suit said, "I'm sorry, but these operations are what they are. There will be help for you, assistance for as long as you live to help you understand and form a better world. But as for the men? No, they are hostiles. We cannot allow them to live. That's been tried before. The same culture or something even worse always develops. The only solution for a bad culture is complete elimination."

The Voice nodded, realizing that this giant woman did not truly understand her meaning. She would have to use better words. "You misunderstand, sky-woman. *We* would like to serve this one final duty to the masters. We women have always been useful, even in death. We would like the masters to have the opportunity to experience that same kind of final usefulness." Here the Voice paused, smiling a little at the old Hand who remained at her side, then she said, "*Exactly* the same final usefulness as we provide. A cleansing fire and feeding the crops with their ashes. With your help, of course. This is the wish of the Hands assembled here."

Then the Voice bowed her head and waited for an answer. When the answer came, she smiled and vowed that she would bow no more.

Twelve

Tango and Delta got a drink from the portable cantina and found a spot where they could swat at mosquitoes in peace for a few minutes. Nearby, a few Administrators were huddled with some Engineers as they argued the merits of particular type of dam. The engineers would win this one, Tango was sure of that.

"Dude, this sucks!" Delta said with a sigh as she dropped down onto a newly fabricated bench next to Tango.

"Yes, yes it does," she agreed, sipping her drink. It was ridiculously hot near the equator when compared the ship, but the women of this world didn't even seem to notice it. While Tango poured sweat and pounded electrolytes, their foreheads barely glistened.

Delta took a long drink and then belched loudly, earning a giggle from some nearby women. The giggles sounded strange, which was okay. The Administrators—which included the Medical Corps as well as a host of other sub-specialties—had decided the best solution for this world of mutes was the easiest one: the same voice transmitters that the suits utilized.

It had taken them many months, but most of the women could communicate well enough. Not all of them, but most. It was a start. The ones who were not mute, but who had no arms? Well, again the suits provided the answer and new, smaller metal arms were now displayed with pride.

Twining her hand in Tango's, Delta leaned close and said, "When do we leave? I'm tired of being a pack mule. And I only got to shoot once. I'm ready for a new battle."

"Soon enough. This planet isn't ideal, but it's theirs. The asteroids will continue to come, but one of the ships is making good progress in clearing up the bigger pieces out there. The briefing this morning was good. Only a few million more big rocks to blast into smaller, not so dangerous, rocks.

It will take a while. You know how much they hate wasting resources, so it's either this or sleeping. Just be glad we're not sleeping through it. We get some time together before the next long nap. That's good, right?"

Delta rubbed her cheek against Tango's shoulder and said, "That's true. I don't mind aging a year for that." Her dreamy smile spoke to the many warm nights made much warmer by the activity in their shared shelter at night.

Tango looked out at the new city being constructed, the green land around them, the many soldiers who carried out tasks to complete this no-two-stones operation. The old cities—the so-called palaces—were gone into dust. The green band around the equator would be the new home for these people. It was battle, only a different kind.

"Just think of it this way. We'll have a story no other division can match," Tango said. Then she swatted at another mosquito and sighed.

Q&A with Ann Christy

The concept of dedicating a human to be either a "Voice" or a "Hand" is horrible and fascinating. And I love the way the reality of those terms creeps up on the reader. How did you come up with such a chilling planetary society?

In truth, it just sort of crept up on me. In this case, a small subset of the population believes they are the chosen ones and this is how they manifest that belief in their physical world. And because those who are not the chosen ones know of nothing that would contradict this insanity, they simply accept it as truth. We see this mirrored in our world, though not with that level of mutilation. It's really about how we can become blinded by belief and how disastrous that can be for anyone caught in such a web.

Has SF always been your favorite genre to read and write?

I love the mind-expanding nature of SF and it has always been my favorite genre to read. I'm still only a few years into this life as a writer, but I find that I can express myself so much better through the SF genre. And really, that's what it is for me. I express all that's in my head, only in creative ways.

What's up next for you in terms of new stories?

Lots of stuff! I'm always cooking up more stories. Right now I'm working on the Perfect Partners, Incorporated series, which is generally focused on sentient androids. I rather like looking at humanity from the lens of an outsider as I'm doing in these books. Also, the next book in the Strikers series is slated for an early summer release, which is exciting!

Where should readers find out about you and your other books?

My website is http://www.annchristy.com, but I'm also on social media (mostly Facebook) and I love interacting with people there. Just ignore all my crazy photos and dog memes.

The Immortals: Anchorage

by David Adams

Monsters don't sleep
under your bed.
They scream forever
inside your head.
— *Extract from 'A Dance of Dreams and*
Nightmares', an Uynovian poem

Ever since the Founding, Colonial settlers whispered of ghost
ships; silent, empty vessels drifting between the stars, steel tombs
for their crew. Ships that set out from Earth and, for whatever
reason, never made it to the stars.

The causes were innumerable. A leaking reactor. A pathogen.
An unstable passenger who took a knife and obeyed the voices
in her head.

Or worse.

Recruited into the mysterious Synapse Foundation, Nicholas Caddy—still bearing the scars of an interstellar war—is dispatched on his first mission with the Immortals. A passenger liner, the Anchorage, has gone silent. Their task is simple: find the ship, salvage what they can, report what happened. Simple.

Simple.

This is Part two of The Immortals series set in the Universe of War, thirteen years before the events of Symphony of War: The Polema Campaign.

Anchorage
DT-Y 44 Transport Lahore
Deep space
0025
January 1st
2231 AD

Three years after *The Immortals: Kronis Valley*; thirteen years before the events of *Symphony of War: The Polema Campaign*

"HAPPY NEW YEAR, Caddy," said Golovanov as he threw a dossier on my chest, the feeling jolting me awake. "Here's your present."

It took me a second to process all of this. I sat up in my bunk, shielding my eyes with my prosthetic hand, squinting in the harsh glare of the *Lahore*'s overhead lights. I sent my implants a mental command to dim the lights and the ship mercifully complied, dropping the illumination down to a manageable level.

"Wait," I said, swinging my legs over the side of the bunk and opening the steel-grey dossier. "We got a job?" The screen lit up, showing a bunch of writing and ship schematics.

"Yup," said Golovanov. "The Synapse Foundation is putting us in the field. You'll like this one: it's gas."

I brought the lights back up as my eyes adjusted. Seemed like all we did every day was train. Adjust to the Immortal Armour. Working in a team with the other Immortals. Fire drills.

I skimmed over the documents, absorbing as much as I could as we spoke. Something about a ship in distress. "What's the deal?"

"The *Anchorage*," Golovanov said. "A DT-Y 44 just like this one. Passenger liner. It went silent about three days ago and has been drifting through Polema's space since. Not responding to hails. Long range scans show low power and thermal signatures, but spectrographic analysis suggests there's at least some atmosphere left. So we get to take a look-see."

Any excitement I had at the potential for action slowly faded. "A bunch of civilians bought it out in the black? This is a job for the Coast Guard."

"It is, and they're contracting it out to us."

"What a beating," I said, and considered a moment. That was very odd. The Polema Coast Guard—named for their nautical forbearers—were tasked with sorting out this kind of garbage. "Wait, why the hell would they do that? The Coast Guard is one of the best funded agencies in the colonies. Why do they need us?"

Golovanov sat at the edge of my bed. "Maybe you should save your questions until you finish reading," he said.

"Reading is for nerds," I said. I switched off the dossier with a mental command. "So. Are we mercenaries now?"

"Eh." He shrugged. "I prefer to use the term *Private Third-Party Offshore Conflict Resolution Engineers*. You can tell how fancy it is by how many words it has."

"So, mercenaries."

"There's no money in integrity. You got a problem with that?"

"Naw," I said. "Like they say on Eris, *money doesn't buy happiness, but poverty doesn't buy anything*. If we're here to do dodgy stuff, and we're going to make a buck doing it, that's fine by me." I stretched out my arms. "But I thought we were supposed to be tracking down and recovering Earthborn technology. Who cares about some civvie freighter?"

"The Coast Guard suspects," said Golovanov, "that the *Anchorage* was attacked by Earthborn raiders."

Well. That would explain a lot of things. "Why not call in the Colonial fleet?" I asked. "If the Earthborn are pushing up into our space, we should hit them hard. Another Reclamation would be…" I didn't even want to think about it.

"Money talks, but wealth whispers." Golovanov's eyes met mine. "Polema wants to avoid making waves—their economy is only just beginning to recover from the Reclamation. If the Earthborn really did hit the *Anchorage*, this might be just an isolated incident. You know, some renegades blowing off steam, or maybe a bunch of clones went rogue. Not an organised attack."

My thoughts went to the same place. "And if that's true, and Polema raises the alarm, and it all turns out to be nothing, they'll lose tens of trillions of creds. They want this whole mess to be taken care of quietly."

"Right," he said. "A few hundred civvies die, but the rich get richer and that's the important thing."

It was as it always was. "The Prophets Wept."

"It's not all bad," said Golovanov. "This is a gas opportunity for us, too. If the Earthborn really did hit the *Anchorage*, they probably left stuff behind. Stuff we could use."

"Right," I said, standing and stretching out my cramping legs. "Whatever. It's gotta be better than more drills."

* * *

I splashed some water on my face and adjusted my chrono implant. It began feeding my body chemicals to suppress drowsiness. By the time I left my quarters, I felt like I'd slept for a year then chugged ten cups of coffee.

Almost. Synthetic sleep was never the same; it was too perfect, too fake, as though some part of my brain were silently screaming in protest. They said it was bad for you.

But so was falling asleep during a firefight.

My suit of Immortal Armour was waiting in the cargo hold, an empty space at the rear of the ship. The Synapse Foundation had converted the area to a hangar. My armour, like the others, hung suspended from the ceiling by thick cables, a ten foot tall ape-like monster, boxy and metal. A caged hunter begging to be unleashed.

"Caddy," said Angel, from behind her suit, one of the

seven others. She seemed to be in a particularly bad mood. "You're late."

"Came as fast as I could," I said. "How far out are we?"

"Six hours," said Angel, stepping into view—shaved hair, muscled frame and all—and reached into the suit's cockpit. She pulled something out that sparked before it went silent. "The *Anchorage* should be coming up on external sensors momentarily. Golovanov said he'd pipe the feed down here. AI, let me know when we have eyes on it."

"Of course," said the voice from her machine. Genderless. Empty.

I didn't know how I felt about Angel. We'd been training together for months now. Things had been very professional. We hadn't bonded properly yet; the Immortals and I. Angel least of all.

She was from a world called Uynov. They called themselves The First to Suffer. Uynov had been trashed by the Earthborn during the Reclamation; their bio-weapons turned it from a watery paradise to a shit-hole full of toxins and quarantined areas. Most Uynovians lived in space these days and they tended to be broody and aloof.

There didn't seem to be anything Angel loved more than weapons drills, or practising endlessly with her armour. Angel might as well be a robot, an observation compounded by her heavy cybernetic augmentation. Prosthetics jutted from almost all parts of her flesh, blunt chrome slivers. Her face was hard, hair shaved, skin rough as cracked desert earth. She couldn't have been older than twenty five but looked in her forties.

She was the first Uynovian I'd ever met. I wasn't sure what

I expected. But, you know, a smile occasionally wouldn't go amiss.

"Hey Caddy," said Stanco, clapping me on the shoulder from behind. "You ready to do this?"

I *also* didn't know how I felt about Maddisynne Stanco. He was built like a bull with biceps like fire hydrants. Fun fact: he was also born a she. A trans-man. Not that there was anything wrong with that.

Although we were all supposed to be enlightened these days, and we'd been taught to accept trans people for what they wanted to be, I couldn't. I tried. I knew it wasn't right— if someone wanted to identify as an eggplant or something, why couldn't they?—but, sometimes, I couldn't look past the parts of Stanco's facial structure that were effeminate. The way he sometimes looked at me or others.

Eris, my home, was very traditional. Osmeon, Stanco's world, was viewed by most Erisians as decadent and hedonistic. Of course, they saw us as uptight, bigoted prudes.

But now, at the end of the day, we were all in this together. They had to accept us, and we had to accept them.

I was trying.

"Yeah buddy," I said, trying to smile my best. "Our first real mission, huh?"

Stanco leaned up against Angel's suit, folding his big hands behind his head. "Fuck yeah. It's going to be gas, my friend."

"I'm sure," I said, and I took a few steps to my suit.

Tall and strong, a mirror of the others, a hunchback made of steel.

"Morning Caddy," said the suit's AI, smooth and feminine. I had named her Sandy, after Sandhya, a woman I'd fought alongside during the Reclamation.

I probably shouldn't have done that. Sandhya hadn't come home. We'd been close: we shared ammo magazines, tactical info, and far too often, a bedroll.

I probably shouldn't have done that either. I had been married to Valérie at the time. Valérie, who had stood by me after I'd been wounded. Valérie, who'd been endlessly understanding, endlessly loving, endlessly patient.

Almost endlessly. We were divorced now. I hadn't seen her in years.

"Morning Sandy," I said. "How's your diagnostic coming?"

"Coming along nicely," she said. "I think I've narrowed down the stability issue; the gyros weren't aligned correctly. It shouldn't happen again."

That was gas. The suits were new technology—not only were they inherently unstable, to give us better maneuverability, they required an AI to operate. We were the guinea pigs, working out the kinks.

I wanted to ask Sandy more about exactly how she was fixing this complex problem in software, but Golovanov stepped into the hangar and everyone fell silent.

"Immortals," he said, casually folding his hands behind his back. Just like the old days.

"Ho," we said in chorus. Only Angel, Stanco and I were here. We had eight suits. Where was everyone else? Nobody seemed concerned. Maybe I should actually read the mission briefings in future.

Golovanov's eyes flicked to me, then he addressed the group. "We're coming up on the *Anchorage*," he said. "Should have eyes in a few minutes. Based on the large amount of debris, it's starting to look like someone did, in fact, attack the ship."

"Cunts," spat Angel. "Of course the Earthborn would prey on civilians."

"Any information from the distress beacon?" I asked. "Maybe they mentioned who was attacking them."

"It's just an automated beacon." Golovanov narrowed his eyes. "So if it was the Earthborn, they struck fast."

That was their MO.

"Deployment is three suits," said Golovanov. "That's you guys. The rest of the Immortals will cover you. Float over from the *Lahore*, get inside the ship, find what you can. Take some emergency bulkheads in case you need to secure an area and dismount, but have someone maintain overwatch. Deployment is with standard layouts for Angel and Caddy, Stanco as fire support with the assault gun."

Standard layout was an autocannon, grenade launcher, and flamethrower. "Fire support on a boarding mission, sir? Don't you think that assault guns are kind of overkill?"

"Hell no," said Stanco. "Automatic weapons are the most casualty producing weapon in the fire team. It's more than simply fire support and suppression." His face lit up in a wide, cheesy grin. "Plus they're fucking *rad*. I feel like a god when I spin that thing up."

"Deific posturing aside," said Golovanov, "we have no idea what's going on aboard that ship, and if the Earthborn are aboard, we want a firepower advantage. Even if it's in close quarters."

"Sounds gas," I said. "I'd rather have it and not use it than need it and not have it."

"Exactly," said Golovanov. "Any questions?"

Angel raised a hand. "Who's lead suit?"

All eyes fell upon her. She was the obvious choice.

"Angel is leading this op," said Golovanov, as we expected she would. "Don't get me wrong—you'll all get your turn. Next time is Stanco. Caddy, you're next."

"Sounds gas," I said. "Gives me time enough for everyone else to make the mistakes."

Stanco laughed. "Gee, thanks."

"Never forget that your eyes are connected to your brain." Golovanov pointed to my suit. "Go suit up. Make sure you're comfortable. I'll put through any more info as it becomes available. Learn what you can, and get back here ASAP."

"Right," I said. Six hours locked in a metal box. No worries.

Come on, I sent to Sandy via my implants. *It's time to go to work.*

Sandy's chest opened up, peeling back like a blooming flower. I turned around and stepped backwards into the suit, the metal petals closing in around me. Thin cables snaked out from the suit and latched into my exposed implants, magnetically attaching to the metal. Three, two, one…

My vision went dark and a numbness enveloped my whole body. The quiet hum of the hangar disappeared; I felt as though I'd been thrown into a bucket of ice water, silent, black as night.

Then I was standing in the hangar, eight feet tall and strapped to the ceiling, as the suit's body became mine. My eyes could see so much now: the heat of the booting up suits, green boxes around the other suits, and text floating in air giving me ammunition counts, power levels, and whatever Sandy wanted to highlight for me. My world was fish-eyed. I could feel one of the cables brushing against the EVA pack on my back.

I was ready for the activation but it was always disconcerting.

"Looking gas," said Golovanov. He looked so small now, like a child who only came up to my waist. He gave me a thumbs up.

I returned it. "Connection is solid," I said, my voice synthetic, an approximation of my natural voice, just deeper. "Ready to go."

Angel's portrait appeared on the left side of my vision. "Immortal Armour active," she said.

Stanco's face appeared below her. "Ready to chew arse and kick bubble gum," he said. "And I'm all out of arse."

"Right." I chuckled, trying to sound natural. Why did he have to sexualize everything? Not *every* guy was like that. It reeked of over overcompensation.

Not that there was anything wrong with that. I kept telling myself that.

Golovanov left, leaving the three of us hanging from the ceiling. I couldn't feel my real body; I knew it was hanging there, limp and immobile, inside my chest cavity, weak as a baby.

"Incoming transmission," said Sandy. AIs couldn't give suggestions or advice, it was against their programming. "From Operations."

"Put it through," I said.

A floating box appeared in front of my eyes, labelled *An-*

chorage. It was a vision of space, untwinkling white dots on a black field. At the centre of it, barely perceptible, was a ship.

The optics zoomed, straining to show us more. The screen pixelated for a moment, and then in the harsh light of false-color optics, I could see a ship floating in space, tumbling slowly, unlit and unpowered. Even its emergency navigation lights were off, and it was surrounded by a sparkling field of debris, like the tail of a comet stretching out beyond the edges of the screen. Readouts showed no infra-red or electromagnetic activity. No radiation, either, so the reactor was intact. Just a lump of steel crying in the depths of the black.

"What a fucking wreck," said Stanco, blowing a low whistle—a prerecorded sound composed by his AI.

The ship tumbled, revealing a jagged, oval gash along one side, about eight meters on its longest edge. It reached right to the name emblazoned on the side in stark white lettering. *Anchorage.*

"I'm reading a pronounced hole in the starboard side," said Angel. "That should serve as our entry point."

Gas plan. I looked over the information Sandy provided. "No sign of internal fuel or ammunition detonation," I said. "No sign of external scoring, either, or buckling on the hull... no stress or micro-fractures. It wasn't weapons fire or a high-speed impact."

"Something caused that big hole," said Stanco. "What else but weapons fire?"

"Maybe the crew cut it out," I said. "It looks like the kind of damage an untrained worker with a plasma cutter would make. Could be they were trying to vent a section manually..."

"Well," said Stanco, "at least we know they weren't attacked."

"They didn't put up a fight," said Angel. "There's a difference."

Curious. "You saying whoever did this was invited in?"

"No," she said, "but it's possible the *Anchorage* didn't see them coming. Someone cutting on the hull might not have triggered their decompression alarms; passenger ships sometimes only treat their safety equipment with indifferent maintenance."

Silence reigned for a time, and I watched the corpse of the ship tumble over and over endlessly. There weren't any other holes.

"Asteroid impact, maybe?" said Stanco. "Something that slipped past their sensors? Or maybe they had a reactor leak. It's possible they wanted to eject their reactor core, failed, so tried to cut it out…"

All this guesswork was frustrating. "Maybe, maybe," I said. "Does it really matter? We're going in anyway, so let's just focus on the mission until we get there."

"Couldn't agree more," said Angel, then her portrait disappeared.

"Wow," said Stanco. "Rude."

"You know what she's like," I said.

Stanco snorted. "She sounds like she needs a dicking."

"Not like you could do that," I said, the words slipping out before I had a chance to rein them in.

Silence. Angry silence. "You don't need a dick to be a dude," Stanco said. "Fucking Erisians."

"I didn't mean it," I said.

"Yeah you did."

It was difficult to deny that. "Look," I said, "I'm trying, okay?"

"I know," said Stanco, without any conviction at all.

I probably should have let it go but I didn't. "It doesn't bother me what you identify as. I'm just saying… it's weird enough seeing women and gays in the military, let alone trans people. There's a reason most of Eris has their own units, rather than integrating with the rest of the Colonial armies."

"I know," he said again, again, not believing a word I said. "It's fine."

I took a breath—not something my suit could do, but the armour's metal muscles and articulators moved in the same way—and used my implants to give my body a shot of a mild sedative.

"I'm sorry," I said, and I tried to genuinely mean it. I resisted the urge to add qualifiers after that. *It was just how I was raised, I don't know any better, I'm wrong but…*

"Yeah," said Stanco, a little hint of levity returning. "It's all gas, bro. Shit takes time to sink in. It just sucks when you get all the shit for being a guy, expectations of being a manly-man, but also shit for being trans, too. All the downsides, none of the perks. Makes you a little defensive. So, you know, I'm sorry too."

"I'm trying," I said again, and then added, "bro."

"I appreciate that." Stanco's suit turned to face mine. "Don't worry. Angel's a bigger weirdo than you are."

Small comfort.

I returned my attention to the feed of the *Anchorage*. The closer we got, the higher the resolution climbed.

Closer and closer.

* * *

Six hours later

The last of the air was sucked out of the hangar, hissing faintly around my suit's microphones before fading to the eerie silence that was deep space.

"Decompression complete," said Angel. She'd rejoined our channel when it was time to do something productive. "Disable artificial gravity. Commence decoupling."

With a lurch, I felt gravity shut off. I sent a mental push that detached the cables that suspended my suit from the hangar's ceiling. I floated in the zero gravity, small puffs of nitrogen from the EVA pack keeping my position steady. Attached to the pack were several emergency bulkheads, heavy and bulky.

Silently, the hangar door began to open. Normally it would be groaning and loud, but with no atmosphere I could hear nothing.

"Move out," said Angel, and we flew slowly out the open doors into the void of space.

Although I'd spent plenty of time in space, protected from the vacuum of space only by the metal of a ship's hull, it was different being in a suit. A starship's hull was measured in meters; the suit was substantially smaller than that. Although it was forged from advanced polymers and composite plates, my face—my real face—was only a meter or so away from the void.

If something went wrong…

I turned away from the *Lahore* and navigated towards

the *Anchorage*. As I looked at it, Sandy outlined it in a box and zoomed in, giving me a clear look at the ship.

I tried to focus on something other than my unconscious body encased within an armoured steel box, where even the tiniest hole would drain away my air and, thanks to my neural link to the suit, the first I'd know about it was when I started to pass out… way, way too late to do anything but die.

"Your heart rate is increasing," said Sandy, her voice tinged with genuine concern. "You okay, boss man?"

"I'm fine," I said.

"Sounds like you need a drink," she said.

I definitely did not. Sobriety was one of the conditions of joining the Immortals. Golovanov knew my weakness. "Thanks," I said, "but I don't think you come equipped with a mini bar."

"Well," she said, "I have full control of your implants at this point. I could give you a shot of alcohol, straight into your veins if you want, so you don't even have to taste it."

"No thanks."

She laughed. "You sure? I mean, I could—"

"*No.*" The fierceness in which I answered surprised even me.

"I'm sorry," said Sandy. "I won't ask again."

I'd pissed off both Stanco and Sandy, and we hadn't even reached the *Anchorage* yet. "It's fine," I said. "We can talk about it after the mission."

"If I had feelings," said Sandy, "I'd think you were brushing me off." Her voice turned chirpy. "But I don't. So that's fine."

The ship, our target, drew closer and closer. In my fish-eyed vision, I could see the *Lahore* behind us, shrinking away. Soon it appeared in a box, zoomed in so I could see it clearly.

Sandy was helping me out in subtle ways. Just like Sandhya, her namesake.

Suddenly I missed her. Naming my AI after my dead lover was a stupid mistake. Stupid.

"You okay?" asked Sandy. "Your heart rate is—"

"I'm *fine*," I said, giving myself another shot of mild sedative. "Just… please don't ask me about my heart rate unless it's much more serious than this."

"I'll increase the threshold by 20%," said Sandy.

Closer. Closer. We drifted through the inky black, three hunchbacked suits of steel stabilised by puffs of gas. Behind us, the five other suits left the *Lahore*, taking up an escort formation.

Although they were there to cover our approach, I couldn't help but feel that they were also pointing weapons at our back.

Soon, the zooming effect disappeared from my vision and I saw the ship *au naturale*. A flood of sensor information floated beside it. Minimal heat. Clouds of debris. Almost no atmosphere present in sections near the outer hull, smaller amounts within—maybe a few air pockets, but the temperature within was well below freezing.

"This ship is a tomb," I said. "Nobody's alive over there."

"We're here to investigate," said Angel. "There are taxpayers on that ship."

"Taxpayer's bodies," said Stanco.

Retrieving those was not even on our mission objectives,

but I couldn't see the harm. Civvies deserved a decent burial too.

"So why us?" asked Stanco. "Why can't the Coast Guard clean up this mess?"

"Because," said Angel, slightly condescendingly, "if your house is on fire, you can't put it out from inside. There are some problems the Colonial agencies can't fix. That's why we're here."

"Oh," said Stanco. "Got it. By the way, don't take this the wrong way, but you're not anywhere near as stupid as you look."

"You are," said Angel.

Brutal.

"Right," said Stanco, clicking his tongue. "Whatever."

The *Anchorage* soon swallowed the stars below, the tumbling steel wall of its hull forming a floor. We aimed for the pivot point at the centre, EVA suits straining to push us forward, then slow us down. Sandy did all the work; piloting a metal suit through a field of sparkling debris, landing on a spinning and structurally compromised space ship, was a job better suited for computers.

My boots clunked down on the metal, magnetising with a faint hum that vibrated throughout the entire suit.

Angel's voice filled my suit. "*Lahore*, this is the away team. We have reached the *Anchorage*."

"Confirmed," said Golovanov. "Stabilise the ship."

We walked along the slowly spinning hull until we reached the stern. The three of us lined up at the edge of the ship and knelt down. I set my magnetized hands on the metal and locked my knees in against the hull. My suit's EVA pack roared to life, firing at full power; Stanco's and Angel's did the same thing.

The *Anchorage* strained in protest, slowed down its spin, and then, after a minute's work, stopped completely in space.

"Gas," said Golovanov. "Proceed into the hull."

Angel, Stanco and I walked on the hull, from port to starboard, putting one magnetized foot in front of the other. As we got closer, we got a better look at the hole.

It was nearly thirty meters wide and fifty long, roughly oval. The edges were melted, blackened and jagged, as though the metal had been dissolved. The floor below was pitted and scored, like the surface of Eris's moon, or an asteroid; hundreds of tiny holes and divots were cut into the exposed bulkhead.

Sandy drew a box over a section of the melted hull and enhanced it.

"What kind of weapon could do this?" I asked her. "There's no scorching away from the impact site. Not even the best Earthborn torpedoes could cause something like this."

"It looks like fluid erosion," she said, confusion in her artificial voice. "Some kind of acid."

Angel looked to me. "No acid could possibly melt through starship hull. It would take days and days, weeks even. Surely someone would notice."

Nobody had any answers.

"Lights are out," Stanco observed. "Even emergency power has run out."

"Hello darkness my old friend," I said.

The tension evaporated. Stanco laughed. "Darkness never returns my damn calls. Sometimes I think I barely know her any more."

I couldn't help but chortle. "Darkness is a strong black woman who don't need no man."

"Cut the chatter," said Angel. Humorless Uynovian. "Split up. Stanco, head toward the stern. Caddy, head toward the bow. I'll make for the reactor at the core."

"In we go," said Stanco, climbing down to the hole and swinging into the corridor. His huge suit had to crouch to move forward, magnetized limbs keeping him pressed against one of the walls.

I crawled into the hole as well. Sandy magnetized my hands and I carefully made my way in the opposite direction.

After a few minutes crawling, I came to a door. The centre of it had dissolved, leaving a hole almost a meter radius.

No. Half that; one meter diameter. I had to remember I was twice as large as I normally was.

"Got a bulkhead," I said. "Emergency decompression door. Something burned its way through… looks to be whatever cut through the hull."

"Yeah," said Stanco. "I got one too. Same deal."

"Employ a manual bypass," said Angel. That was the euphemism of the day. *Manual bypass.*

A simple instruction easily followed. I reached out with my hands, prying the metal. The suit's articulators groaned faintly and, for a moment, I didn't think it would bend; then the metal peeled back and the gap widened.

I pulled myself in, wiggling and kicking, pushing through the metal gap. The metal of my suit's armour scraped against the edges of the hole, but I fit.

The corridor on the other side was stained with blood, splashed down with rust-colored gore and a strange black fluid. The bulkheads were riddled with holes from high velocity bullets. A rifle floated oddly in space, along with dozens of shell casings and debris. I recognized the type; standard civilian Polema issue Type 1. It wasn't Earthborn.

"Someone actually did put up a fight," I said. "Got a gun and signs of a struggle."

"Act tough, die rough," said Stanco. "Any Earthborn shit?"

"Unless you want me to scrape their blood off the walls, no."

"Don't disturb the bodies," said Angel. "Note the location and have the *Lahore* retrieve them."

I looked around. The corridor had been stripped bare, leaving only stains on the metal. "There aren't any. Just blood, and lots of it."

"Maybe they got sucked out," said Stanco.

"That's *blown* out," said Angel.

"So, okay, maybe they got *blown* out. And I bet you know a fancy word for *killed to death by space* too."

It was unlikely the bodies had been either sucked or blown out. We'd have seen them by now. Anyway, before I'd widened it, the hole was barely big enough for a person to fit. Nothing made sense. "Getting a bit sick of hearing the word *maybe*," I said, a little snappier than I intended.

Sandy pinged my vision, drawing a red dot over something deeper in the ship and painting a red line on the corridor that lead toward it. "Nicholas, I'm reading a room with air. Sealed. Trace amounts of heat."

An intact room? "Pass it along to the others." I changed

direction. "Guys, got a room with atmo'. Looks to be about deck seven, 'bout forty meters away from the hull." Right at the core of the ship.

"No way," said Stanco. "Survivors?"

"Who knows?" With a mental thrust I transferred the information Sandy had compiled for me to my team.

"We'll meet you there," said Angel.

Floating through bloodstained halls, I made my way further and further into the ruined hulk of the *Anchorage*, following the red line deeper into the ship's heart.

* * *

I floated past a lot of things. I saw computer screens powered down and inert, I saw half-melted emergency bulkheads breached and useless, I saw personal effects floating in the nothingness and loose bulkheads and yellow oxygen masks drifting like tentacles, their precious cargo long ago discharged.

But I saw no bodies. Personal effects, plenty. Weapons and shell casings, sure. Blood, and lots of it, including some that looked like the victims had been dragged. Not a single corpse.

Finally, the red line led towards a thick blast door labelled *Secure Hold*. There was a button to open it, but the display glowed with an angry red hue and flashed the words *decompression failure*. The metal had the same acid scoring as every other door we'd seen, but this one had held up, probably due to its significant thickness and anti-theft reinforced polymers.

The shipbuilders valued the passengers' gold more than

it valued their lives. Although, by booking passage with that particular ship, the paying customers were de-facto supporting them.

Whatever. It wasn't my job to feel sorry for anyone.

"Man," said Stanco as he crawled around the corner, "we are going to get so much free shit."

"Salvage of non-Earthborn items isn't one of our objectives," said Angel, appearing right behind him.

"You kidding? What's the point of being a Crisis Exacerbation Specialist if you don't get to loot anything afterwards?"

I shook my head. "Golovanov said we were Private Third-Party... something-or-rather Engineers."

"Golovanov," said Angel, "can also hear you. The audio is piped into mission command."

"We've been through a lot," I said. "He can handle a joke."

Stanco floated toward the door, peering in close.

"Thoughts?" I asked.

He extended a giant metal hand, reaching out and touching the pitted and scarred door. "Knock knock," Stanco said, rapping silently on the metal. Anyone inside could hear us, but we had no hope of hearing them through the vacuum of space. "We should send through a probe first."

That sounded gas. Stanco pulled a small metal oval about the size of a discus off his back and clipped it to the wall. It glowed faintly as it began to cut into the door.

The minutes ticked away.

"How long could someone survive in there?" I asked. "There's air, so presumably they didn't just die."

Angel's suit's head appeared over Stanco's metal shoulder.

I could see her portrait on the side of my vision, but I looked her in her optics, too. Some human habits died hard. "With food and water, a long time. The ship was well stocked, and no matter how strong that acid is, they must have had some time to prepare. There were armed guards at the first door to be breached, after all. As each door went down… they probably stockpiled as much as they could inside and waited it out. Fortunately, these doors won't open if there's no air on our side, so if they're in there thinking they're saved, they'll have to wait a bit longer."

Made sense.

"What do you think they did to pass the time?" asked Stanco. "Played cards? Drank?"

"Sex is an excellent recreational activity," said Angel, matter-of-factly. "Although I imagine that privacy would be at a premium."

"A substantial part of the crew would be Osmeons," said Stanco. "They wouldn't care."

"And some would be Erisians," I said. Just thinking about having sex while someone else watched was super weird.

Finally, the probe flashed a bright green, and Sandy connected the link.

Darkness. The probe's light turned on; the camera was looking at the back of a metal crate. It snaked out around it, thin optic fibre slipping between tiny cracks, weaving its way through a tightly packed maze.

"They barricaded the door," said Angel, the first hints of… something filtering into her voice. Stress, maybe? Relief? Fear? Did crazies from her world even feel fear?

The optic fibre tried to push a box. It didn't move. Its

laser worked again, drilling a tiny hole. This, unlike the rein-forced bulkhead, fell away quickly. Harsh, white light flood-ed in from the other side. The lens adjusted.

The secure storage room was a low-ceilinged metal box fifty meters squared. The far side of it was stacked with box-es, most neatly arranged, although some had been hastily opened. Deep scratches lined the floor where they had been dragged over and welded together to form a crude, addition-al barrier.

In the centre of the room, a pile of people, over thirty of them, lay huddled together on the metal, dressed in thick clothes. Weapons lay scattered all around, close at hand, ready to pull up at a moment's notice. Empty bottles and food wrappers lay scattered all around.

"O2 is solid," said Stanco. "It's pretty cold, though. -10c. Miserable but survivable." He sighed. "No loot for us. Wakey wakey, sleepy heads."

Our view floated toward the huddle. It slid close to one of the people, a woman with long, dark hair who lay on her back. The camera manouvered around to look at her face.

Her eyes were rolled back in her head, skin pale and des-iccated. A rusty stain spread out from underneath her chin, and the pistol she clutched in her hand was held by thin, shrivelled fingers. The camera moved to another one—a young boy. He, too, had blown his brains out on the deck. The camera panned over a half-dozen faces, all dead.

"This is why I don't fly coach," said Stanco.

The camera rose and swung out. "They had plenty of food," said Angel. "Water. Air. Warm clothes. The bulkhead was holding…"

"They probably heard the acid melting down the door," I said. "Decided they didn't want to be prey for the Earthborn."

Angel shook her head, her tone turning venomous. "This isn't their style. Earthborn desecrate the bodies of their enemies, they would never give up just because they were already dead. They couldn't let an opportunity like this go to waste." The only time she seemed to feel anything was discussing our long-lost cousins.

"You okay?" I asked her, using my implants to send the signal just to her.

For a moment, she said nothing, then her suit looked back at me. "We're all animals," she said. "Some just wear clothes."

"They're still people," I said. "Them and us. These dead civvies, the Earthborn, everyone they killed on Polema. All humans."

"What makes a human life inherently so valuable that ending one is so terrible?"

"Life is preferable to death," I said. "For most people."

"Not on Uynov."

I tried to grimace with muscles I didn't have control of any more. "Going to be honest Angel, and don't take it the wrong way, but why didn't you just kill yourself if life on Unyov was so bad? How'd you get to be here?"

"Suicide doesn't end pain," she said. "It just gives it to everyone else. When we die, the only thing we leave behind is the joy we give to others. I don't want my legacy to be distilled suffering."

I digested that. "Erisians believe all life is sacred, and only death is owed to those who cannot abide this simple tenant."

"People only say all human life is valuable because that means the speaker's life is valuable. It's an ultimately selfish action."

It was hard to argue with that.

"So," said Stanco, "if you two are done staring creepily at each other, are we going to head in or what?"

* * *

We sealed each end of the corridor with emergency bulkheads, then retrieved the probe. Air hissed through the tiny hole it had drilled, white and visible as rushed to flood its new home, and slowly the pressure equalized. The *open* button turned from red to green.

Time to dismount. The world went dark again, and then Sandy's suit opened up and rotten, frigid air blew against my face.

I'd almost forgotten that smell. Dead things left to rot in a too-small place. I stepped out of the suit. The ship's corridors were so much bigger when I wasn't crawling through them.

I unclipped a light carbine from the outside of the suit and watched as Angel stepped out of hers, taking a weapon and shouldering it with the detached air of someone who had done so a million times before. I was nervous, and the smell was getting to me, but Angel might well have been taking a stroll down to the mess hall.

"Ready?" I asked, hand hovering over the button.

"Breach it," she said, and so I pushed.

The doors groaned, strained, the metal underfoot vibrating. The motors whined loudly. The reverberation travelled through the metal of the ship, shaking its deckplates, and then with a horrible grinding noise the bent, battered door retreated into the floor.

"Make *more* noise why don't you?" Stanco reached around with his giant metal fist and pushed the box-barrier away, breaking the welds and collapsing it easily. How strong the Immortal Armour seemed as a mere mortal…

Angel and I stepped inside, weapons shouldered. The smell of the dead got stronger as we drew close. I put one hand over my nose, holding my rifle with my prosthetic. It was strong enough to comfortably hold it up.

"We should check them," she said, her nose wrinkled but otherwise seemingly unbothered by the stench. "Whoever attacked this ship was looking for something. I intend to find out what."

I gave one of the corpses a nudge with my boot. "Where are all the bodies aside from these arseholes?"

She didn't answer. I looked her way, then followed her eyes.

One of the dead was wearing combat armour. Where she had found that I had no idea. Maybe she was a soldier, maybe she was a merc'. That didn't matter.

What did matter was the large claw protruding from the ceramic plate covering her gut. It was curved, nearly half a meter long and was wickedly serrated. It was dug in deep, bone yellow and attached to a green, leathery limb which had been severed with a laser cutter.

"What the fuck is *that*?" I asked, crouching over it for a better view. She'd killed herself, just like the others, although instead of using a pistol she'd injected a dozen morphia needles into her leg.

"Caddy," said Golovanov in my ear, "retrieve that corpse when you go."

"Aye aye," I said, staring at the claw, transfixed. Despite all the medication its victim had injected, she still seemed so terrified…

"Sometimes," I said, "I think that if I ever decide to just kill myself… I wonder how it should go. Should I go the painless way, or the painful one? After all, once I'm dead none of it matters anymore. Maybe I can snatch a glimpse of the other side before I go."

"I have had my fill of pain," said Angel. "It is nothing to be romanticized."

I let go of my weapon, switched my rifle into my flesh-hand, then touched the bone; it was smooth, and covered in a thin layer of slime.

The slime began dissolving my prosthetic finger.

"Shit!"

Even though I'd had a metal and polymer arm ever since the war, human instinct was a powerful thing, and hard to override. I flicked my fingers, trying to get rid of the stuff; the array of sensors in my prosthetic fed me information. It felt cold, wet, tasted of brine and salt… and plenty of pain, too.

My finger dissolved up to the third knuckle before the acid became too diluted to do any more damage. I stared at the withered remains of my index finger. It hurt; the prosthetic was wired directly into my nervous system. I used a mental push to lower the implant's sensitivity, turning down the pain on that finger completely. It slowly went numb.

"You okay?" asked Angel.

"Yeah," I said, "but getting the body out is a no-go. That acid is wicked stuff."

Angel inspected the wound on the corpse. "It doesn't seem to be dissolving the victim," she said. "Maybe it reacts only to non-organic material…"

Before I could stop her, she slipped her glove off, and poked the bone with her finger.

Nothing.

"What kind of creature is coated with an acid that only reacts to metal?" I asked. "Some kind of bioweapon?" I felt a vague sinking in my gut. "Is the *Anchorage…* a weapons test?"

A faint sound reached my ears. The sound of rain on a metal roof, from above.

"Contact," said Stanco. "I got movement out here. Vibrations from the deck above. They're moving."

"They?"

Angel and I exchanged a worried look. The sound travelled directly above us, distant but audible, and then toward the stern of the ship. Toward the way we'd come. Drawn by the vibrations of the opening door.

Hundreds of those claws were making pitter-patter rain on the deck.

They were coming for us.

* * *

I ran toward my suit.

"Operations, we are egressing *now*. Right now!" My rifle bounced against my side as I ran. If whatever was coming for us reached the emergency bulkheads we'd set up, and breached them… I didn't want to think about it, but through those thin sheets of metal was the logical way to get to the meat the creatures had too long been denied. Sandy moved towards me, the suit opening up. Angel's AI did the same thing, presenting its open chest for boarding. We passed by the ruined boxes.

Something heavy slammed into the emergency bulkhead. A massive bone claw, just like in the gut of the dead woman, broke through the steel, smoke hissing as it dissolved the barrier.

Air rushed out. Alarms screamed. The button flashed red—the door, hopelessly jammed, strained as it tried in vain to seal off the breach.

Stanco opened up with his assault gun. It fired like a titan ripping cloth, shaking the walls and floor, impossibly loud in the cramped quarters, drowning out the howl of escaping air. Brass shell casings the size of a fist slammed into the bulkheads.

I practically fell into my suit. Darkness enveloped me as the armoured plates closed, and the gunfire became muted and distant. The only thing I could hear was profound ringing in my ears.

"C'mon," I shouted to the darkness. "Boot. Boot, damn you!"

Plugs attached themselves to my implants, then the ringing went away. For a second, there was nothing, and then I was a metal giant once more.

Bugs. A wall of eight legged bugs, each roughly the size of a horse, some smaller, some larger, all tearing down the shredded remains of the emergency bulkhead. Their eyes glowed red in the dimly lit corridor and the deck was soaked in the same black fluid I'd seen before. The blood.

They were all different; some had massive pincers, some huge claws, others were bigger or smaller or weird colors. A myriad of forms, all trying to tear us to pieces.

Stanco fired again. Rushing air blew the spider-like creatures back, and debris—including the bodies of the crew—thumped against them, but still they came, crawling, hissing, reaching for us with a host of teeth and talons.

I ignited the pilot light on my flamethrower and turned that corridor into a tiny piece of hell.

Orange and red consumed everything, the rushing, escaping air twisting the jet of flame and pulling it off in random directions. I saw dozens of the creatures be consumed by the flames, the sticky, high energy fluid seeping between cracks in their carapace. I bought my right arm around too and added autocannon fire to the mix, heavy shells wailing in the rapidly depleting air.

The deck plate underneath me gave way. I nearly slipped and fell, the escaping air buffeting me from behind.

"I got you!" Stanco grabbed hold of my suit's leg. "Hang on!"

I scrambled around, digging my fingers into the skeleton of the ship, trying to hold on. I felt Stanco's metal fingers weaken and a crate slammed into my back.

Then I lost my grip and, torn away from the metal by the rushing air, tumbled down the corridor.

* * *

Sandy fired the EVA pack, trying to stabilise us, but we were a big thing in a narrow box. The suit clanged off metal bulkheads, screamed as it was dragged along the floor, then tumbled head over heels as we were pushed towards the ship's stern.

I hit an exposed beam and bounced off. Then another. My vision went static-y as the suit's cameras took a hit. We spun and spun, puffs of nitrogen trying to stabilise us.

Finally, we got stuck arse-first in a door. This one had been melted through like the others.

My head hurt from the close proximity to gunfire and taking a spin through the insides of a too-small ship. A strange sensation, coming from my real body; fake parts of me hurt. Sandy was trying to tell me I was injured.

"Hey," I said, groaning as I eased myself out of the ruined door. "How about dialing down the pain some?"

"You're already heavily medicated," said Sandy. "Are you sure?"

Uh oh. "Did I break something?"

"A few somethings," said Sandy. "The human body is just not designed to survive these kinds of forces. Fortunately you have lots of implants."

We'd have to do something about that. There were ways to play with gravity, create it and negate it. The suit would have to be modified for future operations.

I couldn't think about that now. Not my job. I'd include it in my after action report, though.

Assuming I survived to write it.

"Let's get going then," I said. "If I need medical treatment…"

"You do," said Sandy, her tone sincere.

Then it was time to go. I magnetized my hands and went to crawl once again, back up the way I'd come, but my limbs didn't stick to the metal.

"Magnetism is damaged," said Sandy.

Dammit. I knew when I was beat. "Send out a distress signal. Have our escorts cut me out of the hull."

"You're not going to like this," said Sandy, "but that's a no-go. The antenna is damaged too, and by now we're deep inside the *Anchorage*. Metal of this size is going to function as a giant Faraday cage. Range is severely reduced. We can maybe talk to Angel or Stanco if the get close enough, but apart from that, we're on our own."

"Fine. We'll get closer to the hull so they can hear us." I started to move back the way we'd been blown, pushing off the metal deck for leverage.

Sandy flashed a red warning. "Lots of movement that way," she said. "Should I warm up weapons?"

AI were forbidden from giving orders or advice. Yet, she always seemed to find a way to let me know what she was thinking.

"So you're saying that we need to go deeper."

"I'm not saying anything," said Sandy. "But we're down to half a tank of flamethrower fuel and only packing a thousand more rounds of autogun ammo. There's a lot of hostiles out there."

I hoped Stanco and Angel were okay.

"Further toward the bow then," I said, and kicked at the burned-through husk of the door until it broke, and we sailed through.

Sandy drew red lines and I followed them. The corridors widened as we got further in, a change I took as a blessing. I was still forced to crawl, though, but it wasn't as hard. On the way we passed more battle sites; blood splatters and scorch marks marred the walls, standing as mute testament to the struggle.

As always, no bodies.

I wanted to talk to Sandy. No, that wasn't true. I wanted to talk to *Sandhya*. The woman I'd loved on Polema. I wanted her to tell me everything was going to be okay, like she used to. I wanted to hold her again. I couldn't focus on the mission.

Maybe my brain was damaged. Sandy had been non-specific about what kind of injuries I had. Everything hurt but I kept going.

We turned a corridor. Frozen drops of ice filled the vacuum like little snowflakes.

"The water processing room," said Sandy. "It must be leaking."

Ice wasn't dangerous in small amounts. The armour on my suit could deflect autocannon fire. The main risk would be that I'd be trapped. "Will that be a problem?"

"Just be careful," she said. "Water expands as it freezes. Structural integrity of the *Anchorage* is going to be low here; those walls will be close to buckling. Float where you can, touch as little as possible."

Again, I tried to guess what she was thinking. "You want to drive?"

"It would be more efficient if I did."

"Go for it," I said, and the EVA pack kicked in again. I

floated amongst the ice crystals, the EVA pack moving the suit in ways I could not, tilting perfectly, tiny puffs of nitrogen guiding me forward.

As we passed the water processing room, I looked inside.

I don't know why I did. Human nature, I guess. I wanted to see the leak. I wanted to see whatever thing was inside there, mundane or mysterious.

I saw the glint of green reflecting in the ice. Definitely more mysterious than mundane. I shouldn't have stopped, I should have kept going, pushed on until I could get free of the hull and send out a signal to get picked up.

"What the hell is that?" I asked. "Stop."

The suit braked. I spun, facing the doorway, then drifted inside.

The room was packed full of chrysalises, olive green and bulbous, ranging in size from a few centimeters to the size of a man. They were sacs of fluid held in place by thin membranes; the majority were clumped together against a broken bulkhead, the others layered the floors and ceiling. Each one extruded thin brown tentacles which burrowed into the ice. Devouring it. Others curled around light fixtures, power outlets, and the door switch. Feeding.

Within were creatures. The smaller ones looked indistinct, just a blob, but the bigger ones... they looked human. An identical person. Androgynous, even genderless, attractive but remarkably plain; olive skin, brown hair. Their skin was markless, fresh, like a child's even though they looked about thirty.

"This is creepy as shit," I said.

"Sometimes I'm glad I'm a robot," said Sandy. "Golovanov will want a sample."

Wordlessly I extended my finger toward one of the larger sacs, and used my implants to activate the sample probe. With a flash of sparks the device broke off. It was broken too. Damn.

The *thing* in the sac looked at me. Did nothing more than move its eyes. They glowed red, faintly, just like the bugs had done. I looked at another one. It, too, reacted to my gaze by staring at me. Soon they were all doing it.

So if my sensitive equipment wouldn't work, I decided to cut to the chase: I punched one. The sac burst like a watermelon and my metal fist slammed into the creature beyond. Its blood exploded, red and rich, all over my fingers. I used my other hand to splatter another one.

"Preliminary examination of the facial structure of these creatures indicates a striking similarity," said Sandy. "Scraping the samples off your fingers. Analyzing. The two bodies we sampled are identical on a genetic level." There was something in her synthetic voice. A mixture of wonder and apprehension. "The DNA strands appear to be a combination of… at least a hundred individuals."

"That's why there were no bodies," I said. "The bug-things took them and, somehow, blended their DNA all together to grow this… person. But why?"

"I can't answer that even if I were allowed to."

I couldn't—simply couldn't—begin to understand what I was seeing, but the cold, empty way their red eyes stared at me told me there was only one thing to do. I floated back to the corridor, ignited my pilot light, and I poured flame into that room until there was nothing left in the tank. The fluid sacs burst, the bodies burned, twitching as flame and vacuum ended them. I emptied a hundred or so high-explosive rounds into the room just to make sure.

"Excellent work," said Sandy. "I was *really* hoping you were going to do that."

"Let's get the fuck out of here," I said, and as Sandy began steering us down the corridor again, I tried to get as far away from that room as possible.

* * *

Left. Right. Right. Left. Right. Right. Right. Right. Left. Straight on.

Without Sandy I'd be hopelessly lost. On the *Lahore* my implants guided me; here, the AI did.

How did people even get around before computers? I remembered they had maps. Gas memories. Or they just got lost a lot. Or…

My mind was wandering when it should be focused. For a moment, I felt odd. Like I was going to throw up; something I couldn't do without a mouth or digestive system. "Hey Sandy?"

"Yes?"

"I don't feel gas."

Sandy said nothing for a moment as the EVA pack guided us around another too-small corner. "You're dying."

So simply stated. My nervous system was linked up to the suit's sensors and inputs, but my brain was within my biological body, and it was screaming.

"How far away are we from the outer hull?" I asked.

"Six minutes," said Sandy. "Maybe less. I'm avoiding unstable areas. We wouldn't want to get pinned in here."

"We would not want that," I said. "Although I'm sure you'd be fine."

"I'd miss you," said Sandy, and I think she actually meant it. The way she said it, though, with Sandhya's voice… that hurt more than all the broken ribs in the world.

"Hey," I said. "Just saying. If it makes you feel better… you suits cost over eight hundred million credits *each*. My death benefit is only about five hundred thousand. Much cheaper for every single one of us to get blown up than one of you guys."

"That actually makes me feel worse."

"It wasn't supposed to make you feel gas, ya' dumb robot."

A few seconds of silence. Then, a yellow bar lit up around Stanco's portrait.

"-addy," came his voice, heavily obfuscated by static, "you out there?"

"Stanco! Sandy, give him our locat—"

"Already done," she said.

"Hey Caddy!" Stanco became clearer by the second. "Buddy, mate, I knew you were too fucking cool to be dead."

"Thanks for the vote of confidence," I said, "but let's not get too far ahead of ourselves. I'm hurting pretty bad. Antenna's damaged. So's my magnetic grip. I'm lost, and running low on ammo and options."

"Right," said Stanco. "I have a fix on your location. Hold tight." Seconds later, Stanco's suit flew around the corner, nearly smashing into me. "Found 'ya."

"You're a sight for sore eyes," I said. "Thanks for coming back for me."

"Angel wanted to exfil," he said, "but Golovanov ordered

us back. You got all the other Immortals out looking for you too. We can't have you ruining our good name on our very first mission now, can we?" He hooked his arm around my EVA pack. "Okay. I'm going to guide you out of here."

"Sounds gas," I said, and again, the world seemed a bit fuzzy.

"Hey buddy," said Stanco. We were moving. He was moving me. "What's Eris like this time of year?"

What a weird question. "It depends on where you are," I said. "Planets are big. Frozen areas, forested areas, deserts… what do you like?"

"I like forests," he said. "Always do. Every time I got married, I'd take the lucky girl or guy to a forest. I like verdant things. Verdancy. Is that a word? Verdancy?"

Osmeons were polygamists. Sandhya had lots of husbands. And wives, too. Girls marrying girls. There was nothing wrong with that.

So I had to keep telling myself.

"Why do you need so many?" I asked. "Why not… just find the one? The person who makes you feel like all the world's right when you're with them?"

"Because," said Stanco. "Sometimes that's more than one person. And it's easier to trust when your marriage is a family." He steered us around a big corridor. "The last guy I married, right? He tried the whole monogamy thing. You know what he told me?"

"What?"

"Something like… *I thought having a vasectomy would stop my wife getting pregnant again. Turns out it just changes the color of the baby.* He was doing the whole monogamy thing but she wasn't. I don't need that shit in my life. If my partners want to fuck around, let them. They're going to anyway. Better we do it on our own terms."

"That's brutal." I felt tired, distant. Too many thoughts of Sandhya, and of what I'd done to my wife. With her. With the soldier I met on a distant world… "Why are you telling me this?"

"Trying to keep you focused."

"'Cuz I'm dying?"

"Pretty much." Stanco steered us up to a tiny gap I didn't think we'd be able to fit through, and then—somewhat roughly—stuffed us through, scraping the hell out of the suit. "It's the game of war, buddy. Play stupid games, win stupid prizes."

"That actually makes me feel worse," I said, stealing Sandy's line.

"Hey," said Stanco. "I can't make *everyone* happy. I'm not pizza."

"I hate pizza."

He laughed down the line. "You can't hate pizza. Nobody hates pizza. You're a fucking monster."

I didn't know what to say to that so said nothing. We flew past various rooms. Quarters. Observatories. A bar.

"Hey Caddy," said Stanco. He just wouldn't leave me alone. "Want a drink?"

More than anything. If I was going to die, I might as well do it with less pain. "Nah. There are demons in there."

"You what?"

"I used to have a drinking problem," I said. It was tempting to mute him but I didn't. "I still do. But I used to have it too."

"Alcoholic, hey?" Stanco blasted open a section of the

wall. The bulkhead splintered into a million shards. I barely heard the explosion. "You know there's an injection for that now."

Was there an injection to take away the pain in my chest when I thought of Sandhya? Was there a jab in the arm that could make the dead come back to me? "I know," I said. "I could just shoot myself in the head. That'd be great too."

"Mmm," he said. "Doesn't sound like a fun way to go. How does someone get like that? All suicidal like Angel?"

Easy answer but hard to say. "For most people, it's when someone dies who you love more than life itself. Substance abuse is gentle suicide."

"You're right where you're supposed to be right now." I could practically hear the smile in his voice. "You couldn't not be, friend."

Where I was supposed to be… "For me, the only thing worse than death is the end of the whisky. And I've been sober for a while now."

He chuckled at that, another prerecorded noise that filtered through the radio. "There's a saying on Uynov," said Stanco. "Angel told me. You treat a wound on the skin with grain alcohol. You treat a wound in the heart with spirits."

"Sounds gas. Spirits keep my spirits up."

"Except you're sober now," said Stanco. "So you've found something else, right?"

Something else? What was there? "Naw. Just because you're sober doesn't mean you don't miss it. Biggest days for relapses are anniversaries: first week, first month, first year, first decade. The shitty truth is, you're never really clean. You're just trying to beat your record for biggest gap between relapses, and eventually you die."

"Not today," said Stanco. "We aren't dying today. I'm far, far too funny to die."

"You're a funny guy," I said, groggily.

"My humour's like a little kid with cancer. Never gets old."

"The Prophets Wept…" I went to banter more, but from around the corner came the sound: rain on a tin roof. A stampede of spider-creatures, howling as they ran toward us.

"Okay," said Stanco, "Yeah. Maybe we *are* dying today."

Then I passed out for a bit.

* * *

"—CC's of adrenaline straight into the heart. Going now. Injecting!"

Something dragged me back to life. A chemical coursing through my body, keeping oxygen in my brain.

"He's back," said Sandy. The relief in her voice was palpable.

I expected to be waking up in the infirmary aboard the *Lahore*. But instead, Stanco was standing by an airlock, his metal back braced against one door, a foot holding it open. He had discarded his assault gun and held my autocannon in one hand. He was firing it in bursts, spraying down some unseen target.

I was still in the suit. I was still aboard the *Anchorage*.

"I took your gun," said Stanco. "That's how you know we're best friends. Sharing guns."

A quick check of my readouts confirmed I was weaponless. "How long was I out?"

"A minute or so," he said, firing off another burst. I

could see red eyes in the dark, and as the shells screamed into the hull and exploded, the flashes showed more of the spider-creatures. "That's super bad for you."

"Super bad," said Sandy.

Two more rounds, a double tap. Stanco threw the rifle away. "Guns are completely dry," he said, and pulled a huge blade from his side. "Good thing I bought this."

I felt vaguely more alert. "Guy I know a long time ago… he practiced knife-fighting techniques. Big guy. Built like a tank. His arms were coiled springs, fingers calloused. He said that the loser of a knife fight dies on the ground, the winner dies in the ambulance."

"No ambulances here," said Stanco, and as the first of the spider-creatures rolled over him, he plunged the blade into its head. "So I'm fine."

I couldn't contest that argument. The spiders bit and tore at his suit, sparks flying. Still he kept the airlock open.

"We gotta get out," I said. "Sandy, can you move us?"

"Yes," she said. "In a moment."

Right as she spoke, Angel clambered in through the open airlock. The instant her autocannon was tracked she fired, portrait in my peripheral vision was iron and unchanging. Strobes of weapons fire lit up the cramped airlock.

The EVA pack moved once more, pushing us out the narrow gap, and then I was in open space again. Behind us, flashes of weapons fire grew distant, and I saw the *Anchorage* shrink away, until it was once more outlined in a red box. Seven little stars, the other suits, raced after me, white tails behind them as their EVA packs pushed them toward us.

"All suits clear," said Angel. "Nuke it."

Missiles flew from the *Lahore*, little falling stars that

streaked across space. They moved so slowly, their movement almost imperceptible until they leapt past us and beyond. Tick tock, seconds passed, and then the *Anchorage* evaporated in a bright white light. When the blast cleared, all that was left was an ever-expanding field of debris.

"Heart rate is down," said Sandy. "Nicholas, you gotta hang on. We're almost there."

"Don't call me Nicholas," I murmured, feeling at once so tired I could barely stay awake, and as though I'd just chugged a crate's worth of stimulants. "Sandhya called me that…"

Sandy said nothing. I should probably rename her. Change her voice—it wasn't right to cling to a ghost, to try and bring my dead lover back to life with a lie. I should probably read the mission dossiers before we launched. I should brush my teeth more often.

I should probably do a lot of things.

So, with a list of all my failings big and small playing in my mind, I passed out again.

* * *

I almost didn't believe I'd actually wake up in a real hospital, but as the world crept back to me, I recognized the familiar ceiling of the *Lahore*. A tray of food, along with a plastic cup of water, sat on my bedside table.

"Good morning," said Golovanov.

"Every time I see you in a hospital, something bad happens to me," I said, taking a deep breath. My whole chest lit up in pain; I shouldn't do that any more. Just shallow breathing. Sandy was right. So many broken ribs… "Or has just happened. Do I have any more prosthetics? Losing the arm was bad enough."

"Nah," said Golovanov, smiling. "You actually pulled through okay. I mean, you're beat up pretty bad, and you have a wicked-sick concussion, but you'll pull through."

"That's what I like to hear." I closed my eyes a moment. "So... what the fuck?"

"Your AI saved your life. Angel and Stanco carried you in. They deserve a fair share of the credit for that, too."

Sandy was saving me, just like her namesake. "I meant with the ship. The *Anchorage*."

Golovanov folded his hands in his lap, sucking in air between his teeth. "Yeah. Not sure what to tell you: appears to be... some kind of spider things. They can survive in space, and they're tough, strong, and adaptable. We got plenty of samples of their blood, along with the recordings from you and your team... so I'm sure Fleet Intelligence is going to have a field day trying to classify them. There's a myriad of breeds we observed, I doubt two are identical."

"The Myriad," I said, shrugging. "Well, hell of a first contact for humanity. Went to shooting in minutes. Mission accomplished, I guess."

Golovanov nodded. "Something like that."

I picked up a piece of stale bread and bit it. "You don't think they're aliens? Some kind of Earthborn bioweapon?"

His expression told me he didn't know. "We'll see," he said, standing up and tugging the front of his uniform down. "I have all seven other suits out there right now, combing over the wreckage, making sure that our nukes got every single one of those bastards—although if we could find one alive for dissection, that'd be useful, too. I've also put out a fleetwide alert. It was tempting to classify this whole thing, but I don't see the point. Not for something this serious. In a few days, all the colonies will know about it. I'm calling them a highly infectious biohazard for now, until we have information that suggests otherwise."

"Hopefully that's the last we'll see of them," I said, sitting up and folding my pillow behind me, making it into a half-chair.

Golovanov tilted his head. "Lots of ships go missing every month," he said. "Most are never found. I'm sure almost all of them have entirely mundane explanations. But what might have happened aboard the *Anchorage* if we didn't show up?" He put on his hat. "Do you really think that this is the first ship these creatures have attacked, or merely the first one that's been discovered?"

A sobering thought. Speaking of…

"I need a drink," I said, cracking a smile.

Golovanov's face darkened. "You know that's not an option," he said, and then without elaboration, turned and left.

"Happy New Year," I said to his back, and then I settled back into my bed, picking up a glass of water and taking a sip.

Mission complete.

Q&A with David Adams

What a creepy, fun story! Did you know what was in that ship before you got to that point?

Oh yeah, totally. :D I've had this story kicking around in my head for about a year and a half, probably more—I knew all the beats, all the characters and the plots, and I just had to find the right venue for it. *Beyond The Stars* is perfect for this piece.

How does this story fit in with the rest of the world you've created?

It's a prequel, kind of, told from a side character from *Symphony of War*. The Myriad are the primary antagonists of the *Symphony of War* series, and I wanted to show how they got to Polema. I also wanted to show, or at least hint that, they had the ability to "create" humans by blending their DNA together. Another short story of mine, *Demon and Emily*, gave insight into what Polema used to be like before the Myriad arrived. *The Immortals: Anchorage* shows something different.

That's what I love about the various short stories and novellas set in the same universe as my novels -- I can show the side stories that "fill in the gaps" of the novels. *Symphony of War* doesn't talk about how the Myriad came to Polema, only that they were there. It's not relevant to that story.

What I want to tell, eventually, is *why*. But that's a story for another day. ;)

What's up next for you in terms of new books?

Wow. So many things...

My next two projects are my two novels being written together, *Ren of Atikala: The Empire of Dust*, the third book in that series, and *Lacuna: The Requiem of Steel*, which is the sixth Lacuna book. I'm working my butt off on both of them, but I also have other novels and short stories kicking around; there's *Symphony of War 2: The Eris Campaign*, which I've got a lot of ideas for, and also *The Immortals: Southport*, which follows up where *The Immortals: Anchorage* left off.

Where can readers find you?

A few places! I have a Facebook page at: http://www.facebook.com/lacunaverse

Or my webpage here: www.lacunaverse.com

I send out a notification for my new books here: http://eepurl.com/toBf9

Or if you just want to talk to me directly, my email is: dave@lacunaverse.com

Pele's Bee-keeper
by Annie Bellet

THE WORLD WAS pain and light. Jackie didn't want to go back to that, but a voice insisted.

"Gensh, amik gensh," the voice said.

"I don't," Jackie started to say, then her mind woke up and the language came to her. "I'm here," she said in rough Farrakhani. She licked her lips, tasting bitter ash and metallic blood. Jackie opened her eyes and blinked against the warm sunlight. A shadow crossed over her and after a moment she realized it was a face.

Her rescuer was covered in a bright purple robe, complete with a veil over her face so that only a small swatch of golden skin surrounding large hazel eyes was revealed. A woman perhaps, Jackie thought, judging by the long lashes and the soft, light tone of her voice.

"Drink this, it will help with the pain," the woman said,

her words clipped and accented, making Jackie wonder if the language wasn't her native one.

She obeyed, hissing as she lifted her head and disturbed her shoulder. *Damn, that's gotta be my collarbone. That's six weeks or more out for me, Miles will whine to no end about the fetch and carry.* She started to chuckle until she remembered. Crash. Miles. His gurgling screams and that horrible warm wetness.

Whatever was in the water, which tasted slightly sweet, started working immediately. Warm relief shoved away the pain and she laid her head back onto the soft thing beneath her body. A blanket maybe? She wasn't sure.

"Miles, my pilot," Jackie asked as the woman's head reappeared above her, "he's injured, too, I think. Did the others get him out?"

"Others?" The woman shook her head and a shadow passed through her green-gold eyes. "There are no others here, only I."

"And Miles?" Jackie was annoyed. Why wouldn't this woman just say? She started to fade again and fought it, reaching with her left hand to grab at the woman. The medication refused to let her win and the dark claimed her again.

* * *

When she awoke she was inside. The lights had multi-colored paper shades and gave the large room a warm glow. Jackie struggled to sit up and leaned against the headboard of the soft bed she'd been placed in. The room had shelves and cabinets along the edges with neat labels on them in a language that she couldn't make out. Opaque jars lined many of the shelves and Jackie smelled fresh brewing coffee. There was no sign of Miles.

A curtain twitched aside and her rescuer entered, carrying a tray. The woman was tall, Jackie thought they'd look eye to eye when standing. Her robe swirled around her body, making her shape impossible to determine, but Jackie guessed she was fit enough to be living out here alone.

"How do you feel?" The woman set the tray down and knelt beside the low bed.

I'm injured, alone, and you won't tell me what the hell happened to Miles. How do you think I feel? Jackie took a deep breath. "Floaty," she said. "The pain isn't so bad. Miles is dead, isn't he?" She forced out the last, making herself look at the possibility head on.

The woman was very still for a moment and then slowly nodded. "If Miles is the red-haired one, yes. He's dead. I stopped the fire in your shuttle."

Grief threatened to shred the bandages the pain medication had laid over her mind. Dead. Nothing she could do there. She took a deep breath and regretted it.

"Careful. Your collarbone is broken, here." The woman touched her right shoulder to demonstrate. "Your arm, too, I had to cast it. Your head just took a little glue, no concussion. I am Darya."

Jackie almost smiled at the quick, clinical delivery of this information. Not a woman used to company, she guessed. A woman in veils with no surname. Curious.

"I'm Jackie, Jackie Banner. Captain of the IOU. I need to contact my crew, get the other shuttle down here. Also, figure out what happened on my ship." What had happened to her crew? Why hadn't the other shuttle come down here yet?

"They are in orbit around the Jewel. Contact from here can't happen for another thirteen standard hours. You need to rest. After you drink this."

"I smell coffee," Jackie said, her mind peeling away again. She did want to rest, wanted to sink into the soft quilts on this strange bed and leave everything behind forever.

"No coffee for you yet. Meds, then sleep."

Jackie obeyed, sliding down into the covers.

* * *

"I went back to your shuttle. To get my cargo." Darya's soft voice broke Jackie out of her dark thoughts.

As soon as she awoke, Darya had made Jackie take more medication and then presented her with a tiny feast of fresh fruit and nuts and smashed, cooked yams. Chewing hurt, but no more than breathing. She forced herself to eat, if only to keep up her strength and pass the time until her ship could be contacted.

"Is, I mean, Miles. His body." She bit her lip.

"I laid him out and put a sheet over him, inside. He is safe." Darya studied her for a moment. "He was more than your pilot? Your lover?"

Is it so obvious? "Sometimes. He's been a friend a long, long time. Was." Another wave of grief slammed into her and she choked on a piece of starfruit.

"I did not mention the ship because of him. I mention because I think you were bombed." Darya set down her water glass and folded her hands in her lap.

Jackie's head snapped up and she raised her left hand to touch her sore head in reflex as it protested the sharp movement. Her braids were crusted and rough above the cut on her forehead. "Bombed? What do you mean?" She wondered if the language barrier were playing tricks with her.

"Your console, it exploded, yes? I looked at it, after moving your pilot. I think it was deliberate, not a malfunction."

"Why would someone want to rig my shuttle?" Jackie glared at Darya. This was a headache she didn't need. It had been weeks since they'd docked anywhere, and no one had been on the ship but her crew. Their cargo was the stuff for this moon, and some bulk plastics for a new Chen Zho station out past Centarus. *And those Mudhemedi documents.* Jackie shoved that thought aside. Not even her crew knew about those.

"You would know better than I," Darya said.

Jackie shook her head, but her thoughts churned with the possibilities.

Laine barely left the engine room and had little interest in the shuttles unless something mechanical was wrong, Carsten had been learning the helm lately, and Aitor always did whatever his cousin, Carsten, told him to. She'd taken Aitor on mostly as muscle for using the lifts and moving cargo.

A bomb. That could have gotten anyone. It made no sense.

"How would you know what a rigged explosion as opposed to a malfunction looks like, anyway?" Jackie asked, dark eyes narrowing.

Darya's expression was impossible to read behind her veil. "I do."

There was no response to that. Jackie looked away. Laine had been buried in manuals when she and Miles had departed. Jackie was going to stay on the ship, but Aitor didn't feel well, and Carsten and Miles had always been at best coldly civil to each other, so she didn't want to send them down together for the drop. So she'd gone with Miles.

Had Aitor's eyes slid away from her when he told her he was sick? Where had Carsten been then, behind her? Had Aitor glanced at his cousin? Why? She tried to replay the events in her mind but it was hazy.

"No," Jackie said. "I'm sorry, you have to be wrong. That explosion could have killed both of us, and without me no one can fly my ship. I've got the codes; I'm the only one with the codes."

She had to keep the codes close, and not just because you could never be sure of anyone, not in space, not out here on the edge. *Can't risk someone finding out about the other missions, the ones that don't pay. Can't risk losing my ship, not now, now when the resistance needs help so badly.*

"Don't trust your crew so much then?" Darya said and her tone stated clearly that she felt Jackie wasn't thinking it through.

"Take me back to my shuttle. I have to see for myself."

Darya looked as though she might protest, her shoulders hunching under the bright fabric. Then she nodded.

"When it is light out, we'll go."

Jackie sank back and sighed. More waiting.

"What was in those cargo crates anyway?" she asked, wondering if perhaps someone had wanted to destroy that cargo. The manifest had said only "agricultural supplies, organic."

"Seeds, and my beehives," Darya said, motioning to the shelves and cabinets.

Abruptly a memory came to Jackie. A large black insect with glinting blue wings resting on her arm in the smoke-filled shuttle. Her arm. Bones all wrong under the dark skin. She glanced down at it in the sling, but the cast covered everything now.

"So that was a bee," Jackie murmured. "Did some get out in the crash?"

"One hive was destroyed, despite the wrappings." There was a hard catch in Darya's voice at this, as though she were stricken with sorrow about it. "Two made it; the bees are waking up now. They must acclimate in the greenhouse, then I'll move the hives outside."

Bees. I lost my best friend and she lost some bees. Thinking about him conjured Miles' laughing freckled face. Bees and a mysterious woman. Miles would have been thrilled about this adventure. *If you hadn't died, it would be an adventure.* A deep shiver went through Jackie and she realized she'd been quiet a long time. Darya just sat, silent and still, watching her.

"Why bees? Why are you here?" *Think about something else. Anything else.*

"Do you feel you can stand? I can show you." Darya rose in a smooth, graceful motion.

Jackie shifted and swung her legs out of the bed, using her left hand to pull away the covers. Her undershirt was still on, though missing the right sleeve now, but she lacked pants with her jumpsuit removed.

Her thighs and knees were mottled with reddish bruising. Jackie was impressed since it took a lot for her dark skin to show damage like that. She knew it should hurt more, but the meds created a squishy barrier against that reality.

She stood. "Pants would be nice." She looked down and realized her ankle holster was missing as well, though she still had socks on. She guessed her sidearm was still in its locker in the shuttle.

"Your jumpsuit is ruined, but your boots and gun are fine. I will find you pants. Please wait." Darya slipped out through one of the three curtained doorways.

She returned and helped Jackie pull on a pair of wrap pants that were soft and smelled herbal, but clean. The boots were harder to get on, but the two women managed. Jackie made no comment as Darya strapped the ankle holster to Jackie's left leg, but she smiled to herself as at least a small piece of the mystery was solved. Darya's long, calloused fingers knew exactly how to fit the holster on, the strange woman barely looking at what her hands were doing as she snugged the gun into place. *Definitely not what she seems.*

The robes, the veil. Her knowledge of guns and explosives. The mysterious woman had seen war, Jackie was sure of that. But which faction? Which war?

Clothed and more or less steady, Jackie followed Darya through another curtain into a dim hallway. Darya hit a code into a solid door panel and it slid aside. Warmth and heady scents of growing things rushed out to greet them. The lights flicked on, revealing an immense greenhouse. Trees, some six feet or more in height, bore heavy fruits while tables full of leafy plants filled the expanse. Flowers of numerous colors and shapes overflowed their pots. The place brimmed with life, a lush paradise enclosed in glass.

Jackie stood just inside for a moment, taking breaths of the humid, earthy air, as deep as her injuries would allow. Slowly the pieces fell into place.

She looked at Darya with a little awe on her face. "You're terraforming. That's what you need the bees for. Right? You're trying to single-handedly transform a barren moon into what? This?" She waved her left arm about and regretted it as her shoulders shifted and the pain stabbed through the medicine blockade.

Darya laughed, low and soft. "Yes. And I will. Pele is not barren or we wouldn't be breathing. The seas are teeming with phytoplankton, and a few other organisms. The land masses are volcanic, the soil here is rich and ripe, a womb awaiting its seed. I am just the sower." Her hazel eyes turned more gold than green under the lights and burned with deep passion.

She's a fanatic. With plants. Weird. Jackie smiled despite herself. It was an ambitious idea. She could admire that. Plenty of people thought running a skeleton crew and dragging all sorts of strange cargo along the galactic rim was crazy too. Those people died old and boring in their beds.

Not screaming and burning and alone. Again the wave, and again she forced it back.

A light touch on her arm drew Jackie's attention. Darya had moved up close enough she could see the veil move as the other woman breathed. Understanding filled those lovely hazel eyes and somehow it was more painful to see than pity would have been.

"Come, Jackie," Darya said, "Come see the bees you brought me."

The hives were two large boxes, almost cone-shaped near the tops, with large slats that turned out to be vertical drawers. The bees were still sluggish from cold storage, but some took flight around the women as they approached. They were black with bluish wings and as long and thick as the first joint of Jackie's thumb.

"Those are honeybees? I thought they were supposed to be yellow and black, and well, smaller."

Darya laughed again. "Some are. These aren't. The gravity here is a little less than standard, the oxygen a little more. These should do well on Pele."

"Pele? My star charts just have a designation and number. Did you name it that?"

"No, not I." Darya turned away so Jackie could not read her face as she added, "It was named by others, long before I came here."

A bee landed on Jackie's arm and she froze, all her questions slipping away. "Is it, do they sting?"

"Yes, but they are nonaggressive. Nasty sting if provoked, however." Darya turned back. "Just lift your hand gently and it should take off."

Jackie did, and the bee vibrated its wings, lifting away and disappearing among the thick, waxy leaves of a breadfruit tree.

The remaining hours until daylight passed quickly. Darya deftly avoided any personal questions and instead distracted Jackie from both her curiosity about the woman and her own problems by explaining the ecology she was trying to produce. It was, as Jackie had suspected, an ambitious project.

The valley they were in was just her test ground; Darya had hope that once she'd unleashed the plants and bees into the environment, nature would take her course and begin working all on its own. If the bees survived, Darya planned to bring in other insects, and maybe bats as well. All Jackie managed to learn was that a settler's conglomerate paid the strange woman to do this.

"Aren't you lonely here, though? Why don't you have assistants?" Jackie asked.

Tension vibrated through the other woman and she turned her face toward the ceiling. "It's daylight now, we should go to your shuttle. If you still want to, that is." Darya said. "Do you need more meds?"

The meds were fading, the pain getting sharper. Jackie shook her head. She wanted the pain. The meds deadened her brain, fogging things over. She needed to think clearly. "Let's go."

The skimmer drifted across the plain towards the glinting wreck and Jackie wondered if running wouldn't have gotten them there faster than this old machine. Darya seemed to read her thoughts and pointed out that there were pockets of sharp volcanic glass beneath the soil, making foot travel dangerous.

Jackie stepped off the skimmer and walked into the dim interior of the shuttle. She paused, staring at the shape under the indigo sheet on the cargo platform. The cloth had slipped, revealing a shock of deep red hair. Miles. Miles grinning, his teeth coffee-stained and slightly crooked, holding the vial of dye. "Just enhancing what the good lord gave me." She gritted her teeth and looked away.

The front of the shuttle was a mess. Jackie forced herself not to think about the dark stains and mangled webbing as she picked her way to the console. It was blown apart, looking very much like something just beneath the screens and control array had torn through. Burning plastic had pocked the entire area and melted wires hung loose like orphaned vines.

"Plastique." Darya's voice startled Jackie. The robed woman slipped past Jackie and bent in front of the torqued plastic and metal where the blast must have originated. "This bit of shielding here; it made it act like a shape charge, pushing it out through the screens. And this fracture here…" She motioned to a deep, long scar in the side of the console.

"No, that was there. Not that big, but there. Laine said it wasn't critical, so I had her leave it." Jackie shivered, ignoring the lance of pain up her neck and then down her right arm. She wanted to reject what Darya was saying, reject the melted, blown apart mess in front of her. She brought her hand up and rubbed it across the bridge of her nose. "It made it worse, didn't it?" Ignoring reality in space got you nowhere but dead.

"Yes."

"So it could have been an accident. This much damage, I mean, not the explosion." Jackie thought about Aitor's face shifting away, Carsten standing big and cool behind her. "Designed to keep me here for a while, keep me busy." She said the last more to herself, slipping back into Esper from Farrakhani. If Darya understood she gave no sign.

"It is possible. But why disable the shuttle? To steal your ship?" The robed woman rose to her feet.

"No. I have a guess." Jackie hesitated. This woman was alone out here, just an employee of a conglomerate. It was unlikely she was a spy for one of the factions, or even involved at all in the various disputes and wars that flared up as regular as a sunrise in the galactic race for wealth and power.

But Darya's strong hands deftly attaching the ankle holster to Jackie's leg was an image she couldn't afford to ignore.

The veils and robe. Farrakhani women sometimes wore a type like this, to signal the loss of family. There was a sect of the Farrakhan faction, the Akkisti, orphaned warriors trained in secret. Supposedly they were responsible for the genocide at Cerebin. 300,000 people had lived there. Then, none. None alive. No one knew what had really happened. The Akkisti had become more legend than anything, these days. Her brain felt slow and jumpy from the meds.

"Are you Akkisti?" Jackie said.

Darya flinched as though struck, eyes narrowing. "Why would you ask this?"

"My gun," she said, motioning to her ankle, "and this, this mess. You can read the explosion; you knew it wasn't from some tech failure. Your accent, your dress. All of it. You're not what you seem."

"Are you, Jackie Banner?"

Those documents, the lists, will save lives. "I am captain of the IOU, yes. I work for no one but myself." *That job isn't work, it's personal, I promised Inri. And the Mudhemedi didn't, don't, deserve what has happened to them.* She lifted her chin. Just as she'd thought, they were of a height, hazel eyes staring into her own black irises.

Darya held very still for a long time. Jackie's hand twitched and she pressed her tongue against the back of her teeth. Then Darya's head dipped, twice, in what might have been a nod. Jackie waited, willing the woman to answer her question.

"I am not just a bee-keeper, no. Before this I lived another life. Here, now, I am what I am. I am terraforming Pele. And keeping an eye on the ansible array in the system."

"What?" Jackie said. There was no listed ansible in this system. She bit back pointing that out. It wouldn't be the first unregistered array.

There was a distant crack, like thunder. Jackie looked questioningly at Darya. "Storm coming in?"

"No, not here. You came in over the ocean, yes? And then made a descent toward here?"

"Damnit. That was our other shuttle then," Jackie said, putting it together. "Out of time."

She walked out of the ruined craft and shielded her eyes from the rising sun. The gunmetal glint of the second shuttle appeared, making a far more controlled glide and landing than she and Miles had managed. Jackie knew who would be on board. She wondered what Carsten's explanation would be and thought about drawing her gun. She glanced behind her as Darya emerged, recalling the sidearm still in its locker in the shuttle. The other shuttle settled, kicking up a haze of black and red dust.

"Maybe I can still get out of this without shooting," she muttered. Darya said nothing as the hatch opened and two figures walked across the field toward the women.

Carsten was six and half feet tall, a head taller than Jackie herself and hulking with biogenetically enhanced muscles. His cousin was shorter, maybe five eight, but just as musclebound. Both men were armed, Aitor carrying a rifle. Jackie had no idea where he'd gotten that.

Maybe Miles and I let ourselves get too distracted, with the easy jobs lately. Or maybe Miles was right to dislike Carsten.

Maybe? She shook her head and winced. Too late to go for the ankle gun now.

"Captain!" Carsten's voice boomed across the closing distance. "Are you all right?"

Jackie hesitated. He looked genuinely concerned, dark brows knitting over light brown eyes. He stopped ten meters or so from her and looked at Darya. Behind him, Aitor stopped farther away, rifle held easy and ready in his hands, but not quite pointing at anyone, yet.

"Who's that? Where's Miles?" Carsten said.

Decision time. Miles would have played it cool, talked them into thinking she was totally in the dark about what might have gone on here. Miles would have made it work without violence or accusations. She glanced behind her and saw the indigo body lying amongst the shadows inside the ruined shuttle.

"Miles is dead," Jackie said evenly. "The bomb killed him. Why'd you do it, Carsten?"

His face shifted like a mask slipping on. Or coming off.

"No one was supposed to get hurt. I mean that, Jackie. I don't know what went wrong." He glanced behind him at Aitor, who now held the rifle pointed at Jackie.

"I got hurt. Miles got dead." Anger rose in her, mingling with grief. These idiots had served with her for a year, and then had killed her best friend by accident, and for what? "What did you want with my ship?" She ground out the words as though chewing gravel.

"You picked up something, a package, last jump stop. We'd heard you were helping those vermin, but couldn't believe it. Not neutral, don't give a damn Jackie. What the hell are you doing with lists of Farrakhani supply caches, Jackie?

Going to hand them over to the Mudhemedi rats?" Aitor called out.

Jackie heard Darya gasp and turned her head sharply to look at the woman. It was a mistake. Her broken collarbone shifted and nauseating pain danced through her. She dropped to her knees with a whimper, trying to breathe through it and focus.

Carsten aimed his gun at her. "I'm sorry it had to be this way. But you're aiding the enemy."

"What damn enemy? Don't tell me you're allying with a faction now." Jackie looked up, fighting another wave of pain. She turned her body slightly, giving him her injured right side and hiding her left as much as she could. She inched her left hand down her leg.

"His accent, the short one." Darya said in Farrakhani. "It is ironic, yes? He is Akkisti."

Aitor tipped his head to one side as Carsten took a couple steps closer. He called out in Farrakhani, "I am. This does not concern you, Mamme. We will not trouble your moon here long."

Carsten glanced back at Aitor again and Jackie slipped her hand under her pant leg. Aitor nodded and Carsten looked almost apologetic.

"Sorry, Jackie. I didn't want it to come to this."

"You can't fly the IOU without me," Jackie said, speaking softly, willing him to come a little closer.

He did, taking a few more steps toward her as he raised his gun. "Yeah, I know. But Aitor says local has to have a way to communicate with somewhere outside this place or we'd have no delivery order for here." Carsten jerked his head toward Darya. "Jewel Box is remote, but we'll figure it out. Too bad our captain got burned up in a shuttle accident."

Jackie took a steadying breath and risked a glance at the other woman. Darya stood a little ways off, green-gold eyes narrowed against the sunlight, her hands tucked into her sleeves. No help there, not for Jackie. She cursed herself for liking the quiet, competent woman.

Saving my life, then standing by while I get murdered. Great, thanks.

"Carsten," she said. "I have a final request."

"Stay out of my line of fire, Carsten," Aitor growled as the big man moved closer to Jackie.

No luck there, but Jackie figured going down with one was better than nothing.

"What is it?" Carsten held his gun steady and towered over her.

"Be like Miles," she said, jaw tight.

"What?" He blinked at her.

"Die screaming, you asshole."

Jackie brought up the .32, squeezing off a close-range shot into Carsten. He collapsed forward as the frangible round tore into his belly.

She threw herself to the left, praying Aitor wasn't a legendary shot. The shock of agony through her body from her broken bones nearly blacked her out again, but she heard the shots clearly.

One, two, then three. Quick, the first almost on top of the next with a slight pause before the third. She waited for impact, something. All she heard were Carsten's horrible gurgling moans.

"Jackie?" Darya's voice was as soft and calm as ever.

Jackie opened her eyes and saw the woman moving toward her, Jackie's own sidearm held loosely in one hand. She forced herself upright and climbed to her feet.

Darya kicked Carsten over and the huge man stared up at her with glassy eyes, his moans turning to garbled begging in both Esper and Farrakhani. Slowly Darya unhooked her veil and then pulled back her hood.

Her face was scarred, a thick rope of whitish tissue disfiguring a full and otherwise lovely mouth. Her head was nearly hairless and the skin had a too smooth, plastic look. Jackie realized they were grafts. On the left side was a deep furrow just above a misshapen ear. Elemental weapons had done this, weapons outlawed by treaty among the major factions since the devastation of the main Mudhemedi colonies on Segina, fifteen years before. Jackie had seen footage. Everything on fire, a fire that spread and spread, burning all it touched. Animals, people, metal buildings. Things that shouldn't burn.

"Misc Mudhemedi," Darya said, "Sor gale, a'mud ismam."

I am Mudhemedi. This death, that life may continue. Inri had taught Jackie a little of his people. Enough.

Carsten's eyes widened and then Darya pulled the trigger and his face spread out over the black and red plain. Jackie looked away and shivered. She walked to Aitor's body.

Two in the chest, one in the head. Perfect shots.

"I am sorry I called you one of them," Jackie said, walking back to Darya.

The woman pulled her hood and veil into place. She shrugged. "I am what I am." She motioned to the bodies. "I will take care of this."

Jackie nodded, suddenly very tired. "I'll take the working shuttle. And Miles. You can do whatever you want with the ruined one. I'm sure I have an extremely confused engineer up on my ship right now. If they left her alive."

She didn't want to think about that. She didn't want to think at all, just collapse and sleep and wake up to a grinning, freckled man and a warm cup of not too stale coffee.

Darya talked her into going back to her compound. Jackie was too drained and in too much pain to argue much. The morphine put her out again and she awoke numb and determined.

Darya handed her a warm cup of fresh coffee and Jackie almost broke down crying right there.

"I wrapped your pilot and put him in your shuttle. We should go now, before you get tired again. You need meds and sleep. Much sleep."

Jackie didn't argue. The skimmer took them out to the plain one last time. There was no sign of the two men other than drag marks that disappeared into the red and black earth.

"Good luck, Darya bee-keeper." Jackie managed a half smile as she nodded. "And thank you."

"Thank you, Jackie Banner. Why would you help the Mudhemedi? We are a lost people."

"I made a promise to a man, once."

"Was he a lover, too?" Darya's eyes crinkled in amusement.

"Sometimes," Jackie replied and smiled back. She turned and stepped into the shuttle, letting the airlock door close behind her.

She settled carefully into the pilot seat and gingerly strapped in, glad for the painkillers. Jackie took a deep breath and hit the controls to start the shuttle. She glanced left to the co-pilot seat, a pang of loss digging deep. Then she did a painful double-take.

Tied into the seat was a large jar of coffee beans with a note scrawled in crisp Esper. "Thank you-—the bees."

Q&A with Annie Bellet

I love the layers in this story... the way the characters are slowly revealed. Is this something you plan out in advance, or does it simply happen in the telling?

I plan it out. I outline everything, including short stories. Once an idea starts to form, I let it percolate and refine in my head. Then I write down what needs to happen, who everyone is, etc.

Your Urban Fantasy series, The Twenty-Sided Sorceress, *is very hot right now. How does writing that differ from writing SF for you?*

It doesn't. I mean, writing a novel is different from writing a short story, the pacing, etc., is different. But at its core, writing any story is about the characters and the problems they face. Science Fiction just means different settings, different sorts of situations you can put characters in, etc., but they are still people dealing with life. Character is always at the core of what I write.

What are you working on now?

I'm finishing up edits on Book 7 of *The Twenty-Sided Sorceress.*

Tell us how to find you online.

Readers can find me at www.anniebellet.com

Services Rendered

by Theresa Kay

LI'HANNA SAT AGAINST the wall with her knees drawn up to her chest, cursing the stars under which humans were born. And her own stupidity.

Her light covering of iridescent fur marked her as a member of the elite colorless clan, but the most important ability that came with that heritage was useless to her now. The two who brought her here had placed rings of tomana, an ore from her home planet with electromagnetic properties, around her neck, wrists, and ankles, effectively depriving her of the ability to shift outside the visible light spectrum. Though her enhanced senses were still functioning, the information they presented her was of little use.

The room itself was featureless, nothing more than smooth metal walls, and there was no datapad to release the door from the inside. Her nose could pick out the various scents around her and it was clear she was no longer on the small passenger ship they had originally used to transport her. Many humans had traveled through the area outside the door since she'd been here and the sound of multiple ships arriving and departing was unmistakable. A space station. Based on the location, this room was a small cargo bay.

And I am the cargo.

A shudder rippled through Li'hanna's body. Nothing good could come of this situation, especially considering who her captors were.

The large one with the offensive odor did not worry her as much as the other—the scentless one. That one was a perversion of human and Kotkaa genetics. Something... other, and certainly not something the elders had anticipated when they allowed some of the clans to be studied by the imperial fleet. Though, to use the word *allowed* was somewhat of a stretch. They had not been given much choice in the matter.

And the elders certainly had no choice in what the humans *did* with the information they garnered from their experiments. The humans created hybrids with Kotkaa abilities and mostly human features.

Her clan—the colorless ones—was the one with the fewest members and Li'hanna was perhaps one of the last. The elders had kept her clan a secret from the humans so how the humans had become aware of her clan and their abilities was a mystery, but what they wanted from her now was not. Her genes. And, after they had everything they needed from her, her pelt would become a one-of-a-kind throw rug for the emperor's quarters. The scentless one had told her as much.

Both of her captors had been gone for some time, but

they could be back at any moment and she had made no progress in releasing the metal entrapping her. She banged the back of her head against the wall. How could she be so stupid as to allow herself to be trapped like an animal and held here against her will? She had to find a way out. One way or another. She would die before bringing dishonor upon her clan and allowing herself to be subjected to what the humans had planned for her.

The door slid open with a hiss and Li'hanna jerked, unnerved that she had not sensed his approach. The scentless one had returned. She hissed and bared her teeth.

"Now, now, that is unnecessary. You and I are practically family." He chuckled as he walked to stand in front of her.

She rose to her feet. "You are a deviant. A mockery of a true Kotkaa."

He made a tsking noise with his tongue and wrapped one hand around her neck just above the narrow metal band. "Do not make the mistake of angering me, creature." His fingers tightened just enough to slightly restrict her airway. "You are helpless here and, although it would be inconvenient, the genetic material we need could be harvested from your corpse."

Rage simmered in Li'hanna's narrowed eyes. She slashed out with one hand as far as the bindings would allow. Unfortunately, it was not far enough to gut the thing in front of her. The hand did drop from her neck, however, as he took a step back. She gave him a feral, sharp-toothed grin. "Death does not scare me. These restraints may hold me now, but, as I'm sure you learned from the mechanical problems your ship encountered, you will not be able to transport me any farther as long as they remain active. Do you imagine me to be a cooperative prisoner? How do you propose getting what you need from anything *other* than my corpse?"

"Simple chemistry," he said as he pulled a slim tube from his pocket and held it up for her to see the pale green liquid inside. "This compound has been specially formulated to work on the biochemistry of your kind. You will sleep through the remainder of our travel time." He moved quickly, striking her in the upper arm before she had a chance to dodge it.

Cold fire expanded from the injection point as the toxin spread through her body. The effect was near immediate. The room spun around Li'hanna's head and she blinked rapidly trying to steady herself. Fog trickled into her mind as she struggled against the bindings and darkness ate away the edges of her vision. Moments later, her chin fell to her chest and her body went limp.

* * *

Jeren Skalos tilted his chair back and interlaced his fingers behind his head, watching the two men by the doorway. He'd pegged the duo as soon as they'd entered the dockside bar and he wasn't happy. At one time his family's shipping company had been one of the largest in the galaxy, but now... here he was, barely more than a smuggler and reduced to dealing with the two shifty-eyed characters scanning the room. With a sigh, he let the front legs of the chair go back to the ground and jerked his hand up to wave the men over.

They made their way toward him, the tubby one squeezing between the packed tables and the shorter, slimmer one following behind. As they drew closer, Jeren's upper lip curled in disgust and he had to resist the urge to get up and walk away, credits be damned. It wasn't the greasy hair and sweaty face of the big one that put Jeren off, but the lithe, quick movements of the other and the way Jeren's eyes slid over him no matter how hard Jeren tried to focus on the man's features. It was bad enough that this job involved the fleet, but working with a Slither, one of the imperial fleet's genetically engineered spooks—and the same type of creature that had murdered his family—was about ten times worse and a hundred times more repulsive.

Slithers were some bastardized combination of human and the cat-like Kotkaa. They didn't necessarily *look* like their feline-esque counterparts, but they moved like them and the alien genes gave them a mild telepathic ability which allowed them to hide their features or to project features a human mind expected to see. It gave Jeren a headache just thinking about it.

"Mr. Skalos." The Slither lowered his chin in a nod. "My associate and I are pleased to make your acquaintance."

"Bradley West," huffed the large man, holding out a hand.

Jeren ran his tongue over his teeth, glanced at West's hand and then back to the Slither. Close up, the mental fog generated by the Slither lessened. This one's true features were more human than feline and sharp-edged: a pointed nose, high-cut cheekbones, and a small mouth. *He actually looks more like a rodent than a cat.* At the thought, the Slither's facial features stuttered, becoming even more rodent-like for a second before settling back. Jeren smirked. "And you are?"

The Slither narrowed his eyes. "Who I am is unimportant."

Jeren felt the subtle push behind the Slither's words. Apparently, this Slither's abilities were a bit stronger than he'd thought. He scowled. "Drop the mind tricks. I know what you are. Now, who the fuck are you and what do you want with me and my ship?"

The twitch of his head was the only evidence of the break in the Slither's composure. "Darbin," he said. "But my name is not important." He lowered himself into a chair across from Jeren and motioned for his companion to do the same. "We are here to talk business, Mr. Skalos. Nothing more."

"And what type of business would a spook have with me? For that matter, what type of business would the imperial fleet have with me? The taxes and tariffs just about killed any small freelance shippers and the new permit regulations have knocked out almost all the rest." *At least those that haven't conveniently disappeared that is. One of the consequences of disobeying the imperial fleet.*

"But not you."

"No." Jeren shrugged. *Not yet anyway.*

"The ship we were traveling in has engine trouble and we are in need of immediate transport to the imperial science station. There are few experienced pilots this far out with ships large enough to meet our requirements, as there will also be cargo involved."

"What exactly is this cargo?"

"Property of the imperial fleet." He cut off Jeren's next question which a brisk shake of his head. "You have a crew, I assume. Are they trustworthy?"

Jeren's jaw tightened as he bit back a sarcastic response. "My mechanic, Arnold, has worked for me for years. Gretchen, my co-pilot, has also been with me for some time. I would trust both of them with my life." *And they hate the fleet just as much as I do.*

"I certainly hope you are correct about them." Darbin narrowed his eyes. "The cargo, and our mission, are both highly classified. Were you or any of your crew to go snooping around…"

Acid churned in Jeren's stomach. This job was sounding less and less like one he wanted. If only he didn't *need* it so fucking bad. He took a deep breath. If he and Gretchen switched off and kept the ship moving around the clock—and the engine held together under that much pressure—this job would mean quick and easy credits. He couldn't afford to turn it down, no matter who he had to work for.

He jerked his chin up in assent. "Half now. Half on arrival."

Darbin gave him a pitying look. "As an agent of the fleet, I do not have access to that many credits on my own." He shrugged. "I can only offer full payment on arrival."

"Fine." Jeren curled his hands into fists. The asshole knew he had him. "But I want a twenty percent bonus for my crew then."

"I believe that can be arranged Mr. Skalos. Please have your ship at dock sixteen for loading in two standard hours."

Jeren pushed back from the table and walked out of the bar. He needed to go round up Gretchen and Arnold and let them know they had a job. And warn them about who they'd be working with. They'd probably be just as *overjoyed* as he was.

* * *

Awareness gradually returned to Li'hanna, her senses checking in one by one. She was no longer at the space station, but not on her captor's tiny ship either. The scentless one had found himself a new ship… and a pilot and crew. Her nose picked up three distinct and unfamiliar human scents. Two males. One female. Interesting. Most imperial ships were crewed with only males. Maybe this was not an imperial ship? Then, why had the scentless one chosen it?

The… box… that contained her still dampened her abilities, but the restraints were no longer in place.

Li'hanna smiled and thanked the stars that the elders had never handed over a live specimen from one of the higher clans. Most of the lower clans were little more than servants, but her clan was one of warriors. Not only trained nearly from birth, she was quicker, stronger, and smarter than many others. And apparently her metabolism was faster as well. The scentless one clearly expected the sedative to last longer than it did.

Her claws cut through the thin layer of metal surrounding her as if it was nothing and she climbed out into the room. Other boxes surrounded her and she had to bend over to avoid hitting her head on the low ceiling. It was a cargo hold and the door to her right was probably meant more to keep people out than to keep people in. This would be even easier than she had anticipated.

She increased her energy levels to shift into a higher spectrum. Now essentially invisible to the occupants of the ship, she slipped through the doorway and glided down the corridor with her back brushing against the wall. Even if they could not see her, they could certainly *feel* her were she to accidentally collide with someone.

She had to decide on a course of action—and quickly. It was possible she could manage to fly the ship, but she was not trained as a pilot and if she murdered everyone on board only to find her skill set was not enough… It would mean a slow death drifting through space. But waiting until the ship reached its destination was not a viable solution. It would be more difficult for her to escape from an occupied planet than it would be to take control of this craft.

Perhaps the crew could be trusted? The scentless one and his human companion certainly could not be, but the rest? Li'hanna's previous interactions with humans had been brief and involved unimportant matters, and she had no way of knowing what to expect from *these* humans. Some investigation was needed before she could come to a decision. Either way, the imperial fleet would not be getting any of her 'genetic material' even if the crew could not be trusted and she had to jettison herself from an airlock.

She continued down the corridor until she reached an open doorway. It was an empty room, someone's quarters by the looks of it. She slipped inside and ran her hand over one of the drawers next to the bed. It slid out from the wall under her touch. Empty. As was the next. In the final drawer, she found two imperial uniforms and an identification card. Her nose wrinkled. *Ugh.* She should have known.

The lettering on the card was unfamiliar to her, but the picture was not. It was the large smelly human and under his picture was what must have been his name: BRADLEY-WEST. Her lip curled up and she snarled softly. She did not like this Bradleywest. Li'hanna tucked the card back into one of the folded uniforms and closed the drawer. Further searching in this room would do her no good.

The next two rooms she encountered were empty. But the third was not. It was occupied by a human female sitting at a small desk and moving her fingers quickly across the tablet resting on it.

Li'hanna moved closer to peer over the human's shoulder. Navigational charts. Flight plans. Trajectory calculations. The human was a pilot. Though both sexes were considered equal within Kotkaa culture, the humans still tended to… coddle their females. That this human female had such a position of influence on this ship boded well for the chance of the crew being sympathetic to Li'hanna's plight. She would start with this one.

Decision made, Li'hanna shifted into sight beside the desk.

The female gasped and stared up at her with wide eyes. "Who…"

"I am Li'hanna of the colorless clan. The scentless one and Bradleywest took me prisoner and appear to have hired your ship to deliver me to one of the imperial labs."

"The scentless one? Do you mean Darbin, the Slither… err the hybrid?" She rose to her feet with a wary look in her eyes.

"The word 'slither' is reminiscent of the Earth animal the snake, correct? I believe that is an apt name for that perversion of genetics."

The female smiled and some of the tension left her body. "I'm Gretchen, the co-pilot."

"And the other crew members? I detected two other males."

The human's—Gretchen's—brow furrowed and she cocked her head to the side. "How…"

Li' hanna tapped the side of her nose with one clawed finger. "Their scent."

"Well, the ship belongs to my friend Jeren and Arnold's our mechanic." She pulled her lower lip into her mouth. "We should go speak with Jeren. You're here against your will and, even though we need the credits, we aren't slavers."

"He would go against the imperial fleet?"

"He has no loyalty to them. None of us do. The fleet—"

"Will now be taking control of this ship," said Bradleywest as he stepped through the doorway, a small blaster pointed at Gretchen's chest. "We only need one pilot to get us the rest of the way and, to be honest, I'd prefer it was you, but it looks like that's no longer an option now that you know about our cargo."

Li'hanna growled low in her throat and sprung forward. Bradleywest's eyes widened and his finger tightened on the trigger as she collided with him. The shot grazed her shoulder, but did not stop her. She grabbed his arm and prepared to swipe a claw across his throat. His other elbow caught her in the face and she took one stumbling step backward, her claw missing its target and slicing his upper arm.

Bradleywest cried out in pain and dropped the blaster. He sent one booted foot into her thigh, pushing her farther back into the room, then spun away and ran out the doorway, one hand over his injury. The door slid shut behind him and a crunching sound met Li'hanna's ears. The datapad? An attempt to lock them in?

Li'hanna stepped closer to the door. Behind it, Bradleywest was breathing heavily and speaking softly. She took another step and placed an ear against the metal.

"…old mechanic is the last of our worries. The Kotkaa is loose. I've managed to contain it for now, but at least one crew member knows. We have to take them out. The course is already set and I can fly this hunk of junk from here. Shut down the ship's communications system and meet me on the flight deck."

She stepped away. The rest of the conversation did not matter. They had to take action now. "They've disabled the communication system and are going to take over the ship. Direct me to the flight deck and I can neutralize them while you check on your mechanic."

Gretchen nodded stiffly and pulled up a diagram of the ship on her tablet. She traced her finger over the most direct route. "Jeren keeps a couple blasters secreted away around the ship. There's one—"

Li'hanna raised her hands and extended her claws to their full two inch length as she shifted out of sight and back in again. "I do not require a blaster. I prefer to bathe my claws in their blood."

* * *

Jeren hit the com button. "Gretchen?" She wasn't answering and, although not unheard of, it was… odd. She knew they'd be docking soon and she should have already been on the flight deck. Something wasn't right and each second that ticked by with no response from the com sent another needle of anxiety into his spine.

"Your co-pilot is unavailable," the Slither said from behind him.

A jolt of alarm ran through his body and he stiffened. "What'd you do to her? Where is she?"

"Unfortunately, some of the classified cargo went missing and your co-pilot then became a liability."

"You killed her. You son of a bitch, I'll—"

Darbin settled a hand on Jeren's shoulder and pinched the bundle of nerves there. "You will continue on to our destination and then you and your remaining crew member may yet be spared."

That's what he *thinks.* Jeren yanked out of Darbin's hold and spun to the right, reaching for the blaster in the holster bolted to the underside of an auxiliary console. Too slow. His fingers scrabbled over empty space. He looked up to find West had the blaster and it was pointing directly at Jeren's forehead.

"Sorry about this, Skalos. We're close enough now that I can fly this thing and with it loose on the ship—"

There was a blur of movement by West's shoulder and the skin of his throat parted as something sliced into his neck, nearly severing his head. Blood splattered across Jeren's face as West fell to his knees and then face first onto the ground. Jeren stared at the motionless body in shock. *What the hell?*

Darbin hissed and took a step backward, his eyes darting around the room." The course has already been set. We will be docking at the imperial science station very soon. You won't be escaping now, creature." Another step back took him outside the doorway as it slowly slid shut, leaving Jeren inside with West's corpse and… whatever had killed the tubby bastard.

Jeren ran to the door and banged his fist against the metal. "Creature? What the fuck—" The question he was going to ask glued itself to his tongue as the air in his peripheral vision shimmered and a female form with cat-like features appeared. A Kotkaa. A full-blooded one. In a color he'd never seen before and nothing like the small-statured ones shown on holovids around the galaxy when the species was discovered.

She smiled, baring sharp teeth. "You have nothing to fear from me, human. I have spoken with your female crew member and decided that you and I are not enemies." She raised one hand to her mouth and licked West's blood from one of her claws. "Unless you would like us to be?"

Jeren glanced at West's limp body. "Well, I'm guessing that wouldn't be particularly good for my health, yeah?" The Kotkaa let out a sound somewhere between a purr and a laugh. Amusement. He hoped. "Wait. A female crew member? Do you mean Gretchen?"

"Yes. Despite what the scentless one said, she is safe and unharmed. She went to check on the other male. The mechanic."

"I need to manually disable the auto-pilot assist in order to alter our course and, with the coms out, I need to get to the engine room." He reached down and pulled the blaster from under West's hand. "I could probably use your help with Darbin if you're willing."

A predatory glee took over the alien's face. "Bradleywest was a coward and a fool who deserved to meet his death quickly, but the scentless one deserves a much worse fate, one that I will deliver with pride."

A little odd, but she was helpful. And she had saved Gretchen's life somehow, so he didn't mind having the alien at his back as he opened the door and moved blaster-first out into the corridor. Empty.

"Can the Slither do that invisibility thing?" Jeren had never heard of one with that ability, but he'd never heard of a Kotkaa with that ability either.

"No. The imperial fleet has never had access to genetic material from the colorless clan, only lesser ones. His abilities pale in comparison to my own."

"Good to know."

The two of them continued toward the engine room in silence. A moan came from behind the door of one of the storage rooms they passed and Jeren paused. He used the datapad to open the door, then moved inside as the automatic light flickered on. Li'hanna followed.

Arnold was leaning against the wall, a bloody gash on his temple. Jeren rushed to his crewmate's side and crouched down next to him.

"Are you okay?"

"Yeah, yeah, yeah, I've had worse." Arnold fluttered a hand in Jeren's direction. "I was expecting Gretchen and that damn thing... it wasn't until he got closer that I recognized him. Bloody idiot. That's what I am. I deserved the knock on the head for not keeping my guard up."

Jeren snorted. "You're a stubborn old bastard, that's for sure. Which way did he go?"

"I dunno for sure. I think he might've been heading for

the pod. I don't know how else he'd get off the ship at this point."

"Shit." Jeren jumped to his feet. "We can't let him take that escape pod. If he gets to that station, they'll launch a full-on attack and there's no way we can withstand that. Arnold, get us turned around while we go deal with the spook." He turned to confer with the alien. She was gone. She could more than likely take care of herself, but he wasn't going to take any chances. He took off down the corridor at a jog.

He needn't have worried.

By the time Jeren reached the escape pod dock, the Slither was already limping and had several bloody slices in various locations on his body. His features were constantly moving, never holding for more than a second or two before rapidly shifting into a different configuration. Darbin moved so the wall was at his back and sent panicked glances around what looked like an empty room. He didn't seem nearly as intimidating as he had before.

A new cut started at his right temple and moved downward to his chin. A few seconds later, a matching one appeared on the left.

The Kotkaa was toying with him.

Jeren lowered his blaster and rested against the opposite wall with his arms crossed over his chest. He had no pity for the spook and the alien deserved her fun.

She drew it out for nearly an hour. Poking, prodding, and slicing through ligaments and tendons. At some point, she'd stopped bothering with the invisibility and her fur shimmered while she performed her deadly dance. It was actually quite pretty in a way.

And, even if *this* Slither hadn't participated in the massacre of his family, fairly satisfying.

Gretchen and Arnold had joined him in watching, their faces hard. Jeren was not the only one who'd been wronged by the imperial fleet. His crew was probably enjoying this just as much as the alien was.

Darbin was on the ground, a pleading and pained look in his eyes, when she finally paused. She met Jeren's eyes and cocked her head to the side. An inquiry. He shook his head and turned to Gretchen.

"Gretch? Would you like to finish him off?" She took the offered blaster and stepped forward.

Li'hanna smiled and moved to stand with Jeren and Arnold.

The blaster shook slightly as Gretchen raised it to point at Darbin's forehead. "This is for my brother, you imperial piece of shit." She pulled the trigger and a small hole sizzled into his skin.

The Slither's eyes rolled back and his body went limp.

Jeren stepped forward and took the blaster from Gretchen's hands. He put an arm around her shoulders and pulled her into his side. "Well, I think we've officially defected now."

She let out a shaky laugh. "Yup. It's definitely official. One ship, two pilots, and one mechanic against the whole imperial fleet."

"And one Kotkaa." Jeren looked up at Li'hanna in surprise. "When the fleet found out our elders deceived them, they wiped out most of my kin. I do not think there is anything for me to go back to and, even if there was, my home planet is under imperial control now."

"It's a start," said Jeren. "There will be others like us. We just have to find them. The downfall of the imperial fleet begins today. With us."

Q&A with Theresa Kay

Photo credit: Marybird Photography

This story sounds like it's the beginning of a possible saga. Did you know that when you started writing?

Not at all. This story was originally supposed to be about a side character from a completely different series, but it turned into something that I'm definitely considering turning into its own series.

I know you have other books. Are they all science fiction, or do you also work in other genres?

All of my released books are scifi, but I've dabbled in other genres as well. Scifi is probably my favorite though.

What's next for you?

I'm working on the final book in my YA Broken Skies series and the next episode of my novella serial.

How can readers find you online?

They can contact me through my website, www.theresakay. com, and I can also be found in the wilds of the internet on Facebook, Twitter, and Instagram.

Spike in a Rail

by Logan Thomas Snyder

SOMETHING ABOUT THE shuttle ride from the surface of Estropo never failed to put Xenecia in a reflective mood. She supposed it helped chase away other, less pleasant thoughts, such as the fact that two inches of hull plating was all that separated her from the diminishing atmosphere turning to true vacuum, or that the civilian operators helming the patched-together death bucket looked adolescent at best. Though she was hardly an expert in human anatomy, she felt her observation was justified given their oily, pock-marked skin and unrepentant body odor, to say nothing of the wispy collection of hairs masquerading as a mustache upon the first one's upper lip.

No matter. The ascent went smoothly enough, allowing Xenecia's mind to wander as they made their approach toward Over/Under Station, the glittering jewel of the Kiilsagi System.

Xenecia clucked with amusement at the thought. Glittering jewel—ha. Hardly. Technically the heap wasn't even a true station, at least in the sense that it hadn't been constructed with such a purpose in mind. Quite the opposite, in fact.

Before being repurposed into its present incarnation, the *Overt Wonder* began service as a super freighter operating under charter of the Capistara Corporation. It was while returning from a routine stretch deep in unincorporated space that a malfunctioning jump drive sent the super freighter straight into the jaws of the Kiilsagi System's first recorded interplanetary war. With their jump drive shot and the battle raging all around them, the captain of the *Overt Wonder* ordered his crew to abandon ship.

The hot war between Estropo and Arathia lasted for over five years. Meanwhile, the super freighter remained unclaimed, adrift in space. In time the Capistara Corporation wrote off its losses—a move they no doubt regretted when both sides abruptly sued for peace the following year. While the local powers haggled over terms and conditions, however, a newly minted triumvirate of the system's most enterprising merchant families invoked the sacred doctrine of right to salvage. Together their crews descended upon the derelict super freighter and, in a display of unprecedented cooperation, successfully jury-rigged and towed it directly into the heart of disputed space.

What followed was an act of hubris rivaling even that which led to it. With all eyes in the system upon them, the Triumvirate declared their prize haul the seat of a de facto neutral zone operating under civilian authority. Five generations later, Over/Under Station remained the undisputed economic hub of the Kiilsagi System. Not that that was saying too much.

Xenecia had heard the station described by the locals as a vast, glittering halo flung out into the middle of empty space. Her own personal view was a touch more prosaic. Even from afar, she thought it more closely resembled the fractured, discarded wheel of some ancient chariot of long-dead gods. The fat slab of a freighter serving as its hub certainly offered little in the way of aesthetic appeal. From that unsightly centerpiece radiated an ever-shifting ring of traffic, lesser vessels coming and going, feeding, consuming, like so many blowflies circling a fetid corpse.

Still, whatever else she thought of the place, there was no denying one thing…

It felt good to be home.

* * *

Technically the station wasn't her true home, nor her birth home. The Tyroshi had made certain she could no longer lay claim to either when they slagged Shih'ra from pole to pole—and the vast majority of her people with it.

Over/Under Station was hardly the first place she had called home as a galactic orphan, nor did she suspect it would be the last. Her experience as one of only thousands of remaining Shih'rahi had hardened her, whittling her down to nothing but sharp edges and a set of skills seldom met with a smile in more civilized ports of call. Over/Under Station, thankfully, suffered no such delusions about itself.

While most opted to live on the station's residential levels, there were many who preferred to make their nests among the hustle and bustle of the market areas. Xenecia was one such boarder, having secured a rack for herself in the back room of a shop owned by a spritely old seamstress. The woman had no use for the space and was only too happy to pocket the extra chits. Xenecia, for her part, was glad not to live behind some filthy, foul-smelling human chophouse.

A cursory glance confirmed that the room was as she had left it one week earlier. Her rack was undisturbed, and anything else she owned she either carried on her person—such as the modified mare's leg carbine that was her constant companion—or otherwise considered an acceptable loss. Even so, nothing had wandered off in her absence. This time.

The downside to living behind a seamstress as opposed to a chophouse was that she had to venture out to procure her meals. While the trip from the surface had done nothing to stir a more conventional appetite, Xenecia had been craving a particular delicacy ever since setting out a week earlier.

Her quest to satisfy that craving took her several levels up to a battered old food stand in a nearly forgotten corner of one of the less popular market spaces. The woman who ran it specialized in only one item, but did she ever nail it. The massive gallon-sized jar sat atop the stand, the briny aubergine liquid within not unlike Xenecia's own amethyst skin. Bending at the waist, she ignored the opaque reflection of her optical implants against the glass. A smile unfurled. She had spied her prey.

Xenecia placed two of the brightly colored translucent plastic chits that were Over/Under Station's preferred currency upon the grimy tabletop. The woman accepted the chits and Xenecia reached for the long, curved fork she indicated, spearing the fattest of those tasty pink baubles from the jar. Her prize secured, she dipped her head in thanks and went on her way. In all the times she frequented the woman's stand, the woman had said not a single word to her.

They were practically soul mates, she had decided.

Xenecia was enjoying the pickled egg—her favorite human treat—when she was stopped at the edge of the market by two women. A glance over her shoulder confirmed that two more blocked her return path. Each of the women wore gauzy white robes garnished with pale sashes of pastel fastened across the breast. The two that stood before her wore sashes of mauve and lilac; behind her, cream and mint. Though their faces were uncovered, they spoke not a word between them—at least, not yet. Their presence alone was enough to communicate their lady's will.

"Very well," Xenecia said. She swallowed the last of the egg before allowing a resigned sigh. "After you."

The Grom's handmaidens led her from the market to a repurposed storage bay that served as home for the station's singular spiritual leader. At last their path terminated before a long dais facing the entrance. A lavish, luxuriously appointed daybed sat atop the dais, all of which was wrapped in a collection of curtains reflecting the colors of Xenecia's escorts. One by one they took their positions upon the platform, standing at its corners with their hands clasped before them. Xenecia followed, picking her way through the overlapping layers of sheer pastel panels that seemed to shift and separate in time with her approach. The last of the panels parted before her, revealing what was left of the Grom. The wizened old woman was as leathery as she was frail, so swaddled beneath a pile of blankets and furs that only her wrinkled, gourd-like head was visible upon the pillow.

Xenecia stood at the foot of the dais for nearly a full minute before the Grom opened her rheumy eyes. This time it was the left eye that opened first, followed by its neighbor, the two working independently of one another as though belonging to some strange hybrid species of marine life. When at last she "spoke," it was the voices of her handmaidens silhouetted beyond the curtains that provided the means for her to be heard.

"Ah, Xenecia. My favorite huntrex," the young woman she thought of as Mauve Sash said, her voice high and clear as a bell. "How timely your return. The stars have recently spoken your name, and here you stand before me to answer their call."

Not this again, she thought. Speaking with the Grom never failed to vex and unnerve Xenecia, none the more so when the conversation turned cosmological. "Can this not wait? I only arrived back aboard station an hour ago."

"The stars spoke of you specifically, Xenecia. You know what that means."

She did, all too well. In this case it meant that catching up on her beauty sleep was going to have to wait. "Very well. What would your stars have of me?"

The next voice belonged to Lilac Sash. Hers was lightly accented, almost sultry. "There is a man aboard this station who should not be here. His presence places it and all the people who call it home in grave danger. "

Xenecia frowned, and not just because of the Grom's habit of switching abruptly between her proxies. "Grave danger?" she repeated, resisting the temptation to direct her reply to the handmaiden currently speaking on the Grom's behalf.

Cream Sash's voice was huskier, but somehow brittle. "Indeed. The stars are in agreement that his presence will have a catastrophic impact upon this station."

"I see. And did the stars have the courtesy to tell you where aboard station I might find this mysterious man?"

"They did not."

Xenecia threaded an exasperated breath between her teeth. "No, of course they did not."

"I apologize. Is locating not a species of hunting?"

Opening her mouth to respond, Xenecia found herself at a loss. "Was that a joke?"

The Grom—Cream Sash—continued undeterred. "And is hunting not what you do as a huntrex?"

Xenecia bit her tongue lest she say something regrettable. "As you say," she forced herself to respond instead.

"Then we are agreed." Of all the handmaidens, Mint Sash's voice was at once the most cheerful yet commanding.

"Can you at least tell me anything else the stars may have shared with you?"

"The vision is indistinct, but I see… bright lights. A struggle. Life and death. The rest is unclear."

"Have I mentioned that I do not normally traffic in rumor and innuendo?"

"Sadly, the stars often speak in such. It falls to me only to deliver their message to the proper vessel."

"Is there anything else I should know before I set out?"

A pause. Then, courtesy of all four Sashes in concert: "That it is most agreeable to see you again."

At that, Xenecia smiled in spite of herself. "And you, as well."

"Splendid. Now, please—I must rest. I trust you can see yourself out."

"Of course. Rest well, Grom."

* * *

Xenecia emerged from the Grom's sanctuary as frustrated as she was flummoxed. It didn't help matters that she had to re-construct the entire exchange in her mind, not least because the Grom required four different voices to communicate her message. Finally, the strange, shifting narrative clarified itself for her. She had a task, but precious little of the information required to make sense of it. Bright lights? A life and death struggle? Not a lot to go on, that.

But not nothing, either. The Grom's vision suggested that the unknown man was involved in some sort of struggle; a struggle suggested the need for medical assistance. Thank-fully, that narrowed down her options significantly. Despite its large population—well above ten thousand, per the last unofficial census—Over/Under Station wasn't exactly teem-ing with medical professionals. The *Overt Wonder* had been purpose-built to operate at peak efficiency with as small a crew as humanly possible. As such it had been designed with only one med bay. The original Triumvirate and subsequent generations had done little to encourage an interest in health and wellness among those who settled aboard the station, the results of which could be measured in its current shortage of life-saving medical care.

For Xenecia, this shortage worked to her advantage.

There were any number of charlatans and snake oil peddlers operating aboard station, but only a handful of actual professionals with the knowledge and skill to care for a man with serious injuries. What that realization didn't earn her was a location.

Not a specific location, anyway, or even one she could ballpark. Aside from the original med bay, dozens of makeshift clinics and offices across the station offered some form of healing service or another. And those were only the ones that advertised. How the hell was she to know which one a dying man might choose, or if he'd had any choice in the matter at all?

Is locating not a species of hunting?

The mocking voice echoing in her head would be disconcerting enough were it simply her own subconscious needling her. With the Grom, though, who could really be sure it wasn't something else? Something... *other*?

The thought made her skin crawl. Fixing her lips and narrowing her mind's eye, she fired off a salvo of what she could only assume was focused psionic thought-speak.

You should be resting, Grom, so I will say this only once in the most polite tone I know how: Get. Out. Of. My. Head.

Xenecia waited one, two, three beats before nodding firmly. There. Apparently that had set the busybody—busybrain?—straight. The inner workings of her mindscape were for her and her alone.

Probably the Grom was having a good laugh at her expense right now, but at least she had made her position clear. With that settled, she turned her focus back to the matter at hand. Her own familiarity with the station informed her that the middle decks received the most foot traffic. If there was a better place for an ambitious young healer to hang their proverbial shingle, she couldn't think of one.

It was worth a shot, she decided. She had precious little else to go on and knew the middle decks better than most others. Hell, at least if the mystery man died she wouldn't have a long walk back to her rack before the station went all catastrophic on her and everyone else.

Somehow that last thought was more reassuring than it had any right to be. That settled that, then. Off she went.

She wrote off her first stop almost immediately. Too busy. The victims of a nearby chophouse fire had descended upon the clinic's doorstep, their burns and shortness of breath demanding the harried attentions of what passed for its staff. One possibility had been shuttered with no explanation, while another was rendered moot by the death of its proprietor days earlier. She heard rumors of a daycare center operating as a front for certain back room procedures, but that proved as erroneous as it sounded at first blush. Still, no stone left unturned and all that.

After nearly an hour of fruitless searching Xenecia was beginning to suspect her methodology was flawed, at least so far as doctor shopping was concerned. One more, she resolved as she approached the clinic ahead of her, and then she was changing tack.

Xenecia was so busy convincing herself she was on the wrong trail that she very nearly overlooked the evidence suggesting otherwise. This particular clinic was wedged catty-corner into an irregular space between a fish fry stand—most of which was hardly catch-of-the-day material by the time it came up from either surface—and a beauty parlor fronting for a numbers racket. And while its location couldn't have been great for word of mouth, she was fairly certain the hand-lettered CLOSED sign hanging awkwardly in the window was out of character even for an outfit as sketchy as this one. And was that a smear of blood retreating from the sign's edge?

Xenecia frowned as she drew the mare's leg from the stubby leather scabbard over her shoulder. Say what you will about the Grom, the kooky old seer knew her shit.

* * *

The clinic's door resisted her initial attempt at entry. Opting for force over finesse in the face of looming catastrophe, Xenecia positioned her carbine above the knob. A quick slam of the mare's leg's molded stock cured the door of its intransigence, so much so that it flung itself wide in invitation to her. Now that was more like it, thank you very much.

Xenecia was all of a foot over the threshold when the sounds of a struggle coming from the back found her ears. Letting the mare's leg lead the way, she followed through the cramped lobby and down a short hall terminating at the clinic's lone exam room. Two men were grappling on a table in the center when she entered. One of the men stood over the other and wore a lab coat that, even from the back, had obviously seen better days; the other was flat on his back and struggling, making some sort of desperate gurgling noise. From Xenecia's vantage point it looked as if doctor and patient were choking the life out of one another. The doctor appeared to have the upper hand, as it were, though not for lack of trying on the part of his patient.

"Take your hands off that man at once," Xenecia demanded, taking aim.

The doctor either didn't hear her or didn't care, still bearing down on his patient with seemingly lethal intent.

"Ahem. I said—"

"Ma'am, I don't know who you are, but I am trying to save this man's life!"

"As am I, doctor."

"By interrupting a delicate procedure?"

"The situation is… complicated."

"Well mine is not," the doctor said, still fighting with his patient. "This man is in neural arrest. Do you understand that? Shoot me and he's as good as dead, guaranteed."

"Do *not* let that happen," a new voice chimed in from behind. "And you! Drop the carbine or I drop you!"

Too late, Xenecia remembered her unprotected backside. She spun on her heel at the sound of the woman's voice, trying to correct for the lapse, but even her well honed reflexes were not enough to balance the scales. The woman had the drop on her but good. Any which way she ran the numbers, she wound up swimming in a column of red. Bad way to go out. With an obliging nod, Xenecia knelt and lowered her mare's leg to the glossy tile.

"Good. Now, step back."

The room didn't allow for much in the way of backpedaling, but somehow Xenecia managed. Staring down the business end of a high-powered pistol proved a great motivator in that regard.

"What now?" she wondered.

"I could use an extra pair of hands if one of you isn't too busy holding the other hostage!" the doctor pleaded in answer.

The woman spared the briefest of glances at the doctor. Xenecia used that moment to take her measure. Human. Mid-to-late twenties, roughly 175 centimeters, 50 kilos or so. Hair: buzzed on the sides and back beneath a slick jet black sweep. Eyes: focused, steely, pissed. Narrow face, pointed chin, angry little mouth. All sharp edges, much like Xenecia herself. Probably Arathian military, if she had to guess.

What she was doing operating in the demilitarized zone, now that was the far more interesting question...

Sensing no threat in the doctor's request, Angry Mouth flicked her pointed chin toward the exam table. "You heard the man. Lend him your hands, won't you?"

That quickly, Xenecia went from huntrex to nursemaid. Swords to ploughshares. Now there was a narrative she never imagined living long enough to claim for her own. Though if she could get her hands on something sharp and throwable, say, a scalpel...

"And no funny business! You do what he says, when he says. Nothing more, got it?"

It proved a moot point. There were no scalpels or surgical tools in sight, nor much else in the way of medical instruments, Xenecia noted. Talk about a fly-by-night operation. Still, she nodded. Best to let Angry Mouth think she had no designs on reclaiming the balance of power.

As for the patient, she could see now that he was not struggling but seizing. Rather hard, too, by the look of things.

"What would you have me do?"

The doctor lifted his head long enough to fix her with

a disbelieving stare beneath bushy, furrowed brows. "What does it look like?" he asked around a stim injector clenched between his front teeth. "Hold him still while I inject him!"

Xenecia stepped over to the head of the table, the hard plastic of a discarded stim cartridge crunching beneath her heavy boot. At least three others lay nearby, a quick glance told her. Then the man flopped a shoulder down hard on the table and she clamped her hand upon it, pinning it in place. She followed suit with the other and while the man continued to seize, he was at least restrained.

The doctor allowed himself all of a moment to take a steadying breath before plunging the injector into the man's neck. It released with a pneumatic hiss, followed by a sharp click as the cartridge was ejected. With a muted clatter it joined its fellows on the floor before falling silent.

The final injection seemed to have the desired effect. The patient calmed, his fits and spasms downgrading to tics and twitches as the stims did their work. The tiny room heaved with a collective sigh of relief... only to be plunged right back into full panic mode when the seizing began anew, harder and fiercer than any before it.

"Give him another dose! Hurry!"

"That was the last one," the doctor barked back at Angry Mouth. "Do I look like I'm stockpiling stims here?"

With nothing left to arrest the violent assault on his brain, the patient didn't stand a chance. At that point all they could do was stand and watch. The veins in his neck bulged; thin streams of white foam poured from his mouth. All at once the man went still, his limbs flopping limply upon the table. His right arm landed not quite flush with its edge, rolling off the side and lolling there haphazardly.

With a heavy sigh the doctor cursed the loss of his patient. Or so Xenecia thought until he fell upon the unfortunate man, riffling through his pockets for payment or anything else of value.

"Damn it."

Apparently he had tapped out his stim supply for nothing. Tough break, that.

"What happened?" Angry Mouth demanded, still trying to make sense of the scene. "Why didn't it work?"

"Something disrupted his neural pathways. The stims should have counteracted it. Why they didn't, I can't tell you. That's the pathologist's problem now." Released from the weight of his duties, the doctor's shoulders slumped. He was a slender man, older and slight of stature. His cheeks were flushed, his brow dappled with sweat. The struggle with the younger, stronger, seizing man had clearly taken its toll. "Look, I have to call this in to station security. If the both of you go right now I'll leave you out of the report."

Angry Mouth eyed the dour doctor suspiciously. "Why would you do that?"

"Are you kidding? Do you have any idea how much more complicated this gets if I mention two armed women burst in here and held me hostage? I just want this bum out of my clinic so I can go home and drink until I forget about this mess."

"'Bum,'" Xenecia repeated. "Some bedside manner you have, doctor."

"It's not bedside manner once they're dead," he countered.

On further reflection, she couldn't deny he had something of a point. "Touché."

The doctor shook his head, waving off her concession. "I'm going to make that call to station security now. You've got five minutes." With that, he shuffled out of the room. On his way down the hall he added, "Oh, and thank you both for not shooting me."

* * *

The doctor had barely cleared the room before Angry Mouth descended upon the dead man. Xenecia didn't think it possible, but the woman's search was even less respectful than that of her predecessor. Shoes pulled off, pockets turned out, coveralls torn open—in a matter of seconds the man looked as if he had been attacked by a gang of ravenous street urchins. Whatever it was she was looking for, the woman seemed to have only the most general idea of where she might find it.

For her part, Xenecia collected her mare's leg from the floor. What little sound it made as she hefted it and placed the stock against her shoulder was lost on Angry Mouth, still too busy fussing over the dead man to notice. Indeed, she seemed to have all but forgotten that Xenecia was even there.

Well, at least until she turned around.

"Whoa…"

"Who are you?" Xenecia demanded as she regarded the woman over the barrel of her carbine.

"Seriously? We're really going to do this over some petty squabble? Come on, you heard the doc. Security will be here any minute. Let's just put our guns down and walk away, yeah?"

"Who. Are. You?"

"Look, sister, from where I'm standing, *you're* the one

holding *me* hostage, so we could always just wait and see who they—"

"Correction: You are being detained. Not only am I authorized by dispensation of the Triumvirate to carry this weapon aboard station, I am also empowered to act as a security surrogate. So yes, we shall wait."

To that, the woman had only one response: "Well, shit."

"Indeed," Xenecia confirmed. "Now, do not make me ask a third time."

The choice between staring down an ultimatum or her carbine proved as easy as Xenecia suspected. Dropping all pretense, Angry Mouth straightened and properly introduced herself. "My name is Sergeant Soshi Anarraham. I'm with Arathian Aerospace Defense, Wraith Division."

Called it, she thought, though she had never heard of this alleged 'Wraith Division.' A branch of AAD spec ops, most likely. It would explain the woman's military bearing, as well as her uncanny presence. Something about Sergeant Anarraham's very being raised the hackles at the base of her neck. As if she were privy to something important, perhaps mortally so.

"Why are you here?"

"What, you're not going to frogmarch me off to get friendly with your security buddies? What are you waiting for?"

"In case it has not already been adequately established, I am the one asking the questions."

"Because your station and the peace of this system are in grave danger."

There was that phrase again. Like the proverbial worm in the apple, the Grom's dire prediction burrowed itself deeper still within Xenecia's brain. What seemed only a minor nuisance an hour before had become an existential threat. Working her lips into a fine, hard line—who had the angry mouth now?—Xenecia made a decision she could only hope she would not come to regret.

She lowered her carbine.

"Come with me."

The self-described wraith was rendered speechless by the sudden display. Speechless, but not motionless. Instinct and years of training spurred Sergeant Anarraham to action, the lack of a snappy one-liner be damned.

Station security was hot on their heels by the time they finally left the clinic. Thankfully neither of the men following up on the doctor's call knew that.

"Hey, doc. Heard you got a stiff one in here," one of the security officers said as they strode into the office, "and not the kind my partner usually comes in for help with."

Xenecia and her new shadow were long gone before they could hear his partner's undoubtedly witty retort.

Even absent the threat of pursuit, the two remained silent until they were safe within the relative privacy of Xenecia's room behind the seamstress's shop. Sergeant Anarraham took one look around and pulled a critical face. Evidently the space was not up to operational standards, at least so far as hideouts and crash pads were concerned. Sadly for her, it was the only space available to Xenecia on such short notice.

"Tell me about your mission," she said, short and to the point as ever.

There was that look again. One part appraisal, two parts dismissal.

"How long have you lived aboard this station?"

"Two years, four months, and twenty-eight days."

"Then you're aware of its history? How it was established as a civilian outpost to check the ambitions of expansionist elements within the planetary governments?"

"I am aware that is the preferred narrative of the Triumvirate. Personally I have always found its plausibility a bit... lacking." Not that it mattered to Xenecia one way or the other. She had no vested interest in the political affairs or wheelings and dealings of the planetary elite, or even those of the Triumvirate, for the matter.

Or rather, she thought she had no vested interest prior to her run-in with Sergeant Anarraham.

"Well, if nothing else you have a finely calibrated bullshit detector," the sergeant allowed with a snort. Something like laughter? Hard to tell with this one. "You're right, the popular narrative is more or less fiction. The real reason the Estropans and Arathians don't turn you into a pretty light show for the people on the ground is that your station has been hosting high-level meetings between the planetary elite for decades. Well, that and the scads and scads of contraband that gets waved through here on a daily basis."

"And the significant loss of life it would represent," Xenecia added. Thousands of Estropan and Arathian expats called Over/Under Station home, with others hailing from elsewhere within the system. No doubt they too would be aggrieved to learn of the calculated slaughter of their own sons and daughters abroad. Surely that had to factor into the equation somehow...

As if reading her mind, Anarraham raised her palm before her, tilting it from side to side. "Ehh, not so much, no. Mostly the secret base and contraband thing."

Xenecia frowned. Not surprising. Not exactly comforting, either, but not surprising. A secret relationship benefitting both the station and the very governments it purported to resist would certainly explain the status quo better than the self-serving narrative pushed by the Triumvirate. As for the planetary elite, they had no shortage of enemies among their own people. Where better to avoid scrutiny or potential attack from extremist groups within than up among the stars themselves?

"I take it one of these meetings is scheduled to take place in the near future?"

"Precisely. What's more, my division of Arathian Aerospace Defense recently received intelligence suggesting the time and location of the meeting had become known to extremist groups with vested interests in rekindling the conflicts of previous generations."

She had no problem believing that, either. While both Estropo and Arathia maintained robust militaries, the outbreak of war after decades of relative peace would kickstart each planet's military industrial establishment. State of the art vehicles would be rushed to production, older vehicles repaired and retrofitted, long-neglected stockpiles suffused with glittering new tech and other vital supplies. The pockets of profiteers on both sides would fatten and swell and it would all begin again, destined never to end.

"And you believe one of these extremist groups was able to smuggle an operative aboard the station?"

Sergeant Anarraham nodded crisply. "Exactly. Intelligence suggests they'll attempt to reactivate the station's secondary self-destruct routine, using the resulting explosion as a false flag to rally support among both sides. I was tracking the man in the doctor's office through your station when I lost him." She worked her bottom lip with her teeth, as much thoughtfully as punishingly. "He must have realized I had spotted him, popped some kind of suicide pill…"

"What was that now?" Xenecia asked, her ears pricking up at the key phrase Anarraham had tossed off so casually. "Something about a self-destruct routine?"

"Correct."

"Would that not have been disabled when the station was first established?"

"The primary self-destruct routine would have, yes. But these old super freighters were built with separate secondary routines that can be easy to overlook. Think about it. Some of these ships were contracted to transport military cargo, including classified prototypes. They had to have multiple layers of security in the event they were ambushed and incapacitated."

"So what you are saying is that the entire station is rigged with an active array of explosives?"

"And has been for five generations, yes. The difference now is that one of the bad guys knows how to make them go boom again."

"Then I suppose it is up to us to make sure they do not succeed."

"'Us?' No way. There's no us here. I'm a trained professional on an off-book black ops mission that my government will disavow in the event I'm captured or killed. The last thing I need right now is to babysit some D-grade mercenary."

Xenecia curled her lip in a display of thinning patience. She was well aware that most military professionals considered the practice of hunting to be a bastardized, even base form of the venerated art of soldiering. Still, this one was pushing her sense of professional decorum to its outermost limits.

"Let me be perfectly clear about two things, " she said in answer. "This station is my home, and whether it is under threat from within or without I intend to do my utmost to assure that no harm comes to it or its people."

The woman shifted her bearing, and for a moment Xenecia thought she detected a note of respect in the way she regarded her. "All right. Point taken. And the second?"

Xenecia allowed her curled lips to spread into a grin. "I was not asking."

At that, Anarraham sighed tellingly. "I thought as much…"

Even if the attack hadn't been telegraphed, Xenecia had been preparing for one from the moment she sealed the door of her space behind them. The struggle that followed was brief—more of a tussle, really—her superior size allowing her to leverage the sergeant's arm behind her back. From there it was only a matter of a few quick steps to force her against the wall.

"You will find the inner workings of this station far more complex than you imagine," Xenecia whispered against the curve of the woman's ear. "Whatever schematics you are drawing from, I guarantee they do not provide you with the full picture you require to navigate the areas you seek."

"Let me guess: you're volunteering to be my friendly neighborhood guide?" Anarraham attempted to use the distraction of her question to dislodge her arm and throw Xenecia off balance, and failed. With a defeated growl she added, "Fine! Get off me already."

At length, Xenecia stepped back and allowed the sergeant to push off the wall. "Who said anything about friendly?"

* * *

The labyrinth that was the station's penetralia unfolded before them under Xenecia's superior guidance. Drawing upon an intimate familiarity with the station's inner workings, she guided them through a twisting warren of seldom-used corridors and passages between levels known primarily to the station's vermin—both human and otherwise—and her. Thankfully during this excursion they came across none of the human variety. Whether the lack of any internal maintenance that day was thanks to a happy accident or good planning on the part of Anarraham's intelligence asset, Xenecia couldn't say. (She did however discover that the sergeant had something of an aversion to rat droppings, which proved a source of private amusement to her, considering how many there were to avoid. So there was that, at least.)

It only got worse from there. The closer their path took them toward the engineering grid, the higher the temperature rose. Incrementally at first, until the change was too significant for Anarraham to ignore. Sweat clung to every inch of her exposed skin, slowing their progress considerably. To her, the salty discharge was an inconvenience, one that required she open her coveralls to the waist and stop repeatedly to swipe at her unprotected eyes.

"How much further?" Anarraham asked in the lowest

of whispers after nearly two hours of creeping and skulking. Without the chatter of the common areas to mask it, speech and other seemingly insignificant noises—the errant scrape of metal on metal, the toe of a boot dragging against ductwork as they crawled through it—had a way of taking on a life of their own within the confined spaces.

"Not much. We should be only a few meters away."

"Should be?" she hissed, a little too animatedly. "I thought you said you knew this place like the back of your—"

Xenecia stopped her abruptly, raising the back of the very hand Anarraham was referring to. Below them, two guards stationed outside the entrance of the engineering grid were chatting in discreet tones. It didn't take long to discern that one of the men was relating the details of an intimate encounter he had recently enjoyed while on leave… a rather vulgar and generously embellished one, at that. Xenecia and Anarraham shared a scowling shake of their heads before continuing forward.

On the plus side, the story would likely hold the men's attention for some time. All the better to ensure they weren't interrupted.

At last, their path terminated before a heavy steel grate. "We are here," Xenecia announced. Producing a multitool from her pants pocket, she set to work on the screws securing the grate. There were several, and the process was painfully slow… but also rewarding. Xenecia was passing the last of the screws back to Anarraham when it slipped through the woman's sweaty palm. The heavy screw hit the ductwork below with an audible *clang*. Xenecia and Anarraham froze, half expecting the guards to start firing up into the ductwork at any moment. No such firestorm came, though. The guards were still engrossed in conversation. They never even heard the screw fall.

With a relieved breath, Xenecia removed the grate. It was the last obstacle in their path, and with nothing else holding them back she slipped through the opening and into the engineering grid. Anarraham dropped down behind her, the sound of her landing all but inaudible. Her spook training at work, no doubt.

"This way," she said.

Xenecia had barely taken the first step toward the central console when she felt a stinging bite against the nape of her neck.

"Sorry, sweetheart," Anarraham said coolly, "but I can take it from here."

Xenecia had all of a second to spin and see Sergeant Anarraham extracting the ultra thin, millimeters-long silver needle from beneath her thumbnail. The paralytic agent lacing its crimson-tipped end had been transferred into her bloodstream, rendering it safe to the touch. Anarraham held the metal sliver between thumb and forefinger, regarding it almost thoughtfully. Then she shrugged and flicked it away as Xenecia collapsed to one knee before her, struggling to breathe.

"Here, let me help you with that." Anarraham gripped Xenecia's shoulder, shoving her roughly to the floor as she strode past her.

The paralytic agent coursed through her, binding Xenecia's limbs more effectively than any external force. Her own body became a prison, her nerves and synapses crying mutiny against the directives they would have so readily obeyed only moments earlier. Her other senses remained unaffected, allowing her to see and hear Anarraham as she went about searching for the input required to activate the secondary self-destruct routine. She hummed to herself all the while, an abominably cheerful melody Xenecia recognized as one of the harvest-time ditties that was so popular during the Arathian equinox.

With a flash of excruciating clarity, Xenecia knew she had allowed herself to be played. She had seen only what Anarraham wanted her to, never stopping to examine the situation from the other side. Anarraham was no special operative, she knew that now, but who or what was she really? An extremist? An opportunist? Disgruntled Arathian military? Perhaps the dying man in the doctor's office could have cleared it up for her, though he was more likely just another link in the chain. Or had been, until he aborted his mission prematurely. Stranded and with no one to help her navigate the station's complicated layout, Anarraham flipped the script, casting herself as the heroic operative in need of a local guide to maneuver through difficult, potentially hostile terrain.

And Xenecia had played right into the role Anarraham auditioned her for.

So much for that "finely calibrated bullshit detector."

Finally the deceitful bitch found the input, the flimsy panel concealing it giving way easily. When revealed, the keypad beneath glowed an eerie golden yellow. The nuclear battery that powered it had not failed, despite Xenecia's most earnest wishes to the contrary.

"Let's see, how long should I give myself to get off station?" Anarraham purred as she pondered the keypad. "Three hours seems a little generous, but two might not be enough if I get hung up making my way back out. What do you think, Xenecia?"

Xenecia scowled—or at least she would have if her facial expression wasn't fixed down to the nerve endings. Then she remembered she was scowling when the paralytic set. Small victory, that, though Anarraham didn't seem to care one way or the other. She was much more concerned with the larger victory.

Well, that and saving her ass.

"Hmm. You're right. Best to split the difference. Two and a half hours, it is."

The moment she inputted the code the keypad turned an angry, accusing red. There were no sirens or klaxons, no computerized warnings announcing the start of the sequence, only the winking flash of the keypad's digital readout as it counted down.

Anarraham crossed the grid and stooped before her, examining Xenecia closely. "Well, it looks like this is goodbye. Sorry it had to go down this way. No hard feelings, yeah?" With a soft pat to her cheek, she took her leave. "Oh, and don't worry, I'll say hello to your friends outside for you."

Xenecia tried to call out as Anarraham approached the door, but of course it was no use. Her vocal cords were as fixed and inflexible as every other part of her body. Two muffled pops sounded as the door swished open, followed by a pair of clipped groans and what could only be the bodies of the guards outside hitting the floor.

So, this is how it ends, she thought, embracing the fatalism of the moment. Even before the wholesale obliteration of her planet and people, she had always imagined herself the hero of her own story. With so few of her kind—her *kin*—

left afterward, it had seemed the only logical explanation. But if this was all she had been spared for—to die alone and imprisoned within herself, the unwitting tool of some double agent used to murder thousands and spark a war she had neither stake nor side in—then what else did that make her but a damnable, blighted fool?

The answer came, of all places, from her twitching toe. The paralytic was wearing off! Perhaps the dose had been improperly prepared; perhaps her body was metabolizing it quicker than a victim with human anatomy. Whatever the case, that lonely little twitch represented the sole hope of the station, if not the entire system.

Fifteen minutes passed before enough of the paralytic ebbed from her system to begin the painful process of moving. The climb to her feet was as slow as it was arduous, her muscles burning in protest through the entire effort. A nearby console proved a handy crutch, for which she was grateful. Without its reassuring presence she surely would have gone right back to ground.

Even attempting to move felt as if three times the normal gravity was crashing down upon her. Only with intense focus was she able to coax her listless legs forward, working inexorably toward the center console. Eventually she ran out of improvised handholds, barely making it to the console before her legs all but gave out on her. There was still half an hour on the timer, she saw. That was good; she could work with that.

But first, she had to get to the guards in the doorway. While they were definitely dead, their radios were not.

Getting to the guards proved less challenging than the

center console. Her adrenaline was flowing now, though traces of the paralytic still lingered in her extremities. Her fingers in particular were slow to respond as she tried to work the radio. She fumbled it once, twice before finally managing to secure it within an awkward, claw-like grip. Holding down the call button proved a fresh challenge, one she had no choice but to master quickly.

"Security," she barked into the radio's mouthpiece once she had the frequency open. "Security, respond immediately!"

"What the—who is this?"

"You are speaking to Xenecia of Shih'ra. Listen to me. You need to alert your people that—"

"Wait, Xenecia of… the huntrex?"

"Yes, the huntrex!" she replied curtly.

"You shouldn't be on this frequency. How did you get on this—"

"I said listen to me, damn it! Alert your people that there is an armed intruder aboard station, but do so quietly. She will likely be attempting to make her way to one of the docking bays." Xenecia described Anarraham, waiting for a response.

"Got it," the dispatcher said after a brief pause. *"Anything else?"*

"Yes. You will need to get someone down to the engineering grid to disengage the secondary self-destruct routine. You have approximately thirty minutes."

"…the what now?"

With five quick strides Xenecia bolted from the engineering grid, the radio squawking in her wake. They would figure it out or they wouldn't; either way, her sole duty was to prevent Soshi Anarraham from escaping whatever judgment awaited her aboard Over/Under Station.

If she had one trump card left, one thing that gave her half a shot of intercepting the conniving little backstabber before she had the chance to slip through security's clumsy fingers, it was her own ego. She had led Anarraham to the engineering grid by a circuitous route, hoping to delay their arrival as long as possible and catch the conspirator in the act. Not only would the reward from the Triumvirate surely have been substantial, but the notoriety of her involvement in preventing the destruction of the station would have earned her bigger jobs, larger paydays, and hopefully someday a one-way ticket out of this backwater system. Win-win all around, she figured.

At least until—well, no need rehashing the past. Her eyes were fixed firmly, unrelentingly forward.

Lo and behold, there she was. Somehow Anarraham had backtracked her way through the guts of the station with time to spare… or so she thought, anyway.

Xenecia came flying out of the intersecting passageway at full speed, shoulder checking Anarraham into the unforgiving bulkhead. The side of the woman's head slapped against the thick metal along with the rest of her body, and yet she still came away swinging. Xenecia easily deflected the attempts before slipping in to deliver two quick strikes to Anarraham's midsection. She followed that combination with a stunning uppercut, the blow nearly taking the woman off her feet. Punch drunk, barely standing, Anarraham refused to give up. She made one last play, charging desperately. The attempt was so futile, so pathetic that Xenecia almost felt pity for the woman as she demolished her with a standing high kick. The kick found its mark beneath her chin, snapping Anarraham's head back and spinning her around like a top before dropping her face-first to the floor.

This time she didn't resist when Xenecia moved to secure her. "Do you recall what you said earlier?" she asked, forcing Anarraham's hands behind her back.

The woman laughed as Xenecia hauled her up once more, the sound as thick and slurred as her words. "About you being a D-grade mercenary? Sorry, a cheap shot like that isn't about to change my mind."

"I meant about me frogmarching you off to meet my security friends."

"Ah." Anarraham spat a bloody wad at their feet. At least one of her teeth clattered to the floor with it. "That."

"Yes, that. *This* is that part."

* * *

The Triumvirate was an unusual bunch. Isolated and elevated above all others from birth, they had a removed, almost casual affectation about them. Far from awkward—no, they were too comfortable with themselves and one another for that—they projected the airy, dynastic confidence of those who take their people's approval for granted.

Such was the extent of their own species of self-worship that the Triumvirate required every meeting begin with a display of homage, no matter how small or seemingly mundane. As a result their chamber all but overflowed with an apparent random, altogether haphazard assortment of trinkets and baubles, knickknacks and curios, all of it stacked floor to ceiling and around and between their makeshift thrones. Some items were exceedingly valuable; others could only be charitably described as junk. The Triumvirate seemed to care not for the monetary value of any particular item, but rather what it represented to the giver.

For her tribute, Xenecia offered one of the teeth she had knocked free of Sergeant Anarrahamm's skull.

"How droll," said the first of the regents, as they preferred to be called individually, upon receipt of the tooth. "The offering is accepted. Let it be noted in the station log that this proceeding has commenced officially."

"Welcome, Xenecia of Shih'ra," the second regent continued. "We would first like to thank you for your service. The people of Over/Under Station owe you a great debt."

"A great debt, indeed," the third regent agreed. "Absent your actions, there is no telling what might have transpired."

Xenecia pursed her lips, waiting while the regents cycled through their script.

"Unfortunately, word of your exploits cannot leave this room," the first regent said in a thin, piping voice. His was the most removed, dispassionate.

Their ruling in and of itself was not entirely unexpected. Xenecia was hardly foolish enough to believe she would be celebrated for her role in preventing the station's destruction, not after leading its would-be saboteur directly to her objective. She knew that now. Still, something about their demeanor, the way they were feting her, stroking her ego… it gave her the unnerving sense that it was all in preparation for something much less desirable.

"Furthermore," he continued, "it is the summation of

this Triumvirate that all involved would benefit most were you to relocate your residency off-station."

And there it was. The other shoe dropping. Her role in saving the station wasn't simply being covered up…

She was being exiled.

"You will be provided with a generous parting stipend, of course, as well as transportation to the surface of Arathia. No doubt their intelligence service will want to debrief you about your experiences with this… what was her name?"

"Sergeant Soshi Anarraham," one of the regents' attendants supplied.

"Yes, that was it." Said as if he had not asked the sergeant's name to begin with, Xenecia noted with a stifled smirk.

"We're certain you shall find ample opportunities for yourself on the surface."

"And, really, who couldn't use a change of scenery once in a while?"

Her jaw tightening, Xenecia eyed the children of the Triumvirate with thinly veiled contempt. For to her that was exactly what they were: children. Fatuous, narcissistic wastrels, each and every one. She regarded them for so long from behind her vacuum-dark lenses that they began to shift uncomfortably under the glare of their own truth reflected back at them.

"Is there anything else we can do for you?" the third regent asked, hoping to hasten along her departure.

On that point, at least, they were in complete agreement. "Spare me the effort," Xenecia said as she turned her back on the Triumvirate for the last time. "I would not wish you to overexert yourselves."

* * *

The ruling of the Triumvirate was absolute. There was no higher authority to appeal to, no one with enough personal cache to—well, perhaps one... but no. She would not reduce herself to such petty groveling.

It took Xenecia little time to gather her effects. She preferred to travel light, after all. Her mare's leg, a bedroll, and a small bag with a few other choice provisions would more than adequately see her to the surface of Arathia. From there she would let instinct point her upon the right path, bullshit detector be damned.

The boarding line for the short-hop shuttle to the surface was dozens deep and still growing by the time Xenecia arrived. Flashing her writ from the Triumvirate, she was escorted to the front of the line to an accompanying chorus of moans from those already waiting. At least one of them was sure to be displaced by her unexpected arrival.

Not her problem, she reminded herself.

As she took her place at the head of the line a figure rose to greet her. Of all the people Xenecia would have expected to come see her off, the young woman with the lilac sash was among the last. Perhaps even more surprising was the realization that she was alone. Her three sisters were nowhere to be seen.

"I have no time to indulge the whims of your master," she said as Lilac Sash approached the boarding line. "Have you not heard? The Triumvirate has declared me *persona non grata*."

"I come on behalf of the Grom, though I speak for myself."

So, the Grom had not forsaken her, after all. Her interest piqued, she gestured for the woman to follow as she stepped off to the side of the waiting area. "Very well," she said, crossing her arms over chest. "You may speak."

"The Grom is grateful for the service you have provided the station. She wishes me to express her sincerest regret that she is unable to sway the Triumvirate in your favor."

At times such as this Xenecia envied humans their eyebrows and the ability to raise them dramatically. She settled for a look of smirking disbelief instead, one well honed through years of enduring conversations eerily similar to the one unfolding before her. "Unable? Or unwilling?"

Lilac Sash canted her head, the thin smile that played across her lips revealing nothing. "Does it matter?"

"I suppose not. Is that all, then?"

"The Grom wishes me to remind you that while this exile may seem as though an ending, it is also a new beginning. There is much in store for you yet, Xenecia of Shih'ra. Your destiny has always been written among the stars."

"Yes, well, sadly, destiny does not put food on my plate or build a shelter around me."

"Alas, no," Lilac Sash allowed. Then she smiled, almost sadly, and bowed. "Farewell, Xenecia."

Watching the *swish-swish-swish* of the handmaiden's gown trailing her toward the exit, Xenecia felt the anticlimax of the moment. That was it? That was all the Grom had for her? She wasn't sure what she had expected, only that she had imagined it being something palpable, substantial. Something she could carry with her going forward, not some damned windy, timeworn cliche.

"What is your name?"

The handmaiden stopped, her body tensing visibly beneath the elegant flow of her gown. The question was a trespass, she knew, yet she had no intention of withdrawing. Even if it was only the young woman's name, she was intent on taking something meaningful into exile with her.

Finally, the handmaiden chanced a glance over her shoulder, her voice hushed when she spoke. "Iliana."

"That is a very pretty name. Thank you, Iliana."

Iliana dipped her head in acknowledgement before fixing her gaze forward. The last Xenecia ever saw of the handmaiden was the swishing of her gown as she rounded the corner and disappeared in a trail of grace and ephemera.

A commotion on the far end of the deck drew Xenecia out of her reverie. There, the captain of an outward-bound freighter was berating one of his crew for some perceived slight or another. That was hardly her concern, though.

No, the object of her interest was the freighter itself. Long and sleek of body, it was certainly easy on the eyes. The telltale configuration of its jump-ready engines was even more attractive, especially as juxtaposed with the flying scrap heap waiting to condemn her to life on the surface of Arathia.

Overtaken by instinct—and perhaps to some extent the parting notes of her conversation with Iliana—Xenecia strode straight up to the captain and asked, "What is this vessel's charter?"

The captain paid her no heed initially, too busy consulting his flexpad for their position on the star chart to lift his eyes as he answered. "You, my good woman, are looking at the *Pursuit of Capital*, bound for Morgenthau-Hale incorporated space."

That augured well for her odds, she thought. "How much to secure a spot aboard?"

"In case you hadn't noticed, we're not exactly a passenger ship…"

Not exactly a strong no, though the man was still studiously avoiding eye contact. Xenecia produced a substantial ingot from a secret pouch within her vest, the better to negotiate her position. "Perhaps this will be sufficient to convince you otherwise?"

That got his attention and kept it. Tipping his brow, the captain inspected the ingot as she held it aloft. "Hell, that would cover a suite on a long-haul civilian vessel. Nice one, too."

"Then consider it my payment." She placed the valuable metal in his hand.

"Done," the captain said, pocketing the ingot with the swiftness of a man who feared his new passenger might have a sudden change of heart. "Welcome aboard, Miss…?"

Xenecia considered herself before answering the question. "You may call me Iliana." With a wave to the waiting boarding line, she forfeited the seat the Triumvirate had held for her.

Minutes later she was strapping herself in as the *Pursuit of Capital* readied for flight. "Tell me," she asked the young crewman securing himself across from her, "is there good hunting to be had in Morgenthau-Hale territory?"

"What, like criminals? Not so much in the corporate center, but out on the fringes where we're headed, ho yeah, you bet. The Haleys are still expanding and they don't care whose toes they have to step on to shore things up. Lots of strife and unrest going on in the local systems." The crewman paused, studying her critically as if only taking note of her unique disposition for the first time. "Not so sure they're going to like the looks of you much, though…"

Xenecia's lips curled into a sly, crescent smile. Story of her life, she thought. The stars would not have had it any other way.

"I believe I shall take my chances."

Q&A with Logan Thomas Snyder

Very cool world you've built here. What's your favorite part of writing a short story like this, and of writing SF in general?

Thank you! My favorite part about writing SF in general is marrying relatable characters with the scope of the genre. As for this story, it takes place within the same universe as my space opera novel *The Lazarus Particle*. It was a blast to return to the Particleverse, so much so that I intend to expand it into a series of stories over the next few years.

How does this story fit into the timeline of the Particleverse?

This story takes place before the events of *The Lazarus Particle*. It's not exactly a prequel, but it does offer a bit more insight into Xenecia and her motivations. Plus it was just fun to write! *The Lazarus Particle* picks up where this story leaves off, so be sure to check it out if you enjoyed "Spike in a Rail."

How long have you been writing, and what's your long-term plan?

I started writing fiction in late 2010 and took the plunge as an independent author in 2014. Since then I haven't looked back! My long-term plan is to keep writing, expand my audience, and hopefully go full-time in the near future.

What are your current works-in-progress?

Right now I'm finishing up my original contribution to Ann Christy's *Between Life and Death* series, a standalone novel titled *Between Kings and Carnage*. After that I'll be returning to the Particleverse with a follow-up to *The Lazarus Particle* titled *The Nemesis Cabal*. I also have some other projects floating around in my head, but those two are my primary focus for 2016 and beyond.

Where can readers find you?

My official website is LoganThomasSnyder.com. Readers can learn more about me there, plus join my mailing list for updates, free books, and more. I'm also on Facebook and Twitter. I love hearing from readers and fellow authors alike, so feel free to reach out and say hello!

The First to Fall
by Sabrina Locke

MY SANDALS CRUNCH through the top layer of crisp reeds into the damp muck of soil and decomposing plant matter below. I try not to think about what crawls and burrows beneath my feet. Just because I've studied the techniques used on terraformed planets for creating walkways that also develop biomass doesn't mean I want it squishing between my toes.

I'd give anything for a pair of regulation-issue settler boots now. Ducking out of an official cultural reception while, at the same time, avoiding my mother's all-seeing gaze hadn't given me time to change. With any luck, I'll be back before she notices my absence.

Hovering security lights cast the rows of boarded shops and small stalls in a haze of blue light that makes everything look unreal. I imagine the marketplace has been abandoned for generations instead of merely shuttered for the night. Of course, this is impossible because the planet, Lakhish Alpha, hasn't been settled that long. Everything here is raw and primitive and new, and although I am not allowed to have opinions, I like it.

My great flaw (according to my mother) is that I see what I want to see rather than simply note what is. Newsflash: she's the one who sees what she wants to see. My chances of convincing her of this fact? Absolute zero.

A shutter slams, and I spin around.

"Hello?"

Silence.

I'm not supposed to be planetside alone, not that I ever pay attention to that particular listing in the one hundred and eighty-seven regulations regarding the behavior of the children of Galactic Two Ambassadors. We (meaning my parents—the ambassadors—along with their staff and support troops) are leaving Lakhish Alpha in a little over forty-eight standard hours.

Earlier today and in preparation for tonight's affair, my mother went through my things while I was in class. She claimed she needed items of *cultural significance* to gift to the Lakhishan people. Considering that an embassy ship like the *Stanhope* has no waste and little cargo space, she must have been desperate because she gathered an entire box of things to donate for the reception. The justification for her thievery? *You're a young lady now and no longer a child. Time to put away childish toys.*

She had no right.

When I'd returned to my quarters and discovered what she'd done, I'd protested to the ship's steward, Kendall. He'd taken her side, of course. I'm old enough to have started noticing the way he looks at her when he thinks no one is watching.

The things she'd taken were treasures I'd carefully selected when we'd embarked from Triton Station two days after my sixth birthday. We'd departed the Terran system for the second (ever) survey of settled worlds. For ten long standard years, each toy and book and trinket had been my only connection to the past, the only things I can truly call my own. My most precious possession is a small figure I named Paladin.

When I discovered he was missing, I'd torn apart the bulkheads, sending dresses and shoes flying, to no avail. My red-eyed appearance at dinner before the reception extracted no more than a cool glance and a sniff of disapproval from my mother. I think my father might have noticed or even done something if he'd been there. Not only had he missed dinner, but he'd also failed to show up for the reception. Kendall claimed he was sequestered with Lakhishan officials over yet another security crisis.

Whatever.

It's always something, and I rarely see my father these days.

Surprisingly, it was Kendall who came through. He came up to me at the reception and whispered that he might have seen Paladin in the box of gifts that had already been sent down to the planet. It's more likely that he noticed my sullen attitude and taken action before my mother noticed, as well.

I only cared that he'd given me a chance to retrieve Paladin before it was too late.

The small figure looks like a fanciful knight, in my opinion, which is why I'd given him his name. No one knows anything about the culture or species that had created him except that they'd been humanoid and that he was really, really old (no matter how time is measured).

To all appearances, Paladin is a child's toy, about thirty centimeters tall, and made from a very strong, but incredibly lightweight crystalline substance. Depending on available light, Paladin shifts from an opaque bronze to nearly transparent.

He'd been a gift from the people of the first world we'd visited on our trip. I don't remember the name of the planet. Our visit had been more for supplies than for diplomatic reasons.

The first night I'd set Paladin next to my bed. When the ambient lighting in the room dimmed for sleep, he'd begun to glow. Something deep within the form had whirled, sending light like shimmering stars bouncing off the walls and ceiling. I'd remained awake for hours, mesmerized by the play of light and shadow.

I made up stories about him: that he was a relic from some ancient culture or a statue of a forgotten god or the plaything of lost and lonely princess.

I was six.

My mother never liked Paladin. I overheard her arguing with my father. "Poorly crafted," she'd said. "The proportions are not pleasing, and the coloration is rather garish. It looks like one of those cheap lamps from Luna that are supposed to change colors depending upon one's mood. Is that the sort of aesthetic you want to teach your daughter?"

My father had argued it was a gift. "Like it or not, we have no choice but to keep it."

I remember my mother's face turning hard and closed. To my father, she'd said, "In future, please be aware we haven't the space to collect every trinket these people seem to be determined to bestow upon us. They think every old thing is priceless when they cannot possibly understand true value. They've never been off world, for goodness sake, which means they lack true perspective. It's a pity, really, but there's nothing we can do.

She'd turned to me next. "I say this, by way of instruction for you, my dear, and not in a spirit of criticism. We must be better than those with whom we deal. They don't have our advantages."

It was after that argument that she'd started the cultural exchanges with every planet and system we visited. I hated but tolerated them until she'd crossed a line by taking Paladin.

Silence still reigns while my breath forms filmy puffs in the air before me.

In moments like this, it's hard to remember I love my mother. Despite her snooty attitude, I never imagined she'd dare to get rid of Paladin after my father expressly forbade her doing so. Didn't she know what Paladin meant to me? I didn't care about his appearance or the lack of artistry evidenced by his unknown creator.

Muffled voices echo through the marketplace. I freeze.

A man and a woman wearing the loose trousers, tunics and sturdy boots issued to settlers pass underneath the icy blue glow of the security lamps on the street just outside the gate to the marketplace. Another man runs after them, laughing, throwing up clumps of soil and muck as he stumbles along. They reach one of the saloons and disappear inside, leaving me alone once again.

Paladin, where are you?

I'm not afraid of the dark—on the *Stanhope*—but the dark on a settled world is different, deeper, thicker. This is a lesson my father taught me not long after he gave me Paladin. "The planets we settle might appear to be uninhabited by sentient life," he'd said. "But we must never assume, especially when a planet is old."

He'd never explained further what he meant. Aren't all planets old? I'd always taken him to mean we must always be on the lookout for things that hide in the dark.

Focus.

A memory swarms before I can stop it…

My father's face looming over me as the technician places the mask over my lips. I suck a mouthful of the bitter gas.

Panic.

I beat at the technician's hands, trying to push the mask away. My father's warm hands covering mine, holding my arms down.

"Don't be afraid," he whispers. "You're going to go to sleep, that's all. Just like you go to sleep every night. The only difference is that when you wake up, you'll have a new body. Your special body, remember?"

Nausea makes the ceiling spin. I blink rapidly to stay awake. My father's face ripples. "Remember how you got to pick out your special body? You wanted blond hair and blue eyes so you'd look just like your doll."

He strokes my forehead, kisses my cheek and whispers,

"Sleep tight, Pumpkin, and when you wake up, we'll go on a great adventure."

I close my eyes and sink into darkness.

Eventually, I had awakened, as my father promised, in a new body with spiffy, perfect skin and shiny hair just like I'd chosen from the catalog. A body designed by scientists and grown in a tank on Triton Station for space travel because humans had learned the hard way that our original bodies could not pass the outer limits of the Terran system.

I remember that first day in my new body. I felt like a mouse lost in a giant amusement park. My new form felt huge. It was somewhat bigger than my previous six-year-old body, although generally appropriate. The new body would grow slowly over the subsequent five to seven standard years in a process that loosely mimicked the human maturation process.

While I travel the galaxy with my parents on the *Stanhope*, my old body sleeps in a tank on Triton Station. Theoretically, I could take up my old body at any time. As far as I know, no one has ever done so. The very idea seems distasteful, like taking a bite of warm meat that's been left on the counter overnight.

"Paladin?"

A shadowy form slips from between two market stalls.

I gasp, my heart beating faster.

The stranger doesn't say a word. Tension prickles the back of my neck. Sensors in my peripheral vision kick up a notch, signs my body senses immanent threat. I think about all the stories I've read where the heroine encounters a stranger in a dark place, and then terrible things ensue.

All of the inhabitants of Lakhish Alpha had been born

here of human stock from Seed Launches blasted from Earth thousands of generations ago. They are conventional and totally organic beings, born of and for this world, this system, in the same way original Terrans populated Earth—the Heritage World.

I take a deep breath and then another and push back the fear, reminding myself I'm an ambassador: the consciousness of girl housed in the strongest, most advanced body human science has ever imagined. I've been trained in self-defense even though I'd never had occasion to use those skills. It's rare that my internal warning system ever alerts me to anything more serious than a too-hot spoonful of soup.

I take a step back from the stranger and assume the Still Water stance.

A breeze ruffles her long hair. Something long and metal glints under the lights. She glides forward.

She.

Lakhish Alpha is a matriarchal society. I relax. "Do you operate one of the shops?"

If the Lakhishan people are the same as those on other worlds, items from the cultural receptions find their way into shops quickly, which is why I'd headed straight for the marketplace. "I'm looking for something. A figure about this tall?" I open my hands parallel to the ground, palms facing to show Paladin's size.

More silence.

"It was sent down from the embassy earlier by mistake. I will gladly reimburse you for your trouble," I offer.

She moves forward again, more slowly this time. She's one of the oldest humans I've ever seen. Gray hair floats in a cloud around a face etched with lines of age. She wears a wrap of some kind over her tunic. Her shoulders are hunched. Her gnarled hands clutch a basket woven of the same reeds as those strewn over the walkways.

She lifts the basket. A pearly light glows beneath the rough, woven cloth.

My hand drifts toward my mouth. "Paladin?"

The glow intensifies.

I reach for the basket. The old woman hisses and tosses the basket at me, her hands flying in the air as she backs away. I fumble for the basket and miss. It thuds on the ground. The cloth falls away and a translucent, shining Paladin sinks into the mud.

Using the cloth, I wipe the dirt and moisture away and tuck him inside my jacket.

When I'm finished, I look around.

The old woman is gone.

Red blotches stain the cloth as if someone had bled onto it recently. I turn my hands over but find no marks or scratches that could have produced the stains.

From my pocket, I pull three of the small white metal discs that pass for currency here, tie them in the stained cloth, and toss the bundle inside the stall closest to where I'd first seen the woman. I have no way of knowing if the exchange of coins is the proper way to complete a transaction, but I figure that if she'd wanted payment, she would have stuck around.

Paladin's glow warms me as I head back to the ship.

* * *

All mothers have this look, I'm told. The one that says *you really screwed up this time and only the fact that I love you prevents me from killing you.*

My mother has long since perfected this look, which is why I recognize it when the airlock swishes shut behind me. Her perfectly almond brown eyes sweep from my tousled hair to my muddy (ruined) sandals. A tiny muscle ticks under the creamy caramel of her jaw.

"So, how'd the reception go?" No point in acting penitent when I'm feeling anything but sorry for what I've done.

My mother looks too angry to speak. Fortunately, footsteps echo in the corridor, giving each of us a reprieve before one of us launches the first verbal missile in the inevitable argument. She glances over her shoulder. Even though she's in profile, I watch a change come over her expression. It's a look I've noticed often but never understood before.

The ship's steward comes to a halt at my mother's side, and I'm studying them like they're people I've never seen before: my mother, slim and elegant in her red gown, Kendall, equally slim and neat in his black and white dress uniform. They look like a pair who belong on top of a cake.

Kendall and my mother? Why had I never seen this before?

Like all the first level staff members on the *Stanhope*, Kendall had been issued an ambassadorial body. I'd always assumed that he, like everyone else, had selected the physical characteristics of his new body from the catalog. If that were true, why would anyone—given a virtually unlimited array of possible traits—have selected a relatively short and unassuming appearance? He's barely taller than my mother. I've never been able to decide if his lackluster brown hair is thinning due to a minor manufacturing defect or if he'd actually chosen "thinning hair" from the body menu.

Weird.

If I had to do it all over again, I'd ask for bigger boobs. Boobs are not important to your average almost-six-year-old. At the time, I'd focused on looking like my doll, which meant I wanted long arms and legs and to be able to run really, really fast. Boobs only got in the way of that goal.

Not that I had a lot of opportunity to show off boobs of any size. With no one my age aboard the *Stanhope*, an actual date with an actual guy remains something I can only dream about. Procreation had been deemed in conflict with the mission, so that meant no more children for my parents and none for me. Ever. If I ever decided I wanted children in the future, I'd have to go back to Triton Station and get my old body back. They were supposed to be maintained in a pristine state. Like anyone believed the claims.

Before we'd left Triton Station, I remembered my parents arguing about whether or not to take me with them. My father took the *pro* side while my mother pounded him with all the *cons*, chief among them being that I would never have a so-called *normal* life; normal being code for having children. Father had insisted we would make it back some day and our Terran bodies would be waiting for us—good as new. Mother never bought that argument, which is why she hadn't wanted me to accompany them.

I didn't understand a fraction of the science involved in the creation of ambassador bodies, but I believed one thing: centuries or even millennia in a tank couldn't be good for a body. Any body.

Not that I wanted children.

Not that my parents ever stopped arguing about Paladin.

My mother considers my attachment to Paladin to be odd and unnatural and reflects some trauma (imagined or inflicted) related to a child's consciousness being ripped from the body of origin too soon.

Since when had such a thing as switching bodies ever been normal? I wanted to ask, but never had the nerve.

My mother's theory is like a lot of theories. It sounds good and maybe even looks good on the surface, but fails upon closer examination. I love my new body, I don't care about children, and she is dead wrong about Paladin. Period.

I am not a grape plucked from the vine before its time. I am a girl, ordinary homo sapiens, and if there is one thing at which our species excels, it is the ability to adapt.

And then I understand. My mother has adapted as well, and in her own way.

I'm old enough now to see that ten standard years of arguing over everything from policy decisions to which toys I'm allowed must have taken a toll on my parent's marriage. They never agreed on anything, from how to approach newly settled planets to something as trivial as Paladin. Even though my mother is also an ambassador, she's been shut out of critical negotiations and relegated to a merely social role.

Something passes between my mother and Kendall. She gives an almost imperceptible shake of her head and rests her hand on his arm.

Turning back to me, my mother says, "I was worried. Kendall didn't even know where you were." Her delicate nostrils flare.

I wait for Kendall to speak, which is pointless since my mother's hand is still resting on his arm.

I let go of any hope of salvaging the situation. If she didn't want a fight, she shouldn't have stolen Paladin. "Do I get a chance to explain myself or shall we go straight to passing judgment and announcing how long I'll be confined to my quarters for my crimes?"

"You were irresponsible. The planet isn't safe. You should have informed Kendall of your whereabouts."

I wait for Kendall to speak and explain, but he doesn't. *Betrayal noted and logged.* "Can I ask you a question?"

My mother sighs. "Of course, you can. Why would you ask such a thing?"

"Do you care about me at all? Even a little?"

She sucks in a breath and tiny lines crinkle around her eyes. "Fallan Elizabeth Jin-Dahl, that is enough. The ambassador has restricted you to your quarters until further notice."

The ambassador? "Getting a little grand, aren't you, Mom? Referring to yourself in the third person?"

A muscle jumps in her jaw. "The orders come straight from your father."

"I want to talk to him."

"So do I." Then she sighs and mutters, "For all the good it will do me."

I can see fine lines of worry around her eyes and tightness in the skin around her lips. In a conventional, organic Terran body, such evidence of stress would be normal; that they're showing up a scant ten standard years into the life of an ambassadorial body designed for a thousand years of use must be pissing her off royally.

"I want to talk to my father."

"We can't."

"Why not?"

It's Kendall who answers. "Because he's sequestered with the Tengay faction."

I frown. The embassy ship has been orbiting Lakhish Alpha much longer than was usual. The *Stanhope*'s mission, to make contact with all of the worlds settled from the Seed Launches, would require every bit of the vastly long life of our bodies. And that was if we didn't spend too long at each planet in the settled systems.

We should have moved on to the next system already. I'd been told the delay was due to the threat of civil war. My tutor and I researched the situation, but that had been nearly a standard year ago, and the details are foggy in my mind. The main point I'd come away with from that unit of study was that the Seeded planets were designed and engineered to be free of the wars and aggression that had plagued Earth for millennia. As a consequence, any sign of war (civil or otherwise) must be ruthlessly removed, no matter the cost. That being said, I knew my father would do almost anything to settle burgeoning conflicts, including making a deal with the Tengay faction. Yet another subject over which he and my mother had frequently battled, with my mother saying there was no point in negotiating with terrorists like the Tengay.

"When do you think he'll be free?" I ask, softening my tone.

She shrugs as if she doesn't care, but her tone is bitter. "There's no way of telling. You know your father. He won't quit until he's certain he has an agreement that will stand."

"So that means we're not leaving tomorrow, then?"

"I don't know when we're leaving. Your father hasn't bothered to let me know." Silence spools out between us. She strokes my cheek. "I'm so sorry. I never wanted this for you—"

I cut her off and recite the words I've heard her say a million times. "—*because we probably won't ever make it home again and I'm afraid you'll forget what it's like to be human.* Well, guess what, Mom? I like this body, and I don't ever want my old one back."

"You don't know what you're saying, sweetheart."

"I know I'll never be good enough to please you."

She pulls her hand away and then reaches under my jacket, extracting Paladin from where I'd hidden him. "Is this why you're so angry?"

"You had no right to take him."

She stares at the toy for what feels like a long time. Finally, she shakes her head, and it feels like she's admitting defeat. "I've tried. I've done all I can. It's up to you now." She thrusts Paladin into my hands, turns on her heel and stalks down the corridor.

While vague guilt wars with leftover resentment, I stand there feeling confused and oddly bereft.

"If I may—" Kendall begins.

"Way to have my back. Not."

"Matters are more complicated than they appear. Surely you're old enough to understand that now."

I can guess what he's hinting at, but I don't want to go there, and hold up a hand. "Stop. You don't have to explain anything."

He blinks. "I was going to—"

"What part of *stop* did you not understand? If you're

worried I'll tell my father, don't." I have to look away. "I don't even want to think about it, let alone talk to anyone about it."

"If you'll permit me to finish," Kendall says slowly, "I suggested earlier that you go planetside because I thought it would be safer for you. I couldn't very well admit that to your mother, now could I?"

"Safer? What sort of punishment did you think she was going to dish out? Or have you and my mother been spending your alone time thinking up kinky new ones?"

I can tell I've gone too far when the mask of the perfect steward slides over his expression. He bows slightly from the waist and smiles. "I'm pleased you returned safely, Miss Fallan." He gestures toward Paladin, still cradled in my arms. "I'll be happy to tidy him up for you."

Since Paladin is still coated in muck, I pass him to Kendall and allow the steward to escort me to my quarters. I do not protest when I hear him key the locking sequence into the security panel.

* * *

I drift in and out of sleep, dreams crawling up out of the dark like worms from the soil wriggling between my toes. Every so often, I jerk to a semi-awake state, convinced a bright light has been sweeping across the room. I sit upright, my heart pounding in total darkness, before sinking back into sleep.

The third time it happens, I stay awake and swing my legs over the side of the bed.

Darkness looms like an unwelcome guest. Something is very wrong.

Lights embedded in wall panels should have brightened as soon as my feet touched the floor. The room remains shrouded in darkness.

I pat the flat surface next to the bed, searching for Paladin, remembering only moments later that I'd given him to Kendall for cleaning.

Cold wraps itself around me like a wet blanket. I exhale, feeling my breath's chill against my skin. I'm fully capable of adjusting my body's temperature, but that should not be necessary aboard the *Stanhope* with its state-of-the art environmental controls.

Blinking hard to bring up night vision, I scan the room. I'm not alone.

A male form huddles in the tiny study alcove between the door and my closet. I inhale sharply, but he doesn't move. Does he think I can't see him? Any of the upper-level staff would know they can't hide. Temporary personnel hired from Lakhish Alpha, however, wouldn't know that nor would they have access to the ambassador level of the ship.

He clutches a small rectangular device in his left hand. Scanner? That explained the flashes of light that had awakened me. He'd been searching for something.

A wave of weariness sweeps over me, making me want desperately to curl back into the comfort of my bed and close my eyes. I curl my fingers into fists, fighting the sensation.

The door to my quarters swooshes open, the sudden flash of light from the passageway temporarily blinding me.

Someone shouts, "Take him!"

The sounds of scuffling, fighting, bodies pounding into the walls of the corridor echo. In the distance, I hear weapons fire.

I bolt to my feet, bringing up my internal defensive systems. The bitter tang of blood registers in my nose.

I face another intruder, this one silhouetted in the doorway. *Kendall.*

"What's happened?" I asked.

"I'm sorry, Fallan." Kendall's soft voice barely registers over the advancing sounds of fighting in the hallway. "If only you'd listened and stayed on the planet. Your father's going to ruin everything. I can't let that happen."

I shake my head in confusion. "What are you talking about? What's going on?

He mutters to himself before looking back at me. "She said we had to stop him. This was the only way. I promised her I'd save you . . ." His voice trails off, and a sob escapes his lips.

"Kendall?" I reach for him. "Please, tell me—"

Fury contorts his face. "I tried, but it's too late." Something metal glints in his hand. He lunges.

I step aside, barely escaping the swing of his knife. Before I can pivot, the dark form explodes from the corner. He and Kendall go down brawling. Light flashes and flesh sizzles.

I scramble out of the room and fumble with the security panel embedded in the corridor wall, attempting to close and seal the door.

A hand touches my shoulder. "We're not here to hurt you."

I wheel around until our faces are only inches apart—a

guy about my age, wearing a stained and rumpled black and white ambassadorial staff uniform.

I back away from him while glancing up and down the corridor that is now eerily silent. "Who are you?"

"My name is Alden Hendrix, and that's my brother, Finn." He gestures at the guy now standing over Kendall's body. He wears the black vest and body armor emblazoned with the Jin-Dahl crest. The blade Kendall thrust at me now dangles in his long-fingered grasp.

They are both tall and broad-shouldered, strong-looking young men, one light, one dark—like mirrors of each other.

My chest tightens and my breath goes shallow.

Alden leans forward. "Do you need to sit down?"

I look at Kendall's body. "Is he dead?"

Finn nudges him with his foot. "Don't think so, but it's always hard to get the stun settings just right, so I can't make any guarantee." He shrugs.

I remember the smell of burning flesh.

My stomach lurches, and I bolt down the corridor.

"Wait," one of them shouts.

I run for the safe room tucked behind the schoolroom at the end of the hall. Footsteps pound behind me.

I shout the emergency word and press my thumb against the security panel and squeeze through the door and seal it without waiting for the protocols to complete.

I lean against the door, breathing heavily.

The cool metal thuds beneath my shoulder blades. "Fallan, it's Alden," he shouts from the other side. "We don't want to hurt you, I promise."

"Yeah? Tell that to Kendall."

"The guy who tried to kill you? I think you've got things backward."

I still at his words, remembering the creepy mix of regret and anger in Kendall's voice when he'd said, *I tried, but it's too late* before trying to sink a knife in my chest.

Alden pounds on the door again. "We're here to help you. Please let me in."

It's hard to think straight. Who was Kendall? The kindly steward who'd always covered for me when I snitched an extra piece of cake, the friend who'd clued me in on what had happened to Paladin, the man who'd conspired with my mother against my father, the man who'd tried to kill me.

My mother and I might not have the best of relationships, but never would I believe she'd authorize my death.

Or had Kendall been acting without her knowledge? Had he fooled her, as well?

Strange young men I've never seen before managed to evade the ship's security scans, steal uniforms and save my life while the loyal steward who'd signed on to serve my family for the millennium had betrayed us. . .

Nothing made sense.

But one of those young men had been searching my room.

I key the all-clear sequence and open the door.

"What was your brother looking for?"

Alden utters a word I don't understand, which is unusual because I know thirty-eight languages.

"It's a figure of a man about this high." His hands sketch the distance.

"Paladin."

"That's what you call it?"

"It's his name. It's just a toy. I can't imagine what you'd want with it. It has no value. That's why my mother tried to get rid of it with the cultural exchange."

"We know." Alden drags a hand through his white-blond hair. "We also know you brought—" he says the strange name again "—back to the ship. Where is it?"

I fold my arms across my chest. "Well, you could ask Kendall, but you killed him."

Alden swears under his breath. "I don't think he's dead."

I follow him back to my quarters.

When we arrive, I see that Finn has lifted Kendall onto the bed. The steward is trussed at the wrist, knees and ankles with flexible ties and gagged with one of my scarves.

Paladin, clean and shiny as the day my father first put him in my hands, stands next to the bed.

"Where did you find him?" I ask Finn, indicating Paladin.

"When I got done with him," Finn nods at Kendall, "I looked up and there it was. It wasn't there earlier when I scanned the room. I don't know how it got there." He and Alden exchange a look.

Alden walks over to the door and sticks his head out, looking right and left. "It's clear for now, but we need to get out of here."

Both guys stare at me like they're waiting for something. "So go ahead, leave. I won't stop you."

Alden checks a device on his wrist. "You can't stay here. It's not safe."

"He's right," Finn adds. "We're running out of time."

"For what?"

"If you come with us," Finn says in a gentle voice that

shreds my last nerve, "we'll explain later. But we need to go. Now."

"No!" I'm fighting tears that make no sense.

"We're not going to leave you here alone."

"I'm not alone. My father is the ambassador and—"

Alden shakes his head. "Not anymore."

I remember the fighting, the tang of blood in the air.

Before either of them can stop me, I sprint for my parent's quarters.

When I get there, the security panel is jammed and won't open with the emergency word or my retinal scan. I tear open the panel and disable critical circuits. I'm madly ripping wires when Finn and Alden come up behind me. Without words, they help. Even then, it takes all three of us to manually push the door wide enough to enter.

The sitting area, normally light and bright, is dark, the furniture tumbled and my mother's treasures in disarray. My hand curls around the armrest of an antique Terran chair. French and very old. My parents had argued over bringing it with us, but my mother had won that battle.

I creep toward the bedroom, my pace slowed by rising nausea. I keep telling myself silently that everything is going to be all right. My parents wouldn't have been in their quarters, anyway. At the first sign of trouble, they would have escaped to the safe room.

"Mother?"

I pass through the doorway into the bedroom.

The stench of blood and feces hits me, and dread claws at my stomach.

My mother lies curled on her side on the bed, motionless, her head turned at an impossible angle. The black hair she always keeps immaculately styled spills across her face. Red lights flash on and off above the bed.

I want to believe she's asleep. I want to believe I'm having a terrible dream from which I'll awaken any minute.

"Mom?" I approach the bed.

Tears stream down my cheeks. I push her hair away from her too pale face.

The pressure of a hand on my shoulder pulls me backward. I jerk away from the touch.

"You don't want to see this." I don't know if the voice is Finn or Alden. I don't care.

I turn, half-blind with tears. "We can save her. There's a way if we can get her to the infirmary."

I roll my mother onto her back. Her torso gapes open like the lapels of a flesh-toned dressing gown from where she was sliced from sternum to crotch with brutal efficiency. Whoever killed her knew what they were doing. They used the one sure and certain way to kill an ambassadorial body.

Ropes of pink guts spill onto the bedding.

Strong hands drag me away from the bed, off the ship and down to the surface of Lakhish Alpha.

* * *

It could have been days or even weeks later in the way we measured time aboard the *Stanhope*, but Terran standard time didn't matter because the rebels—the Tengay faction—had blown the ship not long after Finn, Alden and I escaped. All I'd taken with me were the clothes on my back and Paladin.

My mother is dead, my father missing and presumed dead, and I am the *guest* of the people of Lakhish Alpha.

Sort of.

They tolerate me because of Paladin. Apparently, we were a matched set, like peanut butter and chocolate; can't have one without the other.

That was one of the things I learned from Alden Hendrix on his frequent visits to the small house I'd been given. At least to my face they call it a house; it feels more like a prison. The guards stationed at every entrance don't help, but considering what happened to my family, I can't complain.

Although, if I had any way of knowing the facts of my situation, it would have helped considerably. Had Kendall been working with the Tengay terrorists? Or were his actions part of some plan he and my mother had hatched in opposition to my father? The only way I could find out for sure would be to talk to my father, but first, I'd have to find him.

On one of his visits, I ask Alden, "You knew they were going to destroy the ship, didn't you?"

We sit on the porch on chairs fashioned from the ever-present reeds they seem to use for everything on the planet. I drag a finger over the sleeve of the shirt I wear. It's blue and made from (guess what?) the same plant material, except that they'd found a way to process the fibers, making them soft and pliable.

"We suspected, but didn't know for sure. All we had to go on were rumors that the ambassador," he hesitates, the pulse at the base of his throat quickening, "that your father had secret orders he would not hesitate to follow if an agreement could not be achieved between the Lakhishan elders and the rebels."

He's told me this story about my father many times. As if it would take multiple tellings to convince me that the ambassador ordered to unilaterally enforce peace had been about to engage the *Stanhope's* powerful laser cannons and eliminate the problem altogether. Along with what passed for civilization in this sector.

That scenario sounded more like a plan my mother would back.

No matter how many times I heard the story, I didn't want to believe it. If destroying the planet had been on my father's agenda, why had he remained in orbit so long? Why had he worked so hard to bring the warring parties to the peace table?

Without my father, I have only questions.

After Alden checks the hour about fifteen times, I stand. "I'm ready."

Finn waits for us in the street, and with one brother on either side, I walk to the Hall of Justice.

* * *

I don't know what I expect. Wait, yes I do. I suspected the hearing should look like something out of the old vids: a simple courtroom in a frame building with lots of windows to let in light. The justice should be a tall male dressed in somber robes. Maybe he will address those gathered to listen to his words of wisdom.

Utter nonsense.

Or wishful thinking.

I studied the various iterations of the Rule of Law, as it's known and practiced in the Terran system. The Seeded worlds were free of such notions, radically free, because they could do as they pleased as long as their actions didn't harm anyone else. That meant there was no standard Rule of Law across the universe.

The Lakhishan elders took pains to point out that *they* had not destroyed my family and the *Stanhope*. The blame fell on the mysterious Tengay faction, the same rebels who threatened Lakhish Alpha.

I would have had some idea of what to do or say if my wishful thinking about trust in the Rule of Law and my father's power had any basis in reality. I let go of my fantasies when I say goodbye to Finn and Alden and walk up the stone steps of the Hall of Justice.

An attendant ushers me into an antechamber. Thickly woven carpets cover the planked floor and soft, brightly colored textiles flank the windows. Three of the walls are lined with low couches layered with a multitude of embroidered cushions.

A round pouf of a seat commands the center of the room. The attendant indicates I am to sit there.

Curtains flutter though there's no breeze. A section of the wall panel slides apart and an old, old woman hobbles through the opening. She supports her weight with a cane that looks as if it has been carved from a thicker, heavier variety of reed. A cloud of silver-white hair haloes her face.

It seems to take an eternity, but she finally makes her way to the bank of cushions in the middle of the wall and lowers herself with great pain and ceremony.

Behind me, the main door swings open. Finn and Alden enter, taking posts on either side of the entrance with their legs spread wide, hands clasped before them, like sentries or soldiers.

Do they fear I'm going to harm the old woman?

I try to make eye contact, but the brothers ignore me, keeping their gazes trained on the invisible horizon.

I turn back to the woman I suppose is my judge, jury, and executioner.

"I am the—" she utters a word I can't make out, "But you may call me Merin." She reaches into the depths of her red robe, pulling out a knotted bundle of cloth. Slowly, reverently, she unfolds the layers of cloth.

Paladin.

She sets the figure on a low, round table. The moment her fingers release him, Paladin begins to glow, his color gradually shifting from a dark, solid bronze color, moving through the light spectrum until he beams a clear, rosy light.

She leans back and folds her hands in her lap. "As you can see, we have followed your wishes and taken good care of your friend."

"Thank you." I'm ridiculously happy to see Paladin again.

Merin is the chief elder of the Lakhishan people and today she will decide my fate. Despite that knowledge, all I can think about when I stare at Paladin is the day my father pressed the toy into my hands. Where is my father now? Is he still alive? Tears well. I have to blink and swallow several times to regain my composure.

"Do you have anything to say in your defense?" Merin asks.

This is what Finn and Alden and I have discussed for weeks. What I knew of the terrorist plot in which Kendall, and possibly my mother, had been deeply embedded, when I knew it, the extent to which I'd been involved, how much my mother had known, including an entire line of questioning where it was clear she was suspected of funding and supporting the terrorists.

I knew almost nothing. My answers satisfied neither Finn nor Alden. There was no reason to think this day and this hearing would be any different.

"I can only tell you that I did not have any knowledge of my mother's plans. I was not aware and remain unconvinced she was allied with the terrorists. I believe the ship's steward, Kendall, took advantage of his relationship with her." I took a breath and gathered my courage. "If you truly believe my mother would have turned the *Stanhope*'s weapons on the people of Lakhish Alpha, I hope your belief is based in fact, not rumors. I would like to see your evidence—if you have any."

The old woman laughs. "Child, child, we are not here to discuss your mother or your missing father, for that matter."

"I don't understand."

"Ambassador Jin-Dahl did, indeed, bring a weapon to Lakhish Alpha aboard his great ship. We knew this from the start." Her expression grows serious. "The Tengay knew this secret, as well. They wanted the weapon, as did we. Despite the efforts of the Tengay to alter the balance of power, the weapon was not destroyed with the ship nor did it fall into their hands."

"Finn and Alden were hunting for the weapon that night."

Merin nods. "Your father alerted us to the possibility of the attack. It is my regret we failed to intervene in time to save your mother. The Tengay blew the ship because they did not want anyone else to possess the weapon."

For a long moment, grief rises in my throat until I cannot bear to think of all I've lost.

Merin sighs heavily and gestures with her cane at Paladin. "You think this thing is a toy. You even gave it a name."

I swipe at the corners of my eyes. "What does a toy have to do with anything?"

She waves the cane in the air again impatiently. "Pick it up. Now."

When I'm seated again with the Paladin in my lap, she says, "Alden tells me you are able to use Paladin to make the stars dance."

"If that's what you want to call it. It makes for a pretty show."

"More than a show. It is a weapon, my girl, one of the most powerful weapons ever created. It links to one user and one user alone. In case you were wondering, that would be you."

"I don't believe you."

She pounds her cane on the floor. "It is hot in here. Open the window."

I start to rise.

She pounds the cane on the floor again, louder this time. "No, with the weapon. Use it. Use the energy of the weapon and open the window." While she had been speaking, the light coming from Paladin has brightened considerably. He's translucent now.

I could pretend I don't know what she's talking about. That would be a lie.

There is no escape.

The first time my father pressed Paladin into my hands, we stood on the *Stanhope's* observation deck in low orbit over the planet whose name I cannot remember. My father asked me to play a game with him.

"Make the stars dance, Fallan."

And I did.

Explosions rocked the clouds layered over the planet far below. Bright like the holiday fireworks I remembered from my early childhood on Earth.

He'd stoked my hair and called me a good girl.

I spent years telling myself Paladin was a toy and lights were merely a pretty display. In the Hall of Justice on Lakhish Alpha, my defenses and justifications crumble.

I lift my chin and meet Merin's hard gaze. "I can open the window as you ask or I can bring this building down around us. It matters not. Which would you prefer?"

She chuckles. "I prefer to live, my child."

"If you've known all along what I can do with Paladin, why didn't you kill me the way you killed my mother?"

"We did not kill your mother," she said softly.

"Then who did?" If she expects me to use Paladin, I want some answers.

"Your steward, Kendall. He was allied with the Tengay and in opposition to your father's goals. He tried to kill you as well, if you recall. Happily, he failed."

Happily?

What is wrong with this woman? Linked to Paladin, I am a human weapon capable of taking out every living thing on this planet without breaking a sweat.

Why isn't she afraid of me?

My mother was.

She feared what I might become, which is why she risked everything—civil war and death and allied herself with terrorists—to save me.

As if in answer to my unspoken question, Merin reaches into the voluminous folds of her skirt and extracts a knotted cloth. It is stained with dark splotches of dried blood. Three coins fall out and clatter to the floor—the same three coins I'd tossed into the market stall as payment for the return of Paladin.

"In our culture, the gift of three white coins is the request of a student for a teacher."

"You know that's not what I meant when I threw the coins into the market stall."

"Your ignorance of our customs changes nothing." She passes her hand over Paladin's head and the glow dims.

I gasp. "How is that possible? I thought you said it only attuned to one person."

She smiles and it is a slow, crafty thing that takes residence on her face. "Yes, I did."

"Then why—"

"Why does the device you call Paladin respond to me?"

I nod.

She strokes the small figure with a fondness I recognize. "It took me weeks to puzzle the meaning of your relationship with the weapon. First, you should know that the device you refer to as Paladin is mine. We are bonded in a very real sense."

My gut twists with a sharp, ugly pang of jealousy.

"And yet you think he is yours, do you not?"

I can't take my eyes from the softly glowing figure. The connection between us throbs in my gut like hunger.

Merin continues, unconcerned with my growing frustration and sounding utterly sure of herself. "You are not wrong. This Paladin belongs to you as certainly as he belongs to me. Yet how can this be?"

I don't know what to say, so I remain silent.

"You, my dear, are not entirely a person, are you?"

If it is possible for the universe to flip upside down and back again, that is what happens in the space between one breath and the next.

"Yet you managed to bond with the device. It is quite remarkable." Merin straightens her back and directs her terrible gaze at me. "There are those among us who think that because of your abilities, you pose a terrible danger. They might be right, however, I think their conclusions are hasty and ill advised. I would prefer that you live and become my student." She gestures at the three white coins on the floor. "The choice is yours. What say you?"

I know what she is asking. With the aid of Paladin, I can use the coins and transform the metal they contain into small projectiles and kill Merin, Finn and Alden. If I do so, there remains the possibility Merin has enough skill and power left that she could also tap into the power of Paladin and stop me. He belongs to both of us, but only one of us of can command him completely at any time. Only one of us would survive the battle.

I stand and cross the room, gathering the three white coins on my way.

I kneel before Merin, bow my head, and open my palms.

Q&A with Sabrina Locke

This is a great big world you've introduced us to. Scary and intriguing at the same time. Did you know what you were getting into when you started the story?

I never think I'm going to create a big world, but that's generally what happens every time I open a blank screen and start making stuff up. The story grew from the premise of a young woman determined to get back something she'd lost. I wrote it without an outline or, as some people refer to the process, into the dark. Occasionally, I'd pause to take notes. It was only then that I realized there was nothing small about the story scope.

Is there a common thread that runs through all of your writing?

My knee-jerk response is to say, "Why no, of course not."

But that's probably because I'm too close. I do think there's a consistent voice in my work that's a bit dark and gritty. I also find myself writing often about loss and redemption. In my own reading and movie/TV watching, I love stories about characters in extreme situations.

Any works in progress?

I'm currently working on a novel titled, *The Breaking*. It's a fantasy/Otherworld novel that will be released in late spring or early summer. On the drawing board are plans for a series of novels based on Fallan, Alden and Finn from *The First to Fall*.

How can readers find out more about you?

Not easily at the moment. However, as soon as *The Breaking* is released, I'll be setting up a website along with the usual social media contacts.

THE
IVORY
TOWER

ELLE CASEY
NEW YORK TIMES BESTSELLING AUTHOR

The Ivory Tower
by Elle Casey

"PLEASE REMAIN STILL, Princess." The fitter, a man of slight build and coiffed hair, looked up at the girl standing on the raised platform before him with a scolding expression. He was very adept at speaking out of the left half of his mouth while the right half held pins at the ready.

The girl exhaled, expelling a sigh of resignation tainted with bitterness. "I wish you would stop calling me Princess. Call me Zelle. That's my name."

The fitter shrugged, holding a new, tighter seam together at her waist with the fingers of one hand as he slid a needle into the material with the other. "I call you what you are."

The girl looked down at the man responsible for dressing her in the finest clothing she would ever see in her lifetime. "Did you know that back on Earth, when our father's father's fathers populated that planet, princesses were given that title only when they were born into a royal family? A royal family that had been in existence for hundreds, if not thousands, of years?"

His answer was toneless, delivered with a distracted air as he maneuvered another pinch of material, readying it for the next pin. "I know our race's history as well as you do."

The girl put her nose slightly in the air. "Then you know it really isn't right to call me Princess. I wasn't born into any special family, I was just born without a Y chromosome."

Having used the last of his pins, the fitter was now free to smile in satisfaction. "And *that's* what makes you *so* special that we consider you royalty." The prim little man stood, wrapping his arms tightly around his ribcage, giving the impression he wished to comfort himself. "You can take the gown off now, *Mistress*." He gave her a perfunctory smile, his use of the title *Mistress* a sign that he had heard what she'd said and wasn't entirely immune to her distress.

The girl bowed out of respect for his small gesture. It probably didn't mean much to him, perhaps it was even a joke, but to her it meant everything. She was tired of being treated like a princess, coddled like a precious gem of Jupiter, all because she'd been born without that Y chromosome. She had always been taught it was a special stroke of luck, but she could only see how it had played out in her life: as a curse.

"Shall I disrobe now, or wait until you've left the room?" She was teasing, hoping to get a rise out of him.

He shrugged. "Makes no difference to me."

She should have known better than to try to get a rise out of a man who had nothing between his legs. Being a eunuch, the fitter was no threat to her cherished virginity, so of course he didn't care if she stripped naked right there or out in the hallway or in the main hall. The only thing he cared about was making sure she was ready for the big day: her eighteenth birthday, when all the fun would begin. When she would be led into her future, like a lamb to the slaughter.

* * *

The fitter left without a word as Zelle slid out of the ceremonial dress and back into her uniform, a shapeless shift of bland color and no discernible style—unless one counted potatoes gathered in a sack as having a style. She thought about the days ahead as the heavy material slid over her soft, pale skin. Three days hence would mark her eighteenth birthday and the day that she would be officially presented to the world. The people would see her one time and perhaps never again as she embarked on her life of servitude.

She left the fitting area and entered the adjoining space, the room she had lived in for the past year. The walls were devoid of color or decor, the bed dressed with simple linens and a single pillow. She had been allowed one thing to keep her company: a bird. It was kept in a golden cage in the corner of her room, just next to a window.

She walked over to see him, mindful of the fact that she wasn't to let him out. "Hello, Bird." His name had been chosen with great care; she never knew when her pets would be replaced, so it was best not to get too attached. "How are you today? Did you see the fitter in there? I do believe his hair has gotten higher since the last time he was here. Soon it will make him nearly as tall as I am."

She smiled sadly as she put a finger into the cage. Bird moved along his perch to allow his head to be reached. Zelle stroked the soft feathers, enjoying the feeling of camaraderie when he turned his head around to make it easier for her to do a proper job of scratching his itches.

"I know how you feel," she whispered. "Stuck in this cage. Being able to see out the window but never being able to leave."

Bird lifted his head up and walked away from her down his perch, turning his attention to his feet.

"One day, you will be free," she said quietly, so that the listeners would not hear. "I will let you go from this cage and you will be able to fly anywhere you want to go. Across the lands and the seas and over to your homeland, if you wish."

She played with the catch on the door, imagining what it would be like, to let a caged creature go to follow whatever destiny he chose for himself. "I wish I could go with you," she said, tears welling in her eyes. "I wish I could grow wings and fly out of here, across the land and the sea. I don't believe what they've been teaching me. I don't believe that I'm lucky to be one of The Four, the mothers of the human race. I don't want this duty. I don't consider it an honor. It's a curse. And this ivory tower is my cage." She rubbed her hand up one side of Bird's home, sighing as she battled the tears back. "You and I are not so different, are we? We both sing, we both walk the perch, we both dream of being free. But neither of us is going anywhere. The bars are too strong and no one is brave enough to open the door."

She walked away and sat down at her small table. There, her tablets and books waited for her to open them and absorb their contents. Her schooling would soon be over as she transitioned into motherhood. When she was younger and forced to endure eight hours of study per day, she never thought that she would miss her tutors or the endless stream of facts that fed her brain morning, noon, and night, but she had been wrong. Now that she only had two days of school remaining, she saw the truth of it; she was going to miss all of it dearly. Clarity and appreciation had come when she'd realized learning was her only connection to the outside world. She had lived on the periphery of that world up until now, but soon, the door would close forever and she'd lose any connection to it, save for the scientists who would surely become her only friends. And her children. Assuming they would let them stay.

Her hand caressed the cover of the text that she had been taught was over four hundred years old. *Moby Dick*: the story of man's futile search for truth beneath a surface he could never penetrate with his puny, human mind. Zelle knew this conundrum well. Truth had always eluded her. No one dared tell her everything, and even the things she was privy to were suspect; one man's torture was often another man's pleasure.

She wondered, as she often did, about the three other girls who were living in their own ivory towers, who were either going through the same motions she was right now or who would be very soon. She was not allowed to know their names, but she did know that they were all born in the same year as she had been. She had been the first, and the others had followed, their births a cruel trick of nature that mankind had not been able to replicate. The other three princesses, humans unlucky enough to be born female, would follow in her footsteps, as reluctantly taken as they might be.

Were they anxious? Did they feel like they were suffocating under the pressure and expectations? Did they wonder what life was like outside of the tower? Zelle had no way of knowing for sure, but she couldn't imagine anyone being content with this life, with being a slave to an entire race.

Zelle had heard through one of her more enlightened tutors, many years ago, that the male children of her people were brought up to believe that the girls of the ivory towers, the princesses of New Earth, were heroes, that they lived in the lap of luxury wanting for nothing and that they were happy to fulfill their duty of repopulating the world, with keeping the human race alive. But what they could never understand was that the girls in the ivory towers were denied the one thing anybody wanted: freedom. The freedom to make a choice about anything that mattered.

Zelle pushed the book away. What was the point in reading that story again? She already knew how it ended, and she already knew what it told her. She was doomed. She would never know why she had been born a girl, or why so few had been born after her, or why since that year, only boys had appeared until all the mothers died away.

She looked at the timepiece that always remained in her front pocket. Two minutes remained until her next lesson. She was not permitted a mirror, but she was allowed a brush. This she ran through her long hair, doing her best to look presentable. She braided it together in one long plait that reached to her waist.

Arno was her favorite tutor. He taught her about history, and he wasn't too much older than she was. He was also one of the few men allowed around her who wasn't a eunuch. She wasn't sure why that was permitted. She had asked him once, but he had avoided the question, leading her to assume that he was connected to someone important. Asking about that connection would have surely resulted in a one-way ticket out of her life for Arno, so she never let her curiosity get the better of her. Not on that subject, anyway.

She left her room, her slippers making slight tapping sounds along the marble floors. She wondered what she and Arno would discuss at their next lesson. Would she learn about the political landscape as it existed before the people of Earth destroyed their planet? Would they discuss the natural resources available to them on various planets in the nearby galaxies?

Arno seemed to know everything. He was a fount of knowledge, and she could never get enough of listening to him speak. The only thing he would not discuss with her was life outside the tower. It was a forbidden subject with all of her tutors, and while Arno didn't always follow all the rules, he did follow that one.

She continued down the hall, taking a left turn and then a right, passing doors she'd never been given access to as she went. She wondered if she would be given a special key that would unlock every door on her eighteenth birthday. And then she wondered if she'd use it. Some secrets, she suspected, might be better left undiscovered.

* * *

Zelle sat across the table from Arno. It was required that two chairs separate them at all times, and because the learning area was monitored, they were always careful to follow the rules. Zelle wondered if the rules chafed Arno as much as they did her, but she'd never built up the courage to ask.

After placing a stack of old books on the table, he rested his hands in his lap. His tailored suit-coat wrinkled at the inner shoulders, the only fault in his carefully constructed appearance. "Do you have a preference today?" He blinked his eyes slowly as he waited for her response.

She bit her lip, wondering if she dared answer the question truthfully. She did have a preference, but it wasn't permitted.

Arno tipped his head to the side. "You have something on your mind." His dark brown eyes never wavered. He stared at her so intently, it was as if he were trying to read her thoughts.

Zelle almost laughed aloud at her folly. As intelligent and intuitive as Arno was, reading minds was not something he could do. It was not something *anyone* could do, much as the scientists were trying. Her mind was the only place Zelle had ever been able to run free, so she fervently hoped they would never succeed with their experiments.

She nodded at her tutor. "Yes. I do have something on my mind." She wondered now if it were worth the risk to share her thoughts with Arno. She didn't want to place him in danger, but time was running out. She was beginning to feel a crushing sensation on her chest at night as she lay in bed, as if a large heavy weight were pushing down on her. She was almost to the point of struggling to breathe when she thought about her predicament too much.

Arno leaned in, selecting a book off the top of the pile and opening it as he spoke to her in murmured tones. "If there is something you wish to discuss, I am open to bending the rules a bit today. We have only a short time remaining before your birthday."

She tried very hard to smother the smile that wanted to consume her face. Arno had taught her some things that were probably on the not-permitted list, but he'd never openly flaunted the rules.

"Are you suggesting a birthday gift?" she teased.

He showed no sign of having heard her suggestion other than to scratch at his temple. He pushed the book closer and opened the cover, speaking while looking at the first page. "I have been told that once you reach your eighteenth birthday, there will no longer be any need of my services."

Zelle's smile disappeared in an instant. She took the book from Arno, centering it on the table in front of her, and flipped through pages, pretending to be occupied with their work when inside her heart felt more than a bit crushed.

"Do they mean to take away my education?" Her hands trembled and bile rose in her throat, burning it and making her feel as though she were choking. She massaged her neck, attempting to rub the discomfort away.

He reached over, running a finger down the page, giving the impression of discussing something in the text with her. "I do not know. I am not privy to the decisions being made by people above me. However, it would be foolish to think that your duties would not change once you've reached … this age."

She shook her head. "I don't want things to change. Or at least, not in the way they want to change them for me."

Several moments of tense silence passed between them before Arno continued. He nodded slowly as he spoke. "I have hesitated to say anything to you until this point, but I know you dream of a life outside the tower."

Her heart raced at the idea that he had seen into her soul, that he knew the things about which she had never spoken. "Yes," she said, her voice rough from nerves.

He turned the page of the book and then rested his forehead in his hand, effectively blocking his lips from being read by the watchers. He spoke low enough to prevent the listeners from picking up the details. "If I were to tell you that there were others who did not agree with your confinement, what would you say to that?" He paused before adding to his statement. "Hypothetically speaking, of course. Because for me to discuss this in reality would be punishable by death."

She nodded, gesturing with her hands and pointing to the book to imitate someone very engaged with the lesson. Her voice was also low enough to avoid detection. "I understand the punishment, although I realize it would be more harsh for others than myself. I would be happy to seek freedom on my own. I merely need to find a way out. Most of the tower is still off-limits to me and therefore a mystery."

He closed the book and put it back on the pile, not looking at her as he straightened the texts and moved the stack to the edge of the table. "I could have a key."

She glanced at her timepiece and then at him. "Is our lesson over already?"

He shook his head, speaking in a normal tone again. "No, our lesson isn't over. I reserved time in the gardens so that we might discuss the botanical names for the flowers on the west side. It's been a while since we've done that, and I fear you have forgotten much of what I tried to teach you before. You know that when you have New Earth's children, you will be expected to take them often to the gardens and share your knowledge of the things growing there."

She tried not to look too excited about the opportunity of having a private and forbidden conversation with her favorite tutor, about life outside the tower. Too much happiness at this point in her life could be dangerous. Any of the watchers or listeners who paid attention to her daily life had to know she hadn't been happy and wasn't looking forward to being a brood queen for the entire human race. To appear happy now would awaken their suspicions that something was amiss.

She looked at her timepiece again. "I suppose I could work it into my schedule. I have weapons training after this, and I must get back in time to change my clothing first."

He folded his hands on top of the books that were now before him. "You must be at expert-level now with the sword, dagger, and wire. How wonderful." His smile was forced.

She nodded, not sure what he expected to hear from her, but doing her best to play along. "Yes, and in several hand-to-hand disciplines. It's helpful to have a way to work off the frustration."

He tilted his head at her. "Frustration? Whatever could you be frustrated about? You have everything you could possibly need right here in the tower, your every wish granted." He gave her a smile that she suspected was meant for the cameras, while the twinkle in his eye seemed to be saying that he did not feel the truth of his words. He was the smartest of her tutors and not necessarily from a family of privilege, though he never gave her the impression of being destitute. Perhaps he knew enough of the real world to see that she was living in a gilded cage, much like Bird.

"You are correct. But I often miss the company of other girls. Men can be so tiresome." That last comment was for those who managed her. They called themselves her fathers, but she knew better. The man who had contributed to her biological makeup no longer lived. She had been informed of this on her fourth birthday.

"Let's take a walk, shall we?" Arno stood and walked to the door.

She nodded and followed him out of the room, tricking herself into believing that she could feel the eyes of the watchers burning brands into her back.

* * *

The gardens were kept for the enjoyment of everyone who worked in the tower, those who catered to Zelle's every need and cared for her, but she was the only visitor. She used to go frequently, but her trips had become fewer over the years. What had once been a beautiful and special corner of her world had become another symbol of her prison. There was a beauty there she could touch, but it never changed. The plants were always kept trimmed to the exact same size, and the colors of the flower petals never varied. It looked exactly the same on this day as it had looked ten and fifteen years ago.

The garden was monitored like all the other rooms in the ivory tower, but there was only so much the microphones could pick up. Zelle had been taught about the technology that the watchers and listeners used, and she had reached the point in her training where she could set up and break down their entire system blindfolded. It was because of this extensive knowledge that she was confident that if she and Arno stuck to the center of the path, where the trees grew too high to have closely overhanging branches, they were assured a relatively private conversation. It felt dangerous and exciting to be there, walking side-by-side with Arno.

"I expect the guards to come and remove you at any moment," Zelle said. She looked over her shoulder to confirm they weren't there. Their blue uniforms with black collars were something both to be feared and admired. They had rescued her as a child when she got lost wandering the ivory tower alone, but they had also been there to stop infractions from occurring. More than one of Zelle's tutors had disappeared from the rolls never to be seen again. She was never told what happened to them, but she feared the worst. It was for that reason that she was always cautious about putting her teachers in danger. But today, it seemed as if Arno were ready to take a risk, and her birthday was too close to play it safe anymore. She decided to take the risk with him.

"I have been given the task by the High Council of preparing you for the transition," Arno said. "I am certain they believe that I am telling you right now what an honor it will be for you to carry the next generation of humans in your womb and to raise them as our ancient ancestors used to."

She worked to keep her expression impassive. "Yes. I'm sure that is what is expected of you. And I'm sure *I* am expected to nod and smile and tell you what a great honor it is, and how I cannot wait to give birth to a minimum of thirty humans, preferably all girls who can be put in their own beautiful ivory towers to become mothers of future generations."

He smiled. "Then we both know our roles and who we should be today."

She couldn't keep the desperation from seeping into her voice. "But I don't want to be that person."

His voice was almost soothing. "Nor do I."

"So where does that leave us?" Her heart was thumping so loudly, she feared the listeners would hear it, that Arno would hear it. She wanted him to think her brave and fearless. She felt confident she could be that person, too … in a moment … after this feeling of incredulity had passed. This was the first time in eighteen years anyone had openly shown scorn for the work of the High Council in her presence.

"My statement earlier about a hypothetical group was not entirely honest," Arno said, his words coming out rushed. He'd never spoken like this before. It made her even more nervous.

"There is a group of people who would like to rescue you from your situation. They do not believe it is fair that you are forced to live under the directives of the High Council. They believe in your right to self-determination." He paused to look at her. "Do you remember that lesson?"

She nodded, her chin lifting ever so slightly. "Self determination: the right of every individual to decide for himself who he should be and what he stands for."

He started walking again. "Exactly. You always were my best pupil. There is something wrong with that maxim, though, is there not?"

She nodded, entirely sure of her answer, even though this had never been a part of their lesson. "They always use the pronoun *his*. As if by simply being a girl, I do not have the right to self-determination. But I don't agree with that. I believe all of the inhabitants of the ivory towers should be allowed to choose for themselves what they do with their lives."

"Then we are agreed. If you wish, I can set you on the road to self-determination."

"How?" Her hands had become sweaty. She slowly rubbed them together and smoothed her hair back in an effort to appear unaffected, concerned only by such things as the botanical name for the oak tree overhead. She and Arno would not be overheard where they were standing, but they would be seen.

Zelle had been the beneficiary of many lessons in self-control and various combat techniques, including how to respond as a prisoner of war. As long as she could remember, the High Council worried about an uprising of men wanting to take part in the pleasures they were denied—those only offered at the ivory tower to a select few male specimens hand-picked by the High Council. Her caretakers were concerned that these desperate men would try to overwhelm the security forces and take her captive, so she had been taught to fight for her own protection. The irony was not lost on her; she was using their training to protect herself from them.

Arno pointed to a bed of red flowers bordered by an ivy-covered stone wall. She expected to hear him say *Dianthus chinensis*, but she was wrong about his intent.

"There is a door on the ground level of the tower that is just off the kitchens on the east side, a delivery entrance. These are the same kitchens in which you've had cooking lessons every Thursday. Just inside that door are the laundry bins that service the entire tower. Each day, those bins are picked up, and new bins and clean linens are delivered. Later this evening, in the third used-laundry bin from the door, there will be a pair of men's trousers, shirt, jacket, boots, gloves, and hat in your size. You must put them on and walk out the door at 8:30 tonight. No earlier, no later."

They were reaching the end of the lane. It was time to turn and walk back. Zelle did the calculation of time, rate, and distance in her mind and knew that they had approximately ninety seconds remaining in their walk to complete their plan for her escape.

* * *

"And how will I do this?" Zelle's mind was racing with possibilities. It would be one thing to deliver men's clothing in a bin without being detected; it was another to put that clothing on and leave without someone seeing, hearing, or being alerted to the subterfuge. The ivory tower was a fortress; no one entered or exited without being watched by many sets of eyes and many electronic devices tuned in to biorhythms and microchip identification. "How will I get past all of the security?"

"We have friends," Arno explained. "It has all been arranged. My job was to determine if you were willing, and you appear to be. All you need to do is put on the clothing, hide your dress in the bin, and go out the door at eight thirty exactly."

She wanted to believe him, but it all seemed too simple. "I know these systems, Arno. The technology was designed to sniff out trouble, and it does a very good job of it. It has never failed as far as I know, and it has caught *many* people trying to enter the tower who did not have the right to be here."

"I cannot tell you any more than I already have. Many

people have put their lives at risk to help you. The more I reveal, the more risk they take on, and I cannot accept more responsibility for their lives than I already have. Just know that if you walk outside that door, there will be someone there to take you, and you will not be detected as you leave the tower. This I can almost guarantee."

Even though Arno had been very clear, she still had to ask the one question that was swirling around in her mind, so that they both could thoroughly agree on what they were talking about doing and what it could mean for them. "And what if I am caught? What happens then?"

He stared straight ahead as his shoulders shrugged very slightly. "Those who helped you would be executed, and you would be returned to the tower to fulfill your duty to the people."

Her smile carried no humor. "Not so terrible for me, but pretty awful for those other people."

He nodded and shoved his hands into his pockets, the first sign that he was not entirely comfortable with everything they were discussing. "You are correct. They will be at great risk. But, I would be remiss if I did not warn you of the risk you take as well. While your life may go back to normal here at the tower on the surface, I don't believe it would feel that way to you. I believe you would notice more eyes on you, more restrictions, and less ..." He paused searching for the right words. "Less forgiveness."

"Do you believe I have been forgiven?"

He took his time answering. "I would say that of the four princesses, you are the one who questions authority most stridently. And yet here you are, walking in the gardens with a fully functioning male and no escort."

Too much of what he said hit her at once and over-whelmed her good sense. She seized his arm for a moment before realizing that this would signal to the watchers that she'd become overly excited. She released him and pointed to the trees, acting as though she'd seen a very special insect or butterfly there. "You know of the other three? You've never told me. I have asked and you've never told me."

"I have not met them, but I know others who have."

"Tell me everything, Arno."

"I cannot. Our time has come to a close." He looked meaningfully at the glass doors that marked the end of the pathway and led into the citrus room. Four guards were standing there awaiting Zelle's approach, two of them her latest training instructors. They would be certifying her competence in expert-level marksmanship and combat maneuvers today.

She paused and turned slightly to face her tutor. "I will be there. And please thank all of your friends for helping me."

He nodded and turned off the path, leaving her with the guards.

* * *

The rest of the day passed in a blur of panic and excitement, the likes of which Zelle had never experienced before. She had, off and on over the years, dreamed of a different life than the one that had been planned for her, but this was the first time a change had felt real, as if it were actually possible. She was not prepared for the depth of emotion this reality

brought with it. Tears were hidden behind he.
was disguised as pride at excelling in combat train.

After careful consideration, she had come up wi.
excuse that would have her down in the kitchens without
supervision at the time arranged for her escape. It wasn't a
perfect plan, but it was the only one she could imagine working. Trying to get from her tower room to the ground level
in the kitchens at night without anyone detecting her movements would be impossible; her best bet was to allow all of
the tower's inhabitants to know where she was but not what
she was really doing.

All of her training and education was over for the day,
and she waited at her window for the sun to go down. She
had showered and changed after her last lesson, emerging
from the bathroom to find a shiny new medallion she could
pin to her dress sitting on the small table in her room, signi-
fying that she had reached the last qualifying combat level.
She would not take it out of its box. She was not proud of
being a warrior, but she wasn't naïve either. What she had
learned here would prepare her for the life that she sought.

She opened the window wide and let the outside air in,
ruffling Bird's feathers. She was seized by an emotion, looking into the creature's eyes. It felt wrong to be leaving this
place and forcing him to stay. She walked closer to the cage
and looked between the bars.

"Bird, do you want to leave? Do you wish to have a different life than the one given to you here?"

He had everything he needed right there in his cage: fresh
water and seed, the occasional piece of fruit. She reached up
and released the clasp on the door, opening it wide as she had

nd if you want to go. You won't hurt

ped back two paces, waiting for him

nd take the freedom she was offering.

g, giving no sign that he even realized

. After a few moments he turned around

faced the wall.

His ac.. confused her and then broke her heart when she realized what they meant; he had given up hope of ever being free. He saw the open door as a cruel joke. Or maybe he lacked the strength to start his life again. Perhaps he didn't want to be alone. Sadly, she realized that this could have happened to her. It was possible if she stayed and gave birth to a child, that she would never want to leave. She would settle into her duty and be glad to remain in her gilded cage. The thought made her desperate to run down to the kitchens now, even though it was too early.

She shook her head and brushed away a tear, turning so the watchers would not see her emotion. She spoke loud enough this time for the listeners to hear. "I will leave the window open so that you may have some fresh air. When I come back later, I will close it."

She wasn't ready to give up on Bird, even though he had given up on himself. She pretended to latch the cage door, but in fact merely closed it most of the way, hoping it was her presence scaring him from exercising his natural curiosity, and that after she left, he would go through the door and out the window before her disappearance was discovered and they were once again made prisoners.

* * *

Checking the timepiece in her pocket against the setting of the sun, Zelle determined it was time to go. She walked over to the communications center near her door and connected to the person she would most likely discuss her coursework with, one of her fathers. She pressed the button and began to speak, not waiting to confirm he was there. There was no need; he was always there.

"Father, I'm going down to the kitchens. There is a sauce that I learned once but I do not remember how to make it. It's important that I remember."

A deep voice devoid of emotion came over the speaker, ringing around the room. "Do you require assistance, daughter?"

"No. It may take me some time, and I'm comfortable alone. I would like to see if I can do it without anyone's help."

There was no answer for a few seconds. Her heart was beating wildly. Had she sounded innocent enough? Would he feel the need to join her? It was not his way, but things were rapidly changing in her world. Perhaps they sensed her restlessness and would feel the need to keep her closer.

"As you wish. Please be back to your room in one hour. You need your sleep. In two days the grand celebration will be upon us."

She could hear the smile in his voice. The pride. The High Council's members were all very pleased with themselves over their accomplishment. They had taken this girl child, raised her from an infant to a woman, and now they would be presenting her to the world. Their Mother. Their Savior. Their whore.

"Yes, Father." She took one last glance at Bird with his beak to the wall before leaving her room.

* * *

There were watchers and listeners in the kitchens, but they were not as concentrated and focused on every corner of the space. Over the years, she had identified the various eyes and ears in the room. There were two areas where one could be working and not be seen: the secondary stovetop and the storage pantry. So long as she was making some noise at this cooking station, she believed she would be safe from prying observers. It was the reason she had selected a sauce as her project. She did not know from Arno how long his friends would have control over the surveillance systems of the tower, and she didn't want to risk the lives of people who were trying to help her.

She pulled out various utensils and a saucepan, placing them over near the stove. She began to whistle, a tune that was easily stuck in one's mind with a repeating chorus that could go on forever. The first several bars of the music she hummed into the recording device at her wrist whenever she was out of sight of the cameras. She managed to go into the back of the kitchen to retrieve ingredients and verify that the clothing promised was in its place.

The only people she had ever seen in the tower were tutors, medical professionals, guards, and her fathers. The rough clothing hidden in the bin was not familiar to her. It made her mission seem even more exciting. Zelle would be in a disguise that would fool even herself.

It was difficult to manage such a mundane chore as making sauce while her mind raced from one drastic scenario to another. Her capture. Her success. Her future. Her past. It all swirled together in one giant maelstrom of emotion. There was plenty of fear there, but overwhelming that emotion was excitement. For the first time in her life, she was actually excited about her future and the potential that it might hold. Always before, there was no potential, only finality.

She began the process of making sauce, measuring the ingredients as if she were really going to accomplish her project, all the while continuing to hum into the recording device. Dressing in the uniform would take her approximately one minute and fifteen seconds. Sweat formed between her shoulder blades and dropped down her back as the night moved on and she got closer to the departure time.

When she was two minutes from the appointed time, she placed her recording device on the small countertop next to the stovetop and pressed *play*. Her voice issued forth from the speaker, soft and haunting. She turned the heat off the stove and slid the pan away from the hot surface. Slowly and quietly, she made her way into the back room. She prayed there were no eyes here now. This was not a place she was expected to be.

Quickly, she removed the shapeless sack that was her night clothing, and once down to her underthings, pulled each item of her new uniform out of the bin with shaking hands. The trousers were a bit short, but the thick, woolen socks that were too long would cover her bare ankles easily. Worn workboots with repaired laces were sturdier than any footwear she had ever been given before. Over her cotton underthings went a scratchy shirt, a heavy vest, and finally an overcoat. She was sweating from her exertions and the adrenaline flowing through her system, so she did not button or zip the jacket. She did, however, tuck her long, thick braid up under the cap provided.

Her last move was to run over to the door and rub her hands along the floor near the entrance, the dirtiest place in the room. She took the grit that she pulled from the hard surface and applied it liberally to her face, hoping it would obscure her very pale skin. She feared she would glow like a candle in the night, otherwise.

The timepiece she'd transferred to the large pocket in the overcoat hung down by her right thigh. She pulled it out one last time and verified the time. Five seconds until departure.

She listened for signs coming from the kitchen that would indicate someone paying her a visit, but there was nothing but the sound of her own voice, humming over and over, the same tune, always the same. Just like her life.

She grasped the handle of the door and turned it, expecting it to be locked. All of the tower doors were always kept locked. But this time it wasn't. It opened easily and swung out into an exterior space.

This space was nothing like her tower's interior. Whereas everything inside was white or cream, this place was dark gray and brown, its odors foreign to her nostrils. Air that carried the heavy stench of oils and fumes hit her in the face. She had smelled hints of these things from time to time on the clothing of various guards, but never fresh in the air like this. She inhaled deeply, taking a moment to orient herself to the room.

It was a garage or hangar of sorts, housing several vehicles, some with wheels, others with hover technology. None of them appeared occupied, but down the line, a single red light flashed on the back of one of them.

She slipped through the door and closed it behind her, experiencing what felt like a small heart attack when she realized there was no going back now; she had officially left the tower for the first time in her life. Zelle had broken the most hard and fast rule she'd ever been issued: *Never, ever leave the tower.* It is not safe, they'd said.

The boots she was wearing made more noise than her slippers, but it was too late for that regret, and too late to go back and retrieve the lighter footwear. This would be her new uniform, come what may.

She reached the vehicle, dismayed to find that it was one with wheels and not hover technology. Her studies had informed her that these craft were less reliable and took a lot longer to reach their destinations. The only benefit to using such a transport was that it would be able to go to some places where hovercraft could not.

She stepped up to the passenger door and peered in the window to find an empty seat. A face leaned over from the other side and spoke. "Get in," the man said in a low voice, easily heard through the thick glass.

The door popped open and Zelle fit her fingers into the seam, pulling it free from its frame so she could enter. This was the first time she had ever been in a vehicle. It was surreal to finally experience something that she had only read about and discussed with people having more knowledge than her, people who lived outside the tower.

It struck her like a bolt of lightning: she was now a person who lived outside the tower. That knowledge made her nearly giddy and then very afraid. She had never been so far out of her element.

The man was old and grizzled. He smelled of someone who did not shower often and did not care to. There had been few occasions in the tower when she had run into people like this. She was always ushered away, and she never knew their purpose for being there, but that didn't stop her from wondering. Perhaps he was a supplicant to the High Council? Or perhaps this was how all people smelled outside of the tower?

She resisted the urge to pinch her nose and instead decided to enjoy it. Her life had always consisted of the same things, recurring over and over again. Finally, this was something different. It was what she had asked for, after all. She was going to embrace these variations from her standards, the differences that made people outside the tower so much more interesting to her than the ones inside.

"Keep your head down. It's good you dirtied your face, but it's still not enough."

She bent over at the waist, placing her face in her hands and her faith in the stranger. "Thank you," was all she could manage.

The reality of what she had done was hitting her hard, the adrenaline making her entire body tremble. The risk she had taken based on the word of a mere tutor was the most foolhardy thing she had ever done in her life. Perhaps it would be the last thing she would do with her life. She had not considered how she could be placing herself in danger by following Arno's instructions before, but now it seemed a distinct possibility.

Where was this man taking her? Would she be brought to a city and left to fend for herself? Did they have a specific place already set up for her? Or maybe they had other intentions. It was impossible to know, and she feared asking. Instead, she braced herself against the sides of her seat as the vehicle moved out of the hangar and into the world.

The vehicle made several stops along the journey, but none of them longer than a few seconds. She wanted to check her timepiece to see if the recording she had left behind was still playing, but she feared moving. Instead, she tried to memorize the directions that the vehicle was taking in case she changed her mind and wanted to go back. That wasn't going to happen, she knew, but it gave her something to think about rather than all of the worst case scenarios that kept floating through her mind.

"We are out of the city," the man said. "You can sit up now."

Zelle pulled her hands off of her sweaty face and slowly sat up. The landscape had changed. Even though it was quite dark, she could see that they were out in a wilderness of sorts. The city lights were behind them, and the road had lost its smooth quality. They were bumping along now, and the force of the tires slamming into the holes tossed her around like she was a mere rag doll.

"Where are we going?" Zelle braced herself against the door, hanging onto it in an effort to keep her body from being bruised.

"Somewhere safe. With my people."

"Are they Arno's people? Are you part of the same … family?" There were families and tribes and clans populating

New Earth. She was almost sure Arno had told her that he was part of a family, but she could be wrong about that. Personal questions had always been discouraged.

He nodded his head and grunted at her, not exactly answering but calming her fears slightly. If Arno was there, everything would be fine. She trusted him. He had opened up the outside world to her mind for many years, even at risk to himself, and now he had opened it to her body, too. That had to mean something.

* * *

She feared taking out her timepiece and aggravating her escort by seeming impatient or distrusting, so it was impossible to know exactly how much time had passed before they arrived at the camp, but it felt to be at least an hour. The vehicle pulled off the road and into a shed made of broken trees. The engine shut down along with all of the interior and exterior lighting. They sat together in the dark for a moment before the man spoke.

"Stay close to me." He left the vehicle after issuing his order, and Zelle scrambled to follow. It took her a few moments to find the release button on the door, and she nearly spilled out of the vehicle when it popped open without warning. She scrambled to her feet, not wanting to be left behind in that dark place, the place where she knew nothing and no one.

The immensity of what she had done was almost overwhelming. The tactical operations officer who had taught her wartime strategies had often made a point of impressing upon her how critically important it was plan movements well in advance. *'Failing to plan, is planning to fail,'* he'd always said. She hadn't planned this maneuver for more than six hours, thereby violating the most important rule of engagement. According to her teachers, this meant she would surely lose. There were so many missteps she could take now, it was mind-boggling, but her only option was to move forward into her unplanned and uncertain future.

She got to her feet and stood as straight as possible. It was time to face her new destiny, and she wouldn't do it cowering like a helpless child, and she wouldn't do it by turning her back and facing the wall like Bird had done. She had not yet lost her will to be free.

At first she saw nothing but the back of the large man in front of her. He was wearing clothing that had been patched in many places and was almost worn through in others. She had difficulty swallowing when she realized this meant she had joined an encampment that could not afford to clothe its members properly. She took another step, reminding herself that she did not need money or material things to be happy. Basic necessities like food, clothing, and shelter would do just fine.

There was a circle of light ahead, and it appeared to be the place where the man was heading. When he reached the edge of it he turned to her. "Don't speak unless I tell you to. Stay close to me."

His words chafed. She had come from a place where her days were ordered and her activities arranged, but she had never been directly ordered not to speak. During her education, questions were encouraged and opinions were shared. Of course she censored her words, careful not to indicate that she wasn't happy, but that was her own limitation. What was happening here did not feel right.

The man moved to the side, exposing a circle of faces before her. They belonged to men, of course, most of them clothed like her driver. There was one, however, who stood out and looked as though he did not belong.

When he stepped closer into the light, Zelle smiled and lifted her hand in greeting. "Hello, Arno."

The large man turned violently to her and leaned in very close, his proximity making it possible to smell his fetid breath and feel his spittle land on her face. "I told you not to speak!"

He lifted his arm, and her instincts took over. As his hand came down to strike, hers went up, easily blocking the blow and sending it sideways. Her driver stumbled, thrown off balance by his own strength being redirected.

Men who had begun to move stopped. Everything froze and went silent. The expression on the driver's face was terrifying; he clearly did not like being subverted. It looked as though he were winding up to try again when Arno's voice cut him off.

"Father. Stop. I told you, she is an innocent. She has no idea what she's doing."

Zelle looked at Arno, not sure she comprehended what was happening. The soft, measured tone that she was used to hearing was missing from Arno's voice; instead, there was a hardness there, something cold she would never have associated with him before.

"Arno, I don't understand." She took a step toward him, but was suddenly barred from further progress by a large arm across her chest. She looked up at the large man who had brought her to this place.

His eyes were dark, his brows drawn together. "Not another step."

There were murmurs in the crowd, everyone taking turns glancing from the man, to Arno, and then to Zelle. Several took a step forward, getting closer.

Arno looked to his people and then moved, stopping just in front of Zelle and the man Zelle now knew as Arno's father.

"Welcome, Zelle. Welcome to the encampment of the Hinter people."

"The Hinter people?" This was not something Arno had ever mentioned in their studies, and he had been the one to tell her of the various tribes around the towers.

"Yes. The Hinter people. Your new family." He turned to the side and gestured to the men standing in the light.

Zelle tried to swallow, but it was as if there was a large lump blocking her throat. None of the men looked as though they had bathed in the last week. They resembled the savages that she and Arno had looked at in pictures in one of his old textbooks. She would not have been surprised to see spears in their hands or knives made of flint hanging from their belts. Because she had been trained to, she did notice the few weapons that were there, most of them on the crude side, but there were also a smattering of other more sophisticated arms that could easily be used against her.

This change in Arno's character and the fact that he referred to this large, brutal man as his father told Zelle all she needed to know about the Hinter people and the game that

Arno had played so well on both her and the High Council. He had always won at chess and now she knew why; he played the long game, and he had a great strategy.

She should have paid more attention to Bird. He had been free once, perhaps. Maybe he had flown the world and seen what was out there. Maybe he knew he was better off in his gilded cage. Regret burned like acid in her chest.

"Is this your entire tribe?" Zelle asked. Her training was kicking in. Add up the numbers, assess the threat. Plans for a diversion and escape required knowledge of many details to be successful.

"This is everyone." Arno once again gestured to the men. "We gathered here to welcome you. Once you get settled in, you can greet each man individually and decide which one or ones you want to bed with."

Disillusionment was replaced with fear. "Bed with?"

His smile was tight. "Yes. You will have the companion or companions of your choosing. Your life will be very different here than it was in the tower. In the tower, the High Council chose companions for you. Here, you will choose for yourself."

She wanted to ask the one most obvious question: What if I don't want to choose anyone? But she already knew the answer. The men were not drooling, but they were definitely looking at her with hunger in their eyes. She wondered how long Arno and his father would be able to hold off the more determined individuals. When she snuck a glance up at the large man, she saw hunger there, too. Surely he would expect to have his chance at being her companion. She suspected he would not take her answer of *No* very kindly.

She nodded. Her only hope was to play along and then

escape. Where she would go, she had no idea. This entire land was alien to her as were these people. All of them were savages as far as she could tell. But the alternative was un-thinkable. She would not lay with any of them.

Her mind buzzed with next steps and possible outcomes. If this was what she could expect from people living outside the tower, her only hope was to find a place where she could be alone. The human race could go on without her and die off if that was what it would take to gain her freedom. She ignored the guilt, telling herself she was no hero and that a human race that enslaved women didn't deserve to carry on. She knew how to protect herself and she could survive in the wilderness. She wasn't helpless, even though she was attempting to appear that way to these men.

For one crazy moment, she wondered if the High Coun-cil had envisioned this particular scenario playing out in her life. Why else would they have taught her all those things—combat, cooking, survival medicine, growing things—and made them a part of her formal education? If she were ex-pected to remain within the tower for her entire life, she would never have needed any of those skills.

But no ... it couldn't be that they meant for this to hap-pen. The High Council would never have wanted this for her. These men, the Hinter people, were not worthy of car-rying on the human race, or so the High Council would say. And she couldn't disagree.

Zelle knew she was no one to judge, but she also knew that Arno had disappointed her as deeply as any other man had, and his people were no better than the other men who had tried to control her life. The men of New Earth were all the same; they fashioned stories for her ears in a way that would cause her to go along with their ideas, but in their hearts they carried a different truth, one of enslavement and denial.

Arno had betrayed her. She would not let him know that she was aware of this, nor would she let him get away with it. She would be the meek little ghost she had been in the tower and bide her time until her moment came. He would be left to deal with the disappointment of his savage family on his own, and she would not feel any regret for that.

She nodded at Arno's explanation. "I accept. I would now like to go to sleep. I am very tired. As you know, I've had a very long day." She looked at the ground and folded her hands in front of her, hoping to give the impression of a frightened young girl needing protection.

"Come with me." Arno took her by the arm and led her through the crowd. She kept her eyes cast downward, fearing visual contact with any of the hungry men. It would not take much to encourage them.

Soon they were past the hot, stinking bodies and out into the darker woods. He led her to a shelter that looked as if it had been pieced together with cast-off garbage from the tower. "There's a bed in there. You should be able to sleep until light. I will come get you for breakfast. Don't leave with anyone else as your escort. I cannot vouch that they will do the right thing."

She warred within herself, wanting to tell him what she thought about his plans, about how disappointed she was that he had betrayed her, but also knowing that revealing her true feelings would place him on alert and cause him to be more vigilant. Her greatest strength now was her false ignorance and subservience. He must believe that she was too cowed to do anything but accept his determination for her.

"Okay. Thank you." She turned away from him and faced the cot that would be her bed.

His footsteps brought him to the door but paused before exiting. "I'm sorry this is not as luxurious as the tower. But I never got the impression that those luxuries were very important to you."

"You are correct. They were not." She was not lying when she said this. Had there been a group of warm, welcoming people there not threatening to force her into repopulating the earth against her will, she wouldn't have minded the hardness of the cot, the cold stickiness of the air, the lack of insulation in the walls or the roof. She would have simply welcomed the freedom these things represented. But this was not her reality; she had merely exchanged one prison for another, one captor for another. Her former instructor had been correct: Zelle's failure to plan had become her plan to fail.

She thought Arno was going to leave, but he hesitated in the doorway.

"Was there something else?" she asked, not facing him.

"Zelle …" His voice had a hitch in it. It was raspy, a tone she'd never heard issuing from his mouth. "Rapunzelle, let down your hair."

She was frozen in place, not sure how to react. "My hair?"

"Let down your long hair. I want to see it."

Goosebumps of fear covered her skin. This was an Arno she had never met before and didn't wish to meet now. Maybe she had dreamed on occasion of a forbidden romance with her tutor, but those thoughts could not be further from her mind now.

She slowly lifted her cap from her head, allowing her braid to fall to her waist.

"Undo it. Let it free of the band that holds it tight."

She shook her head. This felt wrong, like another violation of her free will and an invitation for trouble. And the fact that it was Arno committing this sin made her angry. She feared that she would attack him and ruin her chances at escape. She turned to look at him over her shoulder, begging him with her eyes to stop.

"Arno! What're you doing in there?" someone shouted from beyond.

Arno's gaze hardened, but he stepped backward, walking out the door in reverse. "Another time," he said, closing the door behind him.

* * *

Zelle stood in the center of the room, looking at the small cutout that served as a window. There was no glass there or other covering, and wind whistled through the opening, keeping the room chilled. She would sleep with all of her clothing on if she slept at all.

She lay down on the cot to bide her time. Her escape must be tonight. Tomorrow, after the men had spent this evening imagining what they would do with her, gaining freedom would be impossible; they would all be watching and waiting for their opportunity to have her.

A group of men who were hungry for sex with one of the last four women in the world would need a very strong leader to keep them in line, and neither Arno nor his father seemed to have the strength of character to manage that. Tomorrow or the next day or a week after, it would become a free-for-all and she would be their victim.

Her plan-making kicked into high gear. They had weapons. She had her hands and feet, which were no match for bullets, but they were a match for anything else. She would wait until most of them were asleep, and then she would leave. No one would take the risk of injuring her seriously. They would try to take her by brute strength. And if anyone tried to stop her, she would use the maneuvers she had been taught to get away. If she hurt someone badly in the process, she would not feel sorry for them; they would have brought the pain upon themselves. Arno had promised her self-determination and she was going to get it.

A sound at her window caused her to sit up in a hurry. She thought she imagined it, and yet there was another sound just after the first, like a pecking that pierced the quiet of the night. Something was gently touching the edge of the windowsill. She stood to look out, and had to blink a few times to understand what she was seeing: the silhouette of a small creature.

Chirp. The creature made a sound.

Zelle moved closer. The light of a distant moon brought some color to the creature's feathers.

"Bird!" she exclaimed in a very small whisper. "What are you doing here?"

He flapped his wings once and then turned around and faced outward.

Zelle walked closer and reached her hand out, expecting Bird to fly away, but he didn't move. She stroked his feathers, relief flowing through her. He was just a bird, but he was here. Her only friend in this wild place. "You left the tower, too." Her heart felt like it was swelling in her chest, in danger of bursting. Bird had followed her from the tower. She wasn't alone.

How had Bird known she would be in that vehicle? Did he know she was in trouble? Did he know she was in a terrible place? Maybe all he knew was that men were savages, beasts who put creatures like him and Zelle in cages. But that seemed to be enough.

Looking out the window, Zelle saw bodies sleeping in groups. It appeared she was the only one offered an actual shelter. The scent inside it led her to believe it had been Arno's or his father's before it had been given to her. This was her new ivory tower. She almost laughed at how awful it was.

"It's time for me to go, Bird. Will you come with me?" Zelle turned around and walked over to the door. She tried to push it open, but found it locked. She wanted to scream in frustration, but knew that would be contrary to her goals.

Back at the window, she stepped up on the cot, putting herself closer to the room's only opening. It was small, but she was smaller. She took the borrowed jacket off and draped it over the sill, waiting a few moments to see if it would cause anyone to investigate. When no one came, she put her head and shoulders out of the opening and looked around.

There were two men sleeping on the ground not far from where she was, but they were definitely not awake, their snores blending together in a low hum. Bird took flight, but Zelle did not see where he went. There was no time to worry about her new partner, though. This might be her only chance to escape.

She slowly pulled herself up to and through the opening, delicately balancing on its sill at her belly as she grabbed the window's edge at her hips. With her head pointed at the ground, she allowed her legs to fall in an arch toward the ground below, using her back and abdominal muscles to control their rate of descent.

Her spine slowly bent backward as her legs continued their downward path. Only when she couldn't stand the stretching or the pain any longer did she release her hold on the window and throw herself the remaining distance to her feet, straightening as she went. She waited a moment for the leaves around her to stop rustling before continuing.

The air chilled her enough that she took the time to lift the coat from the sill and put it over her head and shoulders, hoping to make herself less visible as she walked slowly around the back of the shed. There was no one there, and this seemed like the direction she should go. Her eyes adjusted to the dark quickly, allowing her to make out her basic surroundings. There was no trail, but the ground was hard. She began to walk.

Her gaze shared time between the ground, looking for roots and other things bound to cause her to lose her footing, and the branches above, hoping to catch a glimpse of Bird. She felt tied to him now, their destinies entwined. He gave her hope that she could make it out, a feeling that she wasn't completely and totally alone in the world. It was her concentration on what was above her that caused her to miss what had appeared right in front of her in her path.

"Where are you goin'?" the man asked.

Zelle didn't recognize his face, but his clothing labeled him a possible member of the Hinter people.

"For a walk?" she said as he approached.

She waited until he was an arm's length away before unleashing her training on him. She could not afford to wait for him to sound an alarm and spoil her escape.

Her first blow was to his Adam's apple, the second to his larynx, and the third to his diaphragm. He would not be breathing easily or talking clearly for a long time.

The man bent at the waist and his legs began to buckle.

Zelle could not risk him going for his friends or coming after her, so she solved the problem with a swift kick to his knee and a blow to his temple. He fell to his side and his eyes closed as his breathing slowed to that of a person experiencing the deep sleep of the unconscious.

Straightening her clothing, Zelle walked on.

* * *

Zelle checked her timepiece frequently in an attempt to gauge how far she had gone. When the sun began to breach the horizon several hours into her trek, she broke into a run.

The ivory tower had automatic lifts to go from one level to another, but she had often taken the stairs, both as part of her training and because she liked the exercise. When she was running up the many flights of stairs, she would sometimes forget where she was and her mind would wander. It brought her to far-off places that she'd read about in Arno's texts.

She couldn't afford to indulge in daydreams during this run, but it didn't matter; she had the stamina to go as far she needed. When the sun came up more fully, firing the landscape before her, she paused to take a look at her surroundings.

She saw where she had come from, a dark forested area that looked as if it had been burned to ash some years before. The landscape was just starting to grow back, shoots of green intermingling with black, sooty stumps and specters of once grand pines. Ahead of her was a denser forest, untouched by fire, and hills that led to mountains. The city and her tower lay in a valley below, the lights in windows tiny pinpricks that were slowly blinking out as the population greeted the sun's rays.

Zelle needed to put a lot more distance between herself and the Hinter people; they had looked very determined and were smart and connected enough to sneak her out of the tower without any interference. Surely there would be other bands or tribes ahead as well. Her future did not look entirely bright, but Zelle was free, and it was her decision where she went.

A sound behind Zelle caused her to duck behind a tree trunk. Something had fallen on the path. Movement above caught her eye. It was Bird, and he was behind her, moving along the game trail she had been following. She stood and walked out from behind the tree.

"You're following me."

Bird stopped one tree over and took up residence on a low-hanging branch. He turned to face her and begin to clean his feathers.

"I'm leaving here, Bird. I don't know where I'm going, and it could be dangerous, but if you want to come with me, you are welcome. I don't mind having company."

Bird took flight and landed on a closer branch. Zelle

took it as his agreement. She looked out again at the valley below and at the dark, scorched area from which she'd come. A smile settled across her face as she realized that this was the first time in her life she'd taken a step in a direction that she wanted to go, and she wasn't following directives handed down by someone else.

Self-determination. She would fight to keep it. And once she knew the ways of this world and how to hide and protect herself, she would seek out the others, the other girls the High Council had named princesses, trapped in their ivory towers, and forced to await a life they did not choose for themselves. It didn't seem fair that she was the only one who had been given this privilege, so if they wanted it, she was going to see that they had it too. And then they would decide for themselves when and with whom they would populate New Earth.

She jogged on, leaving the path and heading for the hills and the mountains beyond.

Q&A with Elle Casey

I love the way this story starts out looking very conventional—even fairytale-like—and then turns darker. How does it compare to other things you've written?

I would say that The Ivory Tower is on par with my Apocalypsis series which is also post-apocalyptic fiction. I think anything in that genre is going to have a touch of darkness to it. The difference between my other series and this short story is that this new story takes place in a science fiction space realm rather than on Earth. Both feature strong female leads and a good versus evil kind of vibe.

What do you like best about writing SF, and space opera in particular?

I love writing stories about a possible future that perhaps my children might see. Space… the final frontier… I can really let my mind run wild up there.

You're incredibly prolific. What are you writing now?

I'm finishing up a ten-book Urban Fantasy series I started in 2012 called War of the Fae. It's probably my most popular series of all my books and a ton of fun to write. After that I'll be adding to my space opera series Drifters' Alliance.

Please tell readers how and where to find you…

The best place to find me is at www.ElleCasey.com. Links to my social media channels, newsletter, and so on are right there!

*Thanks for reading **Beyond the Stars: A Planet Too Far**.
Please take the time to leave a review. Many sentences
are not necessary—many stars are always welcome!*

*Look for the next space opera anthology in the **Beyond
the Stars** series to be released in August of 2016.*

*Did you miss the first anthology in the series?
Pick up **Dark Beyond the Stars** now.*

Acknowledgments

I'm so proud of the stories in this collection. As each new story reached my inbox, I read it with amazement and delight. The worlds depicted are as many and varied as the tales told... each unique and thrilling. So first, I want to thank the authors who contributed to this anthology.

In addition, thanks are due to the many people who collaborated in putting this volume together...

Julie Dillon, two-time Hugo Award-winning artist, who made the glorious art for our cover, front and back.

Kendall Roderick, who designed the cover, and who was both creative and patient.

Therin Knite, who formatted the digital and print editions of this collection with great dedication.

David Gatewood, who edited our first space opera anthology, *Dark Beyond the Stars,* which stands as a powerful foundation for this series.

Ellen Campbell, our editor, who was a wonderful resource and all-around asset.

Samuel Peralta, whose Future Chronicles anthologies inspired the *Beyond the Stars* series and whose enthusiasm and generous support for authors has created new possibilities for indie writers, especially in the field of science fiction.

I also want to thank the larger indie author community, which remains an incredible resource for writers of any level of experience. There are a lot of authors in particular who meet in private corners of the internet and give generously of their time and expertise, just because. You know who you are.

And of course, as always, I thank my *alpha beta*, Richard.

Patrice Fitzgerald
Series Editor, **Beyond the Stars**

Ellen Campbell
Editor

Ellen Campbell is an editor and voracious reader. Campbell's talent spans multiple genres and her credits include more than a hundred titles, including bestselling authors Peter Cawdron, Nick Cole, and Will Swardstrom. She edited three issues of the international best selling anthology *The Future Chronicles*, and was Editor-in-Charge of the Apocalypse Weird Metaverse.

She currently resides in Huntsville, Alabama with her husband and two canine Egyptian gods (a.k.a. Basenjis).

Ellen can be contacted in connection with editing services at http://ellencampbell.thirdscribe.com

Made in the USA
San Bernardino, CA
10 April 2016